THE
BUTTERFLY
EFFECT

BY

Eve Zaremba

A HELEN KEREMOS
DETECTIVE NOVEL

Second
Story
Press

The "butterfly effect" is the notion that a butterfly beating its wings in one spot today can affect a storm system next month across the globe, i.e., tiny differences in input can produce huge differences in output, and complex outcomes can result from simple causes. Based on Chaos Theory, which describes this phenomenon as "sensitive dependence on initial conditions."

This is a work of fiction. The author has used names of some existing places and organizations in the interest of verisimilitude, but any resemblance to real people, places and organizations is coincidental and unintended.

CANADIAN CATALOGUING IN PUBLICATION DATA

Zaremba, Eve
The butterfly effect

"A Helen Keremos detective novel".

ISBN 0-929005-56-2

I. Title

PS8599.A74B8 1994   C813'.54   C94-930563-4
PR9199.3.Z37B8 1994

Printed and bound in Canada

Edited by Margaret E. Taylor
Copyedited by Lynne Missen

Second Story Press gratefully acknowledges the assistance of the Ontario Arts Council and the Canada Council

Published by
SECOND STORY PRESS
760 Bathurst Street
Toronto, Ontario
M5S 2R6

For all the ex-pats in Japan and every student of Japanese in Canada — especially the one I live with.

PART I

1
Prologue

The tall man with eyebrows like an unclipped hedge juggled the phone from his left to his right ear and tried to keep the eagerness out of his voice.

"So when's delivery?"

"Hey, man, what d'you think this is, UPS? We don't deliver. You're going to have to pick it up."

"Pick it up! ... Oh, okay. Where?"

"Tokyo."

"What the hell do you mean, 'Tokyo'!? I haven't got time to go to Japan ..." Mel Romulu's voice rose, his vowels broadening. "That wasn't our deal!"

"Deal? Our deal was, I was to get the merchandise. Well, I've got it. You want it, you pick it up. In Tokyo. No home delivery, Doctor, you know that." A smiling sort of voice with American intonation coming clearly over the long-distance crackle all the way from Hong Kong into Romulu's ear in Toronto.

"Damn it, Sonny! I can't pick it up myself this time! I'll have to send someone to collect it. It will cost me at least a couple of grand on top of what I'm paying you ..."

"Cheap at the price, Doctor. Right? Hey, cheap at twice the price. You want it or not?" A definite chuckle this time. Sonny Burke was sure of his ground.

"What d'you think? I'll have it picked up. Where and when?"

"Next week. The Tokyo Hilton. Your courier will be contacted there. Just let me know who it is and make sure he's got the 10 grand on him."

"Oh, all right. Call me tomorrow. And don't worry about the money."

"I'm not worried, not for a minute. Nice doin' business with ya."

The line went dead. Doctor of dentistry Melhior Romulu swore and put the phone down gently. Then immediately picked it up again and punched in a familiar number.

"Hal, I need someone to run an errand for me. Out of town, outside Canada, in fact. Be gone three, four days or so. Yes, with passport. Who've you got? ... Of course he must be reliable! Who? Wayne Tillion? ... Sure I remember him, how could I forget! Yeah, I guess he'll do. Strong, sound and not too smart. A good Canadian type, eh? Send him up here as soon as you can. Great. Let me know. Thanks."

Romulu replaced the phone, his good humour restored. It was okay. The merchandise was indeed cheap at twice the price. He rubbed his large hands together and smiled.

2

Getting There

Terminal 3 of Toronto's Pearson International Airport is pretty new. Its claim to fame is that it is more like a covered shopping mall than many shopping malls. Which, as it happens, isn't even true. Still, it's "a user friendly, state-of-the-art facility" with 70 check-in counters, fully automated ticketing facilities, moving sidewalks, computerized baggage routing, dedicated check-in service, 3,300 indoor parking spaces, two luxurious lounges, an on-site hotel and scores of pricy boutiques to take your money. Canadian Airlines International, its chief tenant, likes to call it the home of civilized travel. Wayne Tillion loved it.

He took his time crossing the concourse, rubbernecking as unobtrusively as possible. The glass dome stretched out way above his head, a monstrous air-conditioned greenhouse. He loved the size, the glitz of it. Hefting his brand new garment bag with the shiny brass locks — $98.95 plus tax at Gold's on Queen Street — Tillion reached one of the 70 check-in counters, was given royal treatment, assigned a seat and directed to the International Empress Lounge where he could sit and drink gratis until his Tokyo flight was called. He loved that too.

Wayne Tillion blended perfectly with the business types around him. He was an unexceptional young man in his twenties with a prominent Adam's apple: clean shaven, well barbered, his shoes shined, his fingernails clean. His bespoke suit, although more than two years old, was cut to show off his athletic build while minimizing his extra thick shoulders and neck. (Wayne's hobby was body building.) The suit had been a gift from Rebecca Gurton, a fashionable lawyer who wanted an escort who didn't look too much like Hulk Hogan. Wayne had never had a tailor-made suit before. During their brief but eventful affair, Rebecca had tried to apply some much-needed polish to the rough diamond that was Wayne. Enough of it stuck for Wayne Tillion to be able to pass, at least with his mouth shut, for an up-and-coming MBA, instead of a high-school dropout.

A certain amount of native intelligence combined with ambition and physical strength had made Wayne Tillion highly employable. After his short stint at schooling and a brush with the law — aggravated assault, dismissed — Wayne made a reasonably good living on the fringes of the "hospitality" industry. He filled in where required as desk clerk, bartender, bouncer, security enforcer, gofer, chauffeur and general dogsbody to one Hal Glendenning, a man with interests in a dozen different enterprises, not all of them a 100 percent legit. Glendenning's flagship was a third-rate, near-fleabag on Jarvis Street in downtown Toronto, predictably called Imperial Palace Hotel. That is what Wayne Tillion had been calling home since he'd split up with Rebecca and had to vacate her North Toronto condo.

His boss considered Wayne smart but not too smart, discreet and loyal — a man who did what he was told, yet who could think on his feet if the occasion called for it. This combination of characteristics made Wayne endlessly useful. The Glendennings of this world live and prosper through "connections," a constant flow of favours taken, granted and exchanged. Lending Wayne to Melhior Romulu cost Glendenning nothing while putting the wealthy and influential ex-dentist in his debt. It is on such small civilities that fortunes are built.

Wayne Tillion considered his current assignment a plum. Of all the jobs he'd ever had, surely a trip to Japan (Business Class yet!) with $1,000 dollars in expenses had to top them all. Stay at the Hilton, sample Tokyo's night scene ... the girls! He'd heard about geishas and the like. In movies, the Western male got bathed, massaged and generally serviced by a bevy of totally subservient lovelies. Maybe he couldn't afford a whole bevy but just one ...

The errand Tillion was to run for Romulu was simple. He would be contacted in Tokyo, he would meet someone and receive a sealed package small enough to fit into a suitcase — or a garment bag. In return, he would turn over an envelope, clearly containing money, which he carried in a belt around his waist. A straightforward exchange. He'd done them before. No sweat.

Once on the plane and settled in his Business Class seat, Wayne accepted a glass of champagne from a smiling cabin attendant, female. She was attractive enough to feed his fantasies but not sexy enough to be disturbing. That was fine. He stretched his legs luxuriously; there was almost room enough for all of his two metres. Better still, the adjacent seat was empty. He was offered a newspaper — did he prefer *The Globe and Mail* or the *Financial Times*? He chose the *Globe*, quickly scanning the sport pages before ostentatiously turning to the unfamiliar "Report on Business." Although no one watched him, Wayne was enjoying playing the part of an international businessman. He peered out from behind the paper at his fellow B Class passengers. All were male, all wore suits not unlike his own, all but one were deep in a business paper and all but two drank champagne. Satisfied, he turned back to the *Globe*, looking for Japanese business news. It paid to be knowledgeable.

One movie, two meals, three drinks and four hours later, the DC10 landed in Vancouver for a two-hour pit stop. There was time to check out the place. Tillion left the plane and spent some time looking out of the airport windows trying to get a glimpse of Vancouver. It was nowhere in sight. All he saw were flat acres of grass, a few airport buildings and what might have been a mountain in the far distance. Dullsville. It was his first disappointment of the trip; there had been more to see from the plane. The last two hours he'd been looking down on mountains. Awesome. He'd always imagined the Rockies running all the way to the Pacific with Vancouver sort of hanging in on the edge. How come it was so flat and boring? So much for all that hype about Beautiful British Columbia. He went back to his seat.

Excitement returned; the seat next to his had now been filled, by a Japanese businessman no less. Wayne sat quietly and watched as the man — small, neat, of indeterminate age and in a dark suit (exactly as per expectations) — folded his suit coat just so, and waving aside the hanger offered by a zealous attendant, placed it carefully in the overhead bin. He took out a short "happi coat" from his bag, put it on, sat down and took off his shoes. Tillion was enchanted. Screw Vancouver, it was only a boring Canadian city anyway; here next to him was the real thing, perhaps a genuine Japanese martial arts expert! Kung Fu movies were Tillion's favourite. He wanted to stand up and bow to his neighbour as he knew was proper but it didn't seem cool. Anyway there wasn't room and anyway the man fell asleep almost immediately.

Other people were taking off their shoes and making themselves comfortable for the long transpacific flight. The Business Class cabin was now full. Wayne looked around checking out the newcomers. Still mostly businessmen singly or in pairs, except for one mixed gender couple with kids, a perfect Japanese nuclear family ... Suddenly he went rigid. Was that ...? Couldn't be ... yes, it was! What's her name ... Helen Keremos, that damned dyke snoop, here on the same plane with him, on the way to Tokyo. What a bummer of a coincidence. Was it coincidence? Wayne wasn't given to attacks of paranoia, but for a moment he considered the possibility that the presence of Helen Keremos on the plane was somehow connected with his trip. With his errand for Doc Romulu. Nah, no way, couldn't be! Well, maybe? Maybe she was here to check up on him, to see he did what he'd been told to do, to stop him taking off with the money in the belt around his middle. Nah, didn't make sense. If he hadn't been trusted, he wouldn't have been sent. Duplicating couriers would be a waste of money. Neither Hal Glendenning nor Mel Romulu were exactly famous for that.

So if she wasn't here to watch him what was she doing on the plane? Maybe she was working for the opposition. Whoever they were: Wayne had no idea. The people who were to receive the dough? Maybe they were planning a double-cross: knock him on the head, take the money without giving him whatever it was they were to give him. Nah, that made even less sense. To cheat the Doc all they had to do was not turn over the right item to Wayne. Any sealed parcel would do, since he wasn't even supposed to look inside. Anyway, to do any of that why would they need to import this broad all the way from Vancouver? Her presence on the plane had to be coincidence.

The logic was persuasive but logic isn't everything. For a while Wayne couldn't relax. He sat bolt upright and stared at Helen Keremos across the aisle two rows ahead.

What he saw was a long string bean of a woman, just this side of old, with coarse, black hair going seriously grey at the temples. She sprawled comfortably in her seat wearing dark pants, a cotton sweater and black leather Reebok walkers. He could see only the side of her face, with its long rather prominent nose, high cheek bones and very wide mouth over sharp, carnivorous teeth. He remembered her eyes as dark brown, small for her face and set wide apart. Her ethnicity was unclear. Perhaps because of her name Helen Keremos was sometimes taken for Greek. Yet she didn't look Mediterranean. Or Native Canadian either. Who knew?

Whatever her background, Helen Keremos made Wayne uneasy. She looks like a witch, he thought fancifully, or a blackbird, a raven or maybe a crow. In any case bad luck.

Quite unaware of being stared at, much less of the role she was playing in Wayne Tillion's imagination, Helen sipped her orange juice and continued reading the first of three books she'd saved for this trip. Ten hours of reading time, with meals served at regular intervals seemed like a holiday in itself. She'd used her frequent flyer points, acquired on her many trips to Toronto to see Alice Caplan, to upgrade to Business Class for the comfort of a larger seat and more legroom. Whatever lay ahead for her on the other side of the Pacific, she was determined to get full value from the trip.

There was no way of evaluating in advance how profitable the journey would prove. The letter from Hong Kong suggesting cooperation had certainly been interesting but it was the enclosed international money draft for $1,000 towards the fare that made it a serious proposition worth her time. The letterhead said Ladrone Investigation and Security Agency, Central District, Hong Kong — with the names of the three principals running down the left margin: Ray Choy, Ruth Choy, Angus McGee. Helen thought that it was nice, if unexpected, since she and Ray Choy had only met once on a case in Vancouver, for Choy to consider her for Ladrone's Canadian contact. The situation wasn't easy to figure but there was no harm in checking it out. Business in Vancouver was slow and Alice showed no sign of moving back West from Toronto. A trip to Hong Kong, with a stopover in Tokyo, was just the thing to add some spice to life.

3

Jet Lag

What can be said about Tokyo's Narita Airport that hasn't already been said? For first-time Western visitors to Japan it starts by confirming their worst fears about Japan — it's big, modern, expensive and full of officious people in white gloves. Then it proceeds to undermine these very stereotypes — it's chaotic, badly located too far from Tokyo and has to be protected from attacks by ecologists and local farmers by club-and-gun-toting guards. Hardly a model of Japanese efficiency and order.

Passage through Narita and subsequent trip into Tokyo is not an experience to be treasured under any circumstances. After a day spent 37,000 feet above sea level in a stuffy plane, on a seat engineered for the "average" and therefore nonexistent, human frame, fed on prefabricated food and too much booze, it is in a category of hell all by itself. Memory of the ghastly trip from airport to city fades once in Tokyo when jet lag hits with full force. Much the way pneumonia drives out the memory of a mere cold. A special excruciating feature of Pacific jet travel from North America is crossing the international date line. Few things are as disorienting as "losing" a day. Going west to get to the Far East. Only homo saps, triumphs of evolution that we are, would willingly put ourselves through such an process. Membership in our species has its price.

Wayne Tillion didn't give jet lag a thought. He'd heard all about it, of course, but saw it as just a fancy way of saying "I'm tired," a way of claiming jet-set status. He'd yet to learn that "jet lag" isn't so much about jets as about "lag." In this area, as in many others, experience is the only teacher. Wayne had only flown once before and that was to Atlantic City, which hardly counted. He realized that he was tired and a bit hungover from all that free gin, but so what? He'd navigated the chaos of Narita, found the right line for the Hilton Hotel bus and watched with dazed interest as white-gloved minions expertly lined up, tagged and loaded luggage, including his new garment bag. He was still relatively fine sitting inside the plush bus, listening to the precise, foreign English of the welcoming recording. He even noticed that the seats were a bit small and that the driver sat on the right of the vehicle. They drove on the left in Japan! It hadn't occurred to him that the Japanese, masters of the auto trade, would drive on the left like the Brits, whom he considered quaint.

By the time the bus dropped him off at his hotel almost two hours later, Wayne had a little trouble concentrating. Oh, the Tokyo Hilton was wonderful, he was certainly conscious of the organized smoothness with which he was registered and wafted up to his room. In the best international hotel style, the bellhop turned on the TV and all the lights, showed him the bathroom, relieved him of a couple of dollars and left.

Wayne decided to take a shower. Just as he took off his suit jacket and started to take off his pants, he was hit by a strange sensation. Jet lag. The room spun; he felt sleepy and disconnected. It didn't seem worthwhile to do anything but collapse on the bed.

For three hours he slept like one dead. Then he awoke sweaty, disoriented and still tired. But now sleep proved impossible. He tried everything he could to attain that blessed state but without success. Having no previous experience of insomnia, Wayne felt an irrational and unaccustomed fear. He would never sleep again! He would be this tired and sleepless forever. All the symptoms of insomniac paranoia, this early a.m. panic.

Perhaps a drink or two would help. Wayne dragged himself up from the bed and, staggering slightly as if already drunk, began to investigate the courtesy bar. He had just opened a tiny bottle of Johnny Walker Black when the phone rang. For a few seconds he didn't recognize the odd noise, then couldn't find the instrument, locating it finally back at the bedside table. As he picked it up, his other hand still grasping the bottle, he broke out in a cold sweat. Who could be calling him? He didn't know anybody in Tokyo. What ... what was he doing here anyway? His mind seemed to become a great blank expanse, without content or connections. The voice that came across the line and out of the unfamiliar phone didn't help. It was female, young, cheery and unmistakably Australian.

"Wayne Tillion? Oh, beuwdy! Got you at last. I called hours ago but you didn't answer. Never mind, got you now. Listen mate, get to Tokyo Central as soon as you can, catch me at the Shinkansen platform. The 9:53 train to Nagoya. Got that? Don't forget the necessary. And don't be late. I haven't got time to hang around. See ya. Oh, by the way, my name is Julie. Julie Piper."

Wayne stood there stunned. It had come to him that this was the message he had been waiting for. This Julie Piper was the person he'd been sent halfway across the world to meet. Jesus!

He stood there in his dirty jockey shorts, holding the little bottle of whisky and tried to concentrate. He didn't know what time it was or how to get to Tokyo Central. He didn't know what to do except that whatever it was he had better do it fast. He poured the whisky down his throat, choked, sputtered, turned and stumbled towards the bathroom, tripping over his pants and jacket of his best suit. It was crumbled on the floor. His best suit. His only suit.

4
What Now?

"Doc ? ... Dr. Romulu ... Sir. I'm sorry but I missed her, Julie Piper her name was ... somehow. I was asleep when she called ... and there just wasn't time to get to Tokyo Central, it's, like, a railroad station. She mentioned this train to Nagoya ... I couldn't figure out the name. The Shinkansen. Turned out to be what they call 'The Bullet.' But who knew, eh? I can't understand why she left it so late, our meeting I mean. The taxi got me there okay but I couldn't find my way around this damned place. It's kind of big. So ... it's not easy to ... nobody much speaks English ... and ... she wasn't there, anywhere. I looked ..."

Wayne was back in his hotel room, sputtering into the phone, filling the airwaves with explanations. He didn't want to admit it to himself but he feared Romulu's reaction to his failure. He was mad at himself for blowing a simple job. Romulu would be fully justified in being mad as hell.

"So you missed a meeting, eh Wayne? That's too bad. Just set up another, that's all. No big deal."

Mel Romulu's voice stayed cool and controlled. It only made Wayne feel worse.

"But I don't know how to contact this Julie Piper! I thought maybe you would know, like ... who do I call to set up another meeting, eh?"

"Easy now, easy boy. They'll get in touch with you, of course. Just sit tight and wait. She'll call, don't you sweat. Presumably she had urgent business, maybe out of town.

Anyway couldn't wait. What was that place you said? Nagoya. Right. Once it's done, she'll be back. How far is it from Tokyo anyway?"

"But Doc, how come I haven't heard from her already? It's three o'clock! She's had five hours to get in touch with me here. I've been waiting all this time. I only called you because there's no word. What do I do if she don't call soon, eh?"

"I see. Well, five hours isn't so long. You have to wait, that's all. Stay in the hotel, near the phone. Call me once you hear from her and make sure this time the meeting is someplace you can get to without getting lost! Don't blow it again! Good boy."

The line from Toronto went dead. Wayne slammed down the phone and swore. It was humiliating. He hated having to sit in his room waiting for that damned girl to call. He hated Tokyo, he hated Japan, he hated not understanding the language, not being able to communicate. He hated the feeling of helplessness that being foreign brings with it.

Reaching into the courtesy bar he took out three bottles of liquor, one each of gin, vodka and whisky. All familiar brands. He lined them up on the table next to the phone, flung himself on the bed, counted "eeny, meeny, miny, mo" and started on the gin. He would wait, damn it, as long as it took and he wouldn't blow it again!

Four hours later he was still waiting. He'd finished the three drinks, ordered and eaten a Western-style meal and, to stay awake, forced himself to watch a TV show of which he couldn't follow one word. Finally the phone rang. He grabbed it eagerly.

"Tillion here!" he almost shouted.

"No word yet, eh?" It was Romulu's voice.

Wayne felt hope drain from him.

"No. What do we do now, Doc?"

"Wait. It's all you can do. I'll be in touch."

Again dead air. Wayne collapsed back into the rumpled bed. He'd been in Japan less than 24 hours and it felt like years. He wished he were home.

5

Waltzing Matilda

Sonny Burke was as restless as Sonny Burke ever got. It had been a slow day, only half a dozen phone calls and a few faxes. Just the usual run of business — no crisis, nothing new or exciting. A good time to relax. For Sonny relaxing normally meant working up improvements in existing business and dreaming up new scams. Like any progressive businessman, he looked for more and better ways to increase profit and minimize risk. There his resemblance to most businessmen ended. Sonny did his planning as he did all his business — sitting in his "office" which was the Waltzing Matilda Bar, downstairs from his bedroom, sipping Diet Coke and contemplating his assets. All of them were in his head: he called it "taking inventory of his assets" and took it most seriously. Sonny Burke's major assets consisted of his contacts, phone contacts — he did all his business via the wire (phone or fax) — throughout the world. He could keep literally thousands of names and numbers in his head because he had one of these phenomenal visual/aural memories. Total recall: once seen or heard, never forgotten.

The evening was young. Waltzing Matilda, a second-story bar in the Wanchai district of Hong Kong, was quiet and Sonny's was the only body at the bar. He sat in his regular place in the corner next to the wall, which held the essential tool of his trade — a phone. This was one of three of Sonny's very private phone lines. Two others were upstairs in his room, one of which was dedicated to a fax machine, the other to a smart switching and answering machine, which spewed out and accepted messages with amazing accuracy and frequency. But the bar phone was where Sonny did his most creative work. The instrument hid shyly behind a fly-specked, pop-up poster advertising Heineken. Only bar regulars knew it was there. No regular would have dreamed of using it or even of sitting on the adjacent stool in those rare moments when it was unoccupied by Sonny's slim behind. The spot was Sonny's and had been since he'd bought Waltzing Matilda, both the building and the business, from its bankrupt owner. Other men fantasize about owning and running a bar; Sonny owned it but didn't run Matilda and never intended to. A large smiling Chinese man known as Canton Bill managed the enterprise to suit himself. Sonny just sat safe and anonymous in the corner of the bar with the phone to hand, conducting his business.

Tonight "taking inventory" did not hold his attention. This was most unusual and Sonny didn't like the unusual. Not in his own affairs. He had constructed this perfect life, built around the Matilda and international phone systems, a life over which he had almost total control. Then into his life had walked a leggy Aussie kid called Julia Piper. It was okay as long as she remained in Hong Kong. She would bounce into the bar every couple of days or so, have a drink with the boys and bounce up to Sonny's bedroom with him. That's how he'd liked things to be.

There had always been women as well as men in his life. And both sexes always wanted more from him than he was willing to give. More love, sex, time, money, attention, whatever. Julia didn't seem to want anything, of itself a disturbing circumstance. And what's more, she kept taking off for other parts. Like L.A. or Taipei or Seoul or Singapore. When she was away he couldn't concentrate on business. Which was most unusual and damn worrying.

This time Julia had gone to Japan, for an indeterminate period. Although he hated to see her go, Sonny couldn't prevent himself from manoeuvring her into doing him a favour or two in Japan, "since you're going there anyway." She would deliver an item of merchandise to a North American courier plus pay a small debt he owed to one Kusashita in Nagoya. This and that. Simple chores like that.

For Sonny this was a perfect arrangement in all respects, totally safe. Neither the "item" in question nor the money for his services were ever directly in his personal possession. The delivery of the item to Julia was arranged by phone. Payment for Sonny's services could not be traced to him since the money would stay in Japan.

This was a good example of a system that was at the heart of Sonny's method. He was the quintessential middleman. He never soiled his hands by actually performing any of the tasks for which he was contracted. Using his encyclopaedic knowledge of who, what, where, how and how much, his shtick was to subcontract all jobs for somewhat less than his quoted price and keep the difference. Someone else always did all the work and took all the risks. Business came to him by word of mouth — recommendations from satisfied customers. Much of it was repeat business and no wonder; he was knowledgeable, always available, reliable and not too greedy. If some of his clients, like Mel Romulu, found Sonny's telephone manner obnoxious, that was too bad. They could go elsewhere. But few did. For Sonny was tops. A perfectionist. Much more than money, he loved an elegant plan elegantly executed. And, while every aspect of every deal he undertook was usually meticulously planned and carried out by the very best specialists in the field, Sonny was also adept at taking advantage of opportunities when they presented themselves. As in this case.

Now his pleasure at a perfectly designed deal was being spoiled by Julia. By her absence. He twisted on his seat restlessly, drumming his fingers on the fake oak surface of the bar. Then he waved a thin brown hand and Canton Bill on duty behind the bar immediately refilled his glass.

"What you want to eat tonight, boss?" Canton's voice showed his concern at Sonny's unusual behaviour but if he guessed at the cause of it, he didn't let on. The question about food was a signal for a return to normalcy. It was part of an unacknowledged daily ritual, the existence of which was crucial to the relationship between the two men. It confirmed that all was as it should be.

Gratefully Sonny looked up at Canton's face, saw it was minus its usual smile and tried to snap out of it.

"What's on tonight, Chief?"

"Ribs are good tonight, Sarge. How about ribs?"

"Ribs sound good to me, Top."

"Coming up." Bill turned and spoke quietly in Cantonese into a speaking tube which connected the bar with the restaurant kitchen downstairs.

"Sonny's usual. Send it up."

The two men grinned at each other.

Minutes later, the meal arrived on a creaking dumb-waiter. Bill set the plate of garlic ribs, side order of stir-fried vegetables and a bowl of rice in front of Sonny. As Sonny reached for his chopsticks, the phone rang. He picked it up in one smooth, practised movement and half-turned to face the wall. Canton Bill moved away to serve a newly arrived customer.

"Sonny?" Romulu's voice sounded tentative.

"Yeah! What's up, Doc?"

Romulu ignored the maddening and perfect Looney Tune imitation and plunged straight to the point.

"My courier missed the first rendezvous. We need to set up another."

"Oh? Missed a randyvoos, did he? Who was the lucky girl?"

"Come on, Sonny! This could be serious. Your Julie Piper. She arranged to meet him at a railroad station but he was late. Apparently she took a train to Nagoya and hasn't called back. My man is sitting in Tokyo chewing his nails and costing me a mint. Do something."

"Nagoya. Right," suddenly Sonny was all business. "Now relax, Doc. I'll get on it."

He replaced the receiver and turned to his meal with renewed appetite. Having cleared every dish, he slid off the bar stool, ducked under the counter flap and with a nod at Canton Bill made his way through an unobtrusive door behind the bar to his own private stairs, which led up to his own private space on the floor above the bar. It was one large room plus bathroom taking up the whole of the third floor. The Waltzing Matilda took up all of the second floor while the storefront housed a restaurant run by Canton Bill's large extended family. That family, in turn, occupied the two top floors of the five-story building. Thus Sonny's sanctum was the essential meat in the sandwich as he himself called it, protected top and bottom by the bread and butter.

He walked in and looked around his private domain, experiencing again the thrill that the place never failed to produce. The walls were hung with yellowing momentos of "Nam," Sonny's war. Two of the walls contained large blurry blow-ups of what Sonny called "pic-bites": that famous shot of the last helicopter hovering over the U.S. Embassy right next to a early Saigon street scene of GIs on R & R with Vietnamese girls; a black soldier setting fire to a village hut right next to a *Life* photo of the President with a bunch of white brass hats looking at a map, smiling into the camera; an image of a man with extended arm pointing a gun at the head of the Vietnamese civilian, captured just at the point of execution, etc. Next to the window hung two flags, South Vietnamese crossed with the MIA/POW emblem. Near the computer the wall decorations were smaller and more personal: snapshots of uniformed men — black, white and brown — most of them long dead.

Humming softly with satisfaction, Sonny proceeded into his regular routine. First he checked the fax machine, quickly scanning the printed pages and committing their contents to memory before shredding the pages. Still on his feet, he listened to whatever messages had been picked up and stored by the answering machine. Next he clicked on all three TV monitors simultaneously and spent a few minutes looking in at CNN and at two local news stations, one in Cantonese and the other in English. Finally, after getting himself a Diet Coke from the cooler and still humming, Sonny sat down in front of a large solid oak table containing nothing but a telephone and started his work.

After two calls, both to Japan, he knew the worst. Julia Piper had gone missing. For real. It wasn't just a scare manufactured by Romulu's incompetent courier. His only two contacts with Julia in Japan had come up empty. She had checked out of her Tokyo *ryokan* as per plan but had missed her appointment in Nagoya with Kusashita's representative, Tetsu Nangi. Mr. Nangi was currently unavailable but his displeasure at this turn of events was conveyed to Sonny in excellent English and in unmistakable terms by a young female voice. Mr. Burke was advised to rectify the situation immediately. Preferably before Mr. Kusashita himself had to be apprised ... Bet she wouldn't sound like that in Japanese, he thought.

It took Sonny only a moment to come to the unpalatable conclusion that he had to get help in finding Julia Piper. It was clearly unthinkable to call upon his usual business contacts; the matter was too sensitive. Word that

Sonny had "lost" his sheila would get around. That he'd gotten her to deliver his merchandise and a payoff *and* that she'd run out on him would be just too good to be kept quiet. Like all active businessmen Sonny had competitors and enemies, not to mention so-called friends who could be counted on to delight in taking him down a peg. The story would hurt his reputation and thereby damage his business.

The normal channels being closed in this instance, Sonny had but little choice. He took a deep breath and punched a local Hong Kong number.

6

Ladrone Investigations

"Ladrone Investigations. Good morning."

"Lemme talk t'McGee."

"Who is calling, please?"

"Sonny Burke."

"Please hold on, Mr. Burke."

Pause. Then a soft Scottish burr: "Sonny? How are you, me boy. Now I know you're not calling to pass the time. What can we do for you?"

"I need to find someone in Japan. D'you have an operative there, right now? And I mean *now!* Someone who's already there. There is no time to waste."

"Oh? ..." McGee couldn't quite disguise his surprise. Sonny Burke was notorious for having more contacts throughout the world than American Express. Why would he need to go to a detective agency? One couldn't ask. McGee collected himself and pressed on. "Oh. Right. An operative in Japan. Could be ... Let me find out and call you back. Who is it you're trying to find? Anyone in particular or ...?"

"A young woman. Westerner. Doesn't speak Japanese. Shouldn't be hard to track down for the right person."

"Right. Call you back right away."

Angus McGee replaced the receiver slowly. A small smile appeared under his grey military mustache. Sonny Burke — asking for help from Ladrone! This was unprecedented. Something unusual was in the works. McGee considered the possibilities. Whatever it was it might represent an opportunity. And Angus McGee hadn't let an opportunity pass in all of his 60 years. Accordingly he heaved his beefy frame out of the chair and, pulling down his waistcoat, walked into the office next door. His partner, Ray Choy, looked up expectantly from a computer terminal. In a few words McGee shared the gist of Sonny's request with him.

"What d'you think, old son? Can we oblige him? Do let's!"

"Interesting. Who is the woman? Any idea?"

"Not for sure. But if it is who I think it is ...! Julie Piper, who else, right? Of course we don't have anyone in Japan right now. So we'll have to fudge it somehow. Be worth going to some trouble, don't you think so, old son?"

"Helen Keremos is now in Tokyo. She just called me. Perhaps ..."

"Who? Who d'we have in Tokyo that I don't know about?"

"Calm down, Angus. Helen Keremos. You remember? A private investigator from Vancouver we are vetting as a possible contact for Ladrone in Canada. We agreed. Remember now?" Choy asked.

"Oh, yes, yes. Your Canadian lassie. What about her? Are you suggesting we use her on this job for Sonny Burke? We don't know a thing about her! How could we trust such a delicate situation to an unknown? And a woman!"

"We don't have any choice, Angus. She's in Tokyo. We don't have anyone else. And it would be very interesting to find out more about Mr. Burke and his doings, as you yourself remarked. So, do I call Helen in Tokyo and set it up or do you want to call Sonny and tell him that we can't help?"

It was no contest.

7
Job(s) for Helen

Helen swung the elongated hot water spigot from over the hand basin to a new position above the bathtub and turned on the water in preparation for taking a shower. All without moving from the toilet seat. She was rather enjoying performing the usual ablutions, although millions wouldn't, in this tiny perfect bathroom, which was attached to a tiny perfect hotel room, with a tiny perfect bed and not much else in it. It wasn't just that the bathroom was small but that it seemed like a Rubbermaid product, i.e., tub, sink and toilet, walls, floor and ceiling appeared to have been moulded all in one piece from the same pale beige, hard-impact vinyl. It was like being inside an egg; every time she vacated this seamless cocoon, Helen felt like a hatchling. Under the influence of jet lag she had felt like a real yoke but had managed to get over it since.

A more lasting impression produced by staying in a room in a Japanese "business" hotel — as opposed to an "international" tourist hotel — is that of being on a small boat. Unlike the traditional Japanese *ryokan* with a futon on the floor, it has a bed (bunk) and a Western-type bathroom (head). As on a boat, everything in it is built-in, tidy and tiny, with no space wasted on anything extraneous. It makes for a simpler life and this too suited Helen just fine. She always liked boats.

Wrapped in a blue and white *yukata* supplied by the management, a clean and relaxed Helen sat on the bed — there were no chairs or room for them — doing her nails when the phone produced an odd sound. She took it, correctly, for a ring.

"Hallo, Helen?" Ray Choy's voice sounded tentative, as if he wasn't sure of his purpose in calling. Curious, since they had spoken just a few hours ago and she wasn't expecting another call from him. Helen made affirmative noises.

"Well, Helen, I am sorry to interrupt your holiday in Tokyo but my partner and I wondered whether you would mind doing a little job for us while you're in Japan. It shouldn't take you long ..."

"What kind of a job did you have in mind?" Helen interrupted. "And hey, Ray, is this a real job or a test to see whether I measure up to Ladrone standards? Because if it is, then forget it. You guys can take your business and shove it."

"Not at all, not at all!" Grateful that his partner couldn't hear Helen, Ray Choy continued, "A real job, and you would be doing us a favour if you could see your way to help us out."

"A favour?" Helen asked suspiciously. Favours came free.

"Yes! Of course, I mean at your usual rates. Plus expenses, of course."

"Of course, of course. What's the deal?"

"A missing person, a woman."

"A Westerner, I trust. You wouldn't hire me to find a Japanese person in Japan."

"Naturally a Westerner. We have an urgent commission to find her. You will need to get started right away. There is no time to spare."

"So brief me."

"The client insists on briefing you himself. He will phone, then probably fax you details. I will give him your number. His name is Burke, Sonny Burke."

"Who am I working for? Ladrone Investigations or Sonny Burke?"

"For us, for Ladrone. Absolutely."

"Good. Okay. I'll be waiting. The meter is on as of right now."

Half an hour later, a fully dressed Helen picked up the phone again. Sonny Burke was on the line, his telephone manner professionally faultless. She listened carefully, noting the flat American accent as he sketched out the case.

"Julia Piper, 'Julie' to her friends. Australian. About 28. Tall, thin, fair, good looking. Should stand out in Japan like a pig at a Muslim wedding. Flashy dresser but I don't know exactly what she had on last. Checked out of her hotel in Tokyo, then missed an important contact at the Tokaido/Sanyo Shinkansen platform at Tokyo Station. She seemed to have taken the train to Nagoya. However, didn't make her appointment there. Now see, she's got valuable merchandise on her. My merchandise."

"How valuable? How portable? Diamonds, drugs, gold?"

"Just valuable. Worth $10,000 to me. On the open market, many times that. And it's portable. Not like diamonds but portable. Not drugs, not gold. Nothing like that."

"You thinking she took off with your loot? I need to know the chances that she's in hiding. It makes a difference. People who don't want to be found are harder to track down. Does she want to be found?"

"I don't know. Can't be sure. But most likely, yeah, she wants to be found."

"Good. I need to know what it is she's carrying. These appointments she didn't make. First here and later in Nagoya. They have anything to do with this 'merchandise' of yours?"

"Yes. At the station she was to exchange the merchandise

for 10 grand. She set up the meeting herself so presumably she'd meant to make it. But the courier was late, the Nagoya train had left. So I'm assuming she left for Nagoya. But I don't understand why she didn't wait, take a later train or contact the courier and make another appointment."

"I'll need to talk to that courier. Now what's with Nagoya?"

For the first time in the conversation Sonny Burke hesitated just slightly. They'd reached the tricky part. Helen picked this up as if he'd spelled it out aloud.

"I don't understand it. Her job was to make the delivery and get that $10,000 in Tokyo then make a pay-off in Nagoya for me. Why would she go to nagoya first? And she didn't make it there either ..."

"Right. If she'd intended to rip you off and disappear she would have been smart to get the maney first, right? Except you just told me that this merchandise is worth more than 10 grand. So. Complicated situation."

"My hunch is that something happened to her either on the train or in Nagoya. Anyway, I don't believe she'd double-cross me for a lousy eight grand. You see, she was to keep two for her trouble anyway."

"Hum. Generous. Did she have any other reason to go to Nagoya? Other than to deliver the eight grand to your associate? By the way, I'll need his name and way to reach him. He's Japanese, right?"

"Yeah. His name is Tetsu Nangi. She didn't show."

"Do we believe him about that? And even if we do, where did they plan to meet? How and by whom were the arrangements made? That's what he'd know and that's what I need to find out. Just what sort of business are you in, Mr. Burke?"

Helen heard Sonny sigh at the other end of the phone.

"Yeah, yeah. Got to hand it to Ladrone. They sure got

smart operators. Listen, Helen Keremos, I can't wait for Julie to be found before I make that payoff in Nagoya. You dig? I need you to make it for me. So, here's the goods. Nangi works for Kusashita, the man I owe money to. Kusashita is the chief of the Nagoya area yakuza. You know what 'yakuza' means?"

"Like the mob or something."

"Oh, baby! Mafia, the syndicate, Unione Siciliano. Like that."

"So?"

"How about Wah Ching? That's Chinese. United Bamboo out of Taiwan? Our own triads here in Hong Kong? Know anything about them?"

"Secret criminal societies? Not much, I guess. So tell me."

"Secret criminal societies, sure. But forget most of that comic book stuff. In Japan, yakuza are part of the way things are run. They are criminal all right, but lately there hasn't been much secret about them. They got so powerful in the eighties they don't have to hide much. But make no mistake. They can be very, very bad dudes. It isn't healthy to cross Kusashita, for instance."

"You owe him money and you've fouled up the delivery."

"He don't know that. Yet. And with luck he'll never know we fouled up. Here's what I propose. You take Julie's place. I wire you the money in Tokyo, you hightail it to Nagoya and get it to Nangi. You being a woman makes it perfect. They were expecting a woman, see. What d'you say? Make it worth your while."

"Why not just wire the money directly?"

"You don't understand. That's not the way things are done. Anyway it sends the wrong message. When you show up it's just a slight delay in delivery, is all. Much easier to explain than having my courier disappear completely. I have to think of my long-term business prospects with the Japanese. With Kusashita for sure. Major screwup would blow it for me. Make me seem unreliable, see what I mean? You getting that money to Nangi ASAP takes him off the hook too. See, any screwup he's connected with is bad for his rep, regardless of whose fault it is. Nangi is an important contact for me."

"I get it. Supposing I do it. What's it worth?"

"I'll wire 9K. You give Nangi 8K."

"What about Ladrone?"

"What about them?"

"They're paying me to find Julie Piper. What do I tell them about this deal?"

"Nothing. None of their business. You go on looking for Julie. I want her found and I'm paying that shot as well. You've got two separate gigs with no conflict. What's the problem? Just do the delivery first."

Helen considered. The ethics of the proposition were murky. For sure, Ladrone would expect her to report on her conversation with Burke. As far as they were concerned, she was working for them and not for Burke directly. It suited Burke to discount the possibility but experience told Helen that once she was in the middle, the chances of conflict were very high, practically 100 percent. She knew that she would be smart to turn him down now. These complications apart, it was crazy to take a job over the phone from someone she'd never met, whose real agenda she could only guess at, to deal with a strange mob in a country like Japan. She would be stepping into a situation, the ramifications of which she could know nothing. And with no support, no network, no language! She knew she was nuts to consider the possibility even. She also knew she couldn't turn down the opportunity.

"Let me think about this. Meanwhile let's get back to finding Julie since you say you do want her found. I want to know what 'merchandise' she was carrying for you. Plus, I still have to talk with your client's courier here in Tokyo before I go to Nagoya. What's his name and where do I contact him?"

"Look, Helen. Telling you the nature of the merchandise is a no-no in my book. The item belongs to my client. The matter is confidential, see? You wouldn't blab your client's business, I hope, right? We're professionals, you and I. You understand. All I'll say is that my client is an art lover." Pause. "Now about my client's courier. He's at the Tokyo Hilton and his name is Wayne Tillion. Got that?"

"Wayne Tillion? Yes, I got it." Helen managed to keep her amazement from showing. There had to be more than one Wayne Tillion in the world.

"For the record he's Canadian. So are you, they tell me. No offence, Helen Keremos, but if you ask me, this Tillion guy's an asshole. Since he fucked up the original meeting with Julie at the station he's been waiting for another call from her and crying on his boss's shoulder for help. Naturally my client called me. He wants his merchandise. I don't blame him. So Helen, your job — should you decide to accept it — is to find Julie, get the merchandise to Tillion, get paid and bring me the money. Simple. But cover for me with Kusashita first. How about it?"

"Mission impossible, eh Sonny? I'm a sucker to even think of it. Hell, I'll do it."

"Atta girl. I'll fax you all the information I have on Julie and the Nagoya situation. The money for Kusashita will be at the Tokyo AmEx office in your name. All you'll need is your passport. Okay? Call me as soon as you can. My numbers will be on the fax. Good luck, Helen. And thanks. I owe you one."

"Better believe it."

8
Surprise!

The girl called Miko crouching between his thighs lifted her head and looked up at Wayne Tillion. Then she swallowed his cum with ostentatious indications of pleasure.

Tillion had had professional blow jobs before but this was something else! Worth every penny of the outrageous price the bellhop had quoted after a substantial tip changed hands. Whoever said there was no tipping in Japan! If he had to be cooped up in this hotel room waiting for that Piper bitch to call, then at least he could have perfect room service! Wayne leaned back in the armchair and sighed with contentment. Miko stood up, adjusted her black garter-belt and stockings, which were all she was wearing, blew him a kiss and disappeared into the bathroom. The phone rang.

"Wayne Tillion?" At the sound of the voice Tillion froze. That witch Keremos had found him! What the hell could she want? His paranoid fears returned double strength.

"Yes? What do you want? Get off the line! I'm waiting for a call."

"From Julie Piper I presume. Still no word from her, eh? Too bad. That means that you will have to help me find her. That's a fun prospect! ... Don't interrupt. I've been hired to find the disappearing Ms. Piper. I need everything you can tell me about her. So I'm coming up right now."

"Right now? No! What's all this about? Who ... who

hired you anyway? Mel never told me ..."

"Mel? Dr. Melhior Romulu of good old Diamond Plaza Towers? He sent you here to collect his merchandise? This is getting more and more interesting. I'm on my way up. Get your pants on."

The phone went dead. It took a moment to sink in that Keremos had called from the lobby and was indeed on her way right up. And how did she know that he didn't have his pants on? Damn! He hurried to make himself presentable when a knock on the door announced the arrival of his bête noire. Damn, damn, damn and blast! He zipped up and opened the door.

Helen walked past him into the room, took a quick look around, noting the state of the bed, the liquor bottles, the unmistakable smell of sex and Tillion's sheepish scowl. Just then a perfectly dressed Miko walked in from the bathroom. She smiled at them both, took out a leather card holder and dropped a couple of her business cards on the table. Helen laughed.

"Just a lucky guess, Cookie, just a lucky guess. It figured you would want your Japanese culture in the flesh and not just from TV. And that bellhop downstairs doesn't have the look of a guy living on what he gets for carrying bags. It's okay Wayne, relax. I won't tell Papa Mel how you're spending your time and his dollars. Let the lady out of here and let's get to business."

Smiling beatifically Helen picked up one of Miko's cards and looked at it. It was beautifully executed on linen paper, with MIKO in kanji and English, with a three-quarter picture in full colour of the lady in question and a phone number. The other side featured the words "Perfecting English." Meanwhile Miko stared at Helen curiously, trying to grasp her relationship to Wayne. Miko's personal experience with Western women wasn't extensive and clearly she was interested.

"Mama? Yes?" she asked reasonably. Helen laughed again, harder.

"She takes me for your mother! How's that grab you, Cookie? What a hoot! No, not 'Mama,' my dear. Helen Keremos, very glad to meet you. Here's my card."

"Heren Keremosu-san?" Miko read Helen's name from her freshly minted business card in katakana, complete with Ladrone's Hong Kong address. In turn she whipped out another one of her own and handed it to Helen with a bow. Wayne could take it no longer. He grabbed Miko's arm and frog-marched her to the door.

"You've got your money. Now git."

The door closed behind Miko. He turned to Helen.

"What d'you want from me? I don't know where that Piper woman has gotten to. All I know is, she hasn't called me back. Anyway why should I tell you anything? Who you working for? Tell me that. It sure isn't Mel."

"No. So let's call him, shall we?"

"Oh? Oh! Yeah. Good idea."

Tillion almost leaped at the phone, punched in the numbers and waited impatiently, jiggling the change in his pocket and glowering at Helen. She sat down in the arm-chair he'd been occupying just a few minutes previously and continued her calm examination of Tillion and the room.

They were lucky. After a short delay Mel Romulu came on the line.

"Yes, Wayne. What gives? Any news of Piper?"

"No, none. Listen Doc, I've got this dyke detective Helen Keremos here with me. She's bugging me to tell her all I know about Piper. She says she's been hired to find her but she don't tell me who she's working for. What do I do? Throw her out on her ear? That's what I'd like to do. Just give the word."

"Helen Keremos! Let me talk to her."

"Oh, shit, Doc, why do we have to deal with her? ..."

"Wayne, I said put her on the line!"

Tillion turned in slow motion and handed Helen the phone.

"Go take a shower, Cookie, while I talk to your boss. You can talk to him again afterwards."

With obvious reluctance Tillion moved off towards the bathroom. Helen waited until he was inside before addressing herself to the phone in her hand.

"Mel? I'm surprised at you. How did you manage to get caught out in the middle of this scenario?"

"My, you don't waste any time, do you? What's your interest?"

"I've been hired by an agency in Hong Kong to find Julie Piper. And you know damn well who's paying the freight for this, so don't let's get coy. But just for the record it's Sonny. You provide his last name and we'll both be sure we're on the same track."

"Fair enough. Sonny Burke."

"Right. As I understand it you also have an interest in having her found, eh? Now to do my job, I need cooperation from your lad Wayne. It's too bad you had to pick such a horse's ass for a courier. But never mind, I'll cope. Just instruct him to be a good boy and do what he's told."

"Hold on there, Helen. I'm not in any way concerned about this Julie Piper ... only in what she's carrying. It belongs to me and I want it. Wayne is in Japan to get it and bring it back. As far as I'm concerned, that's all that matters. It doesn't fill me with confidence to realize that Burke entrusted my merchandise to someone who turned out to be so unreliable. Sonny has a very good reputation but he certainly fell down on this one. He doesn't know much about this Piper woman or her connections in Japan. Else why would he hire you, an outsider, to find her? Frankly, I'm disappointed in him."

"Look, I'm just hired help. Who cares about Burke's rep? So never mind all that. You want your merchandise, right? Well, since Julie Piper has it, she's got to be found, wherever she is. So what's the problem? We cooperate. How else are you going to get what you want? My instructions are to find Julie, get the merchandise from her and turn it over to Tillion on payment of 10 big ones."

"That's different. That sounds okay. So how are you going to go about looking for this woman? How's your Japanese?"

"Nonexistent. I'll have to improvise. Starting on the train to Nagoya. That's where she was going, I'm told."

"Look, take Wayne with you. You are underestimating that boy. Give him a chance. He might be useful."

"Oh, yeah? Mel, you just don't want to pick up Wayne's tab for screwing around at the Tokyo Hilton. I don't blame you. But getting me stuck with him ... come on!"

"Do it, Helen. Have him tag along. He'll do what he's told, I promise you. Don't tell me this job wouldn't be easier with a partner?"

"With a partner, yes. But Wayne Tillion? Give me a break, Mel."

"Wayne is all we've got. Take him."

There was a moment of silence on the long-distance line as Helen considered her options. Finally she said:

"Okay, I'll take him along. Muscle can come in useful. But if he gets out of line just once ...!"

"He won't. Now let me talk to him."

"Yeah."

She put down the receiver, walked to the bathroom door, opened it and shouted over the sound of the running water.

"Wayne! Mel wants to talk to you." Then she sat down in the armchair again and watched Wayne, wrapped in a hotel towel and dripping with water, pick up the phone.

He ignored her.

"Yeah."

"Wayne, I'm only going to say it once. Helen is looking for Julie Piper and you're going to help her. Understood?"

"Sure, sure, Doc. What d'you want me to do?"

"You're going to get off your butt, check out of that hotel and go with Helen to Nagoya and do what she tells you. Make yourself useful, you hear? Once this Piper woman is found, you're to make sure you get the item you've been sent to Japan to get and bring it back. No if, buts or delays. Follow?"

"Oh, sure. I'll be looking after your interests, like. That's cool. What about the money? Do I pay it or ..."

"Or nothing. Don't even think about it. Once the item is in your possession you pay Helen. Then you get on the next plane here. That's all you have to remember."

"But, but how do I know when I find the right item, Doc? I don't know what it is," Wayne inquired reasonably.

Behind him Helen chuckled. Out of the mouths of babes! Maybe having Wayne around wouldn't be a dead loss.

"Never mind! Once Piper is located you call me. I'll take it from there."

"But ..."

"No buts. Just do it."

"Okay, okay. Hell, I don't mind. It will be great to get out of this place. Get moving again. I'm going nuts just sitting on my can."

Wayne ignored Helen's loud chuckles behind him. Next thing he knew she was taking the receiver out of his hand and hanging up.

"Get dressed, Wayne. Time to go."

9

Bullet Train

Tillion's previous unsuccessful trip to Tokyo station hadn't been a total waste. At least he could find the Shinkansen tracks and had learned to cope with that underground maze that is any large Japanese railroad station. He bull-dozed his way through the mass of unresponsive people, giving way for nobody and ruthlessly using his size. Helen followed sedately in his tracks, her way cleared by his bulk augmented by his garment bag. Still, it took them three tries to acquire tickets and the track number of the next train to Nagoya. Once on Track 16 and out of breath, they joined one of the orderly lines of passengers at numbered points along the platform. Yellow lines indicated where each car door would be once the train arrived. Cars 1 through 5 were for those without reservations; they chose the lineup for Car 4. The train arrived and departed dead on time.

The trip itself was a pleasant relief. Airplane-style seats, air conditioning, great views of miles of suburbs punctuat-ed by little plots of rice paddies, a glimpse of Mount Fuji and a supply of beer, soft drinks and box lunches of inter-esting Japanese food. Tillion sat on the aisle and did all the negotiating with a series of young women constantly going by pushing little food carts and calling their wares. He spoke to them in English, loudly and clearly, as if to chil-dren or slow learners. They understood none of it but the translations were nevertheless completed satisfactorily. Such is the universality of the language of commerce.

Helen sat absorbed in the view, enjoying the unaccustomed experience of having someone else deal with the exigencies of travel in a strange land. She was in the grips of a strong feeling of unreality. Travelling through Japan in the company of Wayne Tillion, whom she remembered as a bit of a thug, to a city called Nagoya, which she hadn't even heard of a few hours ago, to deal with the local mobster and locate a missing Australian, at the behest of a Hong Kong detective agency and a shady character called Burke whom she'd never met ... was it crazy or what? Strangely she felt no anxiety at the prospect. Which in itself was a warning and an indication of how out of it she was.

"So. How's your jet lag?" Tillion broke the ice with a non-question. He had fed and was pulling contentedly on a beer, watching the passing scene. Feeling mellow and inclined to make contact with his travelling companion who hadn't said a word since they left Tokyo. It would do no harm to make peace, sort of, with this strange woman. "I saw you on the plane from Vancouver. What are you doing here anyway?"

"I was on vacation 'til this crazy gig came along. Some coincidence, you and Mel involved in this thing. Hope it doesn't get too messy."

"What's to get messy? Either we find this broad or we don't, right? We find her, we get what I came here for, we leave. We don't find her, we leave. No sweat."

Keremos laughed aloud.

"Dream on, Cookie, dream on. Still, may as well think positive. I would love for this to be short and sweet, so let's not waste time. You got any bright ideas of how we find this Julie? What d'we do when we get to Nagoya, eh?"

To her surprise Tillion leapt in eagerly: "Well, I figure she must have checked in somewheres. A hotel, right? So first off, we check hotels. By phone, I guess. Till we find where she's at. How about that?"

"Good luck, Cookie. *You* do that. And while you're asking Japanese hotel staff questions about their guests and trying to make sense of any answers you may get, I'll go see this Nangi guy that Piper was supposed to meet. Deal?"

"Deal. Listen, I looked up this Nagoya. It's big, you know, big as Toronto. Over two mil. Business travellers, tourists, that's what the hotel business is about. All over the world. I know. And you can't get by without English in this business. Trust me."

"I guess you could be right. Suggestion. Make it easy on yourself and try the local tourist information centre. Probably be one at the station. Like you say, in a city this size they are likely to have English-speaking staff. And a list of hotels if nothing else. And if you could get someone there to make the calls for you, that would sure help."

"Good idea, I'll do that. And I'll get us checked into the hotel she's at. While you're pissing around with this Nangi character. How about that?"

"Go ahead. Assuming she checked in some place and you can find it."

"So let's hope so, right?"

Talking companionably Helen and Wayne planned their future moves. They reached Nagoya two hours after leaving Tokyo. Right on schedule.

10

Nagoya

Nagoya station is a complicated place. The JR (Japan Rail) station proper is merely the centrepiece of a complex of underground passages, shopping arcades, entrances and exits leading to a private railroad line, three subway lines, a bus terminal, central post office and a flock of hotels, office buildings and department stores. There are literally miles of passages weaving in and out of hundreds of stores, restaurants and coffee shops, twists and turns, dead ends and sudden stairwells that land you up on unfamiliar streets. Carefully designed to confuse and confound any stranger, foreign or domestic. Most domestic strangers can read the signs; foreigners are on their own. Of course, since it calls itself proudly "International City Nagoya" there are signs transliterated in romaji (Roman alphabet) and even signs in English. All together many, many signs. Too many. The challenge is to spot consistently and somehow follow the useful ones in the cacophony of numbers, images and icons that from every direction assault the senses of the weary traveller.

Helen and Wayne started out lucky. Almost immediately on hitting the main concourse, they spotted the sign for the Nagoya City Tourist Information Centre and vigorously plowed through the crowds in the indicated direction. That is, Wayne plowed ahead through the indifferent masses and Helen once again followed in his wake hugging her carry-on case to her side.

"Let me see a list of Nagoya hotels," Wayne demanded

of the neat, middle-aged man behind the counter. The man looked at the large, rough-looking *gaijin* who had so arrogantly assumed that his English would be understood. Wayne picked up an English-language brochure, flipped through the glossy illustrated pages and stopped at a map of the downtown area of Nagoya with a list of hotels running down the side. There were 49 names and phone numbers. Tillion printed JULIE PIPER in block letters on the margin of the brochure and turned it around so it faced the clerk again.

"Great. Now I want you to call these hotels one by one and find the one where a woman called Julie Piper is registered." The man gaped at him, started to say something, changed his mind and reached for the phone. Helen watched this encounter while another clerk transcribed Nangi's address for her into something a taxi driver could read. As is usual in Japan's public areas there was nowhere to sit. Helen turned away from the counter, leaned against the wall and gazed out the window at the busy concourse.

"Bingo!" Wayne came up to her waving a map of Nagoya station triumphantly. "Piper's registered at the Nagoya Miyako Hotel. It's right here near the station, through this passage at the end of the Miyako Mall. Don't need a taxi or even to go out on the street."

"That was quick."

"Yeah, it was third on the list. Lucky, eh? Or we could have been here all day." Wayne was pleased with himself. He hefted his garment bag and in a magnanimous gesture picked up Helen's bag as well. "I'll take that and get us registered at this Miyako Hotel. Meet me there after you've done with this Nangi. Okay?"

"Okay."

"Hey, it's working out just like I said on the train, right?"

"Yeah, so it is."

"Tonight drinks are on me." Laughing, Wayne took off into the maze that was to take him to Miyako Mall.

11

Meeting Keiko

Nangi's accounting firm was on the eighth floor of a downtown office building. At first glance it seemed to consist of one large room with a dozen or so people sitting in front of computers and accounting machines. As Helen entered looking around tentatively, a middle-aged woman at the desk nearest the door sprang up and walked towards her. Smiling and bobbing her head, the Office Lady engulfed Helen in an incomprehensible stream of words.

"Do you speak English? I do not speak Japanese. My name is Julie Piper. I have come to see Mr. Nangi."

Helen spoke loudly and clearly as is the wont of anglophones faced with a foreign language. No response. Clearly the woman knew no English. Not a head turned, but Helen felt the whole room waiting for her to solve this problem. She tried out some of her minimal Japanese from Berlitz *Japanese for Travellers*:

"*Koko ni dareka eigo o hanasu hito ga imasu ka? Nihongo o hanashimasen. Watashi wa* Julie Piper." (Does anyone here speak English? I do not speak Japanese. I am Julie Piper.)

The woman burst into a further spate of Japanese. Knowing enough of a language to ask questions is useless if you don't understand the answers. Helen shook her head and slowly in careful English again enunciated the stock phrase:

"I do not understand Japanese. I am sorry. Is there someone here who speaks English?"

At the back of the room a young woman rose. She spoke briefly to the Office Lady who backed away in evident relief. Then she turned to Helen:

"I am Keiko Ueki. It is so nice to meet you. We have been waiting for you. Please come with me."

And she led the way between the desks to a well-hidden door, which turned out to lead to a small private office. It contained two desks, a couple of chairs and a file cabinet but was otherwise empty. Helen guessed that it belonged to Nangi. His would likely be the only private office in the business. Keiko sat down at one of the chairs and motioned Helen to the other.

"I am sorry Mr. Nangi couldn't be here today to meet you. It's good you are here. We worried about you. Mr. Burke called to inquire if you arrived. I hope everything is all right. No problems?" Keiko said in fluent English.

She was a woman in her late twenties, petite with a beautifully oval, white face framed by shoulder length hair. She was dressed in a blue blazer and matching skirt with a white silk blouse and black pumps. Her look and manner proclaimed a degree of sophistication that, correctly or not, Helen equated with Western influence.

"Thank you, I am fine. Sorry to have caused you any anxiety. Please accept my apologies for being so late. Unforseen circumstances ... Anyway, I am here now on behalf of Mr. Burke ready to discharge his obligation to Mr. Kusashita."

At the mention of the name Kusashita, a small frown appeared on Keiko's perfect brow.

"Yes, good. Very good. Nangi-san will be pleased. We handle business for Mr. Kusashita. He has a lot of business. Very important, busy man."

"So I understand." Helen noted with interest the slight slippage in the fluency of Keiko's English. "I hope the delay in repayment of this sum of $8,000 dollars has not inconvenienced Mr. Kusashita unduly," Helen said raising her eyebrows. Could a man as important as Mr. Kusashita be inconvenienced by the lack of so meagre a sum was the unspoken comment.

"No, no. It is of no matter. I was only concerned about you, Ms. Piper. Since Mr. Burke called, you know. Something seemed to be wrong. That's all. The money is of no importance at all."

The phone on the desk in front of Keiko rang. Helen leaned back in her chair and became very still, making herself as inconspicuous as possible. This "becoming forgotten" was a trick she'd perfected long ago. Then she concentrated on getting all she could out of the short conversation in a foreign language. On the strength of the fact that Keiko's voice had gone up a full octave and that she bobbed her head constantly and said *Hai* and *Hai wakarimashita* every two seconds, Helen surmised that a male superior was at the other end of the line. Perhaps Nangi. Perhaps Kusashita. Whoever it was, Keiko's swift glance at Helen at one point in the dialogue was a dead giveaway that he'd asked about her. After Keiko's answer — presumably a description of her visitor — came the longest stretch of silence as she listened, followed by a flurry of nods and *Hais*. Keiko was getting instructions. Had to be about Helen. Or rather, about Julie Piper Helen had to remind herself.

In the half hour that followed, Keiko offered Helen tea, which she ordered politely over the phone and was brought on a tray by the Office Lady, still bobbing and smiling. They sat sipping green tea and chatted mostly about Helen's impressions of Japan. Keiko was interested in how long Helen — Julie — had been in the country, what she'd seen, where she was staying in Nagoya and for how long and where she was planning to go next. Perfect tourist questions by a perfect host. Helen mentioned the station hotel where Wayne presumably was checking them in and was otherwise politely noncommittal. She hoped to get to Kyoto she told Keiko off the top of her head — it was a tourist must, so surely she would go there soon. In turn, Keiko hoped that Helen would have time to visit the sights of Nagoya, for instance Nagoya Castle, temples and museums. Perhaps she could show Helen around? She didn't want to presume but could she join Helen for dinner? Make plans for sightseeing the next day? Nagoya was worth it, Keiko assured Helen. Helen took pains to be delighted. She didn't mention the existence of Wayne Tillion.

The tea and the oh so courteous interrogation completed, it was time to return to business. Helen turned over 80 crisp one hundred dollar bills and received a receipt on a piece of high-quality, buff-coloured paper written in beautiful script in both languages, signed and sealed with Keiko's personal seal. Neither woman cared to mention that transactions in foreign funds were illegal in Japan.

Keiko walked Helen back to the front door through the room full of busily bowed heads. After many expressions of mutual esteem, Helen left.

12

Bar Talk

"So what have we got?"

Having found Wayne in the gloom of the hotel bar, Helen sat down beside him and ordered a bottle of Ebisu beer. Wayne handed her a room key.

"This is yours and I'm right next door. And guess whose room is down the hall?" He sounded pleased with himself.

"Julie Piper? No shit! So you got us on the same floor. Hum. When did she check in? And for how long? Did you get that?"

"Natch. She checked in yesterday just about the time you would expect if she'd arrived from Tokyo on the train I missed. And she booked for two days but left it open, sort of. The bellhop remembers taking her to her room. She left again right away and hasn't been back. What d'you think?"

"She had an appointment here that she didn't want to miss. That's why she didn't wait for you at the station in Tokyo. Hum. Now she's disappeared. Hum. How well did you lubricate the bellhop? Any chance we could get into her room? Check her luggage?"

"Hey, good plan! But I don't know about the bellhop. Hard to figure these Nips. Maybe yes, maybe no. I can try."

"No. Better not. No point spooking the natives." Helen looked at the room key on the table next to her beer glass. It was of the standard Yale type but larger and with the brand name GOAL featured prominently. The usual Lucite tag was attached, with the number 614 on it. "We'll do without help. Shouldn't be too hard."

"You gonna break in?" Wayne asked eagerly.

"No. *We* are going to slip in like two little mice and not *break* a thing. Our rooms are on the same floor you said, right?"

"Yeah. Hey, you're right. Breaking ... getting into hotel rooms is easy. Let me think ... how about pretending you're this Piper woman, telling the room maid you locked yourself out of the room and getting her to open the door for you? Works like a charm nine times out of ten."

"Maybe back home it works. I bet it won't here. Bet the maid won't understand and even if she did wouldn't do anything on her own initiative. She would call down for direction, permission, whatever. Haven't you noticed that? Any divergence from the expected routine throws most Japanese for a loop. No, we'll just have to pick the lock. It shouldn't be too hard. Good thing they haven't gone hi-tech here yet. Those electronic gizmos controlled by pre-coded cards can be trouble."

"Pick the lock, eh? Okay, if you think you can do it. I still think getting a key from the maid, one way or another, is a hell of a lot easier. While she's making up our rooms tomorrow, for instance."

"Who said anything about tomorrow? Tonight's the night as far as I'm concerned."

"You try your way tonight and if it don't work I'll try my way tomorrow. How's that?"

"Sure, makes sense." Helen sounded amused. Wayne was clearly pleased. He called for another drink and went on eagerly.

"Okay, now tell me about this Nangi. What happened there?"

"He wasn't there. But I met a woman called Keiko

Ueki." She spelled it out for him. "And you'll be glad to hear she's coming over tonight to have dinner with us. Seems very interested in me, that is, Julie Piper. Too, too accommodating. So watch your step. Incidentally, I didn't tell her about you or what you are here for. So handle yourself accordingly."

"Hey, what's she like? A looker?"

"I'd say. She makes Miko look like Commander Data. But don't get your hopes up, Cookie. Or anything else. She is all business and I bet smart as a whip. So keep your hormones under control."

"Sure, sure, Mama-san, whatever you say. You've got your eye on her yourself, right?"

"Give it a rest, Cookie. You haven't even seen her yet. I am going up to my room now. I arranged to meet her in the lobby at eight. You be there and on your best behaviour, you hear?"

Wayne nodded and waved at the bartender.

Once alone in their rooms, each made one international phone call to their respective employers.

13

Dinner for Three

They sat in an Indian restaurant that Keiko had recommended once she'd recovered from the shock of meeting Wayne Tillion. She had arrived expecting an informal dinner with an older, foreign female. She had her instructions and had no doubt of her own abilities. But the addition of a large, young, male *gaijin* just bursting with sexual vibes was throwing her off her stride. Keiko hadn't had this problem since her days as a student in Hawaii with her first experience of Western men. Working for Nangi back in Nagoya she'd met horny American businessmen and dealt with them more than capably. Her ability to do so was almost as useful in her job as her almost perfect English.

Sitting between Helen and Wayne in the restaurant pungent with cardamom, she felt surrounded and invaded. It was difficult to concentrate on Helen, talking with her, drawing her out while feeling the presence of Wayne's heavy body on the other side, his knee touching hers.

Wayne wasn't saying much, happy to leave the business end of the affair to Helen, whom he had trouble remembering to call Julie. He couldn't think of what to say to impress Keiko, overcome as he was by her delicate, feminine beauty. In some deep part of him, Wayne Tillion was a traditional man for whom sexually attractive women came in two distinct categories — whores and angels. The place for whores like Miko was on their backs; the place for angels like Keiko was on a pedestal. It's not that he didn't yearn for Keiko on her back, merely that he didn't know how to go about getting her there. At the same time, he felt a bit uncomfortable, even sacrilegious for wanting to try.

For her part, Helen gave no indication that she had any clue to the predicaments of the two young people. As she told Keiko much, much later and in very different circumstances, she had been prepared for sexual tension between Wayne and Keiko. It was almost inevitable. In the event she found that she couldn't read exactly what was going on. The vibes were strong but different from her expectations. As was her wont in situations she couldn't pin down, Helen carried on as if unaware, giving herself time to sort out the situation and the other two to deal with their feelings. She was pleased but not surprised that Keiko was concentrating on her, the woman, and ignoring Wayne, the man, as much as a well-trained Japanese woman could. After all, Helen was Keiko's job. But Wayne seemed quite satisfied with only a small part of Keiko's attention, which wasn't at all in character.

Over a so-so tandoori chicken, Helen listened solemnly while Keiko continued to exhault the attractions of Nagoya, again offering to act as tourist guide the next day. With Wayne grinning delightedly at the prospect, Helen permited herself to be persuaded to stay in Nagoya for "another day or two." Now they had an excuse to remain here and continue looking for Julie and Mel's precious item. They agreed to meet in the hotel lobby at 10:00 a.m. the next day.

Mission accomplished, having eaten very little and drunk even less, Keiko hurried to leave before coffee was served. She was tired, she pleaded, and so must they be and with a long day of sightseeing tomorrow ... Wayne demurred, but Keiko was adamant and Helen went along. Wayne started by insisting on taking Keiko home — no, she said. If not home then to a taxi — no, she said, her car was just a few blocks away. Could he see her to her car then? Not an offer Keiko could courteously refuse. Wayne was on his feet helping her into her coat. They left Helen sitting at table as an attentive Indian waiter brought coffee.

Wayne was back just as Helen signalled for more coffee.

"Wow!" Wayne almost exploded. "Wow!"

"Indeed."

"What d'ya mean 'indeed'? Fucking gorgeous is all!" Now that the object of his dreams had left, Wayne couldn't contain his excitement. "Wow!"

"How come you were so quiet all through dinner, eh?"

"Couldn't make a move on her with you sitting there, now could I?" Wayne defended himself.

"Why not? Admit it, you didn't have the nerve."

"Oh, yeah? Just watch me. She's real keen to see me again, did you notice? Tomorrow ..."

"Tomorrow we go looking for Julie Piper. Remember? That's what we are here for. Or rather you'll go looking for her. Alone. Checking hospitals for a start ... I'll play tourist with Keiko."

Watching him almost choke on a mouthful of coffee, Helen took pity on Wayne.

"Look, Cookie. I'm not trying to spoil your fun but we've stepped into some funny business here, or haven't you noticed? Keiko was already angling to show me Nagoya before she even knew of your existence. You really think she can just take a day from her job to show two perfect strangers the sights, unless we *are* her job? She's been instructed to keep tabs on us. Your manly charms have zip to do with it. So cool your jets. This isn't about sex. It's something to do with this Piper character that I've been impersonating and wish I hadn't started. So you'd better find her soon — and her precious bundle, whatever it is — so we can get the hell out of here."

Wayne sobered immediately. Helen continued: "Like I said before, we need to take a look in Piper's luggage. A long shot but what else have we got? So let's do her room."

"Now?"

"Now."

14

Julie's Luggage

Julie Piper had gotten one of the best corner rooms in the hotel. Luckily for lock pickers, its door was away from any neighbours and partly hidden in a small alcove at the right-angle junction of two corridors, with elevators almost equidistant along them, on the hypotenuse corridor. Helen and Wayne walked softly along the rose-coloured carpet meeting no one. At the door marked 608, Helen bent down to her task, leaving Wayne the job of protecting her back.

Gripping a tiny "Legend" flashlight in her teeth, she probed the lock with a flexible steel instrument rather like a dental pick. The rest of her collection of small tools, which travelled in the guise of a manicure set in a nice leather zippered case, sagged down her shirt pocket. She was practised in getting at them fast and without fumbling. Wayne had watched as she prepared in her room just down the hall, restless with having nothing to do. Now he did. He stood at the intersection of the two corridors listening for footsteps, for doors opening, for voices in either direction. It was best not to be spotted and they had agreed that the risks of being challenged were small. Who could know that this wasn't Helen's room, that she wasn't having trouble with the key? It was 1:00 a.m. and it was more than reasonable to assume that anyone coming in at this hour would have a certain amount of alcohol in their blood. Wayne could be a gentleman escorting her to her room or an invited bed-partner. It was a totally persuasive scenario but ... it was still better not to be seen. They were just too notice-able even among the small number of non-Japanese hotel guests.

Helen was having problems with the heavy lock. It was proving harder to open than the dead bolts she was used to, possibly because of its larger size and weight. Swearing softly under her breath, she changed tools and chose a harder, less flexible pick with which she hoped to move the tumblers.

Wayne's loud breath and impatient pacing behind her didn't help. She felt herself sweating heavily and for a few painful moments contemplating the possibility of failure. Surely it was sheer hubris on her part to think she could open this door in an unknown city in this very foreign country. Surely she would lose all credibility with Wayne if she didn't.

But a lock is a lock and once she made herself breathe deeply and steadied her hands, it gave up. They tiptoed into the room.

Julie Piper travelled light and smart. There were two pieces of luggage in her room, both still packed, both top-of-the-line matching green Mandarina Duck cases, both small. Helen went first for the over-the-shoulder carry-on. A blue T-shirt with "Now-You-See-It-Now-You-Don't" in old-fashioned script on the front, a pair of sneakers, two pairs of socks, a bag of toiletries, box of tampons, bottle of extra-strength Tylenol, two magazines, a pocket mystery, a pair of sunglasses, a flashlight, a tourist guide to Japan, a Swiss army knife, three flavours of Lifesavers ... plus a mass of flotsam that always accumulates at the bottom of travel bags. Helen went over these extra carefully: a comb, four paper clips, broken nail file, a Cathay Pacific airline board-ing pass to Tokyo, a ballpoint from the Ambassador Hotel in Hong Kong, a much-folded slip of paper with a phone number on one side and what looked like a shopping list on the other, magnifying glass in a leather case, a used tube of sunblock, matches advertising a bar called Waltzing Matilda with no address, a handful of Hong Kong small change, a tangle of rubber bands, a Yale-type key, British Airways coffee spoon ... on and on. She replaced everything as close to the way it had been as possible.

Helen then turned to the suitcase, while Wayne watched with interest. Whatever Julie Piper was wearing when she left, she'd packed for all eventualities. There was a sweatsuit in British racing green with matching running shorts. A tank-top with the crest of a Melbourne Rugby Club. A slinky jumpsuit in black silk with hot pink facings at neck, wrists and ankles. A pair of expensive-looking slacks in beige cavalry twill, with three blouses and a matching vest to go with them. A light jacket of leather and wool, a skirt of the same leather and two pairs of Italian shoes of impossible elegance. Six pairs of new panties in assorted colours, two bras and two pantyhose, four pairs of nylon knee-highs. A magazine. Pad of note paper, blank. Pair of rubber gloves. Small box with costume jewelry, nothing showy or expensive.

No photographs, notes or personal papers of any kind. Nothing that could constitute Mel's item or help them trace the owner. Helen closed the lid gently.

"I guess we struck out, eh?" Wayne said.

Helen slowly nodded her head.

"Looks like it. Sure nothing there to take back to your boss. Or tell us where to find her. Anything personal or important must be in her purse. Which she took with her, naturally. Notice that she hadn't washed or changed? She split out of here in the clothes she travelled in. Jeans, I bet, judging from what's left in that suitcase. Had to be in a hurry. Which suggests that she had to meet someone who couldn't be put off or kept waiting. Not much to go on. Still, now we know a few things about her. Or can guess."

"Yeah, what?"

"She's got expensive tastes, for one."

"Hell, doesn't take Sherlock Holmes to figure that out!"

"She sleeps in the raw, for two."

Wayne chuckled appreciatively.

"You noticed, eh?"

"Sure I noticed. I'm a trained detective. Let's get out of here." Casually Helen picked up the magazine that had been in Piper's bag and put it under her arm.

They snuck out of the room into the dim corridor and made their way into Wayne's room without incident. A bit of an anticlimax after all the problems with the lock but still a relief. They continued over mini bar whisky.

"Try this for size. She's used to travelling. She's smart and sophisticated. She is very, very careful, gives nothing away. She is here in Japan on her own business, which is much more important than the chores she agreed to do for my client. But ... "

"But ... what?"

"But it doesn't mean it's unconnected. In fact, I bet it is. What's your hunch?"

"Dunno. But what I'd like to know is how she makes a living. Regular, I mean. What does she do for eating money, like? That stuff in her bags ... and doing little jobs for guys ... she sounds like a high-priced whore to me."

"Oh? Interesting, yes. There are other possibilities, you know. How about showbiz?"

"Same difference. By me they're all whores. I've seen plenty of the type working hotels, looking for some rich boob to latch onto. Walking around all tarted up with that too-good-for-you look, treating the help like shit. You know the type?"

"Somehow I don't think so. No, we've got quite another breed of cat here. Look at this magazine, *PC NETWORKING*."

"So she reads that computer stuff, so what? So maybe

she went to college. You think that means she couldn't be a whore? Get real!"

"Have it your way, Cookie. I bow to your superior knowledge of the subject."

"Yeah! And stop calling me 'Cookie'! And what did you take it for, anyway?"

"I am interested in computers, so why not? As for 'Cookie,' don't take it to heart so. Just a pet name to show my regard for you. Yo! Have another drink. What will it be, Cookie? How about Suntory Scotch? Like to try that? Or Gordon's?"

"Oh, gimme the gin. You can drink their phony Scotch."

"Right. Up the rebels!"

"Nuts to that. Hope we find this Piper dame soon! You couldn't get me out of this fucking country soon enough to suit me!"

The evening ended with the mini bar empty.

15

Helen Unmasked

Helen and Keiko had spent almost two hours visiting the Atsuta Shrine dedicated to the Kusanagi Sword, one of the Three Sacred Treasures of the Imperial family.

They walked, admired and talked, getting to know and like each other. They ate local kishimen noodles with tempura, and talked. They sat by the little pond watching people watching turtles and talked. They admired the Sacred Tree and the colourful strutting roosters and talked. They dodged groups of Japanese tourists singlemindedly following a little flag carried by their guide and talked.

Helen congratulated Keiko on her English; Keiko described her education and her stay in Hawaii. At first Helen was careful what she said about herself since she was supposed to be Julie Piper but as it soon became clear that Keiko had no idea who Piper might be, Helen felt safe in sticking to the truth, more or less, and merely changing her name to Julie's. Inventing a phony life story was unnecessary.

Finally, when Keiko pulled out a list of half a dozen more tourist attractions that she insisted they had to visit, Helen called a halt.

"Enough already. I need to collapse over a cup of coffee. Honourable Tour-guide, how about finding us a spot with good coffee, preferably for less than five bucks a cup. Know of such a spot?"

"Sorry to have tired you. I know a nice coffee shop near my office. We'll have coffee and I'll go pick up messages and you can rest. Then we go to Tokugawa Art Museum and Nagoya Castle ..."

"You never give up, do you? Do I have to see everything?"

"Well, since you claim to be a tourist, you must act like one, don't you?"

"Touché!" said Helen and the two women looked at each other, laughing.

Presently Helen sat by herself over a second cup of cappuccino, comfortably waiting for Keiko. In spite of the difficulty of remembering to "be" Julie Piper and her suspicions of Keiko's motives in being so accommodating, she had enjoyed their morning excursion. She had to remind herself not to get too interested in the young Japanese woman. Perhaps she'd better sic Wayne on Keiko in the afternoon. Mix and match, mix and match until they could find Piper and get out of here ... Suddenly Keiko was beside her, her manner changed.

"Please don't pretend any more. I don't know who you are or why you are here, but I know you aren't Julie Piper."

Helen stared at her for a minute. "Oh, damn! Well, I guess I knew the masquerade wouldn't hold if we stayed around. Anyway, I never liked playing this 'Julie Piper' character so maybe it's just as well. My name is Helen Keremos of Vancouver, Canada."

Helen scrambled lamely to make the best of a bad job. She produced a dog-eared business card with her name, Vancouver address and PRIVATE INVESTIGATOR printed on it. Printed, not engraved. This proved that she'd told Keiko the truth about herself, just changing her name to protect ... the innocent? Ever careful she'd decided not to use her new bilingual card with the Ladrone name and Hong Kong address.

"Here's my card. I am very sorry."

"Helen Keremos. Yes, so please explain why, what was

your purpose?"

"Fair enough. Well, those were my instructions from Sonny Burke. He's my client. When Julie Piper disappeared on him carrying the payoff for Mr. Kusashita, he hired me to find her. And to complete the transaction by pretending to be her. That way her getting lost wouldn't make any waves over here. So ..."

"Making waves? What do you mean?"

"He thought your Mr. Kusashita would think he was unreliable and wouldn't want to do more business with him. I guess mislaying a courier, especially one carrying a payoff, loses you a lot of brownie points."

For a moment Keiko looked baffled.

"Oh, you make a joke. It is not funny, you know. And it is all wrong. Very bad!"

"Oh, come on! No big deal. What can be so wrong about it? I mean, I am sorry but no harm done. I just substituted for the original courier without telling you of the substitution. You client got his money, and my client covered his ass. What does it matter who the real Julie Piper is? Look, I didn't like it but Burke insisted and it was his call."

"Then Mr. Burke is not very smart man and deserves to lose his business with us. It's not how we do things in Japan. You tell me this story. Now, how do I know it is truth? We can have no more trust in you. How can more business be possible?"

Keiko was enjoying the rare freedom of speaking her mind. She was putting into practice what she knew to be the way Westerners dealt with each other. She'd gotten a taste of it in Hawaii and had never forgotten how good it felt.

Helen leaned forward with interest. She was surprised and somewhat taken aback at Keiko's directness. It ran dead against all she'd read about the Japanese. Weren't they supposed to hate confrontation and strive for social harmony? Weren't the women especially socialized to be agreeable, no matter what? And here was this young, well-brought-up woman pulling no punches.

"Okay, so tell me, how do you do things in Japan? I keep hearing it's so different. You can't be telling me that Kusashita and Nangi wouldn't have held it against Burke that his courier disappeared? Don't tell me that in Japan that wouldn't be seen as a royal fuck-up! You don't mean that!"

"Yes, of course. It is bad for business reputation, yes. Mr. Burke is right about that. But what he asked you to do is worse, much worse. Never can trust him again, cannot do business with a man like that."

"I think what you really mean is that we broke the eleventh commandment ... you know ... 'Don't Get Caught.'"

"Oh, you make jokes all the time! I mean it was very unwise of Mr. Burke to risk our trust. Not necessary at all. There is a better strategy for avoiding problems like that."

"How should he have handled it?"

"Your Mr. Burke should have learned about the Naniwabushi strategy while negotiating with us."

Keiko Ueki laughed, pleased with herself.

"Okay, I'll bite. What or who is Nani ... Naniwabushi?"

"Old Edo ballads," Keiko grinned.

"You aren't going to tell me, are you? Taking the piss out of me, eh? I guess I deserve it. But how about telling me how you found out I wasn't Julie Piper? How did I blow it?"

Although disappointed that Helen wasn't pressing her to explain what old ballads had to do with Japanese business practice, Keiko answered quite readily:

"You didn't blow it. I received a message from Nagoya National Hospital that they have a *gaijin* woman called

71

Julie Piper very sick since two days. I have to go there and sign for her so they can treat her and make her well. That interests you, I think."

Helen was on her feet.

"You think right. Let us go to this hospital and meet Ms. Piper. And on the way, you can tell me all about this Naniwabushi tactic. Deal?"

16

Inspector Haruo Suzuki

Haruo Suzuki had finished his rice, raw egg and miso soup, which he had for breakfast every day. He was sipping his first cup of coffee when his landlady, a stooped grey-haired woman in a worn kimono, apologized for disturbing his morning peace with the news that there was a phone call for him. He grunted, wiped his mouth, stood up and walked past her to the door. He had, of course, heard the phone ring through the thin walls of the traditional house and knew the call was for him since they all were. But he didn't move until properly advised of this fact. His landlord, a more aged male twin of the woman, stood by the front door holding out the receiver. As Suzuki took it from him with a nod, he bowed and disappeared having fulfilled his assigned role.

"*Moshi-moshi.*" Suzuki "helloed" into the phone.

"Inspector-san. I regret to disturb you but ..."

"Get on with it, Sergeant."

"*Hai!* An *omawari-san* found a body in the Uni Mall. Male. A car is on its way to pick you up ... ?"

"Good."

Suzuki hung up. He picked up his raincoat and briefcase and stepped out the door to await his transportation.

On the surface, Haruo Suzuki was indistinguishable from an army of other Japanese salarymen. He was in his mid-thirties, of middle height and weight, with dark brown hair cut short and heavy glasses. He dressed in the regulation dark suit, with white shirt and nondescript tie.

He could have been a middle manager in any one of the thousands of large Japanese corporations. In fact, he was a Police Inspector, First Section (Homicide) the Nagoya Prefectural Police. More than that, Haruo Suzuki was of the elite class, a Tokyo University law faculty graduate. He had been one of only a handful who each year successfully pass the National Public Service examination and so started his career as an Assistant Police Inspector rather than a lowly patrolman. His way was open all the way to the top. Barring accidents, he could count on ending his career as Chief of one of Japan's 47 prefectural police agencies or in a high post in the National Police Agency in Tokyo.

Working in Nagoya in homicide was a good posting for an ambitious policeman, but he didn't expect to stay in Nagoya forever. In fact, he was due for promotion to Police Superintendent and relocation. With luck his new posting would be to Tokyo, which, as well as being the hub of the nation and of his profession, was where his wife and two children lived in a recently purchased modern two-bedroom apartment. He visited them on his days off. In Nagoya he had chosen to lodge in an old-fashioned quarter in the house of a retired policeman and his wife, both of whom considered themselves honoured by Suzuki's presence in their home. For his part, Suzuki a very modern man, much enjoyed living in traditional Japanese atmosphere and being treated like a shogun.

The unmarked police car arrived in minutes. A smartly uniformed officer leaped out and opened the door for Suzuki, saluting punctiliously.

At the Uni Mall, the patrolman who had found the body snapped to attention at Suzuki's approach. A Sergeant in plainclothes remained kneeling, watching as the "scene of the crime" officers meticulously attended to their business. On the other side of the body, a youngish doctor wrote rapidly on a notepad.

Suzuki stopped a metre away and looked around. The body was that of a man in late middle age. It was lying on its side behind a service door well out of traffic flow, on the edge of a wide public space. It was screened from casual view by a set of stairs leading up to one of the many exits to the street. In one direction from this area ran a tiled corridor leading after twists and turns to a subway entrance and on to the basement elevators of Nagoya's International House. In the other direction was the shopping concourse. Brightly lit aquaria full of colourful tropical fish lined the walls, clearly designed to counteract the sterility of this transition zone but with little success. There were no benches; no one lingered here.

"Was the door locked?" Suzuki asked, not seeming to address anyone in particular. The kneeling Sergeant answered immediately.

"Not when he was found."

"How did he die?"

"Garroted. With a piece of common cord. No leads there." Suzuki looked down without expression at the distorted features of the dead man and nodded to himself.

The Sergeant lifted a massive head and stood up. He towered over his younger superior. "He's missing the tip of one of his fingers. Not recently, though."

Suzuki nodded again. There was no need to comment.

"What do we know about him?"

"Tetsu Nangi. Accountant. Had his own business, employed about a dozen people. Working mostly for the construction industry."

Again, no comment was necessary.

"Private life?"

"Unmarried. Lived in Myoon-dori with his sister, a widow. I've sent two men there to make sure nothing is touched until we can get to it."

"Good. Anything interesting on him?"

"Nothing yet."

"And the office?"

"I thought you would want to go there first. It's not far."

"Yes, in a minute." Suzuki turned.

"Doctor, how long since he died? Approximately will do for now."

"Twelve hours, maybe more. Sometime last night, I would say. Can't be sure, you understand ..."

"I understand. Thank you. All right, Sergeant, let's go.

"*Hai!*"

17
Nangi's Office Lady

The Office Lady was badly flustered by the large silent Sergeant and even more by the formal Inspector. Whether willfully or not she managed to misunderstand every question, repeating coherently only a statement to the effect that she couldn't tell them anything, she didn't know anything and they must ask Mr. Nangi. Hiding his exasperation behind the wall of proper politeness Suzuki told her:

"I am so sorry to inform you that Mr. Nangi is dead. That is why we are here ..."

"Some mistake, so sorry. Mr. Nangi just away from the office for a few days. He called in yesterday and talked to Miss Ueki. I know because I took the call ..."

"Then perhaps I might speak to Miss Ueki?" asked Suzuki swiftly changing tactics.

"So sorry. She isn't in the office now. She came in a little while ago, picked up her messages and left right away. Most unusual. She was upset I think by the message from National Hospital. It's nothing serious, I hope."

"What isn't serious? What was the message from National Hospital?"

"About this *gaijin* woman, tall and dark, I don't remember her name, so sorry. Very difficult. I don't speak English so Miss Ueki spoke to her. Now she is in hospital ... So sorry cannot help you. I'll tell Mr. Nangi you called."

She continued to bob and weave, an elderly widow much out of her depth, firm in her resolve not to acknowledge the death of her employer.

"Just one more question. What is Miss Ueki's position here?"

"She has very good job, she's an accountant. Mr. Nangi trusts her with everything, more than anybody else. She handles everything for the most important clients. Very good job, yes."

"I see. Thank you, thank you very much." Suzuki bowed stiffly and continued with heavy authority. "We will leave you for now. There will be other officers here soon. Please extend your cooperation to them."

"Of course, of course. We are always to cooperate with the authorities, Mr. Nangi insists." She continued bowing them out.

"I'll bet! I'll just bet Mr. Nangi cooperated with the authorities! Cooking books for the yakuza is what Mr. Nangi did! And this Ueki woman. I don't think I know a woman accountant, bookkeepers yes, but not accountants." Once out the door, the Sergeant had turned voluble.

"There are quite a few. My wife's sister is an accountant. In Tokyo. She works for one of the foreign banks."

"Ah, foreign. Yes. A foreign woman came to see Ueki yesterday and now she's in hospital. Bet we find Ueki there too."

"No bet. Sergeant, I am going back to the station now, then to National Hospital. You can meet me there. I'll send you a female officer and a couple of men. Interview every employee. Search the place, especially Nangi's and Ueki's desks. If there is a private office, seal it. Make sure nothing is removed. Tomorrow we'll get experts in on this. Fraud Squad."

The Sergeant made a face. He wasn't high on the Fraud Squad. And he wasn't keen on dealing with the elderly Office Lady either. He preferred them young.

18
Meeting Julie

The enormous three-story lobby looked to Helen more like a cross between a railroad concourse and an auditorium than a waiting room of a modern hospital. It was crowded virtually wall to wall with rows upon rows of chairs in white-and-blue plastic. It was the only waiting place in Japan that Helen was to come across where more than enough seating was provided. All the chairs faced one way — onto an ugly semi-abstract mural that stretched over one side of the hall. Above rose a fancy gilded ceiling. The hospital was almost new, built in the expansive eighties. It felt half empty, overbuilt and outsized for current needs.

Walking in from the parking lot, Helen noted a pharmacy on the right and a flower, gift and variety store on the left of the entrance. She was relieved at their familiar, utilitarian aspect.

A few people sat looking at the mural on the wall and smoking. A few stood smoking just outside the doors by the umbrella racks, which in Japan are a feature of entrances to public buildings. There was only one lonely, uncomfortable-looking nonsmoking *gaijin*.

"Wayne! So you found her. Good for you!" said Helen, pleased to see him.

"Yeah. Hi, Keiko, how you doing?" Wayne glanced from Helen to Keiko uncertainly, not knowing what to make of their presence there together.

"I'm fine, thank you. You found the real Julie Piper! So

soon. How did you do it?" Keiko smiled at him brightly.

Wayne looked at Helen for help.

"It's all right, Wayne. Keiko knows I'm not Piper. She heard from the hospital that Piper is here. So how did you find her?"

"Easy — checking city hospitals. I figured the closest hospital to the station first. She'd booked into a hotel just across the street from the station so wasn't apt to be going far, right? Bingo! She's here. I just called the hotel and left a message for you. I guess you didn't need it." He looked put out.

"You're smarter than you look, you know that? Had any problem getting to see her? What's the story?"

"Nah, no problem. This place is so wide open a gorilla could waltz in here carrying a Christmas tree. Nobody stops you. There's no security."

It's true there was little security, but, in fact, there wasn't a soul in the whole hospital complex who didn't know that Wayne was there and whom he'd come to find.

"And I bet you're the nearest to a gorilla they've seen here in a week," Helen said affectionately. "So what'd she tell you?"

"Nothing. She didn't talk. Took one look at me and waved me away. Besides, she's damn sick, if you ask me."

"Oh? So what's the matter with her?"

"Damn it, I don't know! She looks bad! But nobody else here will speak English. The nurses just giggle, bow and split. I couldn't get any answers from anybody. But she looks bad to me." Wayne spoke with evident frustration.

"Never mind, now that Keiko is here, we'll get some answers. Do your stuff, Kei. The hospital authorities called you so they need you. To guarantee the bill, I guess. Don't sign anything until we find out what happened to Piper and what her condition is."

"That wouldn't be correct. First I must do what the

hospital needs from me. Then they will know I'm to be trusted. You see ..." Keiko was all ready to plunge into another discourse on Japanese customs and morés. Helen had other priorities.

"Whatever you say. Let's go. Cookie, you stay here. Have a nice can of coffee." Helen waved at one of the omnipresent coin machines, which in Japan dispense everything from whisky, pornographic comics and beverages designed to boost the virility of overworked salarymen to cold or hot coffee in cans.

"Where's she at?"

"Gynecology/obstetrics, fourth floor. Room 401. Seems very quiet, very few people around. The elevators are slow; it's faster to walk up. Room is just past the nurses' station."

"Obstetrics, eh? She having a baby or what?"

Wayne shrugged and ignoring Helen's suggestion about coffee, sat down on one of the plastic chairs. Stretching his long legs in front of him, he prepared to wait.

While Keiko stopped to talk to the duty nurse on the fourth floor, Helen walked into Julie Piper's room. For a moment she stood looking down on the motionless figure in the regulation hospital bed. The figure stirred, revealing a narrow face, shadowy gray eyes wracked with pain, and a mop of blond hair. A pair of elegant feet poked their way out at the foot of the bed. A bed that was clearly too short.

"Julie Piper?" Helen asked.

"Guess so. Who wants to know?"

"Helen Keremos. Sonny sent me."

"Sonny? Christ!"

"Not hardly."

The woman in the bed chuckled feebly. She turned her head with some effort and visibly tried to concentrate on her visitor. Helen continued.

"You disappeared, you know. He's sort of worried."

"I'll bet!"

"What happened? What's the matter with you?"

"Who knows? — I don't. I'm bloody crook, is all I know."

"What?"

"I'm sick, ill, wrecked, crook. Silly cow, don't you understand English?"

"Some. So speak. Talk to me. What do I tell Sonny?"

"Whatever you like. I'm not going anywhere for a while. These local pill pushers reckon it's real serious, something in my tubes. You know about tubes?"

"No, but I'll find out. Keiko Ueki is here with me so communication with the natives should be no problem from now on."

"Keiko. Well, then I guess you must know at least part of the story. Sonny gave you her name, did he?"

"Yes. And I paid her what was owing to Kusashita."

"Good. Then it's all taken care of." Julie Piper's voice was fading. Helen pressed on.

"Is it? Wayne Tillion is downstairs."

Julie groaned.

"The no-neck wonder who bounced in here a while ago? I was afraid it was him but hoped it wasn't. Well, well. Quite a party." She looked at Helen, then looked away again and closed her eyes. "Sorry. I can't cope right now. He will have to wait."

"We'll all wait. You get well. I'll be back. Anything I can get for you?"

"Other than a couple of jars of Foster's, all I need is a real pillow. Look at it, it's full of rice husks. Made for Japanese necks, not for Aussie heads. Otherwise, no worries." The last words came out in a whisper that belied their content.

"Done," said Helen, left the room and went looking for Keiko.

19
Doctors

Helen found Keiko in a small office down the hall talking, or rather listening, to two male doctors while a female nurse stood by and nodded vigorously at every word. Helen's entrance created a small stir of interest combined with discomfort. Out of courtesy it was now necessary to continue the conversation in English. This was something the senior doctor was loathe to do since it was difficult to be authoritative in a foreign tongue, even one with which he was professionally familiar. His English wasn't quite perfect and only absolute perfection was good enough for him. He therefore left the explication of Julie Piper's condition to his younger colleague while interrupting and correcting the junior man's stumblingly but passable English. Having confirmed his superior status, the senior doctor bowed out followed by the nurse, leaving the other man to cope with Helen.

That young man was now free to admit that the medical staff wasn't quite sure yet what was wrong with Julie.

Helen watched him draw a sketch of the reproductive system of the human female in cross-section. It look very much like the muzzle and spreading horns of a steer. Pointing to one of the horns he said:

"We think that problem there, in the fallopian tube. Maybe ectopic pregnancy."

"What's 'ectopic pregnancy,' Doctor? I've never heard of it."

"Most fortunate to be so unaware. It is fertilized egg

not getting to uterus. Get stuck in tube."

"Oh? How serious is that?"

"Very serious, if so. Must operate. Then take two or three weeks for patient to get better."

"I doubt that Julie Piper will put up with staying here that long. Tell me, how soon will you know enough to get on with the operation, should it be necessary?"

"Soon, very soon. We have done tests, results maybe this afternoon. Now that Miss Ueki is here to take responsibility for patient, we will do operation as soon as possible. Dangerous to wait."

"Who will do the operation? You or Doctor-know-it-all ...?" Helen nodded towards the door just exited by the other man. The young doctor, while still smiling at Helen, kept glancing at Keiko. It was her role to help him with this crude *gaijin*. Well-socialized Japanese women spend their lives making the way smooth for Japanese men, at least in public.

Whether Keiko would have leaped to it will never be known. She was interrupted by the sudden entrance of Police Detective Inspector Haruo Suzuki, followed by the large Sergeant. Bringing up the rear was the senior doctor, who wasn't about to be left out of this exciting development.

20

Suzuki at the Hospital

Suzuki had noted with interest the large male foreigner in the hospital lobby, sprawled on a blue-and-white chair too small for him. He looked to be waiting for someone or something. Suzuki couldn't help connecting him with the mysterious *gaijin* woman he himself had come to find. A good cop is suspicious of coincidence. There just weren't that many Westerners to be found in hospital lobbies. A matter to be looked into in good time. His immediate objective was the sick woman and, of course, Keiko Ueki.

There was only one *gaijin* patient in the hospital and every one had heard about her. By the time he'd made it to the administration block he had already been assured that she was two metres tall, that she was dead, that she was found naked in the mall the night before, that it was two nights ago, that she'd been raped, that she'd been shot, that she was pregnant, that no one knew who she was, that she was ugly, that she was beautiful ... He took in that she'd had visitors and that one of them was the large *gaijin* in the lobby. Also two women who'd just come in, one of them also *gaijin*. As is normal in police experience, everyone knew much that was none of their business and not necessarily accurate. Everyone was eager to know more, accurate or not.

Hospital administration was housed in a separate building, even more empty, luxurious and dull than the hospital proper. A series of polite functionaries directed the Inspector to a counter in the middle of a large office where he introduced himself to the assistant chief administrator and explained his guest. As was to be expected he received full cooperation.

"The name of *gaijin* woman is Julia Piper. She was admitted, let me see, two nights ago, quite late. Brought here by a gentleman in a taxi. Unfortunately, he left without giving his name. She had no identification on her so we didn't know who she was until she came around this morning. Gave us her name and her contact in Nagoya. Yes, Miss Keiko Ueki. Miss Ueki was here just a moment ago and has gone to speak to the doctors who are looking after the patient Piper. You will find her in the gynecology/obstetrics floor ... no, I cannot tell you what's wrong with her, sorry. You will have to ask the doctors. Not at all, very pleased to be of service to the police."

On his way to the gynecology/obstetrics floor, Suzuki met his Sergeant and minutes later both of them were walking in on Helen, Keiko and the puzzled young doctor.

21

Meeting Helen

Suzuki sorted out the complicated situation with masterly efficiency and precision. The medical contingent was shooed out to be interrogated about Julie Piper by the Sergeant. Suzuki stayed to concentrate on Keiko Ueki and Helen Keremos, the mysterious visitor to Nangi's office. Proud of his English and, unlike the pompous senior doctor, not a bit shy at using it, he introduced himself and demanded identification. Helen took out her passport and her Vancouver business card. Suzuki looked at them with attention.

"Ms. Keremos, how very pleasant to meeting fellow detective. Have never before. You visiting Mr. Nangi's office yesterday, yes?"

"Yes."

"Perhaps you were Julie Piper, now sadly very ill here in hospital. So glad to find you well. Regrettable misunderstanding, yes?"

"Yes."

"You and Miss Ueki now here to visit Ms. Julie Piper, yes?"

"Yes."

"Ms. Keremos, please be so good to help. Why do you come to Nagoya? Please don't say for tourism."

"I won't. I came to find Miss Piper."

"Ah. Together with large gentleman downstairs?"

"Yes."

"Whose name is ...?"

"Wayne Tillion."

"Thank you. Now please be more helpful. Who is Ms. Piper and why is she here?"

"I don't know."

"Please explain circumstance for looking for someone you don't know."

"I'm sorry. That's confidential."

"Not confidential from police. I regret you must tell me. This is homicide investigation."

"Murder you mean. Whose murder?"

Suzuki swung around from facing Helen to Keiko and answered:

"Miss Ueki's employer. Mr. Tetsu Nangi."

"Nangi has been murdered?! How? When?" Helen tried to keep Suzuki's attention on her, giving Keiko more time to take in the information.

"It seems last night. When did you see Mr. Nangi last, please?"

"I've never clapped eyes on him."

"'Clapped eyes' ... ? Oh, you mean you never saw him. Then perhaps I better ask this of Miss Ueki?"

Suzuki continued in Japanese:

"When did you last see your employer? Or hear from him, perhaps?"

"He really is dead! Oh, I must call his sister. How she must be feeling badly! It's terrible, terrible."

Keiko had fallen immediately into that twittering manner of speech common among Japanese women that appears so obsequious to Westerners. She found that she couldn't do otherwise when addressed and answering in Japanese. It is virtually a cultural imperative of the language. "So sorry, Inspector, so sorry. I don't remember. Oh, dear! He called, yesterday, I believe. I haven't seen him in a number of days. He hasn't been to the office since ...? Perhaps someone there will know. So sorry."

"You spoke to him on the phone, did you say? Yesterday? What time? What about?" Suzuki barked out his questions, confidently pressing his advantage, wanting to keep her off-balance. Intimidating a young Japanese female, even a well-educated one, wasn't hard. He knew he was at a disadvantage with Helen Keremos, an older Western woman who wasn't used to being bullied and could easily make a fool out of him in English. Although Helen didn't understand Japanese, she understood the dynamics perfectly. She moved in.

"Go easy on her, Inspector. Can't you see Miss Ueki is upset? Give her a little time to pull herself together and I'm sure she will answer your questions. Here, Keiko, sit down. Would you like a drink of water? Perhaps coffee. Inspector Suzuki, we need some coffee for Miss Ueki. Please. Now, Keiko, take it easy. I know it's a shock but you must pull yourself together. All right? No, I won't leave you. I'll be right here."

Being a smart cop means knowing when to retreat graciously. Suzuki picked up the phone, asked for his Sergeant and told him to produce lots of coffee and to collect Wayne Tillion while he was at it. He then returned to questioning the two women until he'd gotten as much out of them as he could.

It took another hour. The matter of Keiko's recent contact with Nangi was soon cleared up. She hadn't seen him for days and didn't know what he'd been up to. She had spoken to him only that one time the day before when he'd given her instructions about an account she was having trouble with. Nothing to do with Julie Piper, Keiko insisted. Helen knew she was lying at least about the subject of the call. What Suzuki suspected only Suzuki knew.

Disentangling Helen from her unfortunate masquerade as Julie Piper also didn't take long. Helen had decided to insist that the poor old Office Lady had gotten it all wrong; she'd never claimed to be Julie Piper. It was just miscommunication due to lack of a common language. Keiko looked at her when she said this but clearly wasn't about to give her away. Now they had each lied to Suzuki and both knew it. A cozy feeling.

Helen then allowed herself to be persuaded to tell Suzuki why she and Wayne Tillion were in Nagoya. She said that they were friends of the sick Miss Julie Piper and had arrived to look after her. Helen's visit to Nangi's office was pure coincidence. She'd come to talk to Miss Ueki whom she knew to be Miss Piper's friend. No connection with Nangi.

The next hurdle was Wayne. What would he tell the police? There was no way of priming him to tell the same story before Suzuki took him aside. But there were no flies on Wayne. His answers were short and his position simple. His story didn't differ markedly from Helen's: they'd come to find and look after Julie Piper ... he'd never entered Nangi's office or had any no connection with him alive or dead.

All of this did sound sort of plausible. There was no way of judging how much of it Suzuki believed. It didn't much matter as long as he couldn't prove otherwise.

The three of them were finally allowed to leave with the usual proviso that they stay in Nagoya and present themselves at the station the next day. They piled into Keiko's car under the watchful eye of the Sergeant and took off for the hotel. There was silence for a few minutes broken by Keiko: "What will Julie Piper tell Inspector Suzuki?"

"You can be sure she won't mention your boss Kusashita or any money changing hands. You can relax about that. As for anything else she might say, who knows? A better question is what are *you* going to report to your bosses about Piper, Wayne and me, eh? Let's be frank with each other. You might have worked for Nangi but he really worked for the yakuza. Yes?"

Keiko remained unfazed.

"Yes. But I don't know much about you so there isn't that much I can tell them. Of course you're right, I will report and very likely you will have to meet one of Mr. Kusashita's senior men."

"Oh yeah? And not with Mr. Kusashita himself?"

"Who is this guy Kusashita anyway?" Wayne Tillion interrupted impatiently from the backseat of the car. He'd been rehearsing in his mind a report to Mel Romulu whom he intended to call immediately on arrival at the hotel. He wasn't looking forward to it. Bad enough that Mel's precious item was still unrecovered. Getting involved, no matter how indirectly, in a murder in this strange land guaranteed trouble. Mel would not be pleased.

"Head of the local mob, that's who."

"The mob! Christ, that's all I need! So what about the mob? What do I tell Mel?"

"Let's save it for later, dig? Now look at the bright side. We've found Piper, haven't we?"

"Oh? Right." And he fell silent again digesting what he'd been told. His job for Mel was no business of Keiko's. Or her employers.

The implications of this conversation did not escape Keiko. She twigged that Wayne Tillion wasn't Helen's partner in any real sense. He didn't know what Helen knew. They had been looking for Julie Piper together but it seemed to be only a matter of temporary convenience. Keiko Ueki surmised quite correctly that they served different employers. She hoped that this information would be of interest to her bosses.

22

Sonny Burke

A tiny thrill ran through Sonny Burke's body. He sat up in bed almost pulling the sheet off his still sleeping companion. But the thrill had nothing to do with Canton Bill's muscular, virile body. It was caused by the almost inaudible tone of Sonny's phone. Specially designed to alert him to an urgent incoming call or fax no matter what he was doing: reading, sleeping or having sex.

Rather than use the bedside extension, Sonny padded across his large cluttered living quarters to the long table that held the tools of his trade. He was naked, his bronze skin shining with the sweat of recent sex. He picked up a towel, made a stab at wiping himself, then sat down on it at the table.

"Yes." He spoke softly into the instrument so as not to wake Canton.

"Sonny? Helen Keremos. I have news."

"Sounds ominous. What gives?"

"We've found Julie Piper. She's in hospital. And that's the good news."

"Whoa! What's the matter? How is she?"

"Not good. Seems she'll need an operation. They aren't sure yet just what it is but a tubal pregnancy has been mentioned. The term is 'ectopic.' Look it up."

"Julie is pregnant! That's great! A kid ... "

"Sonny, you aren't listening. There's no baby coming and Julie might die. The egg didn't get to the right place or something. Like I said look it up."

"Okay, okay, I get it. But what d'you mean Julie might die? Fuck, she's stronger than a horse. Where is she, in Nagoya? Gotta get her out of there and away from those little Nip doctors. Get her to an American hospital with proper medical attention ..." his voice broke off.

"Better start listening to what I'm telling you, Sonny. Julie isn't going anywhere for a while. And these quacks are probably as good as any. Now listen up. Julie's health is not the only problem we've got. Like I told you that was the good news. The bad is that Nangi got wasted last night. Murdered."

"Nangi? He's Kusashita's boy. These guys ice each other all the time. Why is that my problem? Nothing to do with me."

"Oh, yeah? So it's not your problem? Well it sure as hell isn't mine. But I have to deal with it and I work for you, remember? Wake up, Sonny, and listen good. Julie arrives here one day to meet somebody. It was Nangi, right! She must have gotten real sick soon after she arrived so probably set the meeting up near her hotel. It's right by this big mall they have here. Some guy drives her to hospital and disappears. Next day Nangi is found dead. In the mall. You getting this Sonny, or do I have to spell it out?"

"Hell, I get it. I wish I didn't. What about the cops?"

"What about them? Inspector Haruo Suzuki. Elite cop, sharp, nothing much will get by him. Speaks English. He won't let us leave until this is cleared up."

"Has he connected this guy who dropped off Julie in hospital with Nangi?"

"What d'you think? No Japanese would disappear like that unless he had something to hide. Then next day I waltz into Nangi's office asking for Julie Piper. Or pretending to be Julie Piper. Either way the connection is made."

"She couldn't have killed him, for Christ's sake!"

"No, but I could. And I work for you."

For a few seconds the line between Nagoya and Hong Kong went silent. Then Sonny said softly:

"Did you find it? What Julie was carrying?"

"No."

"She tell you where it is?"

"No and doesn't seem to intend to. She had nothing with her when she got to the hospital. And we've checked her luggage here in the hotel. Nothing in there but her personal things, clothes and such."

"That 'we' is you and my client's courier, right?"

"Right. I know your client. And his courier. Met them both a couple of years ago on a case in Toronto."

"Small world."

"You would say that. Enough of this chit chat. What next?"

"Keep an eye on Julie for me, that's first priority. And you may as well go on looking for that item, since you cannot leave. Maybe she'll give you some clue ..."

"My first priority is to stay out of the local slammer. I wouldn't do so good bedding down on the floor. As for Julie, sure I'll look after her as best as I can. But she isn't exactly outgoing, you know. How about you call her at Nagoya National Hospital? Tomorrow should be okay. Maybe she'll tell you something useful."

"I'll do that. Hey, buy her some flowers. On my account."

"Done. This pregnancy, you believe it's your doing?"

"A man can never be sure, can he?"

"You're breaking my heart. Just answer the question."

"Likely. Very likely. Hell, yes. Had to be."

"It didn't have to be but you think it was. Right?"

"Right. Say, how did Nangi die?"

"Garroted."

"Bah, that makes it a professional job and you've nothing to worry about."

"If you say so, Mr. Burke. Meanwhile send another couple of grand. This isn't the job I signed up for."

"How about Ladrone? You talked to them yet?"

"No. They are next."

"Well, hit them for money. That way I'll be paying you through them. Not directly."

"Bit late to worry about that, isn't it? What about that draft at the AmEx office? Think the cops won't be able to trace it?"

"They can try. Won't get them anywheres. Least ways not to me."

"You sure cover your ass like mustard plaster, Mr. Burke."

Sonny looked down at himself and for the first time since the conversation began, he laughed.

"Not as you'd notice it! Bye now. And don't forget the flowers."

He hung up, his face grave again. Across the room Bill sat up in bed. The two men looked at each other.

"Bad news, chief?" Bill broke the silence.

"Yes. Julie's in hospital. You better git now, Bill. I've got work to do."

"So do I. Christ, look at the time. A quick shower and I'm gone."

"No time for that. Take yourself out of here. Now, go!"

"Right."

Clad only in a pair of Hawaiian pattern beach shorts Canton Bill left the room. Went first upstairs to shower and change in his family quarters and then down to the bar where the evening rush was just beginning. If he felt any sorrow at Julie Piper's illness, it didn't show.

23

CHNOPS

Sonny called Mel Romulu in Toronto. The line was busy. Entering his professional phone mode, he waited without impatience pressing the redial button three times before Mel answered.

"You've heard."

"Yes. What do we do?"

"Nothing."

"I could recall Wayne, give up on the ... merchandise."

"You're dreaming, man! You know pulling out now won't do no good. If the cops keep on digging, you're in deep doo-doo."

"*We* are in deep doo-doo my friend, please don't forget that. Anyway who can say what the cops will turn up. Maybe nothing. In which case ..."

"In which case you would've sacrificed that very fine item for nothing. Can't have it both ways. Better stay in and try to fake it. This Keremos broad, who incidentally says she knows you, she's staying. She'll keep on at it, looking for your item and keeping me informed. How about it?"

"Helen Keremos is very good. She gave me a hard time once. But she's only staying because the cops won't let her go. But they've got nothing on Wayne. He can leave anytime I tell him. Break contact, finito. I'll be out of it."

"Like they say, 'you can run but you can't hide.' You're in too deep, Doc, and you know it. If the cops find that item before we do and start connecting all the dots ... our little scam will be history. Hell, it won't matter a damn who killed Nangi or why."

"What's your point, Burke?" Romulu was finally showing impatience.

"Don't do nothing, Doc. Don't pull out Tillion, it will look bad. Our gal Helen will find that merchandise, you just bet on it. Then Tillion can pay her and vamoose. So ... leave it to me."

"I have left it to you, damn it, and look where it got me! Oh, all right, what choice have I got? I'll tell Wayne to stay put. He'll want more money, I bet. Christ!"

"Be cool now, man. You're in the big leagues now. You'll be hearing from me soon." Sonny hung up.

Mel Romulu stared at the dead phone for some time pondering what Burke had said. Big leagues, eh?

Sonny didn't hurry to take his much-needed shower. Instead he wandered uneasily around his domain, still carrying his towel on which he kept wiping his hands. Once he stopped in front of his work table and stared at his computer. He was weighing possibilities, trying to come to a decision. Finally he made up his mind and acted on it immediately. He turned on the computer, activated the modem and dialed. Moments later he was in an international network and his message sat in the designated board waiting for the right recipient to find it. The message was short: "CHNOPS, MAYDAY, HK."

Sonny didn't like computers and used his only when it was unavoidable. Reluctantly he'd decided that contacting CHNOPS was unavoidable and this was the only way. Having followed instructions he had no doubts that he would hear from CHNOPS within two hours. Now there was plenty of time to take a shower.

24
Suzuki's Men

Loud banter died and a dozen well-barbered heads bowed towards Inspector Haruo Suzuki as he entered the room. It was full of homicide detectives and cigarette smoke. Most of the men — no women were present — were in their thirties and wore charcoal-grey suits, white shirts and neutral ties. They had been lounging about, smoking, talking and making plans for the evening *enkai*, the squad drinking party. At the entrance of the Inspector they all stood at attention and bowed from the waist with hands on their thighs. His bow was measurably less deep and less prolonged.

"It is good to see you all here, in good spirits. We have an important case to solve. We must all do our best and work hard for the honour of the Nagoya homicide squad."

"*Hai!*" the squad replied as one man and bowed again.

"We will now hear reports from everyone. We must all listen so that nothing escapes us. If anyone has any comments, speak up. Sergeant!"

"*Hai!*" The largest man in the room looked around and indicated the most junior detective. This was a man still in his twenties, one of the few in jeans and leather jacket. Taking out his notebook, he cleared his throat and reported:

"As for my assignment, I checked out the two *gaijin*: Helen Keremos, female, and Wayne Tillion, male. They arrived in town together on the train from Tokyo the afternoon of the murder. Keremos went immediately to

Nangi's office. Tillion booked them both into Miyako Hotel, same hotel where Piper had booked the day before. One of the hotel clerks reports — the one who speaks good English — that the American asked many questions about the Piper woman, when she arrived, when she left, what she was wearing, like that. That evening both of them met Miss Ueki in the lobby — another clerk recognized her from a photograph — and went out. We traced them to The Mogul, an Indian restaurant in the mall, where they had dinner. The waiter remembers that Miss Ueki and the American went out together before the end of the meal and Tillion returned alone soon afterwards."

The speaker paused as one of his colleagues interrupted: "Excuse me, Inspector, but the Mogul is just a couple of hundred metres from where Nangi was found; it's the same mall. And the time checks out. Could it be that Miss Keiko Ueki left the restaurant to meet her boss? And killed him?"

"Interesting possibility. But remember, Means, Motive and Opportunity. The garrote is not a woman's method. Is she strong enough to overpower a grown man? Why would they meet at night in the mall when they could see each other in the office every day? What motive? Many unanswered questions. However, since she did have opportunity, Miss Ueki can be considered a suspect. Anything else?"

"Perhaps the American she left with? He could have done it."

"According to the waiters, there wasn't enough time. He was only gone about 10 minutes. It would have taken him that long to get back from escorting Miss Ueki to her car. So unless they were in it together, which seems far-fetched, he is clean. As is the older woman with him. She never left the restaurant. Carry on."

The original speaker looked down at his notes and

continued: "The two *gaijin* then came back to the hotel where they stayed up late, drinking. Mini bars were empty in both rooms according to the room service supervisor. But no sex. Hotel staff assumed at first that they were mother and son but now they are sure they are business partners of some sort. No one can figure them out. The American male uses the Hotel Health Club, he does weights, is very strong according to ..."

"Do we need all these details, Inspector?" someone asked.

"It is best to have it all now. Who can tell at this time what is relevant. A point, they are not Americans but Canadians. It is important to be accurate even in minor matters. Please go on with your report."

"... the physical training instructor." This time the junior detective continued just where he left off as if no interruption had occurred. "Yesterday Ueki again came to the hotel and went out with Keremos. Tillion went out alone. The two women went to the Atsuta Shrine, seemed to be sightseeing. Tillion got a taxi driver who speaks some English and had himself driven to the hospital. There he tried to get information about Piper. Took him quite a long time, but he was most insistent and even ill-mannered, according to the nurses. He went in to see her finally, but left almost immediately. Nurses said that she wouldn't talk to him."

There were sniggers from the back of the room at this. The detective looked up at Suzuki, then continued: "Sometime later the two women arrived, spoke to Tillion in the hospital lobby. Keremos went up to Piper and talked to her for a few minutes. According to the duty nurse who saw her afterwards, Piper was glad to see Keremos. Then Ueki went to administration and then both of them talked to the doctors about Piper's health. That is when you arrived, Inspector. All three left together in Ueki's car directly to the hotel. She then went home. Both Canadians made long-distance phone calls from their respective rooms soon after arrival. We are getting the numbers they called. Neither of them left the hotel last night, as far as we could tell. In addition to the main entrance, there are two side exits to the street from the hotel, as well as one underground exit to the mall so we could have missed them.

"This morning Keremos went to the hospital with a parcel containing a hotel pillow, a new *yukata* and some toilet things for Piper. However, Piper was being prepared for surgery and not having visitors so they didn't speak. Tillion went to the Health Club. He pressed 100 kilos."

There was an appreciative murmur from the detectives.

"This afternoon, Ueki picked up the Canadians and took them to the offices of the Kusashita Construction Company where they stayed 56 minutes."

The young man stopped. The room broke up in exclamations of surprise and interest. Everyone knew that Kusashita was the local *oyabun*, a yakuza chief. Obviously pleased with the reaction, the detective continued: "They returned to the hotel where I left my partner, Detective Ito, to continue surveillance. That is all." He closed his notebook, bowed and stepped back into the crowd.

"Very good, Detective Okuda. Please continue surveillance. And follow up on the phone numbers, of course. Now, who's next?"

A grey-suited man stepped forward and gave his report in a sullen monotone.

"My partner and I went to the home of the deceased where we interviewed his sister, a widow. The deceased is unmarried. She knows nothing about his work but to her knowledge he had no enemies. He left for work as usual on the morning of his death and did not return." He stopped. The Sergeant moved his shoulders impatiently.

"Well, keep going," the Sergeant snapped. "Why didn't she report him missing when he didn't come home that night? What did you find in his rooms? Go on!"

"She says that he often stayed away overnight. She didn't ask where or what he did."

There was knowing laughter and a voice at the back of the room said something about "love hotels."

The sullen detective continued, "We tossed his room but found nothing. Except this."

He handed the Sergeant a matchbox. Everyone craned forward to see it. The Sergeant read the name, "FineFun," aloud and handed it to the Inspector with a snort, "A fag! This is a hangout for faggots."

"Beg your pardon, Sergeant, yes, but not necessarily. Many *gaijin* of all kinds go there. It's very fashionable," one of the men volunteered. Someone else poked him on the back laughing, "How would you know? You just got married! Who can afford those fancy places?"

Banter continued until the Inspector spoke: "We are progressing. There are a number of possibilities. One, Nangi was killed on orders from his boss. Two, he was killed by a gay lover. Three, one of the *gaijin* killed him. We will pursue all three lines of inquiry. Sergeant, check out this bar. Find out if they know Nangi, who he spent time with. Who goes there ... you know the drill."

"*Hai!* Who's next?"

The next man stepped forward, looking pleased with himself.

"We searched the mall very thoroughly but found nothing of interest. Until we checked in the Lost and Found, as you suggested, Inspector. We found the handbag of Piper! It was turned in at closing time the evening Piper was brought to hospital. A man answering Nangi's description came around the next day and tried to claim it but the clerk wouldn't give it to him because he had no authorization from the owner."

The handbag was passed to the Inspector, who nodded in a satisfied manner and tucked it under his arm.

"Sergeant, find anything of interest in Nangi's offices?"

"Can't tell, Inspector. We're working on it."

"And the Fraud Squad?"

"They are getting in our way as usual. But yes, they've sent a whole unit to go over every detail."

"Anything to suggest Nangi was a homosexual?"

"Sir, we are doing all we can."

"Of course you are, Sergeant. I am sure everyone here is. We must all redouble our efforts. Thank you."

25

Helen's Knees

Wayne Tillion was enjoying himself. For him the visit to Kusashita Construction had been a success. He'd loved the formality, he'd loved sitting on his haunches in front of a little table and being served tea by exotic babes with powdered faces and fancy kimonos! He wasn't much bothered by the four silent men who sat across the room and stared at him and Helen. He leaned back and let Helen talk with a young man in sunglasses whose name they didn't catch and who asked questions in smooth American-English. Wayne couldn't take the whole thing seriously. It was just like the movies! Nipponland Theme Park! Virtual Reality!

But the best thing about it was that Helen Keremos hated the whole experience! In the past few days they had gotten along well enough; in fact, he'd decided Helen was okay. He even admitted to himself that he was glad of the companionship. Nevertheless, ever since Helen had invaded his room in Tokyo he had felt at a disadvantage. More than that, once in a while her face would go stony and strange. He would see the witch in her and feel a momentary twinge of ... discomfort is all he would admit to. But hey, no more! Now that feeling was gone. She was just an ancient female with creaky joints. He felt almost euphoric.

Humming softly under his breath Wayne made his way down the hall to Helen's room and knocked: "Tum-tu-tum-tum tam tam."

"It's me. Time for dinner. How about buying me a drink first?" he sang out.

He heard her limping towards the door. She was wearing a *yukata* supplied by the hotel and a pained expression. Her hair was dishevelled.

"Come in. Help yourself to a drink. I won't be long." She marched into the bathroom and closed the door.

"Take your time." Wayne opened a beer and sat down on one of the beds. "Your knees still bothering you, eh? Gee, that's too bad. Guess it's something you have to get used to while you're young, sitting on the floor like that, I mean."

There was no answer from behind the bathroom door. Finally it opened and Helen walked back into the room. She was dressed, her hair was combed and she had a "don't mess with me" look on her face.

"Quit your gloating and get off that bed. Make me a drink while you're at it." Wayne moved and she took his place, stretching out as comfortably as her ailing knees allowed. He handed her a glass of whisky and sat down on a chair. Helen took a long drink and continued, "Yes, my knees hurt. Yes, I'm too old to be comfortable on the floor. That's not all that's bothering me."

"Hey, you aren't worried about the guy who asked us all those questions, are you? Whoever he was. He wasn't the boss, right? I thought we were going to see this mob boss, Kusashita. How come we didn't?"

"Maybe we did but didn't know it. One of the other four guys could easily have been Kusashita."

"No shit! Which one? They all looked alike to me. Why would the boss hide like that?"

"What did you expect? A Japanese Godfather? Throwing his weight around, giving orders 'or else'? I don't think the Japanese work that way. Most probably Kusashita wanted to look us over without actually dealing with us directly."

"Sneaky bastards!" Tillion was struck by a thought. "So

what was all that malarkey about then? Why d'you think they got us there? That room with tatami mats, geishas and all that tea paraphernalia? Why not a regular office? That's an office building with regular meeting rooms with chairs and tables, just like in an office back home. So why the traditional number?"

Helen took that as a rhetorical question and just sipped her drink. Tillion continued: "I guess I thought it was an honour! Felt that way, anyway. How come it matters to you? Just because you were uncomfortable there ... aha."

"Right. That's why. I figure it was a little light intimidation. Discomfort to put us at a disadvantage."

"If you're right then it didn't work," Wayne laughed. "Not with me, anyway."

"Yeah, well it sure worked on me," Helen admitted ruefully.

"So what d'you think they wanted from us, eh?"

"I got the distinct impression from the way the questioning went that to them Nangi's murder was of secondary interest. It was us they were interested in, primarily. Like, what were we doing in Nagoya. And Julie — lot of attention on Julie. They wanted to figure out how we all three related to Nangi, to his death."

"Yeah, could be. Now you mention it ... I guess I wasn't paying attention. So what do you think it means?" Wayne was conscious of losing control of the situation to Helen. Again. He took a stab at regaining it. "Maybe they did him themselves. You think?"

"Maybe. Or they know or suspect who did. But not *why!* That is what's worrying Mr. Kusashita and his boys. They believe it had something to do with us being here. Or at least with Piper."

"But what if they did have him killed? It was a professional hit, right? And these guys sure look professional to me!"

"Damn it, Cookie, I just said that!" Helen made no effort to tone down her irritation. "But not necessarily. Anyone can buy a hit like that if they know where to go. Anyway, whether this bunch is guilty or not, the point is that they are confused about me impersonating Piper, about who I am and who you are and why we followed Piper here. *And* I bet they are sure that Nangi met Julie the day she arrived and that it was he who took her to hospital. I'll bet he didn't report any of this to them. Working on his own. That they wouldn't like. So maybe they killed him for trying to freelance. And now they are nervous about all the things they don't know. Like how Julie and you and I fit in."

"They and me both. How *do* we fit in?"

"Wake up Cookie! We're after something Piper is supposed to be carrying, right? Well, look here. I've something to show you."

Helen reached down to the floor next to the bedside table and picked up the computer magazine she'd "borrowed" from Julie Piper's bag. She passed it to Wayne and leaned back again, bending her knees up to ease her back.

"Check out the centre spread."

"What the hell?" Wayne flipped carefully through to the middle of the magazine as if it was going to explode in his hands. In the centre of the glossy coloured pages was a black-and-white four-page insert. "One of those mail-order sections. What about it?"

Helen didn't answer. He looked closer. Each page was divided into numbered boxes and each box contained a description of an object with a blurry picture above it. A mail-order catalogue to the life.

It was desktop published with numbered descriptions — in English — of paintings, prints, sculptures and objets d'art. At the end was what appeared to be a price list, with prices running up to $50,000 U.S. Wayne turned it over and looked at every page. There were no markings of any kind. He looked again, impatiently. There was no name or title, no indication of source, no address or phone number — nothing. The thing was totally anonymous.

"What are these things? Let's see, this one says *The Stag Hunt*, Lucas Cranach, 1472-1555 — it's a painting! They are all, like, art. Sculpture and stuff. Someone selling these things by mail order? Anonymously? Out'a computer book?"

"Strange, isn't it? Yeah, that's how it struck me too. What do you reckon, is this what you've been sent all this way to collect? A fire sale catalogue of art objects, most probably stolen, considering the low prices, camouflaged in a magazine?"

"No way! This shit could be sent in a letter or fax and not be spotted. Wouldn't make sense to send me all this way for it. I was told a 'package,' not big but definitely not this." Wayne paused and considered the full implications of what Helen had suggested, "But now I think about it, Mel *is* a bit of an art freak. His fancy place up there at the Diamond Plaza Towers, it's full of pieces like this, I mean paintings and stuff. Could be a connection, must be. Let's call and ask him." He looked at Helen expectantly. She took the magazine out of his hand and threw it down on the floor.

"You do that. Then we'll go down to eat."

Wayne reached for the phone. "Hey, what time is it back home in Toronto anyway? I've lost track."

"Don't blame you. It's about three in the morning. Something like that."

"No shit! So we'll get him up, eh?"

But Mel Romulu didn't answer his phone. Wayne had to be satisfied with leaving a message on his machine.

26
Piper's Purse

Piper's purse was a handsome over-the-shoulder affair in blond leather. Suzuki emptied it onto his desk. As he opened each zipper and checked for hidden compartments, the pile of items in front of him grew. Carefully he examined each item, replacing most of them and putting a few aside — wallet, a tiny address book, airline tickets, two maps and a small bundle of letters.

Wallet contained a passport, AmEx traveller's cheques, a wad of Japanese currency, four credit cards, a cheque-book for a Hong Kong bank, a slim Parker pen and a Casio card-size solar calculator.

Address book looked new and held only 10 names and phone numbers, seven of them in Hong Kong and three in Japan. None of the former meant anything to Suzuki. The latter were Wayne Tillion at the Tokyo Hilton, Nangi at his office and Keiko at her home. Suzuki grunted in disappointment.

Airline tickets were an open return Narita/Hong Kong on Cathay Pacific.

One of the maps was of the city of Nagoya. There was nothing on it. The other was of the station complex. Hotel Miyako, where Piper had registered, was marked with a discreet cross. As was entrance number 15 to the Uni Mall. It happened to be the nearest entrance to where Nangi's body had been found. No coincidence, Suzuki was sure.

There turned out to be three letters. One, signed

"Mum" (clearly a keen gardener) contained very little except a lament about pest-infested roses. Another, signed only "J" was on European-type airmail paper and appeared to be from a friend of Julia Piper who hadn't seen her for a long time and hoped to see her soon. Neither letter included a return address and there were no envelopes. The third letter was more promising. It was a short note on the letterhead of a journal called *ARTrace*, with a phone number in Las Vegas, Nevada, U.S.A., no return address. It was signed "Bob" and seemed to be merely confirmation of something received, presumably from Piper.

In short order, the contents of the address book and all three letters were copied and all items replaced in the bag. Suzuki planned to take it to Julie with the compliments of the ever-efficient Nagoya Police Department. He intended to interview her personally just as soon as doctors at the hospital decided that she was well enough to have visitors.

Suzuki was a good cop because he held to the truism that investigators always missed something the first time around. He knew that it was never a waste of time to go over everything again. Only differently the second time. For the following morning he scheduled a follow-up sweep of Nangi's house and the mall area where his body had been found and re-interrogation of everyone concerned. Different teams of detectives would examine with fresh eyes and interrogate with fresh minds.

Two detectives were given the task of checking out the "Who" and "What" of the seven Hong Kong names. Another was to go the library and get whatever was available on *ARTrace*. Suzuki looked at the purse on his desk and ordered the Lost and Found checked again. What else had been turned in during the two days preceding Nangi's death? It was best to be thorough.

Since his English was the best in the department he intended to concentrate on the *gaijin*. The owner of the purse would be unavailable for a while so he decided to take on Helen Keremos. Not waiting till next day, but immediately that evening.

27

Escape Plans

Helen, by now familiar with the echoing corridors of the half-empty hospital, found Julie Piper's new post-op room with little trouble. She was here at Piper's invitation, a phone call to her hotel room at an ungodly hour of the morning. Piper's voice had been low and toneless, emphasizing only her illness and the requirement of confidentiality.

"Come alone and don't tell anyone, okay? For public consumption I'm still not well enough to see anybody."

"And are you? It's just 48 hours since the operation."

"You're telling me! These jokers would keep me here for weeks, given the chance. Anyway, I'm well enough to see you. I must see you." There was pleading in the tired voice.

"I'll be there."

And here she was. Julie Piper's room was dim with early morning light seeping through the windows. In the half-light she appeared to be sleeping, flat on her back in the too short bed. But her eyes were open, shining, alert. She moved her body over and motioned Helen to sit next to her on the edge of the bed.

"Hi! How you feeling this morning?" Helen began.

"Lousy, thank you. What d'you think?" Julie waved Helen's pleasantries aside. "Thanks for getting here so promptly. This place will come to life in about half an hour. You must be gone by then so listen closely. I have to get out of here and I need your help."

"How come? You're in no shape to leave the hospital."

"Leave my shape out of it. There is a myth around here that after the kind of operation I've had, women have to stay in bed for weeks, very sick. Woman the weak vessel, you know. It's bullshit but useful. The authority of these god-like doctors protects me, see. Keeps the cops off my back — they can't get to me. But only for so long. Another day maybe. I must be out of here before they call my bluff."

She stopped speaking. They looked at each other. Helen said nothing.

Julie continued: "You get it, I hope. Sonny called just before the operation. Bloody good timing, mate, bloody good. Told me about you, said to use your help. He's paying for it, right? The merchandise you came to collect, remember? It's in my umbrella. Find it. Get me out of here and we can all split this crummy place."

"Umbrella! Where did you leave it?"

"Hell, I can't remember. I think I dropped it along with my purse in that fiendish mall where I met Nangi. Near Exit 15, that's where we met, his choice. I remember fishes, an aquarium or something. Then I passed out from the pain I guess and the next thing I remember I was in this hospital. Nangi must have brought me here, how I don't know. So I guess the umbrella is lost. Unless he took it. In which case ..."

She stopped again. Helen was nodding.

"I don't know about any umbrella but your purse was found. Police retrieved it yesterday from the Lost and Found office in the mall."

Helen didn't bother to mention to Julie that Inspector Suzuki had questioned her till late into the night and that among other matters, he'd asked her about *ARTrace* and about a man called Bob in Las Vegas. Helen had never heard of any of them and told him so, quite truthfully.

"Shit! I wonder ... never mind. Go find the umbrella. It might still be at the Lost and Found. I think it's possible that if the cops hadn't asked specifically for an umbrella, then the clerk might not have mentioned it."

"You could be right. It's worth a try. But will he give it to me? Describe it."

"Long and green with a curved handle like a walking stick. Expensive. Gucci or some such fancy brand. Can't miss it. When you get it, *don't* open it there. Take it back to your hotel. Then open it. Your merchandise will be, I hope, still inside. Taped tight to the stem. Get me?"

"I get you."

"Good. Now tell me why you aren't curious about the merchandise? Sonny didn't tell you. Why aren't you asking me?"

"Because I think I know, or can guess. A painting, right?"

"Yeah, but how ...?"

"Tillion and I went through your baggage. I found a computer magazine, took it away and ..."

"Found a copy of a catalogue of stolen art in the middle. Damn!"

"Yes. You were meeting Nangi to give or show him a copy, right? Show 'n Tell. A sales pitch, eh?"

"Right, right. I gave him a copy before I passed out. So if the cops haven't got it then the murderer probably does. Unless Nangi stashed it somewhere. Bloody hell!"

"And the umbrella with the painting?"

"Had to show him the real merchandise to prove ... hey, you aren't thinking I was out to screw Sonny's client and sell the painting to Nangi, are you?"

"Ever upright and honest. Sure, I didn't doubt it for a moment." Helen laughed, then sobered, "What was your meeting about then? What exactly were you selling?"

"Information. Nangi had contacted a friend of mine

who runs an art newsletter saying that he'd come across some information about art thefts. He wanted to exchange information, a quid pro quo. My friend asked me to check it out. Nangi wanted to make sure he was talking to the right people, who could tell him what he wanted to know in exchange for what he'd found out. You see?"

Helen nodded. She didn't exactly "see" but she did now have an idea who and what Bob of *ARTrace* could be. Too bad this didn't seem the right moment to probe the subject any further. She had to get to the point, which was the painting.

"So this painting you were carrying in your umbrella is one of those listed in the catalogue, eh? So maybe Nangi took off with it."

"He didn't know I had it or that it was in the umbrella. I hadn't had time to show him anything except that damn catalogue. We were going to go somewhere safer than a shopping mall to do business. But ..."

"You passed out. Like a good Samaritan Nangi brought you here, forgetting your purse and umbrella. He must have been some spooked to have done that. By the time he got back to the mall, both items had been picked up by some law-abiding citizen and turned in to the Lost and Found."

"Only in Japan!"

"Yeah." Helen was amazed at Julie's strength.

"Now this top cop of theirs is hounding me. In person. He was here last night trying to get at me. If the cops find *my* umbrella ... with a stolen painting inside ... it's game over. I'll be in a prison hospital in the next hour. I can't even wait until tomorrow, I must disappear immediately, if not sooner. Like I said, you must help me. Will you?"

"Sure. And not because Sonny Burke is paying me."

"I didn't think so," Julie smiled at Helen, her relief showing in spite of herself. "But it's nice that your time's valuable, isn't it? And he can afford it."

"You have a plan of getting out of here." It was a statement. Julie nodded.

"Come back about noon like a regular visitor with stuff for me. You know flowers, toiletries, books. Like for a long stay in here. My clothes are here. I'll dress and we will walk out together."

"Just like that. Walk out. Can you walk? Sure you're not going to pass out on me? I couldn't carry you very far, you know."

"I can walk. I walked to the toilet for the first time this morning. How do you think I got to call you? There are no private phones in these rooms."

"Walking all the way out is something different. But assuming you can do it, and I wouldn't put it past you, then what? Catch a taxi to the station? How long before the cops find you? Where do you plan to go to, to hide?"

"If it was easy I wouldn't be asking for your help. Of course we can't just take a taxi from here to anywhere! A little misdirection is called for. First of all, can we trust that muscleman you've got with you? What's his name, Wayne ... something? Will he help and keep his mouth shut?"

"Wayne Tillion. Yeah, under the circumstances, I think he will. What's the plan? And we had better hurry. It's getting on."

"Listen. I came up with this idea ... maybe it's crazy. Maybe I'm crazy. See what you think."

In an urgent whisper Julie spelled out her plan of escape from the hospital and ultimately from Japan. Helen listened, fascinated.

"It's got style this plan of yours, I'll give you that. But whether it will fly in Japan, who knows? Back home I could at least figure out our chances of making it work, but here ..."

"Precisely in Japan it will work. They can't tell one *gai-jin* from another. I know, trust me. It will work; it has to work! Can you think of anything better? Will you go with it? And Wayne? Please! I've got no alternative."

"Oh, I'm in. 'Course I can't be sure about Wayne but my bet is he'll love it. Mind you it's a bit rough in places, this plan of yours. We'd better take it a piece at a time. First, out of this hospital. I'll be back at noon. Be ready."

"No worries."

28
Nagoya Castle

"And don't forget to shave real close, Cookie. Like a baby's bottom, eh?"

In spite of himself, Wayne Tillion had gotten quite excited as Helen elaborated on Julie's plan. At first a little doubtful and full of questions about his part in it, he ended up eager to take on the challenge. By unspoken agreement neither of them expressed any real qualifications nor second thoughts as to the wisdom of helping Julie Piper. It was a "go" for both of them, no question about it. Sitting knee to knee in Wayne's room, they filled out the details of the action to come, went over options and contingencies.

By 9:30 a.m., Helen and Wayne were having breakfast downstairs. Soon after, Helen left to check the Lost and Found, returning in less than fifteen minutes empty-handed. Police had been there first and even the barely understandable "Japlish" of the clerk couldn't hide the fact that they had departed with a green umbrella — gureem burera. There was no time for niceties.

At 10:30, Wayne was in the gym warming up. This was the routine he'd established over the past couple of days, and keeping things as much as usual as possible was part of the plan. By a little past 11:00, he jogged out of the hotel in his sweats just as he had done on two other occasions. Within moments, Helen, burdened with parcels, was on her way by taxi to the hospital. The game was on.

Wayne's route led him past the tiny parkette next to the

hotel. It was occupied at all hours by half a dozen or so street people of both sexes with long matted hair and dark faces: Burakumin, outcasts. Wrapped in blankets and raggedy clothes they monopolized the park benches, sleeping or smoking, drinking and eating. This morning, as usual, there was a good-sized cooking fire going right there in the middle of the park. And right next to a first-class hotel! Yet nobody bothered them or came near them. Passersby totally ignored these their fellow citizens. But everyone noticed and would remember the large *gaijin* passing by, with legs moving like pistons in pumped-up running shoes.

Wayne trotted easily on the route he'd taken the day before, towards Shirakawa Park, which housed the painfully new Nagoya Science Museum and the self-conscious Nagoya Art Gallery. If necessary, he would be able to describe in some detail the park and the two examples of conspicuous expenditure on Western-style High Culture. No one should be able to prove that this morning he had cheated by taking the subway at Fushimi station and going two stops in the opposite direction from the park, to Sengen-cho. From there it was just a short walk through the Main Gate into Meijo Park, the location of Nagoya Castle, the city's major tourist attraction. The castle and the surrounding complex of watchtowers, teahouses, gardens, moats, walls, ramparts, gates, bridges and monuments are uniquely impressive examples of the art of fortification, as well as symbols of the dignity and power of the Tokugawa Shoguns. Parts of the complex count as "Important Cultural Properties" and are treated with much reverence. Tourists don't care that the original 16th-century castle was destroyed in 1945 and has been rebuilt out of concrete.

Wayne bought a ticket as unobtrusively as possible. For a few moments while crossing the moat and going through the Main Gate he was just another *gaijin* tourist in pursuit of Japanese culture. The whole journey had taken him 35 minutes.

His objective was the East Gate to the park. By no coincidence it faced the National Nagoya Hospital from which Julie and Helen were shortly to emerge. Propped up against a tree, well out of sight of the path leading to the impressive structure of Nagoya Castle, Wayne consulted a map of the area. Like most free tourist maps, it wasn't a real map at all but an out-of-scale schematic representation, more decorative than useful. Still, it would have to do.

At the outset he moved with the flow of tourists towards the castle through the second gate and over the inner moat. It was deep and empty containing nothing but tufts of grass and weeds and acres of hard-packed mud marked with hoof prints of a herd of deer. Out of curiosity he stopped for a moment to check out what Japanese deer looked like. He was a little disappointed to find them quite ordinary and even a touch shabby.

Now he had to diverge from the direct path, which led past the ruins of Honmaru Palace towards the prime attraction. With a wistful glance at the overhanging roofs tapering up at each story of the structure, he turned right onto the path out of the inner garden, over the dry moat again and towards the East Gate and the exit. He wished he had binoculars to view the pair of eight-foot Golden Dolphins on top of the castle roof better. Wow! He'd never seen anything like this; Toronto's Casa Loma didn't compare. He was sorely tempted to stop and sightsee.

Regretfully he returned to the job at hand. That was to get within sight of the East Gate without being seen — especially by park staff who were the most likely to be questioned by police once the hew and cry started after Piper. It wasn't hard to avoid being seen; the park was well wooded. Wayne had lots of ornamental shrubs to hide behind while virtually everyone else stuck to the well-marked paths.

He dodged an important-looking uniformed official on a bicycle and then almost stumbled onto a necking couple, a rare sight in Japan, but they were too busy to notice. In the immediate vicinity of the East Gate he looked for a good hiding place. Spotting a large spreading rhododendron, he dived under it and settled down to wait for Helen and Julie to appear. It was almost noon.

While Wayne was brushing ants from the legs of his sweatpants, across the road in her hospital room, Julie was painfully putting on her own jeans. She had refused Helen's assistance.

"Shit! I can't close this zipper over the bandages! I need a longer belt to keep my pants up."

Helen burrowed through the bag of Wayne's clothes she'd brought from the hotel, found a belt and handed it to Julie.

"Here. This should do."

"Perfect. Now, shoes. Just as well they're loafers. Okay. Next, where's that hat you promised me?"

"Here." Almost reluctantly Helen handed Julie a Tilley hat of beige canvas. It had been a birthday gift from Alice. Helen had long lusted for a Tilley but could never bring herself to buy one. She hoped she would see it again.

"No worries. I'll take good care of it." Julie read her mind. She pulled the hat over her blond head, then took it off again to tightened the thong under her chin. "Good oh. Ready or not, here we go."

And the two women walked out of the room into the empty corridor. They passed the nurses' station without attracting attention and made their way to the elevators. Soon one arrived empty as usual and took them down to the ground floor without stopping. With Julie leaning heavily on Helen's arm, they slipped out the door on the west side of the building. They crossed the small parking lot and stopped at the corner of a wide boulevard called Otsu-dori. On the other side was the tall stone wall surrounding Meijo Park, with the East Gate just half a block up.

"This country has the longest traffic lights in the world."

Although impatient with the delay, Helen was nevertheless glad of the halt. She shifted her support of Julie just a little. Her knees were feeling the strain.

"You noticed that too? At last! Hey, let me try walking alone, okay? Here goes."

As the light changed to green, Julie removed her weight from Helen's shoulder and started across the wide street.

"Don't be an asshole, Julie. You will have plenty of opportunity to prove how tough you are. This is no time to be grandstanding."

Gratefully Julie felt Helen's arm around her again. They reached the gate, Helen bought two tickets, they were in — out of sight of the street and the hospital windows!

"Now what?" Julie had stopped and leaned against the wall. There were no benches right there; there are very few in Japanese parks. A scattering of park visitors, all Japanese, flowed past them.

"Stay here. I'll nose around and see if I can find Wayne."

Helen strolled away slowly in the direction of a large grove of shrubbery close by yet well clear of any direct path. That's where she would have hidden in Wayne's place.

Wayne watched her walk towards him, swinging her bag. Surely she couldn't see him? No, she just figured this to be the place he would be. Smart. He had to give her that. He sat very still waiting for her to get right up close.

"Pssst. Here!" His voice came to her soto voce from the centre of the large clump of rhododendrons. She stopped as if to admire it. Then she moved around it.

"Hi! This a good place for the switch, eh? Can we get Julie down there with you? What say?" She muttered.

"Yeah, it's as good as any I've seen. Where is she? How is she?"

"By the wall. She's pretty weak. Lots of guts though."

"Just get her here. Then both of you sit down right in this little dip here. Now hand me my clothes and we can do the switch right here."

"Done." Helen dropped the bag containing Wayne's jeans, shirt and loafers within his reach and strolled away. Wayne pulled off his sweatshirt and started unlacing his running shoes. He was in his underwear by the time Helen returned with Julie. Quick glance around to make sure they weren't being observed and the two women were on the ground, well-hidden by the dense folliage. Helen peered in at Wayne. He was struggling to get into his jeans, not an easy task while sitting down under a bush.

"Damn! Where's my belt?"

"Do without. I hope you can. Julie needs it. Her jeans won't button over her bandages."

"Should've thought of that. Never mind. I won't embarrass you, I promise. Now, what's next?"

"Hat. My Tilley. I want it back, so be careful with it. How does it fit?"

"Not bad. What size is it? Oh, 7 3/8. Take a large hat size, don't you?"

"As large as it needs to be, Cookie."

Julie lay back in the grass with rhododendron branches brushing her face. She said nothing, merely listening to the banter of the other two that seemed to come to her from a long distance. It wasn't the pain so much as a great tiredness. Her body felt like it was melting. There was no strength or energy in it. She couldn't believe that she'd been able to get this far. Getting out of bed, dressing, walking out of the hospital, crossing the street ... how could she have done all that when now she could hardly extend a finger? There was something digging into her back, but she couldn't move even to make herself more comfortable. She giggled.

"I'm glad you find it funny. You look like death warmed over." Julie heard Helen's voice. She giggled some more, tried to hum and finally mouthed the words of a song she'd learned as a kid: "the dog is howling cause it's sitting on a thorn but it's too lazy to move over" just loud enough for Helen to pick up the words.

"I know that! It's 'Life Gets Tedious Don't It.' My, you Aussies are well educated! But you can't sing worth a damn, you know that? So hush up. Listen Julie, concentrate just a moment. You have to get in deeper, right in there where Wayne was. Okay? Nobody can see you there. Then you can take a rest. Sleep maybe. Be a while, few hours before we can get you out. You hear?"

With a little pulling and pushing, they got Julie hidden and as comfortable as possible.

"Whose idea was all this anyway? Mine, I guess," Julie whispered once she'd settled down flat on her back, holding in her hand a plastic bottle of water that Helen had brought along.

"God, I feel weak! Go, I'll sleep. Lucky it's not raining. I miss my umbrella ..."

"Julie, Julie." Helen said urgently. Wayne touched her shoulder.

"Nothing you can do. Leave her. Let's go. Like she said it was her idea."

"Yeah, I guess. All we can do is try and make it work."

"Yeah? How? How the hell are we going to get her out of there? She's in no shape to walk out any distance under her own steam. We need a car. Which we ain't got."

"True. And we can't use a taxi or rent a car, either. Too easy to trace. So we have to beg, borrow or steal."

"Steal? I sure hope you have a better idea than that."

"I do. Tell you later. Now, let's get out of here. And try to remember who you are: female and ill."

So, two *gaijin* proceeded down the path towards the castle and on to the Main Gate. The taller one wore jeans, loafers and a Tilley hat and walked supported by the older one in black pants and sweater. Exactly like the pair who, just a few minutes earlier, had left the hospital, crossed the street and entered Meijo Park through the East Gate.

29

Brass Tacks

The long green umbrella lay on Suzuki's desk for an hour and a half while he and his Sergeant were at a conference on the Nangi case.

In addition to the two homicide detectives present at the meeting were Police Inspector Koshi, who was involved in the investigation on behalf of the Fraud Squad, his boss, the Superintendent in charge of the Second Section, a youngish Sergeant from the Fourth Section and the Public Prosecutor, who was in nominal charge of the investigation. The Senior Prefectural Superintendent was unavoidably detained elsewhere and couldn't make the meeting.

The young Fourth Section Sergeant had recently been transferred from Tokyo where he'd specialized in the Inagawa-kai criminal organization. Fourth Section is concerned with criminal gangs, i.e., the yakuza. This yakuza specialist spoke first, with evident satisfaction.

"Collection and laundering of money, tax avoidance, bribery. We've known for some time, of course, that Nangi performed these functions for the Kusashita-kai criminal organization. But until now we've had no opportunity to get in there and properly investigate. With Nangi murdered, we can really do a job. We managed to get almost all the documents, computer files, names and addresses ... now it's just a matter of going through them with our accountants and Inspector Koshi's men ..."

"Almost all? What couldn't you get?" Inspector Suzuki

asked alertly.

"It looks as if some of Nangi's very personal papers are missing. Two drawers of his desk, which were always locked, were found empty. Miss Ueki, that's the young accountant who appears to have been Nangi's right hand," the Sergeant explained for the benefit of the Public Prosecutor, "says she doesn't know what happened to them or what they were. She claims that she didn't touch anything or take any material out of the office. The other employees confirm that and also claim they don't know who could have removed these papers. Which proves nothing. They could be lying or someone could have entered the office at night when the office was empty."

"If Nangi's secret papers are gone, what are you likely to get out of all the material you do have? Surely the incriminating material would have been removed?"

"As to that, we seemed to have found much that is incriminating. A great mass of files about payoffs, collections, bribery ... of course it's very early yet but even without whatever was in these two drawers, we are sure that there will be lots of useful material."

"Ah, useful, yes. Money laundering, tax evasion! I have a murder to solve. Have you got anything for me?"

Inspector Suzuki wasn't interested in what he privately called "paper crimes." But of course it was necessary to appear impressed.

"So sorry, Inspector. Nothing yet. Inspector Koshi's men and I have barely started sorting it out."

"Inspector Koshi, how long before you know what you've got there?"

"It will take months just to catalogue all the documents. Then we will seal everything that pertains to taxes and pass it on to the tax department. Then we'll see whether there are charges to be brought and against whom. As you must be aware, our work takes time, attention and patience, Inspector," Inspector Koshi of the Fraud Squad reminded his colleague. Suzuki kept his cool.

"Months and months of paperwork. You'll do a super job of it, Inspector Koshi, I'm sure. But it won't help me very much. Have you anything specific on Keiko Ueki?"

"Not yet. But I'm sure there is much information ..."

"Isn't it rather strange that she's been left in charge of that office?"

"What are you suggesting, Inspector?" the Fraud Squad Superintendent asked Suzuki.

"I think that she's been thrown to the wolves. That's us, I mean. It is she who will have to account for whatever Inspector Koshi and his crew find in that office."

"You believe that Kusashita-kai can just write the whole operation off? Surely Nangi's operation was too important for that?"

"That is for Inspector Koshi to establish. In any case, I doubt that it has any bearing on the murder investigation. There are a number of questions that interest me a lot more. What did the murdered man keep in those secret drawers? Did it have anything to do with his death? Who emptied them? The murderer? Was it Ueki? She could have. Why? Most of all, what did these three *gaijin* who suddenly appeared have to do with Nangi's death? What ...?"

"You are saying, Inspector, that you don't think that Nangi's death is related to his job for Kusashita? That it wasn't a professional mob hit?"

"A professional hit, most certainly, Superintendent. But not necessarily related to the Kusashita-kai. As you so acutely pointed out, surely Nangi's function was too important to be put in such jeopardy. Had he been killed on the orders of his bosses, that office would have been cleared out of anything incriminating, saving Inspector Koshi many months of work."

Inspector Koshi opened his mouth to retort, then closed it again. He lit a cigarette instead. His boss, the Fraud Squad Superintendent, was clearly taking on Suzuki.

"Very interesting, Inspector. And how are the *gaijin* involved, in your view? Let me see, a young American accompanied by an older woman arrived just before Nangi was killed. You suspect that he is a professional killer?"

"No sir, not at all."

"Good. There is nothing to connect this man and Nangi, is there?"

"Not directly. But the woman went to Nangi's office and spoke to Ueki. All three had dinner together the night of the murder."

"And that is the only connection you have found between the two *gaijin* and Nangi? Not much is it? Now about the other woman, the one in hospital, it is your view that she and Nangi met the night before his death and it was he who took her to hospital?"

"There is much evidence to confirm that. Plus there is the matter of her purse. Nangi tried to recover it from the Lost and Found."

"Was there anything in that purse to give any indication of her business in Nagoya with Nangi?"

"As to that, I have a theory ..."

"Thank you, Inspector. In other words, there is no evidence that this *gaijin* woman is involved in anything criminal?"

"Nothing concrete yet, Superintendent. I hope to interrogate her soon. I'm sure the other two foreigners are tied up with Nangi through her. I don't want them to leave Nagoya, or at least Japan, until I've found out all about them."

"Without evidence of a clear connection, we cannot prevent them leaving for very long. If you can get something concrete, fine. But a complicated 'theory' will not do. Let's keep it simple. There is nothing up to now to contradict the assumption that the yakuza disposed of Nangi for some reason. And good riddance."

Satisfied that he'd properly disposed of the issue, the Fraud Squad Superintendent turned for confirmation to the Public Prosecutor. That official, who had enough to do and not enough time to do it, drew slowly on his cigarette, nodded and spoke for the first time:

"It is best to be sure just why these foreigners are here, you will agree, Superintendent. I'll be interested to hear what you find out about these people, Inspector Suzuki. Keep me informed." The Public Prosecutor rose. The meeting was over. He didn't bother to acquaint the police officers with the fact that Kusashita himself had called, showing little interest in Nangi but urgently insisting that the foreigners be investigated. The two men had agreed that it was in both their interest to get to the bottom of a matter involving unusual and noncooperative foreigners. Neither the law nor the mob much liked being without full control on their own turf.

30
Piper's Umbrella

"How long has this umbrella been sitting on my desk?" barked out Suzuki. Having kept his cool admirably throughout the meeting with the brass, he now allowed himself to vent his frustration at the wasted time. He glared at Julie's green umbrella and, without waiting for an answer, picked it up, shook it, hefted it in his hand, grunted and put it down again. He waved at his Sergeant: "Get it open." The large man leaped up immediately.

Minutes later, the two men were carefully unrolling an oil painting that had been hidden in the now dismembered umbrella. Curious detectives crowded around looking, touching, commenting. What they saw was a small — 14" x 10"— painting of a well-dressed 19th-century European gentleman in a top hat with what looked like a stall with prints and paintings in the background. The dark brilliance of the work produced a collective "Aaah" from the stunned onlookers. The Sergeant looked up and chased them away with a wave of his hand.

"French," Suzuki declared. "It's by a French painter ... I don't remember his name ... Never mind, we'll find out. Now, no more waiting. Sergeant, get over to that hospital. Make sure that that Piper woman is ready to talk to me. I'll be there in a few minutes. We'll soon get to the bottom of this."

Suzuki continued to study the extraordinary painting with fierce concentration. He had every reason to believe he could take his time, since Police Headquarters, together with the City Hall and the Prefectural Government offices, was just kitty-corner from the Nagoya National Hospital. He believed that he could be interrogating the bed-bound Julie any time he chose. Not until he heard a few minutes later from an out-of-breath Sergeant that Piper had disappeared did Suzuki fully realize that he'd been snookered. Drawing in a deep breath he gave orders for the fugitive to be traced with all speed. As Julie had feared, now that he had a reason to hold her, Suzuki intended to pursue her with all the resources at his command.

It was a very angry and determined Suzuki who sat musing silently for a while. Then he reached for the phone. The squad room went silent, listening. Suzuki said:

"Get me Tokyo. INTERPOL. Cultural Property Unit."

There was a collective expulsion of breath and an exchange of knowing grins among the remaining Homicide Department detectives. Calling INTERPOL wouldn't have occurred to any of them, only to Inspector Suzuki. Their superior was deservedly one of the elite. The First Section was indeed Number One. Everyone lucky enough to be in it under Suzuki's command partook of its successes. The men went back to their work with renewed dedication.

Comfortably ensconced in an old grey building at Kasumigaseki, right next to the National Police Agency in Tokyo, INTERPOL proved supremely uninterested in Suzuki's find. The responsible person of the Cultural Property Unit was out of town, maybe out of the country. Anyway unavailable. The remaining staff was polite; by all means ready to accept and perhaps even examine a photograph of the painting the Nagoya police had come across. Inspector Suzuki thought it might be by a French master? How interesting. Inspector Suzuki was, of course, an expert in European painting. No? Oh. If it was identified and proved to be stolen ... well ... that would have to be established first, wouldn't it? Any photo sent to them would certainly be filed for future reference.

Disappointed but unsurprised, Suzuki hung up. A photograph of the strange painting from Julie Piper's umbrella would be sent to INTERPOL in Toyko. But it was up to him and his squad to find out what it was, its provenance and how it connected to Nangi's death. For he was sure it did.

31

Among the Burakumin

Something woke Julie Piper under the sheltering rhododendron. She awoke refreshed and needing to pee. Struggling to her knees she managed to crawl out. Just as she hoisted her body to a vertical position, she felt a hand on her arm. A strange Japanese woman was smiling up at her. Julie panicked. "Oh! NO!" She shook off the restraining hand and tried to push past the young woman who stood her ground and said urgently in English: "It's all right! Please! Calm yourself. I am Keiko. Keiko Ueki. Helen sent me. I will help you get out of this place. Please come with me. My car is outside."

Tucking her arm under Julie's, Keiko led the tall woman from her hiding place behind the trees onto the path to the East Gate of the park.

"Oh?" Julie stumbled along as directed, gathering her sleep-fuddled wits as she went. "How come? Helen really ... asked you to get me out of there? But ..."

"Yes, yes she did. Don't worry. It's all right. I am happy to help ..."

"Why? Why would you do this? Did she tell you about ... the police ..."

They had passed safely through the gate, turned left and were walking along by a high stone fence.

"I know all about it. Please trust me. It's the only way. Ah, here's the car." Quickly Keiko opened the passenger door, thrust the unresisting Julie down onto the seat, walked briskly around to the other side, started the engine and moved away from the curb. All in one fluid motion taking no more than 20 seconds. They sped along. Traffic was light. It was still hours until the evening rush hour.

"Please to relax now."

Keiko, now secure behind the wheel, smiled encouragingly at her passenger. Julie glared back at her.

"How can I relax? Give me a break! Where are we going? This wasn't in the plan! ... Anyway I need to pee. Damn, I wet my pants! Sorry ..."

Distressed and distracted from her larger problem, Julie groped in her pockets for tissues. Considering that cars are sacred to the Japanese, who treat them as family treasures, Keiko showed admirable self-control at this unfortunate accident. She remained unfazed, passing Julie a whole box of tissues and speaking to her soothingly.

"Do not distress yourself. It's going to be all right. To answer your question, we are going to the Miyako Hotel. That was in your plan, wasn't it? To hide in Helen's room, yes? Until you can leave Japan, yes?"

"Yeah, that's right. But how d'you know all that? Helen must have told you, of course. But why — and why are you helping me? You might get into trouble with the police."

"Yes, if they find out that I helped your escape. We do our best to see that they don't. Yes?"

"Yeah, sure, sure. I still don't understand. But thanks anyway. Let's hope we don't all live to regret this. Hey, let's just hope we all live ..."

Julie closed her eyes and fell silent.

Minutes later Keiko stopped the car. They were on a narrow street running beside the hotel, next to the little parkette taken over by the outcasts huddling around the dying fire. Keiko handed Julie a large tattered quilted robe and motioned for her to get out of the car.

"Please to wrap yourself in that so as little shows of you

as possible. Especially hide your face. Now please and go sit on that empty bench. Wait. Wayne Tillion will come for you when it's safe. He will take you into the hotel. I must go now. Good luck."

And before the startled Julie could react, Keiko closed the door and sped away.

Julie did as she had been told. She sat and waited huddled under the dirty quilt, invisible to the passing throng among the Burakumin.

32

Julie v. Helen

"It's by the French painter Honoré Daumier, titled *The Collector*. Stolen, of course, a year ago from a gallery in Scotland. Now you know what that Romulu bloke was out to buy from Sonny. Stolen property I carried here in my cute little umbrella." Julie paused and waited for Helen's reaction. None came. She continued. "Are we worried?"

Julie lay in one of the beds in Helen's hotel room drinking orange juice. She was clean, fed and rested after her adventures under bushes and on park benches. Smuggled safely by Wayne into the hotel, she faced her next challenge, which was Helen. Her bright grey eyes followed Helen as she moved restlessly around the room.

"'We' should be worried, I guess. Me, I'm more pissed off. I've been sparring with that fancy cop Suzuki for two hours and I see no end to it. I have no business here any longer; you've been found and the police have the painting, which probably means that it's lost to Mel permanently. But that Suzuki won't let me leave. He's mad as hell that I helped you get away and of course he is convinced I know more than I'm telling, which is true, and that I had something to do with Nangi's death, which isn't.

"Once that stolen painting is properly identified, we'll have more investigators on our necks — Japan's INTERPOL National Central Bureau in Tokyo and most likely Scotland Yard. Your Sonny and my Hong Kong employers are getting antsy, and I can't blame them. Now Wayne's getting ready to split; Mel called him home as soon as it was clear cops had the painting. That leaves you and me and you are underground, you lucky bitch. Which leaves me as their only 'lead,' if you can call it that. Nice, nice prospect for yours truly. Damn!"

Impatiently Helen plonked herself down on Julie's bed and stared back into her eyes. Julie said: "Fair go, mate. I sure sympathize but note that I am not volunteering to surface from this safe place and help you out. After all, you went to some trouble to save my bacon, be ungrateful of me to waste your efforts. You'll cope."

For a moment Helen's face remained closed. Then it broke into a grudging smile.

"You have a nerve on you! You know damn well that now that I've fished you out I'm not going to throw you back. Wouldn't help me to have you in Suzuki's clutches. I'd rather keep an eye on you right here. Make sure you don't get into any more trouble."

"Good on yer, mate. I knew there was a good reason for this Good Samaritan caper. You want to interrogate me yourself. Well, go ahead. I'd rather be in your clutches than Suzuki's any day."

Julie smiled flirtatiously.

"Don't tempt me, you are in no shape to put out. Seriously, this situation stinks. I have to know the nature of the dog shit I've stepped into in all innocence. I need to know how to avoid stepping into any more. I reckon you are my best source of information. That's why you are here."

"I didn't think altruism had much to do with it. Maybe just a little ...?" Julie said, coaxing another reluctant smile from Helen. "Before you get out the thumbscrews, tell me why Wayne helped out and especially that Keiko! How and why did she get involved?"

"We needed a vehicle to move you. Keiko was our best chance. It was that simple. I called her; she agreed. And she did great, didn't she? Picked you up without a hitch, right? She also supplied these fresh bandages. As for Wayne, he's an okay guy, as guys like that go, I guess. He just loved the challenge. Enjoyed himself no end fooling the natives. No ulterior motive there."

"Glad to hear it. But don't avoid the issue. What about Keiko's motive? You're not going to tell me that she just 'enjoyed fooling the natives.' Give me a break!"

Helen laughed. "Not hardly. I took a gamble in telling her about getting you out of that hospital and the spot we were in not having wheels to move you further. Calculated risk, you might say. I just had that feeling about her ... She could have squealed on us to Suzuki, gotten some brownie points with the cops. But she didn't. I don't know for sure why she helped us hide you. I'll ask her next time I see her."

"Some feeling! Keiko Ueki works for the yakuza, and don't you forget it, mate! How do we know they aren't in on this? Maybe she killed Nangi on orders? And now they are just letting you keep me on ice to keep the cops looking everywhere but at them? Who knows? Hell, I can't even be sure that *you* don't work for them."

"You know better than that. As it happens ... oh, never mind. Look, there is no point having paranoid fantasies about things you cannot help anyway. If Keiko acted under yakuza orders, there isn't a hell of a lot we can do about it now."

"You're a beuwdy, Helen, you are. I couldn't be in better hands, I can see that. I'm ready to spill all. You got questions? Shoot."

Helen didn't waste any time.

"Right. Let's start with who the bloody hell are you, Julie Piper and what's your connection to Sonny Burke and stolen art? That should do to start with."

Julie brushed a wisp of still damp hair away from her

face and sat up carefully in bed, arranging the bedclothes around her. Her thin arms stuck out of the plain white T-shirt supplied by Helen. Bandages bulged around her middle. She knew she looked fragile. Her grey eyes looked innocently into Helen's hard brown ones. A well-practiced look. All of which was clearly cutting no ice with Helen. Julie answered fast and convincingly:

"It's a long story. To cut it short, my name really is Julia Piper, my home town is Sydney and my favourite beer is Toohey's. There I go talking about beer, like the stereotypical Aussie! Never mind, I'll try to do better. Well, sometime in my youth I must have been impressed by that libellous riddle 'Question: What do you call a sophisticated Australian? Answer: A New Zealander.' I did my bit to prove it a horrible lie. I took Fine Arts in college, then went to the U.S. for graduate work in art history. Got my PhD there. A doctorate in art history is nice but hardly a secure meal ticket. Like many Aussies I took to travelling, working at whatever came along. About three years ago I struck it lucky: in L.A. I got a job ghostwriting a book for a gallery owner and 'art expert' who was totally illiterate. You can imagine the hype. It was good pay, all under the table, tax free. I have no green card, of course. Great opportunity for a humble little girl from Oz. I met a lot of people in and around the art biz, galleries, auction houses. And not merely in California. That gave me a start. I wrote anonymous pieces for art journals, catalogues, collectors. Julie of all-work, that's me. I got to travel here and there: to New York, Europe and finally to Asia. In Hong Kong I met Sonny Burke."

Julie stopped. She was coming to the crux of the matter and needed to gauge the effect her story was having. Helen's face gave nothing away.

"You want to know about Sonny, right? Well, he's quite a character. He's from Detroit — an African-American as they say these days, although he prefers 'black.' He wouldn't like being hyphenated maybe because he hasn't been in the U.S. since the seventies and isn't up on what's politically correct there these days. He's a Vietnam veteran, ended up a Sergeant. I think maybe he went back to the U.S. and couldn't hack it there but I'm not sure. In any case he's been living in Asia a long time. Settled in Hong Kong oh, years ago, I don't know when exactly. Sonny owns this sleazy bar called 'Waltzing Matilda,' I think he owns the whole building. Understand, mate, he didn't tell me any of this in so many words. He doesn't talk about himself much. What I know from my own experience is that he's a bit nuts, also strange and wonderful, a great lover. But you know, he won't leave that building for any reason, I guess it's called agoraphobia. He has a phenomenal memory; anything once seen or heard is never forgotten. It's really eerie. So ..."

"Where did the dough come from for that building? How did a U.S. army Sergeant come up with the money it takes to buy Hong Kong real estate?"

"Oh? I don't know! Isn't that funny! That question never occurred to me. It just seems so natural for him to be there, sitting on his stool in the bar, on the phone to a client or shooting the shit with his friend Canton Bill who runs the business for him. Where or how he'd come up with the money ...? Probably from some scam or other. Illegal for sure. So what? I have no problem with that. It's the way of the world these days. Sex, Drugs and Rock 'n Roll."

Julie looked up at Helen cheerfully, again trying to gauge the effect of her words. Helen remained impassive.

"I see," she said without inflection. "Go on. What does he do now? Run a mail-order house in stolen property? Did he produce that 'art catalogue'?"

"No, no. It's not his racket. Sonny's only a middleman.

In everything. He's just, well, one of the points at which a client can access this stolen art marketplace."

"He arranged for the delivery of the Daumier painting from the unknown seller to Mel Romulu. That's what you're telling me. But you carried it. How come? Get to your part in all this."

"I was just doing my bloke a favour. He'd asked me to deliver this item to your Wayne, pick up the money and deliver it to Nangi. It didn't work out that way but ..."

"Oh, cut the crap. Sweet, innocent Aussie kid being manipulated by 'her bloke,' doing his dirty work because he asked her, taking a fall for him. Nuts. Back in your hospital bed, when we were talking about the umbrella, you told me you and Nangi were exchanging information about this art scam. For a friend you said. Remember?"

"Well, Sonny did want to know what Nangi knew ..."

Helen allowed herself to show more signs of temper.

"You know what I think? You weren't working for Sonny and he wasn't using you — *you* were using *him!* You didn't just 'happen' to meet Sonny Burke and fall into his bed, did you? You planned to get next to him, use his connections to get inside this art scam. And you did. You and whoever is behind you have your own agenda. I don't know exactly who you're working with and on what but I know that much. So get real, Julie Piper. You are in deep shit, need all the help you can get. Lying to me is a dumb thing to be doing. Now, try again."

Julie considered her options. She didn't have many, but there was no harm in having one more try. She gave a rueful laugh and started on a new tack:

"Fair cop, mate! My bad luck to hit a smart woman who won't be conned. Now, if only I had Wayne Tillion or some other bloke to deal with, they would be eating out of my hand by now. Look, you can't blame me for trying. I thought, you being gay, you might be susceptible. I guess I should've known better. Sorry."

"Oh, Jesus. Yes, you should've known better. Not many lesbians are flattered to be viewed as dickless straight men. Susceptible we may be, as you call it, but we don't think with our clits. At least I don't. Now, if you've any more bull for me, get it over with. You don't have all the time in the world. Nor do I. One more chance to tell it like it is."

Before Julie could respond, there was a knock on the door. Tum-Ta-Tum-Tam-Tam. Wayne's signal that the coast was clear. It was time to move Julie into his room because the hotel maid had to be allowed to come in to clean Helen's. It was imperative for all their sakes that no one know of Julie's presence in the hotel. Swearing under her breath, Helen abandoned her interrogation, helped the patient into sweatpants and escorted her to the door. Here Wayne took over.

Moving like whirlwind Helen removed any signs indicating that she wasn't the sole inhabitant of the room. A few minutes later she gave the room one last glance, placed a 'Please Make Up This Room' sign in English and Japanese on the outside door handle and made her way to Wayne's room down the hall. She wasn't about to let Julie bamboozle him.

She need not have worried. Julie was too smart for that. By the time Helen got to Wayne's, Julie was on his bed her face to the wall and Wayne had a finger to his lips.

"Shush! Let her sleep. Come on, time for dinner."

It took them a few heated minutes to agree on a restaurant. Wayne tended towards either the more gaudy or the frankly sleazy. Neither of these types suited Helen. Feeling stubborn she insisted and they finally made their way downstairs to a little sushi place in the mall under the hotel. It was Helen's favourite eating place among the many in the underground maze. Here prices were reasonable by Japanese standards, the food to her liking and the middle-aged serving women were obliging and patient. The restaurant even had a "No Smoking" section. That had been the deciding factor.

Helen quickly settled for a set meal of soup and sashimi with a Kirin beer, but Wayne took his time, joking with the smiling woman, extravagantly ordering à la cart sushi and beef sukiyaki.

"Well, Cookie, I guess this means you're about to go home. Blowing a hundred bucks on a dinner. Got your marching orders, eh? When are you leaving this fair city?"

"Pretty soon. Maybe even tomorrow."

"Oh yeah? Tomorrow. You're going to leave me to cope with that Piper woman all alone, are you? With you gone I won't have anywhere to stash her while they're doing my room."

"Yeah, I know. It's a bitch ... It could be that I'll stay a day or two longer ... like I said, hopefully tomorrow, but maybe not."

Helen put down her glass and gave Wayne her full attention.

"Hallo! What gives here, Cookie? What's with this 'maybe tomorrow/maybe not?' You want out of here, don't you? Now the cops have given up trying to hold you, your job here is up the spout so Mel has zipped up his wallet and your boss wants you back. So what's keeping you? It sure isn't my problem with Piper ... Oh, don't tell me! Love's young dream!"

Wayne looked more pleased than embarrassed.

"Yeah, I've asked Keiko to come back to Toronto with me. Like, we've been seeing each other these last few days. And I think she'd like it there. She hates working for these Kusashita sleazeballs. This is her chance to split this crummy place. So ..."

"So you're planning to get her 'away from all this,' Sir Galahad. Well!" Helen considered the situation for a second then shook her head unbelievingly. "Has she really promised you she will go home with you or this is just a wet dream of yours? Eh?"

"Not exactly 'promised' but I've got her half-persuaded. I'm going to see her tonight; I'll keep working on her and with luck she'll come. She wants to, you know, believe it or not."

"She wants *you* or she wants a way out of Nagoya and the mess with Kusashita? Which is it?"

"I don't care! Both I guess. Anyway, why shouldn't she want to be with me? We've been getting along just great. What's the matter, Mama-san? You jealous or something?"

"Or something."

"I'll bet. Can't fool me, you kind of took to Keiko yourself. Of course, she isn't that way, so you are way out of luck. A real man's woman, Keiko is. She'd never go for a woman."

Wayne's rather ordinary face glowed when he spoke of Keiko and turned almost handsome. Youth, love and sex is a hard combination to beat, Helen thought, looking at him. Not a permanent situation, however.

"Never say never, Cookie. Never is a long time. Regardless, if you can get Keiko to take off with you, my blessings on you both."

"Thanks." Wayne seemed really pleased. "Now all I have to do is persuade her. By tomorrow I'll know."

For a few minutes they concentrated on their food, thinking their private thoughts. Finally Helen said: "While you and your hormones are having fun, I'm still stuck with the Piper problem. We have to figure out a way of getting her out of here. You and I did such a great job of misdirection that Suzuki is still looking for her in Tokyo. I hope, I hope. That's in our favour. But he's got her passport. Makes it hard to get out of this damn island country. Burke is supposed to smuggle in a phony passport for her.

That shouldn't present a problem, given time. This Burke character knows his way around Hong Kong, which is just about the world capital of forgery, counterfeiting and smuggling. But ... if you leave tomorrow, that one won't fly. There won't be time to get the passport and get Julie out of here before you leave. If you aren't going to be around to help out, at least let's have some ideas. Well?"

Wayne woke from his daydream of Keiko and switched to the Piper problem.

"Shit, I don't know what we can do. Not much choice ... unless Keiko — Keiko could come up with something! I don't know what but I'll ask her. I think she likes Julie."

"Bravo, Cookie! Great minds ... I've been thinking the same thing. I'm going to miss you, you know."

Momentarily Wayne Tillion was thrown off his stride. He couldn't help being pleased at this accolade from this witch of a dyke. Part of him wished he could stay and continue adventuring with her, another part thought only of being rid of her and couldn't wait to be back home in Toronto — with Keiko.

Helen was amused by the young man's reaction. She raised her beer glass to him: "Cheers, Cookie! Give my regards to old Hogtown. And may the Blue Jays win the pennant!"

"Cheers, Mama-san! Gimme a call next time you're in T.O. I'll get you tickets for the SkyDome. And the Jays will win the Series again, never mind the pennant. Just you watch!"

They left the restaurant amicably together. Wayne was to deliver Julie back to Helen's room, and then go and keep his date with Keiko. While she waited for them to arrive Helen called Keiko at home and arranged to meet her next day, in the morning. The conversation was short and guarded. Helen was sure that Wayne wouldn't hear about it.

Then she gave some serious thought to the situation presented by Keiko. First of all by her oh-so-willing cooperation in Julie's rescue from the cops, now in this potential plan for taking off with Wayne to Canada. It just didn't sit right with Helen. Too pat somehow. No matter what she'd said to Julie or to Wayne, Helen wasn't convinced of Keiko's motive or of her past and potential role in the "Nagoya mess," as she'd started to think of it.

Keiko had played a major part in keeping Julie out of the hands of the police. It was reasonable to conclude that that had indeed been the objective. In other words, Keiko's bosses, the yakuza, didn't want Suzuki interrogating Julie. Why? What did *they* want from Julie? Would they instruct Keiko to continue to cooperate? Would Julie be allowed to slip out of the country with Keiko's help? Or would they reel her in when they were ready or throw her back to Suzuki?

Helen resolved to question Keiko closely when they met the next day and not take any bullshit for an answer.

Then there was that fascinating prevaricator, Julie Piper, Helen reminded herself happily. It was all very promising.

33

Nerves in Nagoya

"How come this sudden trip to Tokyo? You gotta yen for big city fleshpots or something?" Wayne asked, watching Helen pack her shoulder bag.

It was two days later and there was more resignation than curiosity in Wayne's voice. He had been making a flying visit to his hotel room to pick up clean clothes, having spent most of the past 48 hours blissfully in the arms of Keiko Ueki. He'd intended merely to check in with Helen, to see how she and Julie were faring without him and to be on his way to Keiko's arms again certain that sooner or later he would persuade her to leave Japan with him for the delights of Toronto.

Now Helen had just sprung it on him that his bliss was over, at least temporarily. She was going to Tokyo and he had to stick around and look after Julie. Feed her, keep her company, move her between his room and Helen's when the maids came around to clean. Out of the corner of his eye, he looked at Julie. She lay on the other bed in Helen's room drinking orange juice and smirking at him over the rim of the glass. She was clearly improved.

Helen didn't answer. She'd finished packing, picked up her jacket, waved farewell to them both and left Wayne and Julie alone together.

As soon as the door closed behind her Julie said: "She's gone to get my new passport. Be back tomorrow. No worries, mate. Get that gorgeous lotus flower to come over here. You two can use Helen's bed and all. Too bad I'm still crook; we could've made it a threesome."

Even knowing that she was deliberately taking the piss out of him, Wayne couldn't help being momentarily flustered. He laughed unconvincingly.

"Why not, eh? I'll call her." But he didn't move towards the phone.

"Great. Tell her to bring over more orange juice. I'm almost out. And a magazine, like *Time*. In English, natch."

And Julie smiled at him. Wayne felt trapped. Now he had to call Keiko, ask her to come over to the Miyako Hotel. And then explain the situation. What then? He didn't know but instinctively suspected that he would be no match for the two women together. While he was picking up the phone, Julie continued:

"Has Keiko agreed to go to Canada with you yet? You've had lots of time. In the sack. To be persuasive, I mean. So when are you leaving?"

"Just as soon as we can get rid of you!" Wayne snapped, just as the connection was made to Keiko. "Oh, I don't mean you, honey! It's … J..just Helen. She's leaving for Tokyo. How about you joining me here? We've so much to talk about."

On the bed Julie was going through silent clapping motions, applauding his instant recovery. The phone was tapped, or so they believed. Using Julie's name could have sicked the "dreaded Suzuki," as they had taken to calling the Inspector, on their necks and perhaps landed Julie in a prison hospital.

After Keiko agreed to come over, Wayne slammed down the receiver. "Get out of my face, you hear me!" He turned to Julie, his temper totally lost. "Bad enough that I'm stuck with you, I've to put up with your shit. One more crack out of you in front of Keiko and she and I are out of here! See how you like staying in that bed on your lonesome, bitch! No one to feed your face or keep you out of sight! Maybe I'll even call the cops on you.

T'would serve you right !"

"I guess it would at that. Be cool, mate, I'll be a good girl from now on." Wayne glared at her, nodded as if a bit mollified and sat down. They waited in silence for Keiko's arrival.

Keiko came in carefully as if on tiptoe, looking beautiful in an expensive casual jacket and tailored slacks. She murmured lovingly to Wayne but concentrated on Julie to whom she was properly cordial, inquiring about her well-being, her needs and wants. Watching her warily, Julie specified orange juice and magazines. Immediately a reluctant Wayne was sent out to get them. He didn't like leaving Keiko alone with Julie, "that mouthy cunt." He hurried out, muttering under his breath.

Once the two women were alone Keiko sat down on the edge of the bed and leaned over towards Julie, her carefully made-up face full of concern.

"Are you well enough to leave your bed? To travel? Could you manage?"

"Could I! Nothing could be better for my health than to leave this place! Just find me a way to do it and I'm outta' here. Believe it!"

"Good. As long as you're sure ... I know the doctors didn't recommend it ... but if you're sure ..."

"Hell yes, I'm sure. No worries, mate. You got any ideas how?"

"Well, we might be able to get you out through the Nagoya airport. On a flight to Seoul perhaps. I have friend at Korean Airlines. If the police are not watching for you very hard it might be possible to get you past the routine checkpoints. But you still need a passport for that. And you don't have one so ..."

"Hallelujah! Our troubles are over then! Helen's getting me a passport as we speak. She'll be back tomorrow with it, she said. That's what she went to Tokyo for! Listen,

Keiko, arrange it as soon as you can, will you? Please! Day after tomorrow be possible? Please! Sooner the better. Boy, do I want to get out of here ... you can't imagine!"

Keiko smiled and nodded at Julie's intensity.

"I can imagine. I too want to get out of here."

"Oh?" Julie was taken aback. For a few moments she'd been too preoccupied with her own situation to see Keiko other than as a means of escape. Now she recovered quickly. She shouldn't have had to be reminded that Keiko had her own agenda. "So. You're planning to take off with young Tillion! And here we thought he was just boasting! It's love ... or what?"

"Oh yes! Wayne is such a nice boy. He'd promised to look after me in Canada. We'll be so happy!" Keiko beamed radiantly, her eyes wet with emotion.

Julie was a Westerner brought up on notions of romantic love. For all her sophistication, she could believe that Keiko would leave her family, job, city, country and culture for love of Wayne Tillion. All the same, she wasn't a fool.

"Well, good luck to you, mate. But my advice to you is 'keep your day job.' You know what I mean? Like, make sure you've got a return ticket and cash on hand. You never can tell."

"Oh, yes. 'Keep my day job.' Very true." Keiko wiped her eyes and laughed. "And what will you do, Julie? Where will you go once you leave Japan? Will you be all right? I worry about you."

"No worries, mate. I'll slip back to Hong Kong, my old haunt. Keep my head down for a while. You don't think Suzuki will try to find me there, do you? What a bummer that would be!" Julie sounded anxious, as if the possibility had just occurred.

"I think better you do not stay in Hong Kong too long. Could be danger for you. Not from Inspector Suzuki but whoever killed Mr. Nangi might want to do you harm also. Very bad situation."

This brought Julie up short. Clearly Keiko was warning her.

"Oh? How 'bad situation'? What are you saying, Keiko? You know who killed Nangi?"

"No, no. Not exactly. But I hear things. I hear about a 'Mr. Tan.' That maybe he killed Nangi because he was meeting with you. So I thought you could be in danger also."

"Who the hell is 'Mr. Tan'? Not a Japanese name, is it?"

"I don't know who he is. Is not Japanese, I think Chinese. Maybe from Taiwan."

"Taiwan! Bloody hell, another country heard from! Why Taiwan? What would a Mr. Tan from Taiwan have to do with my meeting with Nangi?"

Not expecting an answer from Keiko, Julie fell silent, thinking. What if Nangi's information, which he never got a chance to pass on to her, was something to do with Taiwan? It could be, she decided. She looked up to see Keiko watching her carefully.

"Yes, is better you go somewhere safe, soon. Hong Kong is nice but ... too dangerous for you, maybe," Keiko reiterated.

"I'll be too easy to find in Hong Kong, you mean. You could be right," Julie agreed. "Well, thanks, Keiko. For everything. For your help." She smiled a tired smile up at her visitor, wishing Keiko would leave her alone to think about the implications of the conversation. "Thanks for telling me this. Okay by you if I tell Helen about this Mr. Tan?"

"Oh, she knows. I've already told her. We had a long talk a couple of days ago."

"You did? Oh, that Helen! Not a peep out of her. Well, she and I are going to have a real barney one of these days! ... Well here's our boy Wayne back with my orange juice. Thanks guys. Now get out of here and let me rest. And have a nice day."

34
Helen Goes to Tokyo

Helen's Shinkansen ride to Tokyo was as uneventful as such things go. All the same, without Wayne to carry the baggage, to plough ahead of her through the crowds, to negotiate for tickets, seats, bento boxes and drinks, she found the experience surprisingly disturbing. Tokyo's chaotic cityscape of miles of massed odd-shaped structures, predominantly dirty-white against a dirty-white sky had a depressing effect. With her nose pressed to the large plate glass window, she tried to spot the Shinto shrines on postage-stamp lots squeezed in among gargantuan buildings. Paradoxically, these reminders of Japanese traditions acted as an antidote; they seemed familiar and somehow comforting. It was the ocean of just slightly off-key "modern," "Western" architecture that Helen found alienating. Riding through the endless suburban sprawl, she looked out at potted plants and flowering shrubs crowding the stoops and hugging the walls of shabby houses without front or backyards, on narrow streets without sidewalks. Although curious about the people who lived there, Helen didn't for one moment want to be one of them.

At Tokyo station she again braved the crowds and took the subway. It is, after all, the only sensible way of moving around Tokyo. Her destination was Shibuya Station and a private detective agency euphemistically called Aido Tagata Private Research Bureau. She was following a lead provided by Keiko Ueki. Keiko claimed that Nangi had dealings with the Aido Tagata organization shortly before his murder. She had found some letters in Nangi's desk that indicated he'd hired Tagata to do some "research" for him. Helen was curious. She also didn't have much faith in this interesting lead Keiko had provided. It could be she'd been sent on a wild goose chase. There might be no Aido Tagata Private Research Bureau at the address and if there were, would anyone there tell her anything? For that matter, would anyone there speak English?

First of all she had to find the address just to establish that such an agency existed. This could easily prove impossible. Helen was lucky: on the windows of a grungy six-story building, the full name in English was printed in white letters. Helen had been in Japan long enough to know that this didn't mean a thing; chances were that nobody there knew a word of English. Using English or what passes for English in advertising is terminally trendy in Japan. She took the dirty elevator, walked in and attempted to communicate with the very young woman in the front office. It was no use. The woman, who spoke only Japanese and seemed frightened of Helen's Berlitz, was alone. At least nobody appeared from behind the door that clearly led to other offices. Helen took out her business card, wrote "I will be back" on it and handed it to the woman who took it and watched with evident relief as Helen closed the door behind her.

Out on the street again, Helen considered her next move. She didn't intend to take the easy way out and admit that it was hopeless to ply her trade in Japan. It's a fool's game trying to be an investigator where you don't blend with the population and can't speak the language. Maybe so, but Helen wasn't given to buying into such accepted wisdom. There had always been something she could do, some way of getting at what she wanted. Overcoming difficulties was what she did best; she had lots of experience in doing things the hard way.

Helen hefted her shoulder bag, which was getting heavier by the second, and looked around for a green payphone to make a local call. What she needed was an interpreter, for starters. And a Tokyo guide. She dug into her bag and recovered a dog-eared business card. Nothing ventured ...

35

Mar's Bar

When Miko walked into the bar Helen didn't recognize her — in spite of the fact that she'd been on the lookout for Miko for 20 minutes. It had taken Helen that long to find the small lesbian bar on the third floor of a corner building in the "gay" section of Shinjuku district. Like many Japanese drinking and eating places, Mar's Bar consisted of only one small room. The 20 women inside it made it feel crowded. Helen sat down at the bar, under the covert and not-so-covert glances of women who occupied all but three of eight stools. Groups of women crowded the two large tables. Soft rock played. All the women were young, sexy and Japanese.

Helen felt right at home. This didn't differ very much from the many dyke bars she'd frequented over a busy and varied life. She relaxed and ordered a beer in English, sure it would be understood. The motherly, long-haired bar-keep had smiled and pulled her a litre. Miko had said over the phone when suggesting a place for them to meet that Western lesbians were frequent visitors to the Mar's bar. It was definitely on the circuit for travelling dykes.

Miko's entrance didn't go unnoticed. One of the women at the bar made an appreciative noise and there was a welcoming shout from someone at one of the tables. Miko smiled at her audience and sat down next to Helen. She was wearing designer jeans, an embroidered Western-style shirt in denim with pearl buttons and hand-tooled cowboy boots. No wonder Helen didn't recognize her immediately; even Miko's makeup differed dramatically from that which she wore when servicing Wayne Tillion. Helen had only seen Miko in her work mode: clearly it bore little resemblance to her private persona.

"Ah, Herren. So nice of you to phone! Very preasant to see you again." Helen noticed that Miko had that proverbial trouble with pronouncing the letter "l"; there is no true "l" sound in Japanese. It was a problem Keiko didn't seem to have. Miko's English was much simpler and less sophisticated than Keiko's but Helen thought that it was fluent and clear enough for their purpose. As they talked she became used to the l/r confusion and soon could ignore it completely.

Miko ordered a margarita, lit a Marlboro and listened to Helen while looking intently into her face. Cigarette in hand, she leaned an elbow on the bartop. The cigarette smoke drifted between them and she waved it away with graceful movements of her free hand, which she then rested on Helen's knee as if accidentally. Helen felt the warmth through the thin cotton but continued with her exposition, for the time being choosing to ignore the obvious implication of the wandering hand.

Miko heard her out with the usual nods, exclamations and smiles by which the Japanese indicate their attention, not necessarily agreement. Once Helen paused, obviously having completed the gist of what she wanted to communicate, Miko gave her knee a squeeze, stubbed out her cigarette and said:

"That's good. No problem. I think I go alone to this Aido Tagata agency. Talk to girl, maybe see boss also. Get you what you want about Nangi. You go to your hotel and wait for me. I come back soon we have dinner and good time. Okay, yes?"

Clearly Miko was a woman of decision and action. A fast worker.

"Sure, sounds great. Except that I don't have a hotel room yet. I guess I should check in somewhere. Where do you recommend?"

"No hotel?" In Miko's mouth it sounded more like "hoterru." "No problem. I know nice place. I take you there, then we have good time. Okay, yes?"

Miko was holding Helen's hand in both of hers and caressing the palm with her fingertips.

"Yes, sure. And how much is it going to cost me?"

It's been so long, Helen thought, too long since ... She was more than game but did want matters clarified.

"Cost?" Miko was puzzled momentarily. "No cost! You think I work? No, no, we play! Yes?" Play came out sounding like "pray."

Helen laughed. "Sure, let's play. But first you go get me that information from Tagata." It felt as if she was the one negotiating for payment! What the hell!

"No probremu. Now we go."

Miko picked up Helen's shoulder bag from the floor and led the way out of the bar. Behind them the place erupted with whistles and applause. Helen was following a prime butch of the local lesbian community.

Somewhat bemused by Mar's Bar habitués' reaction to her companion, Helen scrambled into Miko's car illegally parked against an alley wall. She noticed that Miko's Honda wasn't the usual white, like 80 percent of cars in Japan. It was wine red like Keiko's. Coincidence. The only other thing the two women had in common, apart from being Japanese and beautiful, was that they both spoke English. And that was certainly enough to make them different from the majority.

Miko drove to Harajuku area smoking and cursing the other drivers all the way. Their destination was a block-long apartment complex on Omote-sando Street. Helen examined it with amazement. The Aoyama apartments were old for Tokyo, probably built in the forties soon after the war. The complex consisted of a series of long, low-rise stucco buildings separated from the sidewalk by a strip of green. Between them, walkways opened out into court-yards rich in shrubs, flowers and weeds in undisciplined profusion. Dingy façades, balconies in disrepair, crumbly stoops: all the signs of neglect and lack of money. The place was a total anomaly in this trendy, upscale, touristy section of the city. Architecturally it could have been in Seattle or Moose Jaw. Sitting on some of the most expensive real estate in the world, surrounded by oddly situated and badly designed post-modern monstrosities, it was difficult to understand how something like this had survived so long. Looking grungy and vulnerable the complex exuded a joyful and vital anarchy such as Helen had not experienced since her arrival in Japan.

Every window sported a plant, an odd sign or extravagant poster advertising imported sunglasses or other trendy objects of specialized interest. Seductively lit paintings announced that inside lurked art objects for sale or a gallery for rent. Anything could be hiding behind these windows, anything. All manner of people walked in and out of the many doors front and back and sides looking, planning, buying, selling, stealing. This was work and living space for artists, petty entrepreneurs, charlatans and outright nut cases. Definitely *not* housing for the notorious super-disciplined salarymen and office ladies or other two-dimensional caricatures of the Japanese that scare Westerners and at the same time permit them to feel superior. For the likes of Helen there was little that was foreign or exotic in a place like Aoyama Apartments. It reminded her of home at its best.

Helen loved the place and told Miko so as they wound their way up the creaky stairs to the top floor. Miko was delighted. She opened the door with a flourish: "Ah, you like it! Good, good. Now rest here; it's nice place belongs to a friend of mine. She rents gallery space but she's away on business. Here have whisky, very good Suntory Scotch. I'm going get you information from this Tagata. Be back soon. No problem."

Miko took both Helen's hands in hers and kissed her firmly on the lips. Then she walked out, leaving Helen in a strange apartment.

36

Sex in the Afternoon

Miko ran up the stairs with eager anticipation. Getting information out of Aido Tagata had been boringly easy; now came the good part. Ever since she'd met that tall, mysterious female *gaijin* in the Hilton hotel room — was it the Hilton? yes, — she'd fantasized about making love to her but never expected to see her again. What luck that she'd phoned, that she needed help, that she'd come along so willingly! What luck that at second meeting she'd turned out to be even more exciting than at the first!

Miko could hardly contain her excitement as she opened the apartment door, stopping only to take off her shoes. Where would Helen be? The apartment had four rooms, of which two served as the "gallery," stacked with paintings and empty of any furniture. There was an eight-mat living room/bedroom with a chest, table and three chairs and bedroll folded in the corner. The small kitchen was adjacent to the bathroom. What would Helen look like? What would she say? Miko hurried through the gallery rooms to the bedroom.

Helen was there. She sat on one of the chairs wearing only socks, a blue tank-top and panties. Her shoulder bag, jacket, shirt and pants lay on one of the other chairs. The futon was unrolled at her feet. She smiled at the out-of-breath Miko, held out both her hands and said, "Hello."

"Oh! Herrow, herrow!" Miko dropped her bag, her jacket where she stood and seized Helen's hands. She held them to her face and kissed first one then the other palm.

Her eyes caught Helen's and also held them. There wasn't anymore need to bother with language.

Her arms around Helen's neck, lifting up her face to be kissed, Miko felt Helen at her waist unbuttoning and unzipping her jeans. She loosened her hold and moved her body slightly, allowing Helen's large, strong hands to find her bare buttocks. She felt herself lifted up by them until she stood on tiptoe with Helen's knee between her legs. Next moment they were sprawled down on the futon, giggling.

Miko quickly divested herself of her shirt and tank-top and kicked off her jeans. She wore no panties or bra. She kneeled beside Helen who lay stretched out and proceeded to undress her.

First socks.

"Leave them, Miko, please," Helen whispered, "I like to leave my socks on."

Miko grinned, amused at this very minor sexual fetish. Then the tank-top was peeled off and Miko's fingers lingered for a moment at Helen's breasts. The breasts were small and hung down loosely as if empty, but the dark nipples proved fully alive and responsive. Then Miko rolled the panties down and off with Helen obligingly lifting her hips. Helen's belly, indented by a small deep button, was the whitest and smoothest part of her. Her mound was hard and almost hairless. Below that her thighs were two long muscled columns seeming to gleam in the dim light, continuing to scarred knees and ending in pair of — probably — skinny and unattractive feet hidden by socks.

Slowly Miko ran her hands down Helen's body, exploring it. She made her way across the side of the nose to the mouth and chin, from the line of the throat to the chest. She lifted Helen's breasts as if to weigh them, then lowered her face momentarily to lick the nipples. Her hands moved down the rib cage stopping at the waist, which they tried to span. Helen gasped as Miko's thumbs dug into her belly. Miko continued, palms down each side of the belly button down to the sweaty grooves where thighs and torso meet, exploring the hip hollows. Skilled fingers found the slight ovarian hardness on each side and above the mound, moved over the crease and down the firm silky thighs.

Her eyes tightly shut, Helen lay virtually immobile under Miko's touch, all her senses concentrated on pleasures brought by those hands. The sight of the unfamiliar room, the smell of paint and dust, the aftertaste of local whisky, the sound of traffic outside and inside the darkening walls were all wiped out. Her whole body was wired into Miko: her skin, nerve ends, muscles, glands, the flesh of her mouth, nipples, clit, vagina. All primed and ready to react, to obey, to go wherever Miko chose to take them.

With particular firmness Miko plunged her hands between Helen's thighs, which opened at her touch. She wedged her body between them, spreading them as far apart as they would go and simultaneously lifting Helen's knees to expose her genitals. Propped up on one elbow with her hair tickling Helen's stomach, Miko ran her fingers along the engorged outer lips of the vulva, along the inside of the thighs and down to the anus. For long teasing minutes she explored Helen's hidden crevices. Fingers, thumbs, one hand then the other, down and up, alternatively probing and caressing, now slowly, now faster. Helen's body moved slightly in concert, clenching and unclenching with every touch.

Opening the vulva wide with one hand, Miko plunged her face down into it. Helen made a groaning sound, which started small then rose and fell again. She grasped Miko's hair in both hands and tightened her knees around the voracious head in her groin. She rocked their locked bodies from side to side. Finally she came in a deep, hard spasm. Then her body relaxed and she lay still.

Miko lifted her wet, shining face and took a few deep breaths. She licked her lips and looked up at Helen whose eyes were finally open, focusing. The two women smiled at each other, a small smile of satisfaction, of secrets shared. Helen lifted herself up on her elbows and said:

"Hallelujah! You sure don't waste any time! Don't believe in long preliminaries, eh?"

"Okay, yes!?"

"I'll say! I haven't come so fast and hard for years! Now I'm thirsty." And she fell back on the futon as Miko extricated herself from her position between Helen's legs.

"I bring Coke. Okay, yes!" Miko stood up, stretched her expert pale body, smiled down at Helen and walked to where she'd dropped her bag. From it she produced two cans of cola, opened one, took a swig and handed it to Helen. It was too warm and too fizzy but Helen drank it down.

"Come back here." Helen dropped the empty can and held out her arms towards Miko. Miko moved into them, pressing the whole of her smaller body along Helen's lanky length. Helen's lips were there to meet her mouth, which tasted of Coke and ocean brine.

For the next two hours the two women continued to pleasure each other in all the ways that two experienced and aroused women can. The last thing that came into Helen's mind as she finally fell into a deep satisfied sleep was, "would it have been as good as this with Keiko?" The thought of Alice in far-off Toronto didn't enter her head.

37

Self-investigation

Miko and Helen awoke hungry. They washed and dressed hurriedly.

"Look at that! What a place to have a hickey! See? And this, this will grow up to be quite a bruise. Oh, hey, and look at you! Did I do that? Ouch!"

"Good loving is okay, yes, very nice."

"Best I've had for months. I'm going to be sore in more places than I care to mention. I feel great. Now food. We never had that dinner you promised me, you know that?"

"So sorry. This was better, yes? Now we can go to eat."

"This was better, yes. And yes, let's go eat. I'm starving!"

"You don't ask about Tagata? What I find out for you?"

"Sure I ask. You can tell me while we eat."

"Sandwich okay, yes? Salad?"

"Sandwich? Salad? Oh, okay if you insist. Just lead me to it."

They left the apartment just as it started to get dark. The street was packed with people. Miko led them to a trendy Western-style self-service restaurant just off Omote-sando Street. It was full of teenagers, yuppies and tourists. The food was good, fresh, carefully prepared and relatively inexpensive. The noise level, however, was fierce. Miko beat a group of young salarymen to a table by a window. They sat down and without a word started on their sandwiches. Once all the food was demolished and Helen was on her second draft, Miko told her what she'd learned from Aido Tagata. She had actually talked to someone who said he was Tagata but Miko doubted the truth of that.

"I think Tagata just name for agency. Maybe it's the founder's name and has reputation. Every client want to deal with boss, so they use this name. This man I talked to probably have other name, I don't know it. Sorry."

"Doesn't matter. You talked to someone and got something out of him. Which is more than I could've done. So what did Nangi want them to do for him?"

"Self-investigation."

"Self-investigation? What the hell's that?"

"He asked Tagata to investigate him, himself — that is, Nangi. Find out what others knew about him, what they thought of him. Their opinions, you see. His co-workers, his bosses, his clients."

"No kidding! I've never heard of such a thing. It's a great idea. I hope it catches on back home. Be great for business. What did they find out?"

"So sorry. He wouldn't give me copy of report. It was sent to Nagoya two weeks ago."

"Report? So there was a report, eh? I wonder who's got it. Keiko? Never mind, just knowing about this 'self-investigation' is a bonus. How did you get him to tell you that? It's supposed to be confidential. Private investigators don't talk about their clients to anyone. Or are things different in Japan?"

"Yes, confidential, yes! I told him I was Nangi-san's good friend in Tokyo. I said Nangi-san asked me to find out if there was anything 'new.' He said no and explained how hard it was to get the information Nangi-san had requested. He told me how good their agency was. He thought I might maybe make good investigator ..." Miko laughed. "That's how I find out that it was a self-investigation. It was clear from what this man told me. You see?"

"He gave the game away! Boastful idiot! Couldn't resist you. I can relate. I couldn't resist you either."

"He was a man. You wouldn't have told me so much to show off."

"He thought you were stupid, eh? You're right. It's not a mistake a woman would make," Helen said.

Miko shook her head. "Maybe he didn't think I was stupid; maybe he didn't think about me, Miko, at all. In my job I know how men think about us. Mostly they don't think. That we are real. Yes."

"Yes. I've forgotten about your job. How's it going?"

"Good money. Hard for a girl to make money like that any other way."

"I guess. Well, it's none of my business. But you know, my mother was on the game. She didn't do so good on the street most of the time. She got beat up a lot. She was an alcoholic. Died years ago. Not a way of making a living that I could ever consider, even when I was younger. No way."

"I am so sorry about your mother. Bad things happen all the time here, too. I'm lucky. I have only good contacts. Tourist hotels, mostly *gaijin*. I speak English, a little German. Lots of money. When I'm 30 I quit work."

"Then what will you do?" Helen asked curiously.

"Run noodle shop daytime. Maybe in Shibaura district near the race track. Have fun with girls. Maybe find one to live with me, help with noodle shop. Maybe you come visit, yes?"

"It's a deal. But ..." Helen wanted to say that she didn't want to wait that long when Miko interrupted:

"Now I have to go to my house. Get ready for work. Here, take key to the apartment. Leave it inside. You can stay there until you go back to Nagoya. Tomorrow, yes?"

"Yeah, sure. Thanks ..." A bit taken aback by the suddenness of Miko's departure, Helen picked up the key and looked at Miko standing up, ready to go.

"Ciao, Helen-san. Very fine time. Yes." Miko picked up her bag, leaned over the table and kissed Helen. Then she was gone, lost in a throng of departing high-school students.

Helen sat there quietly for another 10 minutes and slowly finished her beer.

38
Julie Exits

"It's all here. Aussie passport, looks great, never know it from the real, and properly aged too. Your photograph, your name is now 'Vanessa Hood,' wonder how Burke came up with that one. You gotta remember your new name, Vanessa. And the landing card that has to be turned in to immigration when you leave Japan. Look at that neat little stamp, like a seal. I compared it with my kosher one and it's perfect. Gotta hand it to your Sonny, this is high-class stuff. He knows his forgers!"

Helen was back in her hotel room in Nagoya prowling around Julie's bed, full of energy. That morning the pick-up of Julie's passport at a small travel agency in the Ginza had gone precisely as arranged. The trip back from Tokyo had been no problem. She'd kissed Julie hello and had sung in the shower.

Catching her mood Julie examined her new passport and landing card with rising excitement.

"That's it, mate! I'm off! Keiko's got it all lined up with this Korean bloke to get me on a local flight to Seoul. After that, hey, ho! it's Hong Kong for me and the dreaded Inspector and all his little Nip cops can go piss up a rope!"

"Neat that, the way Keiko has helped you out, eh? You got no problems with that anymore? Seems to me you had some doubts not so long ago about her motives, the beautiful Keiko."

"Fuck her motives! If she can get me out of here, that's all I care about. Wouldn't you?"

"How can I tell? This is your game, not mine. Only you know what danger you're in. After all, it wasn't me carrying a stolen painting in my umbrella. Me and Wayne, we are only innocent bystanders." At this, both Julie and Helen laughed.

"Innocent doesn't exactly describe you, Helen. As for Wayne, you once called him naive. That sounds more accurate than innocent. But I take your point. Well, I can't tell what danger I'm in, not really. But you'll agree that I'm in no shape to stay around to find out, either. As for 'the game' as you call it ... it's not mine. I have seen a corner of it, is all. Really."

"Indeed. Regardless, you know more than I do. You've had a part to play, right? Bringing that painting to Japan, meeting Nangi the night before he got killed. Maybe meeting you is what got him killed, have you considered that possibility? Did he mention anyone he was going to meet the following day? Just what happened that night?"

"You know, Helen, it could be that your interest in Nangi is quite misplaced. His death is just a coincidence, nothing to do with me or ... the painting. To me he seems quite ... extraneous. I wish you would believe me."

"Nuts to that. You may know things that make you believe that but I don't, do I? You haven't told me half of what you know, have you? And you'd lie through your teeth just to save yourself any trouble, wouldn't you? Nangi's death may or may not be 'extraneous,' as you put it. I won't know which until I know who killed him and especially *why*."

"Why do you care about Nangi and his death at all? None of it concerns you. You're just 'an innocent bystander,' you said so yourself."

"We've just gone through all that, for Pete's sake! I said 'innocent,' I didn't say 'dumb.' And neither are you."

"All right. Make what you can of this. When I was

arranging to meet Nangi, he told me that it had to be that night because the next day he had an appointment at that very same spot in the mall by the fish tanks with someone Nangi called 'an insurance agent.' That's why I couldn't wait for Wayne in Tokyo. Nangi said it was that night or never."

"Not bad. And that's all you can tell me? Correction: that's all you *intend* to tell me? How about something about the painting, eh? Just to show there're no hard feelings?"

"I told you, already! I don't know anything about the painting except that Sonny asked me to take it to Japan and give it to Wayne in exchange for $10,000. Wayne didn't show so I went to Nagoya to see Nangi ..." Julie paused and looked at Helen ruefully. "You're right. Sounds pretty weak, that story."

"I'll say! First I'm told that you've been asked to deliver a Daumier painting to Wayne in Tokyo. Then you tell me that you wanted to show it to Nangi to prove your bona fides. And Nangi insisting that it be then or never because he had an appointment with his insurance agent! Which is why you left Wayne standing at the station with the money in his hot little hand. What a mixed-up story! And the little matter of that cute catalogue of stolen art in your suitcase. Come clean, Julie. Just what is your connection to the art scam?"

"Well, I'll tell you this much. I wasn't into selling any stolen art. Then or ever. Believe me or not."

"And that's all you're planning to leave me with, eh?"

"Too right."

Impasse. Julie faced Helen, looking very determined. Helen wasn't having any of it.

"How about *ARTrace?*"

Helen pulled this one out of left field and threw it at Julie. Julie sat up in bed and stared at her.

172

"What ... what about it? Where did you get that from?"

"Aha, goody! Now we have something to 'share.' I'll tell you how I heard about *ARTrace* after you tell me about *ARTrace*. Fair?"

"Damn it, Helen! Get off my case! I'm sick, can't you tell? Have a bit of heart. Quit tormenting me like this!"

With a sob in her voice, Julie turned away to face the wall. Helen looked at the back of her head sceptically. She knew that Julie was full of tricks, but at the same time genuinely ill. Recovery from an ectopic pregnancy is no joke. But this sudden appeal to compassion at this crucial point when Helen seemed to be gaining on her ... it just didn't sit right. Give it one more try.

"So you don't want to hear what I know about *ARTrace*, I guess. That's okay ..."

"Of course I want to hear it, mate!" Julie turned around to face Helen again. Her face was drawn, there were tears in her eyes, but her voice was as strong as ever.

"You first."

"Oh, bloody hell! *ARTrace* is a newsletter about art. Art and museum artifacts and ... things like that. For collectors. It's private, goes only to a select group of subscribers. You won't find it on your neighbourhood newsstand. That's all I'm telling you so you can quit trying to bully me."

"Good start, don't ruin it now! Who runs it and where is it located? Come, spit it out. You'll feel better for it." Helen continued to press her advantage.

"Out of Las Vegas. A friend of mine puts it out. I ... I've been helping. Now leave me alone."

"Does Sonny Burke know about *ARTrace* and your friend in Los Vegas? Stupid question, of course he doesn't. Well, I guess you should know that Suzuki asked me about *ARTrace*. Wanted to know what it stood for and what I knew about it. I told him all I could — nothing. I wouldn't be surprised if the dreaded Inspector was trying to trace *ARTrace* himself. You might be wise to let your friend know. He sounds like the shy type, probably won't enjoy police attention. What's his name, by the way?"

"Bob."

"What a sweet name! Better be the real thing."

"It is."

"Just Bob, eh?"

"Yes. You're a copper-bottomed bitch, Helen."

"Too right, as you Aussies say. Taking advantage of you on your bed of pain! Terrible! But for your own good. Thing is, I could be on your side, if you played it right. Only you don't know how to do that yet." When Julie didn't answer Helen went on: "Okay, that's enough. Now, where is that boy Wayne? He and Keiko are due to switch you to his room. I want my room cleaned. Let's get this show on the road."

39

Case Filed

Suzuki's homicide case was going nowhere. His men might be turning up fascinating information on Nangi and his life but it wasn't getting Suzuki any further in finding out anything useful about his death. This was most unusual in that the death of a murder victim is almost invariably a consequence of the life. The matter of the "FineFun" bar with its gay reputation was diligently pursued. Nangi was a habitué there, well remembered for practising his English on Western visitors. However, nothing definite could be established about his sexual preference. It remained merely a suspicion, a speculation that, to Suzuki's disgust, made it too easy to characterize the murder as just a falling-out among faggots.

Nangi's yakuza connection was another problem for Suzuki. He could have made a case for the yakuza killing one of their own, but the presence of the three foreigners had muddied up the waters considerably. Their involvement and Kusashita's concern about them had convinced the Public Prosecutor that Kusashita didn't order the hit on Nangi. This effectively cut Suzuki off from pursuing that obvious possibility. Of course, there were rumours and hints from informants about Kusashita's foreign connections. Then there were always hints and rumours in cases just as this.

What remained were the *gaijin* and the painting. If they were connected with the murder, how? The painting Suzuki had recovered from Julie Piper's umbrella was taking up much of his time in correspondence and phone calls with INTERPOL in Tokyo but not helping a bit in the investigation of Nangi's death. INTERPOL had gotten interested once it was established that a painting of that description had been reported stolen. Suzuki had been vindicated; INTERPOL files indicated that it was indeed a French masterpiece by Honoré Daumier lifted a year previously from a gallery in Europe. Much good having been right did him. Possession of stolen goods was definitely a crime but where was the last known possessor — i.e., Julie Piper? Slipped right through his fingers. Just as he was about to question her regarding the stolen painting, she had left the hospital, which according to the doctors just wasn't possible two days after an operation, and took off for Tokyo. Disappeared from right under his nose. There were sniggers at this from the Fraud Squad still diligently excavating Nangi's office. It was no consolation to Suzuki that their efforts were unlikely to lead to even one indictment. It was even less consolation that the Tokyo police couldn't find Julie Piper either. Naturally, she would have had friends in Tokyo to hide with, accomplices in the stolen art ring. Like that other foreign female, Helen Keremos. It mattered not at all that this one had stayed in town as instructed and could be interrogated. She'd helped Julie Piper escape from hospital, taking her onto a Tokyo train. Suzuki's men had traced the two women right across town from the hospital door, through the park and to a taxi to Nagoya station. Keremos couldn't deny it. She didn't. Interrogated by the angry Suzuki she stayed maddeningly cool and reasonable. Piper wasn't under arrest, what is the Inspector going on about? There is no law that forbids one person helping another take a train. No, she didn't know where Julie Piper was headed. And so on. There was no profit to be had from that unnaturally hard-nosed woman.

And yet. Piper, her umbrella and the contents of her purse were the only leads he had. Nangi had met Piper the night before his death; he had taken her to hospital. All that had been established through the meticulous work of the Nagoya homicide detectives. Suzuki knew in his bones that Piper and the painting were somehow involved in Nangi's death. The only way he could think of to establish the connection was to backtrack through the letters and phone numbers in Piper's purse.

He'd followed up the two Hong Kong numbers called by Helen Keremos. One of them was to Ladrone Investigations, a quite reputable detective and security agency. They had vouched for her bona fides. The other number had initially been reported as a telephone in a bar. Then out of service. Dead end. Wayne Tillion had called a M. Romulu in Toronto. There wasn't much to be made out of that.

Finding "J" or "Mum" was downright impossible. Tracing *ARTrace* turned out to be no easier. It wasn't listed in any standard directory of U.S. businesses, corporations, foundations or journals. Directory assistance in Las Vegas had no current listing; similarly, the telephone book white pages at the U.S. information centre were of no help.

Suzuki sent a fax of inquiry to the Nevada State police. They merely did what he'd done; checked directories and the phone company and got nowhere. They were sorry, but the name *ARTrace* wasn't much to go on. Clearly, Nevada wasn't enthusiastic about using scarce detective resources on a vague inquiry from Japan.

By the second week after the murder, Suzuki had a thick file on international art thefts and INTERPOL. He'd exhausted the facilities of the Nagoya Art Gallery, the public and university libraries. He had to permit Helen Keremos to leave Nagoya; he couldn't justify stopping her.

Wayne Tillion was already gone. And Keiko Ueki was

on a prolonged leave of absence for health reasons, report-edly staying with an old friend in Hawaii. He doubted that she would ever return to work for Kusashita.

The Nangi case was dying at Suzuki's feet; no one seemed to care about the murder of a gangster. He had other deaths to investigate. He didn't exactly give up, but the case had to go on a back burner. Of course, all murder files stay open, always.

Part II

40

Ladrone Partners

"Angus, you should know this. That CHNOPS business seems to be stirring again."

"Who? Chops? Oh, yes, that funny CHNOPS business." Angus McGee liked to pretend that CHNOPS sometimes slipped his memory. He didn't like to think about it too much; besides, slips like that covered up for the times when he really did forget other matters. For, in fact, CHNOPS was not something either he or Ray Choy were likely ever to forget. "Well, good. Maybe it will be lucrative for us again. Haven't heard anything for a while, have we? Something to do with that Burke fellow, right?"

"Yes. Remember that Nagoya hit? Some mobster got killed. And Burke's girl Julie Piper was involved and then disappeared, remember? We got that Canadian investigator Helen Keremos to check it out. Then Piper turned up hiding out in a hospital. Now she's disappeared again. So just to be on the safe side, CHNOPS went to ground. Temporarily, of course."

"Humph! Why would CHNOPS have done that? How does a yakuza being murdered and a girl disappearing connect with CHNOPS?"

"Nagoya police found one of the CHNOPS paintings. I don't know which one or the circumstances but it's probably not hard to identify. So I guess the fear was that depending how far they go with it, they could unravel much of CHNOPS. Possibly including our past role."

"But you're saying CHNOPS is active again?"

"It seems so."

Ray Choy didn't bother looking at his partner directly as he explained the screw up in Nagoya and the fact that CHNOPS might be active again. He knew exactly what Angus McGee would look like and say in any situation. Including this one.

Angus nodded in an abstracted way as if the subject of CHNOPS had already fled his mind.

"How is your father keeping these days, Ray? I haven't seen him for a while."

This wasn't as much of a non sequitur as it seemed on the surface.

"He's old, Angus, what can I say? Holding up well enough, though. For his age. I'll tell him you asked."

Neither man needed to be reminded that it was at the insistence of Ray's father that Angus became a Ladrone partner. Or that they had become involved in CHNOPS without his knowledge and consent. Ray was bound by filial duty to honour his father's wishes about Angus but he didn't have to like it. He wasn't about to let his father's old-fashioned ideas interfere with the way he ran the business.

His father was traditional. He had arrived in Hong Kong from a village in China in the early years of this century. Charles McGee — Angus's father — had given him his first job. As the McGee Mercantile Company grew from one small warehouse into a major player in the busy Hong Kong market, Choy's position grew with it. At the beginning of World War II, he was McGee's right-hand man, as wealthy and honoured as any Chinese could be in the British colony at the time. Then came the cataclysm of the Japanese conquest. The shock was traumatic in every imaginable way. Charles McGee had sent his wife and the 12-year-old Angus to the safety of Australia in good time but he himself had stayed and carried on. It didn't take long before he and many others were rounded up by the

Japanese. Ray's father had remained, loyally running what was left of the business, squirrelling away money. He never doubted that Charles McGee, his family and Hong Kong's white colonial authorities would be back.

The war ended, the Empire returned, but Charles McGee was never heard of again. He'd died in a Japanese internment camp. Angus and his mother moved to Scotland. What was left of the McGee business in Hong Kong was liquidated for whatever it could fetch. It was barely enough to keep them in genteel poverty.

Choy Senior continued in business, now on his own account, keeping in touch with the McGees by infrequent letters. In the early 1950s he wrote to Angus, now a restless young man at loose ends, and invited him to Hong Kong. Angus McGee arrived in the colony on August 29, 1956, where he was greeted by his father's old companion with open arms and pocketbook. It was a very auspicious date: the very day that Choy's first and only son was born. That son was, of course, Ray.

In spite of Choy Senior's encouragement, McGee didn't settle down in Hong Kong. For the better part of 20 years, he sponged off the old man at long distance from Singapore, Darwin, Honolulu, Glasgow, Taipei, London and Manila. During these years, young Ray studied, worked and grew into an exceptionally bright and bitter man. Bitter at the hold that the memory of Charles McGee had on his father and bitter at the favours this memory showered on Angus McGee.

In 1984, Angus surfaced in Hong Kong, having spent the previous few years running a bar-cum-brothel in Manila. At 56 he was a garrulous, self-important drunk with a reputation throughout Asia as gambler, pimp, ivory smuggler, petty con man and, worst of all, a failure. In spite of Ray's urgent remonstrations, his father insisted on giving McGee a job at Ladrone Investigations, one of the family businesses of which Ray was chief operating officer.

Even Ray had to admit that given this opportunity Angus tried hard to rehabilitate himself and cut down on his boozing. Soon he became an asset to the organization. His forte was playing the role of the expert "old Asia hand" with Western clients, some of whom were more comfortable dealing with a Scot than with a Chinese, notwithstanding Ray's Cambridge degree. In addition, McGee's extensive knowledge of the murky edges of the underworld in some of Asia's biggest, fastest-growing cities came in very useful as Ladrone expanded under Ray's aggressive management. Thus when Choy Senior insisted that Angus be handed a partnership in Ladrone, Ray Choy had no objective arguments to offer against it. The old man felt vindicated.

And the old man was very old. Ray loved his father but he'd found himself looking forward to the old man's inevitable death as the necessary step towards getting rid of Angus. He felt guilty about this and naturally blamed Angus for that feeling. It didn't help that Angus's alcohol-saturated mind was slowly deteriorating, he suffered memory lapses and found it hard to follow simple conversations or to remember when to keep his mouth shut. It made for some explosive situations at Ladrone. The coming of the CHNOPS project had considerably complicated the matter.

Ladrone's first contact with CHNOPS had come through McGee. He'd gone "home" to Scotland the year before but, although on vacation, wasn't above turning up a bit of business. The job had involved tracing the whereabouts of a Glasgow burglar for a local reinsurance company. It was rumoured that after a big score, the burglar had "retired" somewhere in the Far East. Ladrone seemed well placed to track him down. It wasn't a big or particularly lucrative job but McGee was eager to prove his mettle to his pals in Scotland so it came high on his priority list when he returned to Hong Kong. He sent out the usual inquiries through the usual channels.

The results were immediate and unexpected. Ray Choy — not Angus McGee — received a polite invitation to meet a highly placed person at an exclusive Hong Kong club. That person (not to be named) suggested, still politely, that Ladrone drop the matter of the Scottish burglar. No threats were made or bribes offered. Ray Choy said he would think about it. Ray talked to his father and together they agreed to forget the Glasgow burglar.

Not so McGee. He took the first flight back to Glasgow, intending to get more information from his contact at the company that wanted the burglar found. The story was an intriguing one. The Burrell Collection just outside Glasgow had been burgled, burgled very skillfully. McGee's friend, one Alister Brown, was the local agent for the reinsurance syndicate with which Burrell's insurance company had laid off a good part of the risk. He was therefore called in when the theft was discovered. It was clear that the crime had been thoroughly planned and skillfully executed. The thieves managed to break in without setting off any alarms. Once in, they had disarmed the security systems, bound and gagged the guards, took surveillance tapes out of the security cameras. Then they removed five paintings — a Cranach, Corot, Degas, Cézanne and a Daumier — and six Japanese prints. Whoever had planned the theft knew too much of the gallery's security systems for the comfort of the insurance industry. Even more disconcerting was the fact that the thieves had clearly come for only these few selected items. Nothing else had been touched although they had had all night to strip the place bare.

The expertise involved in the crime called for matching expertise for its solution. Jason Forbes, an authority on international art crime and the underground market for

European paintings, was hastily summoned from a lecture tour. He arrived, a small, pale, pipe-smoking man in Savile Row tweeds, and proceeded like the proverbial consultant — i.e., nosing around the case and then producing a lengthy, very detailed summary of everything the police and the insurance investigators already knew. While this part of his report provided no real leads to tracking down the thieves, it was held in high regard by police and insurance investigators, who pirated his educated prose for their own voluminous reports to their superiors. As a bonus in this report, Forbes pontificated about "acceptability of various levels of risk in the light of the perceived adequacy and actual costs of available security systems" and came up with some rather frightening hypothesis about the operation of a ring of international art thieves. This part alone was considered worth his fee and was later widely quoted by the insurance company in its sales presentations.

While Forbes was busy enhancing his reputation and laying the groundwork for future assignments, all the routine things were being done. Known sellers and buyers of questionable art were investigated. Fences were checked, double-checked, threatened and bribed. The stolen masterpieces were recorded in the Art Loss Register, a private data bank in Grosvenor Place, London. All official and semi-official alphabet soup of organizations — INTERPOL Cultural Property units, International Foundation of Art Research (IFAR), Scotland Yard's index of stolen paintings, International Association for Art Security (IAAS) and Insurance Crime Prevention Institute — were duly notified. Nothing.

Only the local police investigation turned up anything and that was almost nothing. Apparently a local burglar of more than average competence had suddenly come into considerable wealth. He'd paid off the mortgage on his home, thrown a big expensive party and disappeared to parts unknown. Extensive checks of airline companies turned up his name on a flight to Hong Kong and some nosy neighbours were found who claimed to have seen him in the company of a man described as a "Chink." The Hong Kong police, notified as a matter of course, shrugged metaphorically. So Ladrone had been hired on the strength of these mighty slim clues, mostly because there were no others. U.K. police couldn't afford to pursue such a nebulous lead across the world with their own personnel; the reinsurance syndicate couldn't afford to ignore it. They were on the hook for millions.

That's where the Burrell case stood when Angus McGee returned to Hong Kong.

He sat in his office recovering from jet lag over a glass of Scotch and mulling over the case when Ray Choy walked in. McGee couldn't hide his surprise; his reluctant partner hardly ever entered his office.

Sitting down in the client chair, Ray wasted no time getting to the point:

"What did you find out about this Glasgow case ?"

Still in mild shock at the invasion, McGee told him all he'd learned from his friend in Scotland.

"I see. Well, I've met your burglar. He came calling while you were away. He wants to do a deal. Immunity from prosecution and a substantial reward in exchange for one of the paintings. Usual sort of thing. Are your pals in Scotland interested?"

"I should think so. I'll ask. We still have a standing commission to find this man. He actually came to see you? Here at Ladrone? Bit of a nerve, don't you think? Besides, why us?"

"I asked him that but he didn't tell me. My guess is that he heard through the usual grapevine that we were looking for him. Checked us out and decided we were worth a try. It turns out he needs money. Lost his nut at the ponies here and is now broke. Having one of the stolen paintings in his possession, he's willing to turn it over. For a price."

Ray paused and looked at his partner for the first time.

"How much?" Angus asked.

"£100,000."

"One hundred thousand pounds! Cash? Sterling?"

"Naturally. He's offering us 10 percent for our services as go-betweens. Keep him safe, make sure the money is good, unmarked and all that. Get the money to him where he wants it, how he wants it. And keep the whole matter from the authorities. For a fee of £10,000. Tax free."

"Good God!"

"Quite so."

Angus McGee shuffled about in his chair uncomfortably. This was a delicate matter and had to be handled with care.

"Well, what did you tell him?"

"I told him that I had to speak to you. After all, we are partners. He'll call again tomorrow for our answer. One way or another."

McGee let out a deep breath and reached for his glass. He swallowed, wiped his mouth and finally asked the key question:

"What ... what does your father say?"

"I didn't tell him about this offer. You know he wouldn't approve."

It was out now. An unprecedented event. The very first time that Ray Choy had not consulted his father. And on a matter that carried such risk — as well as profit. McGee looked at Ray Choy and considered his next move. Perhaps it was safe to play devil's advocate.

"Ah! So you do think we should do it? Well, I don't know. It's pretty risky, old man, isn't it?"

"Yes. It's risky. Could get us into trouble," Choy said calmly. He wasn't going to be put in the position of advocating such a dicey project. If McGee wanted to be "persuaded," he was out of luck.

McGee backpedalled immediately.

"Be worth the risk though, wouldn't it? We could do it without much trouble, couldn't we, old man? Nothing dreadful being a go-between. Journalists do it all the time."

"Yes. If your people in Scotland will play, we could do our part and with very little risk, I think. With great care and total secrecy, of course."

"Of course, of course! I'll call Alister right away. See if they are interested. There may also be a reward ..." McGee couldn't hide his delight.

"Yes, do that. Then we'll see." Ray Choy stood up and left the room. McGee looked after him, a puzzled frown on his face. Then he shook his head, grabbed the phone and dialled.

Within three months the two principal partners of Ladrone Investigations were irrevocably committed. The transfer of money for stolen goods had gone down without a hitch. They had pocketed their payment, all in cash. They didn't know it at the time, but it was just the beginning. They were now part of CHNOPS and up to their armpits in the stolen art business.

41

Helen in Hong Kong

"Ladrone Investigations! Good Morning!"

"Mr. Ray Choy, please."

"Whom shall I say is calling?" A plummy English voice of the receptionist mangling the language.

"Helen Keremos."

"Mr. Choy is not available at the moment. Perhaps someone else can help you?"

"No."

"Oh! What is this in regards to then?"

"Just tell him I'm here in Hong Kong and want to see him."

"Yes. How can he reach you?"

"I'm staying at the Ambassador Hotel in Kowloon. Number's in the book." Helen hung up.

Helen Keremos had arrived in Hong Kong from Tokyo one bright May morning some weeks after the death of Tetsu Nangi. She took the airport bus to the hotel, took a shower, sat and flipped through the solid stack of glossy tourist bumph about Hong Kong provided by the hotel. Then she went out to eat.

She hit the hubbub of Nathan Road. Within two minutes she was urged to buy "a genuine Rolex" watch at a fraction of the price for which it was offered by the Rolex Authorized Dealer in front of whose jewellery store the street merchant carried on his business. Helen turned down the "once in a lifetime offer." She wasn't in the market for a new watch and besides it wasn't hard to figure that brand-name rip-offs were a major Kong Hong industry kept in business by endlessly gullible tourists. Hong Kong is a genuine shoppers' mecca where you can find Swiss watches, German binoculars, French perfume, Japanese camcorders, American notebook computers, Scotch whisky, and a thousand other "world famous" brand-name items cheaper than in their countries of origin. You can also get seriously stung by inferior knockoffs of all these products. Brand names can be a snare and a delusion. Buyer Beware everywhere, but especially in Hong Kong.

While she looked around for a good place to eat, Helen marvelled at the variety and colour of Kowloon street life.

It was great fun. She pushed her way through the crush of people, careful of her wallet. The crowds were as big as those in Tokyo but oh so different. Here was no visual uniformity, no social discipline. People of every cut and colour stopped in the middle of the sidewalk blocking traffic and argued in dozens of tongues. The noise was fabulous. All of southeast Asia was here, much of Europe and Latin America. Not to forget the Lebanese, Egyptians, Saudis, Australians and more than a few Canadians. Hundreds of languages, cultures and tastes all in Hong Kong in the name of trade. Trade, the great — maybe the greatest — cross-cultural phenomenon. Certainly the most potent.

For all that Helen's first Chinese meal in Hong Kong was a disappointment. The "English" menu in a much-touted restaurant was laconic and garbled to the point of misrepresentation. The bored waiter insisted that he understood English when he clearly didn't. The food was okay but no better than that. Not as good as in Helen's favourite restaurants in Vancouver or Toronto. Better luck next time, Helen promised herself. She picked up a copy of the *International Herald Tribune* and went back to her hotel. That's when she phoned Ray Choy at Ladrone.

As she had expected, he returned her call just minutes later welcoming her to Hong Kong. Could she come to his office right away? Yes. She finished the paper and went out again to meet the Ladrone partners.

42

Helen Interrogated

"Helen! So nice to see you again. Hope you've had a good flight from Tokyo. Not too tired?"

"Not tired at all. Ray, I'm here to do business. Let's do it."

"To the point, by all means. First let me introduce my partner Angus McGee."

"Delighted to meet you, Miss Keremos. May I call you Helen?" Angus McGee turned on his avuncular charm. He didn't like the looks of this formidable woman, but having been warned by Ray to behave he was extra careful not to show it. Helen, who didn't like him either, wasn't fooled.

"Sure, Angus. Call me Helen. It's my name."

"Good, good. How about some tea, what? Time for tea! Or perhaps something stronger. Sun must be over the yard arm somewhere!"

"Tea's fine, thanks." Helen ignored his tired humour.

"Oh. Right."

Tea was sent for. The three of them sat at a small round table in Ray's office with a spectacular view of the harbour so hard to ignore it seemed to become a fourth participant. Ladrone offices were on the Hong Kong side, in the district called Central. They were strategically located in a mid-sized, mid-priced skyscraper. Helen had taken the famous Star ferry across the harbour from Kowloon. She viewed the solid phalanx of office towers with mixed feelings. She was finding that she felt about Hong Kong much as she did about New York. The best and the worst of what the world had to offer was here. The frantic beauty, the excitement, the energy of these places is hard to resist; on the other hand, there is cruelty, dirt, exploitation, poverty, violence, greed. Forget it, she said to herself. To business. She turned her attention back to the two men with her.

"We've passed your invoice over to Mr. Burke. I believe he sent you an advance? Good. I'm sure the balance will be forthcoming shortly," Ray began smoothly. Angus poured the tea. Helen accepted a cup, took a sip and waited. Ray continued.

"There hasn't been a report about this missing person case, I notice. When can we expect it?" Ray was careful to voice his demand in neutral third-person terms. Angus didn't notice the subtleties and jumped in.

"Yes, most surprising that you haven't sent in a proper report. One would expect better from a professional, you know."

"My report went directly to the client. Plus, I'm going to see him personally now that I'm here."

"Not the way we do things here, my dear. You were working for us; we must have a report." Angus tried patronizing again.

"Angus is right, you know, Helen. It would be best. For our files we must have something."

"For your files? Okay, I'll send you something for your files."

"Good. A copy of your report to Mr. Burke, that will be fine." Ray looked at Helen questioningly. She smiled and didn't answer. Ray had to know by now that she had no intention of giving them a copy of her report to Burke. But he had to let it go once she offered to send them something for their files.

"Well, now that we've dispensed with the formalities do give us some highlights of your stay in Japan! This missing person — Julia Piper, was it? — you found her but she disappeared again, is that right?"

"Hardly disappeared. She was ill, in hospital. When she felt better, she left. That's all."

"Where did she go, where is she now?"

"I wasn't hired to follow her about. Just to put the client in touch with her. I did that."

"Oh! And the murder of that man ... what's his name?"

"Nangi."

"Nangi, yes. Bad business that murder. Must have created difficulties for you to be involved, even peripherally," Ray continued fishing. Predictably it didn't work.

"It held me up, sure. But since Burke went on paying my expenses, it didn't bother me any."

"I see." Ray Choy lifted his hand to silence his partner who was about to explode. Not being able to contain himself, Angus left the room slamming the door behind him.

Ray shared Angus's exasperation but it wasn't in his personality to show it. He leaned back in his chair and stared at Helen. She looked older and thinner than he remembered her from their first meeting in Canada. Not surprising. Her face was lined and tired, her eyes like small dark smudges, large mouth clamped tight over uneven teeth. She sat quite still in the chair, her legs stretched out in front of her, ankles crossed. She appeared relaxed but Ray Choy was conscious that that was an illusion, a pose. He decided to change tactics, to take a chance. He gave a small chuckle.

"Well! Top marks for inscrutability! And I thought that was our Oriental prerogative." Another small chuckle. "However, I don't see the point. What's so secret about this Piper woman and all the goings on in Nagoya? You've really piqued my curiosity."

"Keeping my mouth shut is what I get paid for, at least partly. It gets to be a habit. If the client wants you in on his business, it's up to him."

"Come now, Helen, we're all grownups here. There is more to it than that! Something is bothering you, if I'm not mistaken. Perhaps I can help, who knows? Why not trust me a little?"

Helen gave a tired shrug.

"Something is bothering me, yes. I'm not sure myself just what. The scene in Nagoya was so strange and so complicated that I haven't got my head around it yet. Once I figure out what it's all about, more or less, you'll be the first person I'll come to for help. Fair enough?"

"Fair enough. I'll look forward to hearing from you." Ray had to be satisfied with Helen's answer since he had no choice. "How long do you intend to stay in Hong Kong? Days? Weeks?"

"I'm not sure. I have an open ticket back. After I see Sonny Burke and give him my verbal report I guess I'd like to finally relax here for a couple of days. You know, do all the touristy things."

"Good idea. You obviously need a rest. But don't forget you came here partly to talk about cooperation between us. Ladrone could use a stringer in Canada. So how do you feel about that now?"

"I haven't forgotten your contribution to my expenses. Business is business. Give me a day or two. I'll get back to you."

"Of course, of course! I didn't intend to press you! Take your time! Rest, relax, enjoy! You'll find Hong Kong a top-notch place for a holiday. Come round when you're ready; I'll show you our facilities. You might be interested. We have just the most up-to-date computer centre and data bank of any private agency in Hong Kong! Nothing but the best. Not much we can't find out for you, just ask."

"Thanks. I'll do that. And sorry I haven't been more forthcoming. I hope I didn't upset your partner too much." She smiled tentatively. Ray was pleased. His tactics were working.

"Oh, don't mind old Angus. He'll get over it. See you again soon."

"Right. Bye."

"Good-bye."

Ray saw Helen to the door. They shook hands most cordially. On his way back to his office Ray was accosted by Angus.

"Well, old man, did you get anything out of that bitch? Well?"

"Not yet but I think I will."

"Oh, How so? Seems to me you'd need a dentist's drill! I'd like to drill her all right! Never heard such insolence! How dare she not answer our questions!"

"Don't take it so personally. She's a smart, experienced operator, knows how to keep confidential matters confidential. Would be an asset to any agency."

"Any employee of ours who behaved like that to me would be looking for work the same hour! I won't have her around, I won't!"

"As you wish, old man. I wasn't going to offer her a job with us, you know. But we do want information that is in her possession, don't we? Get further with honey than with vinegar ..." And he smiled at Angus.

"Yes, yes. Tell me, how are you going to get her to spill the beans?"

"Offered her use of our facilities, data bank and such. She's clearly out of her depth, doesn't know what it's all about. Needs assistance. Once she realizes that we might be able to provide some answers, she'll come to us for help. To me."

"Hope you're right."

"We'll see."

43

Helen and Sonny

"So you're Helen Keremos! Pleased to meet ya. What will ya have? Lee! A drink for the lady."

It was before noon and Waltzing Matilda was almost empty. Sonny sat half-turned on his usual stool at the bar looking Helen over. He seemed to find her acceptable. She sat next to him feeling better and looking less tired after a good night's sleep. She accepted a cup of coffee from Lee, the morning bartender, a look-alike cousin of Canton Bill. Sonny was drinking Diet Coke, as usual. He was a cool-looking, small, black man in his forties, well-built and handsome. He wore chinos and a T-shirt and, except for the Chinese slippers on his feet, looked very American.

"So what's the scoop with this Nagoya business? You and Julie sure cost me a lot of dough. All the money I sent you, the passport and all, wow!"

"It worked. Isn't that what matters?"

"Yeah, sure it worked. But it's all negative cash flow, get me? I'm out thousands. I told Julie that."

"She's better, I hope."

"Yeah, she's okay now, I guess."

"Bad break to lose that baby, eh?"

"Yeah, too bad. I had plans for that kid ... "

"You knew Julie was pregnant before she left for Japan? I thought even she herself didn't realize ..." Helen couldn't hide her surprise.

"I didn't know nothing, damn it! Guess the father is the last to know. I just had plans, hopes like. If I ever had a kid, I'd take him away from here. But it didn't happen, so what? Live with it."

He smiled an automatic smile and took a sip of his drink. So did Helen — to hide her face in the cup. Her stomach felt queasy and it wasn't because of the coffee or anything she'd eaten. It was Sonny Burke. There was something decidedly odd about this man. She recalled what Julie had said about him: an agoraphobic Vietnam vet cursed with total recall. It was on the cards that he would be "disturbed." Euphemism. How badly? It hadn't been obvious over the phone. Quite the contrary. So what changed?

"Yeah? Where would you go?" Idle question to give herself time to figure him out. The answer came like a dam opening.

"Cameroon! West Africa. Area 475 square kilometres, population 9,467,000, GDP per capita $871," Sonny quoted glibly. Probably knew the whole world almanac by heart.

"Sounds small and poor," Helen went along calmly.

"Yeah! But it's home, see. Hey, me and the kid, we would do fine there. Take him outta this crummy place, leave it to the Brits and the Chinese. They deserve each other, yeah!"

"You ever been there? Visited maybe?"

"No. Never been anywheres outside of Nam and here." Sonny gave that automatic smile again, took a deep breath and continued, "And Detroit, Michigan, U.S. of A."

"What if the kid were a girl?"

"A girl?" Sonny was taken aback as if the idea had never occurred. "Hell, I wouldn't have a girl, no way. If it happened that way ... I'd still go. But it wouldn't be the same, see?"

"No, I guess it wouldn't."

"You think I'm nuts." Sonny surprised Helen again.

He'd finished his Coke and turned his fixed smile on her.

"Well, I guess yes, a bit. Cameroon, give me a break! What about Julie? She planning to go with you?"

"She thinks I'm nuts just like you do. But at least you're up-front. Julie, she don't say nothing about it mostly. One time she said 'Rave on.' I reckon there ain't no harm in dreaming, hey!"

"No harm. So where is Julie now? She still hiding or what?"

"She left! Damn it, the cunt left me!!! After all I done for her. I smuggled her here, gave her everything, she was sick like, got a tame pill pusher who owes me to come look after her! Once she's better she splits on me!" Sonny was shaking, his face contorted as if with pain.

"Just like that, she split on you? You didn't have a fight or anything? Without a word?"

"Just like that, without a word!" Sonny was becoming more and more distraught. There was no way to tell where all this would lead. Clearly it was better to lay off any mention of Julie. Best to change the subject. But what would be safe?

"Tough. You want to hear what happened in Japan? I've come to report." She'd also come to collect the balance of her fee and expenses but it didn't seem like the right time to bring that up. Sonny grabbed at the new topic.

"Yeah! Great! Let's go up to my pad, where I do business. You tell me everything. And I'll pay you what I owe, too. Sonny Burke always pays his debts, see."

Relieved, Helen followed Sonny upstairs. On the way up they met Canton Bill coming down. Helen watched the short, wordless meeting between the two men. Bill's quick 'Are you okay?' glance at Sonny and Sonny's reply of a pat on Bill's butt. She'd seen similar looks and gestures a thousand times, between gay men. So that's how it is, she thought. Is that one of the reasons that Julie took off?

How many reasons would she need! Had Julie known that Sonny went both ways? That he was currently actively bisexual? Julie might not have liked finding herself one in a ménage à trois. She would've taken off like a scalded cat. But where? Back home to Australia? Maybe. Maybe not.

Helen took in Sonny's domain with a practised eye. She noted all the Viet Nam paraphernalia, the MIA (Missing in Action) posters, the photographs of events once on every TV screen and front page of every newspaper in North America. A 20-year-old war still alive on Sonny's walls.

"You're old enough to remember Nam, right? Those were the days, man! I had everything, everything you could ever want! I'll sure never forget it, never. Best years of my life. Nothing like Detroit, hey!"

"Yeah? What outfit were you with?"

"82nd Airborne, Supply Sergeant." Sonny sniggered. "Best job in the army. I had my hands in everything, get me? I could get anything — booze, great dope, gooks to do all the dirty work. Two boys fighting to clean my combat boots. A girl for a pack of cigarettes. Hell, for a pack of gum, sometimes."

"You loved it."

"Sure I loved it! Why not? Never had it so good!"

"And combat? Did you see any of that?"

"You kidding? With the Airborne? Sure I was in combat!"

"And how d'you like that?"

"You sort of got used to it, see! Price you paid to be there and not in a stinking slum on welfare. And yes, I lost some buddies, knew you would ask me that. So what? When you gotta go, you gotta go! But ol'Sonny-boy, he made it out. That's me! Hey!"

"So what happened? You went missing or what? They still looking for you?"

"I skipped out before they could ship me back. Went

AWOL. With a nice stash, yeah! No flies on this boy, yeah!" Sonny sang out, his eyes shining. Helen, chilled, had enough.

"Looks like you've got yourself a nice deal here. And all this." She indicated the phones, computer, fax machine, TV sets. Sonny nodded, calming down.

"Tools of the trade. I'm best in the business! Now, you're going to ask me 'what business is that,' right?"

"Not hardly. I can guess the business you're in." Without being invited Helen pulled up a chair and sat down at the table. "I sent you a report."

Sonny sat down across the table from her. He was breathing fast but seemed to have himself under control.

"I read it. Good report. Want to hear me recite it back to you?"

"Spare me. Since I wrote that a few new things have come up. Want to hear?"

"My money's worth!"

"Okay. About the murder of this Nangi guy. Let's see how good you are. Ever hear of something or somebody called Tan or Mr. Tan? Maybe a hit man or something like that?"

"Tan, Tan ... any Taiwanese connection?"

"Could be. Why?" Helen leaned forward with interest.

"Well I've heard it said about the Taiwanese mob. It's a threat, like. Toe the line or else ... else Mr. Tan will get you. One of those boogey-man things. Not a real person. How does it connect with Nangi?"

"Not sure. But the term was mentioned in connection with his death. Another word was 'insurance.' They go together for you, maybe."

"They sure go with Taiwan, that's for sure. Now me, I try to stay as far away as possible from any of the Taipei boys. Bad dudes, that lot. Hong Kong triads, even mainland Wah Ching I can deal with, but United Bamboo, no.

If they are in on this ..."

"United Bamboo, eh? What are they into?"

"Everything. You name it."

"I mean stolen art. You obviously didn't believe they were in on your scam. What would their part be? Insurance suggests protection to me. Is that what you mean?"

"Protection! Right on! It's one of their favourites! Anywhere in the world there are Chinese businesses, U.B. tries to muscle in. Sell them protection. It's a very competitive field, mind. The Vietnamese are in on it now in a big way, not just the Chinese. Turf wars all over the place. Green Turtles are the worst."

"Green Turtles?"

"Yeah, that's what Bill calls the Taiwanese. Fun, eh? All this is real bad news, if true. You got anything else I need to worry about?"

"Ray Choy and Angus McGee. Ladrone partners."

"I know who they are, damn it! What about them?"

"I went to see them yesterday. They seemed very curious. Fishing. About what happened in Nagoya, about Julie, about you. Are they involved in any way with ...?"

"Now who's fishing!" Sonny laughed. He went to the refrigerator, took out a bottle of Diet Coke and a baggie and sat down again. Deliberately he rolled a joint, neat and quick, lit it, inhaled and handed it on to Helen. She toked without comment.

"They know too much to be just curious bystanders. Anyway that's how they struck me. So what's your take?"

"They don't like me, at least that Brit stuffed shirt McGee hates my guts. He came here once and I didn't show proper respect or something."

"You think he wants to get something on you? That's all? Well, I don't believe it. It wasn't McGee alone. Ray was on the case, like in spades. You know about this fantastic data base they claim to have? Well, after I turned out not to be real forthcoming with information, Ray offered to let me have a peek at it. Use it. How does that grab you?"

"I see. What are you planning to ask their magic computer, hey? About Tan? And what else?"

"Maybe about a stolen oil painting by Daumier."

"Hey, why not? Be interesting to know ... what they know." He took one last toke and in a habitual movement broke up the tiny roach. He opened the Coke, took a long drink and handed it to Helen. She drank. Sonny considered for a second, then continued.

"I got something else for you. Ask them about CHNOPS." He spelled it carefully. "See whether they have a file on it and what it says. Let me know, eh?"

"CHNOPS. What's that?"

"Find out!"

"And watch for their reaction, right?"

"Yeah! How about another joint?"

They had another joint. After a while Sonny said:

"I like you, Helen Keremos. Hell, if you were a man I'd fuck you!"

They both laughed.

"Oh? And you don't fuck women?"

"I fuck only beautiful young broads. Like Julie." A grimace moved on and off Sonny's face. "Hey! No offence!"

"No offence taken. I wouldn't fuck you even if you were young and beautiful."

They almost broke up laughing.

44

Ladrone Data Bank

"Fire away, Helen. What do you want me to check for you? Proper names of people and organizations are, of course, easy, so let's try them first, okay? Then we can go on to key words. Follow?"

Ray Choy sat in front of a monitor in a screened corner of the Ladrone computer centre, his fingers poised over the keyboard, and looked expectantly up at Helen standing next to him. She noted that the rest of the room was empty of Ladrone employees. Even Angus was nowhere in sight. She looked down at the computer screen, which indicated they were in LAData.006. She bent down and said: "Try the name Tan."

"Just Tan? We'll find hundreds of Tans here." Quickly he typed in TAN and scrolled down a numbered list of TANs each with either additional names or other identifying characteristics. Helen pointed to numbers 8 and 17. "Try those two first." Ray glanced up at her. "Right. Number 8."

Information flashed on the screen: "TAN, Louis — Taipei. Age 36. Owns travel agency. Tan's Travel. Believed involved in underworld activities. One arrest for extortion, no convictions. Source: LADnet."

"Well?" Ray asked "Is he the man you're interested in?"

"Not sure. Try 17."

"Right you are."

"TAN, Pak — Taipei. Age 62. Retired. Has family members in N. America and Malaysia. Travels there frequently.

Suspected member of U.B. Source: LADnet."

"What have you got on United Bamboo?"

"United Bamboo? Probably quite a bit of generalities but nothing recent or vital, I'm sure. We don't operate in Taiwan." Ray seemed reluctant to pursue the topic. If he was surprised that Helen knew what U.B. stood for, he didn't show it.

"What else are you after? "

"Sonny Burke."

"Right." Without hesitation Ray played with the keys until "Burke, Sonny" came up on the screen. Helen noted that they were now in LAData.008 and knew she would find nothing here of interest. Ray had prepared a special "Sonny Burke" file just for her. The real Burke file remained in LAData.006. Still, she read the doctored file carefully. This was the information Ladrone didn't mind her having.

"Pretty thin. Nothing here I don't know." She managed to sound disappointed. She bent over Ray, her hands on his shoulders.

"Oh, well, sorry. Our information is better in some areas than others. Better luck next try."

"Try 'Daumier, Honoré. French painter.'"

Ray flinched. It wasn't much of a flinch but Helen's hands reported it to her brain. There was no mistake. Ray Choy was sensitive to the name "Daumier." What was more, he was clearly faking his search for a file on the painter. There was something there he didn't want Helen to see.

"I don't think we have anything on this Daumier. Should we? What about him? "

He turned in his chair so Helen had to drop her hands.

"Oh, nothing much. Just curious. The Nagoya police found a painting by him during their investigation of the Nangi murder. A small oil painting of a man in a top hat standing in front of a outdoor display of prints or books. I believe it's called *The Collector*."

Helen had boned up on Daumier and his oeuvre in the library.

"*The Collector?* Never heard of it." The way he said it confirmed for Helen that not only was he lying but that he was gravely disturbed by what she'd just said.

"We struck out again, eh? Perhaps your data base isn't as good as you claim. Okay. I'll give you one more chance. Try CHNOPS. And if you're having trouble finding it, I'll be happy to key it in myself."

Helen was ready to end the game. Ray elected to brazen it out.

"You're smart, Helen. I knew it when I suggested you come to Hong Kong to see us. You're too smart to get yourself into a spot you can't get out of. Drop your interest in CHNOPS. It would be best if you forgot it, immediately. Don't meddle anymore, Helen."

"Just what is your connection with CHNOPS, Ray? With stolen art?"

"I can't — I won't — talk about it. Professional confidence is involved."

"You mean CHNOPS is a client of Ladrone? You have a criminal organization for a client? Tut, tut."

"What makes you think that CHNOPS is a criminal organization? In fact, where did you get CHNOPS from? Who told you about it? Mind you, it's not difficult to guess. Sonny Burke, right? Why should you be grinding his ax for him? What makes any of this your business, anyway?"

"You're changing the subject, Ray. Just tell me about CHNOPS. What's your connection? How does the Daumier painting fit in? "

They were both standing up now, facing each other, voices raised. Then Ray turned his back and walked away.

He opened the door and motioned Helen out.

"No more. I've got nothing more to say. Please leave. Right now."

"I'm going, I'm going! But the issue isn't going away, you know, Ray. This bubble is going to burst one of these days. Better be ready."

Ray didn't answer. He led the way through the reception area to the front door. Heads turned as they walked out. Helen saw Angus's face in a doorway, his eyes frightened. She winked at him.

"Ray, does this mean you don't want me as a stringer? Too bad, we could have made beautiful music —"

Ray closed the door behind her.

45
Sonny Again

"I don't know nothing about this CHNOPS thing. I figured it for some sort of code. Look it, I just do what I'm paid to do. Mostly it's delivering stuff to people, like that picture Julie carried to Japan for me. Making arrangements is my business, see? I set it up with the client, Mel Romulu in this case, where the exchange will be made, how the money is to be delivered. Like that. I'm told where to pick up the merchandise and afterwards I wait until I get the word from CHNOPS, usually by phone, and pass on the payoff as instructed. It's always a deposit to bank accounts right here in Hong Kong. I can give you the numbers but I bet they are all closed and money long gone. It's easy to move money around like that these days. Very hard to trace. That's it. "

"Why Japan?"

"What?"

"Why did you arrange for Romulu to pick up his merchandise in Japan?"

"Why not? Julie was going there, it seemed a good idea. But if I'd known those Ladrone bastards were part of this CHNOPS scam I sure wouldn't have gotten them to look for her."

"We don't know what their part is, or even if they have any active part. But they sure know about CHNOPS and at least one of the paintings, the Daumier specifically."

"Yeah? And how can I be sure they aren't running this scam? Hell, maybe I've been working for them all this time!"

"Don't get your briefs in a knot about Ladrone, Sonny. Ray Choy might have the brains, but he sure doesn't have the nerve to run a business like this. Angus hasn't either. Brains or nerve. They are acting shit scared. That's a good sign in my book. Relax."

"Easy for you to say. You'll be off back home in a day or two, right? You can forget all about it, like they told you. Me, I'm on the hook ..." Sonny stopped.

"Oh? What hook is that? What haven't you told me, Sonny? And here I thought we were going to be up-front with each other!"

"No harm telling you, I guess, you know so much already. It's been very quiet lately, since the Nagoya delivery misfired. Well, it's on again. In fact, I've got a delivery to Romulu right now, just waiting to make the arrangements. That's okay. But there seems to be a big score going down soon, like in the next couple of months. The word is, it's Taipei. And now here you tell me the United Bamboo might be in on the action somehow. But which end of it? I don't like it. Is CHNOPS working with them or ... Like I said, if CHNOPS is tangling with the U.B. boys I'm outta here."

"Can you contact CHNOPS? Ask what's going down? And about Taipei, Mr. Tan, Ladrone and all that? How about it?"

"Yeah. I could do that. I don't like it, though."

"How do you initiate contact? You have a phone number to call? Let's do it now. I'd love to talk to CHNOPS!"

"You kidding? To 'initiate contact' I leave a message on a computer network bulletin board. Someone contacts me. That's what happened the only time I've had to do it. I guess I could do it again now. This big score ... if the Taiwanese are involved, I don't like it. And if Ladrone is in on this deal I want out. I don't like fuckups, especially fuckups close to home. But you can't 'talk to CHNOPS,' Helen. Nuts to that."

"Okay, okay. Can't blame me for trying. But in your own interest you will be in touch with them, right? And you'll report about me too, won't you, Sonny? This Nosy Parker of a private investigator from Canada. Well, I'll bet CHNOPS already knows all about me. Never mind all that." Helen dismissed CHNOPS and Ladrone, United Bamboo and Mr. Tan with a wave of her hand. "How about this new delivery to Mel? How about I do it for you? Take it with me to Toronto. Like you said, I'm on my way out of here momentarily. And I know Mel Romulu. I bet the item is smaller than a breadbox, eh? Be no problem to take it through customs."

Sonny looked at her for a moment, considering. Then he smiled and nodded.

"Why not? I'll have it delivered to your hotel tonight. And it's smaller than a breadbox for sure. It's a picture, like the last item. Small, portable."

"I figured it would be. Replacement?"

"Something like that, I guess. I've never seen this merchandise. Don't want to. You really going to do it?"

"If you trust me with it. And pay me to do it!" Helen laughed. "Speaking of pay. You still owe me for Japan. Remember: 'Sonny Burke always pays his debts,' eh?"

"No sweat, lady, no sweat! Every penny I owe you as per your invoice, plus a couple of hundred for taking the item to Mel and, of course, the item itself, will be in your hands tonight at your hotel."

"Five."

"Five what?"

"Don't be cheap, Sonny. Five hundred."

"Five hundred for taking a piece of rolled up canvas in your suitcase!? It won't cost you nothing! "

"It's all in what you call it. I call it smuggling a stolen painting into Canada and I say five hundred dollars American is a fair price. A bargain."

Sonny laughed, his face alive with pleasure. He patted Helen on the shoulder. His worries about Ladrone, CHNOPS and the Taiwanese appeared to have vanished.

"Girl, you're a peach. Five it is. Say, how about a joint? Good shit that."

"Thanks, no. Wipe me out."

"How about lunch? "

"What d'you serve here? Pizza?"

Sonny laughed. "Let's go down and see," he said.

They both ate Sonny's regular lunch of ribs, stir-fried vegetables and rice, sitting companionably next to each other at the bar. They talked but "business" wasn't mentioned again, directly. Between bites Sonny kept asking Helen about herself, her work, about Canada, Toronto, Vancouver. About herself Helen was not particularly forthcoming — due to her usual reticence on the subject and not any specific reason to hide from Sonny. When she mentioned Alice in Toronto, Sonny said: "So that's the attraction in Toronto! I wondered about that. Like, why not just go back to Vancouver? That's where you live, right? Vancouver, British Columbia." Sonny rolled the words out on his tongue.

"Mostly, yes. So?"

"Nothing, nothing."

"Oh, spit it out, Sonny! What about Vancouver? You thinking maybe moving there after 1997?"

"Could be, hey! "

"You don't think you could carry on business as usual after the Chinese take over?"

"Who can trust the commies, I ask you! The Brits don't, that's for sure. They just want out of this colonial game at any price. And it's us, us Hong Kong folks who will pay it! You betcha. Anyway, living with the commies ... not for this boy."

"Sure. Besides they'll probably take over the telephone

system, fire your friends and raise the squeeze so high it won't be profitable for you to operate. Have to go out of business."

Sonny choked on a mouthful of rice.

"Right, right! The greedy commie bastards will kill this golden goose stone cold dead! "

"Yes. On the other hand, maybe they will get the knack from greedy capitalist bastards and the goose will flourish."

"Yeah! Never can tell with the Chinese. Sneaky types." Sonny dismissed Helen's transparent irony. "Now Vancouver. Give me the scene. Could I carry on my business outta there?"

"With your resources you could go just about any place with a good phone system. They've got that. Great Chinese food in Vancouver, too."

"That's sure a plus!"

"No kidding. Better than in the Republic of Cameroon, I'll bet. And we speak English."

"Cameroons. I'm not going to no Cameroons, hear me?"

"Sure, Sonny," Helen backed off immediately.

Throughout this, their second meeting, Sonny, although volatile, had been quite together. He'd never slipped away into that chasm he'd exhibited the first time they'd met. Perhaps because neither Julie nor a baby had been mentioned. Helen wondered what his reaction would be if she brought them up. They finished their meal and Helen was about to leave when she decided to risk it.

"Where did Julie go, Sonny? When she left here."

He answered readily as if he'd been waiting to be asked.

"She flew Cathay Pacific to LAX. Still on that passport I'd gotten her. Bet you could find her if you tried."

"Should I try, Sonny? "

"Up to you." He avoided her eyes.

They shook hands and Helen made her way out into the bright May sunshine.

46

Angus Talks

Helen reached her hotel after seven, tired after an afternoon at the Happy Valley race track. This was her last full day in Hong Kong and she was making the most of it. She'd enjoyed herself. She'd sat in the stands in the midst of a family group of about 16 people of all ages, from a two year old to a great-grandmother. Most of them were eager and knowledgeable race fans; those who spoke English were very willing to instruct the stranger in the intricacies of Hong Kong racing. As a result, she didn't lose as much money as she might have otherwise. Or so she told herself. Anyway it was worth it. Her companions laughed and kibitzed a lot, some of which Helen even thought she understood. She ate Chinese finger food with them and watched them drink gallons of soft drinks. It was an afternoon she wouldn't soon forget.

Back at her hotel, Helen was given a small parcel. After a shower she sat down and opened it. As promised, it contained a bundle of American dollars, a cardboard tube and a short note on yellow-lined paper. The note said: "In case you run out of cash in L.A."

She counted the money. It came to a thousand more than she'd been expecting. The terse note spoke volumes. She was taking off for Toronto but Sonny was sure she would eventually get to California to look for Julie. He wanted to help finance the search.

The phone rang. She picked it up reluctantly. Who would be calling her and why?

"Miss Keremos? I mean ... Helen? It's Angus McGee. I must see you. Immediately. Please. I'm downstairs in the lobby. Can I come up to see you? Right now. Please ... it's very important ..."

"Come on up," Helen interrupted the scared voice. She swept the parcel and its contents into a dresser drawer.

Minutes later Angus McGee arrived, his breath rasping in his throat as if he'd run all the way upstairs. He stood a second gasping for breath, then said: "Could I have a drink? Scotch would be nice but anything ... "

Without a word Helen got him a glass and poured a miniature bottle of Red Label into it. Still standing at the door McGee drank it all and handed the glass back to Helen. She took it and indicating one of the two chairs in the room suggested they sit down.

"Yes. Good. I was afraid I would miss you. We have to talk."

"Talk away."

"Well, the thing is, Ray told me what happened this morning. You mentioning the Daumier painting and ... CHNOPS. Oh, God! Got me worried, you know. Ray shouldn't have just shown you out. We must talk about it all." His voice had strengthened but his eyes gave away his panic.

"Take it easy, Angus. We are talking. Continue."

"Yes, well. How did you know ... who told you ...?"

"Angus, it doesn't really matter how or who, does it? Fact is that I know and after this morning I also know that you and Ray are involved. In a criminal matter, right?"

"Yes! No! Criminal? Maybe a little off colour, but not really criminal, surely? I don't know! You see it all started so innocently ... "

And Angus McGee proceeded to tell Helen the full story of Ladrone's original involvement with the Glasgow burglary. She listened quietly as a number of facts fell into place.

"All we ever did was act as go-betweens. Between the insurance companies and the ... thieves. Twice we did it, that's all. It all went like clockwork that first time, money was paid, the goods turned over. Everyone was happy!"

"So what's the problem?" Helen asked.

"Don't you understand? The painting recovered was the Daumier! *The Collector* it was called. Now it seems there is a copy around — do the Japanese police have it?"

"Yes, they have something that sounds very much like what you describe."

"Well, don't you see? What if the one that was returned by the thieves is the fake? We are in the middle. The whole thing will come back to haunt us. And if old man Choy finds out ..." Angus took out a handkerchief from his sleeve and wiped his face. The problem of "old man Choy," whom Helen had never heard of, was a new wrinkle that she thought best to ignore, at least for the time being. Probably it was a matter of concern only to Angus, a red herring.

She stuck to the main point. One thing at a time.

"What happened the second time you played go-between? What were the items?"

"Oh, much more minor. Six Japanese prints. We didn't make much on that ... wasn't worth it really, considering. But we couldn't refuse, you see. I understand all that now but ... anyway that's when CHNOPS came in. We hadn't heard about him before, nothing, nobody mentioned him ..." Angus stopped. His panic had increased with the narrative. "How about another ...?" Helen got up and gave him another scotch. He drank it gratefully.

"Him? You're calling CHNOPS 'him.' What do you know about this 'him'? Why not 'them' or 'it' or 'her' for that matter? Isn't it an organization rather than an individual?"

"Organization, yes of course, you're quite right. My error. Ray is forever telling me not to think of CHNOPS as 'him.' Somehow ... well never mind. It's very frightening not to know what one is up against."

"So this CHNOPS surfaced around the return of Japanese prints. How? What happened?"

"Let's see. I'm trying to recall how it worked, it was Ray who dealt with this matter mostly. Right, the first contact was a Chinese. He came in, asked for Ray. After that we got instructions by phone. The whole process was different from the Daumier exchange. We turned over all the money, rather than keeping our share of it and then we were paid off. Cash arrived by messenger. And it wasn't much."

"Yes, but how did CHNOPS come into it?"

"We didn't want to do it, you know. But we had to ... as I was saying this CHNOPS had all the details of the first transaction, which had included that wretched Daumier. So ... "

"They suckered you in by overpaying in the first instance. After that they had you over a barrel. Greed will do it every time. You thought it was safer to go along than to have your connection with art thefts come to light. Plus you didn't want Mr. Choy Senior to know ...?"

"Yes, yes. Old Choy wouldn't stand for it, I know. I can't afford to have him find out." Angus was perspiring heavily.

"I see. Okay, that's clear. But how did this CHNOPS identify himself?"

"Once we were in and the matter was closed, we got a fax. From CHNOPS. Saying 'welcome to the club' and things like that. And instructions on how to get in touch if it was ever necessary. Via computer bulletin board, something like that. I don't like computers, a bit of a Luddite, I'm afraid. Ray handles all of that. He told me the other day that something new is in the wind from CHNOPS. Something big. Then you show up knowing so much. It's damn upsetting. So I thought it best to find out what you have in mind. It's too bad, really. I want to retire, you know. I need the money. Ray is trying to get rid of me. What will I do? Oh, my God, what will become of me ...?" McGee became incoherent.

Fear and booze make an ugly combination. There was little Helen could do, so she left him alone. Helen was only mildly sorry for him. The outlines of at least one section of the story were becoming clearer. Selling stolen property back to insurance companies is not a very original scam. However, it's one that is dangerous to repeat more than once or twice because it's susceptible to sting operations. But CHNOPS seemed to have a sting-proof setup going. Greed works. Helen wondered if the Ladrone partners were the only ones CHNOPS had collected on his string. It had to be quite a complex operation keeping track of it all. No wonder he used computers. He?

At nine Helen finally called the porter for a cab and got rid of McGee. Once alone Helen took Sonny's parcel out again. She put the money away in her money belt, then turned to the cardboard mailing tube. Rolled up inside was a canvas bundle. She unrolled it as carefully as she could. Rolling and unrolling old oil paintings is not recommended. This one had obviously suffered and would require expert attention in Toronto. But Helen felt no qualms in doing what was necessary to identify the "item." As she'd both feared and expected, it proved to be a portrait of a man in a top hat standing in front of a display of prints. Another *The Collector* by Daumier, she was ready to bet. She hadn't seen the painting recovered by Suzuki from Julie's umbrella, but this one matched the description to a tee. Since obviously it wasn't the same painting, it had to be a copy. She let out a sigh. Having just listened to McGee's story, she knew there were not two but three of them — at least.

She re-rolled the canvas into the tube and stuck it into her carry-on bag. This was her last night in Hong Kong. Tomorrow she faced a long, exhausting flight to Canada. What she needed now was a good dinner then rest. Sleep.

Dinner was easy but sleep wouldn't come. Helen did all the things guaranteed to produce sleep — hot shower, cold shower, hot tea, cold drink, read book, watch TV, turn up heat, turn down heat. Everything she could think of. She even took two ASA tablets prophylactically for early-morning knee pain. She remained wide awake. Her mind buzzed like a hungry bee over everything she'd learned. Just before she finally fell asleep she reminded herself of the phone call she would make the next morning.

47

Suzuki's Correspondence

Suzuki replaced the receiver carefully. The call from Keremos had been unexpected and the information she'd provided disturbing. Nangi's murder was over a month old and a bulging file testified that he and his detectives had tried hard to solve it. And had been unsuccessful in finding any evidence of what had happened in the Uni Mall the evening of Nangi's death. No witnesses had come forward; no one remembered seeing Nangi there alone or in company. Of course, there were leads of a kind. Circumstantial suspicions. As in the curious coincidence of the three foreigners. The hidden painting. The yakuza connection. On the murder per se, nothing.

Now here was a name — "Tan," maybe Louis, age 36, or possibly Pak, age 62, and a nationality — Taiwanese, with connection to the underworld. All this plus the word "insurance" handed to him by long-distance telephone by one of the suspicious foreigners. Helen Keremos had carefully waited until she was out of his jurisdiction to present him with this information. The original source of it, assuming it wasn't a red herring designed to mislead him, had to have been the elusive Miss Julia Piper. Whom he'd not been able to lay his hands on, so to speak. It was enough to put a man off his lunch.

Suzuki sighed. This "Taiwanese Tan" would have to be hunted for, hypothetical or not. Japan doesn't officially recognize The Republic of China, as Taiwan calls itself. Its interests are looked after in Tokyo by something called the

Association of East Asian Relations. Not that they were likely to be helpful. Unless he was travelling on a Japanese passport, which wasn't likely, Mr. Tan would have needed a visa. Check visa applications. A lot of police resources would be used up in what Suzuki was sure would prove to be a useless pursuit. Nevertheless a proper inquiry had to be instituted. He made careful note of the conversation and put it in the file. Then he called the large Sergeant and gave instructions.

Helen's phone call hadn't been the only matter that had disturbed Suzuki's equanimity. The previous day two letters had arrived on his desk. One was from Tokyo, from INTERPOL. It advised him in long-winded bureaucratese that with reference to a painting by Daumier, Honoré, of a man in a top hat, etc., which had been stolen from a collection in Scotland, said painting had been recovered with the assistance of Jason Forbes, a well-known expert in these things, and was currently back on display. INTERPOL's Cultural Property Section was deeply honoured to cooperate with the splendid Nagoya police department and hoped it had been of assistance etc., etc., — in short, the painting sitting in his evidence locker was no longer of any interest to INTERPOL.

And the second letter? It came from the United States, California, Los Angeles. Master, Powers & Khayatt, Attorneys-at-Law. It demanded the immediate return of the property of Miss Julia Piper unlawfully confiscated by the Nagoya Prefectural Police on the orders of Inspector Haruo Suzuki. Forthwith. Passport, purse and contents, umbrella. And painting "by unknown artist" of man in top hat etc. Signed: M.D. Khayatt, Ms.

Suzuki had told Helen about both these letters. After telling him about the mysterious Tan, she'd asked about any developments regarding the painting. There hadn't been any reason to keep either of those letters secret. She hadn't seemed surprised at these developments. But she had been interested in the name of the Los Angeles lawyer.

Across the city from Suzuki's spartan office the yakuza chief Kusashita was relaxing in his bath. Kusashita, a broad-shouldered man in his fifties, loved his bath. He was an intense patriot, even a Japanese chauvinist, who took great care to follow traditional Japanese ways as much the exigencies of yakuza business allowed. The contents of his home and personal space at his office could have been lifted from a 19th-century Japanese print. No Western, modern furniture or decorations were permitted, most communication equipment was excluded and the essential was carefully hidden or camouflaged. He wore Japanese clothes as much as possible, reasonably making an exception for golf. On a chair he would sit with his feet up tucked under his body and he would grumble when invited to eat European-type food. Viewing the yakuza as a legitimate and vital part of Japanese heritage, he insisted that its etiquette, as he conceived it, be followed punctiliously by his followers.

The murder of Nangi, his bagman and tax accountant/money launderer, had initially disturbed Kusashita. Nangi hadn't been a favourite of his and there had even been an idea floated that he should be replaced. There had been that hint that Nangi was going into business for himself. That couldn't be borne.

Of course it wasn't Nangi's death as such that was upsetting the great man. The murder investigation lay in the middle of his turf like an unexploded bomb. Was it ticking away? Was it a dud? Was it the beginning of an attack on the Kusashita mob or the end of a private affair?

As a yakuza chief, he couldn't allow one of his men to be killed and not retaliate. But on whom? That was the problem. Unanswerable questions made Kusashita deeply uneasy.

He'd kept in touch with developments via his police contacts; he instituted his own investigation of Nangi; he took in without comment Keiko Ueki's reports on the three foreigners and arranged to see two of them himself. He considered the situation carefully and decided that Julie Piper's departure from Nagoya before being interviewed by the police was in the best interest of his organization. One never knew what she might confide to Inspector Suzuki. Kusashita had a very high opinion of the Inspector and a low one of foreign women.

To cover all bases he allowed Ueki to take off with Wayne Tillion, whom Kusashita took to be the most important of the threesome. Although foreign, Tillion was, after all, male. Besides, Kusashita had watched from the sidelines as Tillion sat relaxed on the floor, sipping tea and letting the older woman do most of the talking for him. To Kusashita this indicated Tillion's higher status. The yakuza chief knew no English.

Over the past weeks the issue of Nangi's death had dissipated somewhat. There had been no sign of a follow-up, no further troubles. The slow dismembering of Nangi's office by the authorities had provided momentary problems but the role of a leader is to cope with such and Kusashita took it in stride. There were many eager to take Nangi's place, including the job of winding the tax and police authorities in endless red tape. Kusashita considered that problem solved.

He stepped out of the super hot water and allowed himself to be dried off. Then he dismissed the servant and, wrapped in a *yukata*, sat back on his haunches on the floor. Before he fully entered meditation mode he contemplated with much pleasure the six beautiful prints of classical Japanese subjects on the walls around him. Fleetingly it occurred to him that he'd received them from Nangi. That fact seemed of no consequence.

48

Mel Romulu

After Eleena left him, Melhior Romulu tore the guts out of the apartments in which they'd lived together and redecorated completely. He had been tempted to leave Diamond Plaza Towers outright but decided against it. Its location north of Toronto just off a major bypass highway and within 20 minutes of Pearson International Airport suited him very well. He was now totally dedicated to the art world — collecting, buying, selling, valuing, restoring — and travelled a great deal in pursuit of those elusive coups that made his life worthwhile. The two side-by-side condominium units were ideally suited for what he intended to transform them into: his own private art gallery. Besides, he would have lost money if he'd sold them during the recession, and Mel wasn't used to losing money.

Thus a section of the 16th floor of DP Towers blossomed into Mel's fantasy. Helen Keremos, who remembered the place quite distinctly from her short stint as the chief of security at the Towers a couple of years before, stood amazed at how perfectly proportioned rooms flowed one into another through archways, the space unbroken by doors or much in the way of mundane furniture. Minute halogen lamps on virtually invisible tracks here illuminated, there cast shadows, the better to exhibit Romulu's art treasures. He had decorated the space and arranged his extensive collection in his own idiosyncratic way. Not by period or genre or country of origin but by colour. For example, predominantly blue objets d'art — whether impressionist paintings, or Chinese porcelain, or Indian rugs, or Inuit sculpture, or Dutch tiles — were displayed in a room of the palest robin's egg blue at floor level, which darkened into midnight blue as it climbed the wall towards the ceiling. There were white, green, red, black, grey, beige, purple and, for all Helen could tell, maroon coloured rooms/spaces. Only two rooms looked like regular living spaces for regular people. One was Romulu's very utilitarian study-cum-office. Although he spent most of his time in there, it betrayed very little about the man. Adjacent to it was his bedroom in yellow. It faced east and felt monastic. Looking into it on a perfect sunny May morning, Helen found it impossibly bright.

"Where are my shades! Sure need them right about now. What a production you got here! Wow! The AGO must be green with envy." And shading her eyes with her hand, Helen swung around. She grinned at the tall, thin man in a yellow jogging suit. "You do take colour coordination a bit far, Mel. I remember that about you. It's effective, I'll give you that. And you've hardly changed at all."

In fact, once seen never forgotten, that was Dr. Melhior Romulu. He would have been a perfect addition to the Addams Family. Unusual height, almost pathological thinness, large bony hands and the face of a clown. His sandy hair was combed back and plastered down like a caricature from the thirties. A wispy mustache clung to his face above a fleshy upper lip and straight, yellowing teeth with prominent gums. The ex-dentist looked as if he needed a periodontist. Yet among all these memorable features one stood out: enormous protruding eyebrows, like a furry shelf over his small, coal-black eyes. Not a man to be lost in a crowd.

"Always nice to see you, Helen. Like my new layout, do you? That's nice. Rather pleased with it myself. Shows off my collection very well, don't you think? Oh! Sit, sit! A drink?"

They had reached the study and Mel was doing the honours.

"No thanks, nothing for me. You do take your enthusiasms a bit past the point of mere eccentricity. Two quarter-million dollar apartments with a colour-coordinated art collection! That's about on par with buying stolen art by mail order."

Mel laughed, throwing back his head and showing his teeth.

"Always one for coming to a sharp point and right away, aren't you, Helen? Didn't even give us time for a small 'hello' before you go for the throat. All right. I'll respond in kind. What business is it of yours how and where I acquire my collection? And why would you care, anyway? You have something for me from Sonny Burke, right? You smuggled it into Canada knowing it was stolen, right? I understand that you started out as just a bystander in this business but you're deep in it now. So please let's dispense with the hypocrisy."

Taken aback at his vehemence, Helen waved a deprecatory hand. It rankled her to be accused of hypocrisy.

"Ease off. What's biting you anyway? I make a tiny crack about your art collection and you jump all over me. You used to be cooler than this."

Mel laughed again and rubbed his enormous hands together in a nervous gesture. She hadn't remembered him like this.

"Quite right. I'm angry, that's all. I must apologize; my anger isn't at you, not at all. Forgive me. This ... this whole business has been very nerve-wracking. Not to mention expensive. Wayne coming back from Japan empty-handed after spending almost every cent of the thousands I gave him. And with a bride! Who works for the yakuza! I feel like throttling that boy. You did know they were here already? After honeymooning in Hawaii at my expense?"

"Yes." Helen thought it wise not to let Mel know that she'd arrived back in Toronto two days previously. Was it hypocritical of her not to reveal that rather than hurrying to DP Towers with the mailing tube from Sonny she'd hunted out Wayne and Keiko? In fact, the previous night the four of them, Alice Caplan having been included, had met over drinks. And Keiko was presently out with Alice sightseeing while Wayne was placating his boss and hoping to get his old job back. She decided to think through the implications of all this later.

She continued: "Yes, I know Keiko and Wayne got hitched. It's not my preference but surely nothing to get so upset about. As I understand it, Sonny isn't asking for payment on this item I've brought for you, so you won't be out anymore, will you? Incidentally, it's damn generous of Sonny, isn't it? I wonder why?"

For a second Romulu looked as if he might laugh again. Then his eyebrows moved even further over his eyes like two small furry animals about to go into hiding. He rubbed his moustache with a long fingernail.

"I've made other arrangements. Not with Sonny, but with the principal. Directly. Much better that way."

"With CHNOPS?" In spite of herself Helen couldn't disguise her surprise and rising interest. Mel noticed and nodded, pleased.

"Yes. CHNOPS. Mail Order House for Art."

"Why CHNOPS? I mean, what does it stand for? It's been bugging me ever since I heard the term. What's it mean, if anything?"

Now Mel looked delighted.

"You weren't able to figure it out? I'm amazed! A knowledgeable woman like you! My, my, but our educational system has much to answer for. CHNOPS is a mnemonic for Carbon, Hydrogen, Nitrogen, Oxygen, Phosphorus and Sulphur. The six atoms, elements if you prefer, from which organic molecules are constructed. We are all constructed. In a sense we're all CHNOPS. I thought everyone knew that."

"Very clever. But what's it mean? What does it tell me about who's using this fancy terminology?" Helen refused to be impressed. In fact, the more she knew about this CHNOPS, the less she liked about it.

"Very clever, yes, it tells you that CHNOPS is very clever. And amusing. I find it so."

"Do you? I don't. It's what hooked you into this scam, I bet. All this redundant mystification. CHNOPS, I ask you!"

"Redundant mystification! Oh, I like that! You have quite a turn of phrase yourself, Helen. I'm surprised you don't appreciate CHNOPS. You know very well that 'redundant mystification' is a very useful device. And yes, you're quite right. That's what piqued my interest. So you see it works. Clever and amusing. Most business transactions, whether lawful or not, are essentially dull. There really isn't much out there to interest a man like me. I suspect that the same goes for CHNOPS. Which is what makes this man so special. Yes, indeed, there is a mind at work there. A truly original mind."

"Then wouldn't you like to meet the owner of this original mind? The person behind it all? Because ... "

"No, no! That would spoil it all, don't you see? The real man behind it all — and let's face it, it is a man, not a woman — will disappoint. He will turn out to be some unwashed computer nerd, with scientific pretensions. A pseudo-artist most likely. Young, probably. No, no, I don't want to meet him. Quite spoil the fun."

"Let's see. So paintings are the objective but it's this odd way of getting them that constitutes the 'fun.' Right?"

"Of course!"

"Tell me about it."

"Why not? I do enjoy talking with you, Helen. You're

so refreshingly down to earth. What can I tell you? Well, first of all you know about the catalogue? We did mention 'mail order,' so you must know about that. Well, it's beautifully simple. I subscribe to a newsletter called *ARTrace*. It keeps me up to date with the inner workings of the art market. Not the art market as in the *New York Times* or gallery glossies. Neither is it a glorified clipping service like most specialized newsletters. Not at all. *ARTrace* knows things before they hit print. Who's gotten what, who's selling under the counter to evade taxes, what is being bought up quietly to keep prices from rising. Which artist is sick and likely to die, increasing the value of his work. Who's looking to unload what and why and for how much. Worldwide. Fascinating stuff. Subscription cost $3,000 U.S. per year for about 20 bulletins. Pricey, eh? It's more than financial advice or stock market newsletters. The cost keeps out the riffraff and the merely curious. I don't imagine their subscription list is more than a few hundred. But what a list! No dilettantes or amateurs. You see the possibilities?"

Mel paused for a second but the question was clearly rhetorical.

"Of course you do. *ARTrace* has an inquiry service, which costs extra. Let them know what kind of items, artists or whatever you're interested in and they'll tell you exactly what your chances are of getting your hands on any of them, including prices."

"Oh? And how d'you get in touch with *ARTrace*? You have an address?"

"Computer networks. Find them on Internet. *ARTrace* will be listed with a bulletin board address. You leave a message for them on the electronic board indicated, then they get in touch with you. Call you with a fax number or a computer password. Next time it might be a different number or different method altogether. Once contact is established, they keep in touch, you can be sure. So. Would you like to venture what comes next?"

"Easy. They offer you just the merchandise you were looking for, by mail at a good price. Just a coincidence of course."

"Not directly, not quite so blatant. Smarter. I received a catalogue in the mail. Included items they knew I was interested in. Also other items, middle-range works of art, all kinds, real mishmash, I suspect, just fillers. Description, a little photo, price. Below market value. Nothing else on it, no return address, nothing. Now what's mail order with no way to order? You've seen one of those catalogues I take it?"

"Better still. I have one."

"Oh!" Mel was momentarily taken aback. He continued: "Well then you know that there is nothing, nothing on that catalogue that can be construed as an offer to sell. If asked they will tell you it's a 'Want to Buy' list *not* a 'Have to Sell' list. Nothing illegal about that. I did say, 'clever,' didn't I?"

"You did. Clever it is. What next?"

"Then someone called. Someone who knew a lot about me, what I collect and that I could afford their prices. Everything."

"That isn't so hard," Helen interrupted. "They credit check all their subscribers, especially those who buy their extra 'inquiry' service. Send them the listings, wait a couple of weeks and then call. Standard operating procedure. It's called 'telemarketing.'"

"Quite so. That's how it works across the board. Someone called me. Male voice speaking North American English, educated, knowledgeable, no discernible idiosyncrasies to identify him. Told me to call him Bob. After that, if you are interested, he tells you Sonny Burke will call you to make arrangements. The price isn't negotiable.

It's take it or leave it. You take it and it all goes like clock-work. You pick up the merchandise and pay Burke in whatever way he suggests. That's it."

"How often have you done this?"

"Three. Three items. Counting the one you're carry-ing." Mel nodded in the direction of Helen's shoulder bag with the mailing tube sticking out of one side.

"And it was always Sonny Burke. In Hong Kong."

"Always. But I didn't know it was Hong Kong until the second time. Until then he only called me; I couldn't call him. And the pick up and delivery was in Montreal."

"And the second?"

"Honolulu. I went myself both times. Montreal in September and Honolulu in January. Had a very nice time in each of those cities in addition to picking up my merchandise."

"Yes, smart. CHNOPS makes it easy to start. Good price, delivery places carefully selected. Once you're hooked he can be less careful. Pattern is very clear. Both at this end and ... elsewhere," Helen said, thinking of the way the Ladrone partners had been manipulated. Their role was different and Helen wasn't sure how it all fit in, but the pattern was revealing. She continued quickly: "I appreciate your frankness. Now tell me, were the items you bought great fakes or genuine but stolen? What did you believe you were buying?"

Mel remained unruffled, having been prepared for this question. He looked at Helen and nodded as if in approbation.

"You've put your finger right on it — what makes CHNOPS so interesting. All these logistical matters we've been talking about so far are minor compared to this. You see, I can't tell whether I've bought forgeries or stolen originals."

"Come on, Mel. I know that sometimes it's hard to tell

and experts have been known to be fooled but surely ... in any case, take this painting I've carried here for you. It's a Daumier and according to INTERPOL, the original is safe in a gallery in Scotland."

"Ah, but is it? I grant you that one of them is a faux Daumier ... but which? It was stolen some time ago and suddenly found again, right? Ha!"

"Surely experts can tell whether it's the original or a copy that was returned?"

"Maybe they can and then maybe not. Who knows? "

"The insurance company is satisfied, so I understand."

"Insurance is satisfied as long as the owners are happy with what's been returned. It's in their interest to have it be accepted as original. Isn't that so? "

"True. You know, this thing gets murkier by the minute."

"Ha! I told you, it's wonderful. And you haven't heard the best yet."

"Oh?"

"About those fakes, forgeries, copies, reproductions. Whatever you choose to call them. They are so good that it's impossible to tell just what they are. Probably impossible to tell them apart from originals even if you have them side by side. Of course, nobody has had the opportunity to compare one of the fake paintings with an original. Yet. And even if someone could get two of them together, who's to tell which is the original? The repros are made only of paintings that have been stolen. Out of the hands of the proper authorities. Their provenance becomes questionable ever after. Who's to tell which is which after that?"

"Isn't there a way of marking paintings and other art objects by some high-tech method? Don't they do that in museums ...?" Helen stopped. She was out of her depth. And Mel was laughing.

"Yes there is some of that. But it costs money. Besides,

anything the poor dumb museums can do, CHNOPS can duplicate! Look, CHNOPS has a method of duplicating the actual molecular structure of the original. You haven't grasped the beauty of it all, you really haven't. Listen. CHNOPS can sell more than one fake of the some original, right? People who buy stolen property don't display it or compare notes with each other. It's a lottery, sort of. Everyone of us, that is, of those who may have bought this Daumier here, thinks, believes and hopes that we have the original. Or perhaps another version of the same subject. Many artists make multiple versions. And since the price is always well below market and the paintings are perfect, everybody is happy." Also happy on his hobbyhorse, Mel Romulu leaned back in his chair. "None of this is new, except the technology, of course. Let me tell you a story. In 1911, 'the unimaginable' happened. Leonardo da Vinci's *Mona Lisa* was stolen from the Louvre in Paris. Did you know about that?"

"No. A bit before my time."

"It seems an Italian carpenter who was working at the Louvre at that time stole it. He was eventually caught and the painting returned. All this is public knowledge. What is less well known is that during the two years the painting was missing very professional copies were made and sold to six collectors for $300,000 each. All six were Americans naturally, each of whom believed that he was the sole owner of the most famous painting in the world! Good story, eh?"

"I like it, yes. But let's get updated. What happens once these fakes start to get on the open market? As they will, sooner or later."

"Hard to palm off one of these as anything but a repro as long as the supposed original is hanging in a gallery somewhere. But if two or more surface at the same time and people finally grasp that there is no way of knowing which is original and which are repros ... well, the art market will be in a mess."

"CHNOPS must choose what to steal and what to fake very carefully," Helen mused almost to herself.

"Absolutely. Another gold star for this guy."

"Go on!"

"Well, there are all kinds of art works that are not on the market any more and probably never will be again. In painting it's mostly European stuff. They are all bought up, by museums and collections of billionaires like the Gettys in California or the British Crown. Some are world famous. Like the *Mona Lisa* and paintings by artists like van Gogh whose *Sunflowers* went for $39 million in 1989. There is a finite number of things like 17th-century Dutch masters or French Impressionists. Like good beach front, they don't make them no more. Consequently there's a shortage, a worldwide shortage of top-flight masterpieces. The market lives on the second-run stuff. Now with CHNOPS almost any piece can be duplicated. Oh, the sheer beauty of it!"

"Then why isn't CHNOPS stealing *Mona Lisa* from the Louvre and reproducing it instead of Daumiers from some obscure private collection in Scotland?"

"Give us time, my dear Helen, give us time. This is just a beginning. Test marketing, so to speak. Working out the bugs, perfecting the repro technique, lining up the logistical support. It's like a military campaign. Takes time and money to organize."

"Us? What makes CHNOPS into 'us' all of a sudden?"

"Would it surprise you that CHNOPS has offered me a partnership?"

"Partnership?" Helen echoed again, stunned in spite of herself.

"Well, an opportunity to invest. I'm considering it."

"Oh, I see." Helen's sceptical nature reasserted itself.

CHNOPS had a lot of innovating ways of fleecing suckers but it was only another fraud after all. She was relieved. "It's just a hustle. 'An opportunity to invest' is how bunko artists describe their scams. Then they take your money and run. You're not going to fall for that, are you, Mel? A smart operator like you."

"Please, Helen, don't insult my intelligence. Look, no matter what you think of CHNOPS, if he's really able to duplicate complex objects like hundred-year-old paintings so they can't be distinguished from the real thing ... well, think about it. The possibilities are endless. Now I happen to be interested in art and so is CHNOPS! Unique objects, one of a kind. Point is that there is no way to cheat in such circumstances. If he can produce a perfect copy of something that is known to be unique then he really can do it! That's all the proof I need.

"I know what you're thinking. Look, this isn't one of those old bait-and-switch hustles! You know, with a counterfeiting machine in the basement supposedly producing 'before your very eyes' perfect hundred dollar bills, which later, after the sucker has bought in or 'invested' in the business, turn out to have been switched. After all, there are millions of hundred dollar bills. How can you tell if the one you're being shown was really a 'perfect counterfeit' and not genuine? But with art or any one-of-a-kind objects, there is no way to 'switch' or substitute another original for a counterfeit. That's why this can't be a scam and why I want a piece of it."

"We talking cloning here or what? DNA duplication?" Helen again felt out of her depth.

"No, no! All that refers to a genetic code for producing exact duplicates of living, organic beings. Paintings aren't produced genetically, for goodness sake, they don't grow! They are manufactured by men ... all right, by people!" Mel laughed.

"So how does CHNOPS do it?"

"I'm not yet privy to the specific technical details, how could I be? I haven't bought my way in. Clearly it's a complex and exacting process. CHNOPS takes time to produce each perfect copy. Which is why he wants investors to come in so the business can expand and speed up production. My guess is that the technique is based on computer scanning. The original is scanned and a sequence of templates is produced layer upon layer in the order in which the painter put down the paint, stroke by stroke. Something like this method is currently being used to make reproductions — I have some examples of such 'legal masterpieces' that I bought in Florida downstairs — but the results are much cruder than CHNOPS's. Clearly he's refined the method way past what others can achieve. A breakthrough of sorts. And CHNOPS claims to duplicate perfectly the chemistry of the paint and canvas and all that, right down to the molecular structure."

"An art-loving chemical engineer?"

"Possibly. And probably a computer whiz. Definitely an organizing genius. Don't forget that — it's important!"

"You said you have 'examples downstairs.' What examples? What's downstairs?"

"Oh, I beg your pardon! Let me show you." And Romulu lifted himself out of the chair. "I didn't explain that I've installed a workroom and storage in one of the second-floor apartments. Got it for a very fair price. Recession, you know. Great time to pick up bargains. That's where I keep the really interesting stuff. Questionable, you know. And do my framing and conservation there. I do my own, of course, can't trust commercial operations and besides, I like the work."

Mel armed the security system and they left. In the half-full elevator Mel fell silent. As she stood next to him, Helen could feel his impatience, his desire to go on expounding on his passion. He couldn't do it in public. There were damn few people he could talk about it under any circumstances, and especially as frankly as he had with her. She clutched the shoulder bag with the mailing tube to her side. That was her passport to Mel Romulu's strange world.

Inside the second-floor suite, Mel carefully disconnected the elaborate security system, a duplicate of the one on the 16th floor. The cost of all these measures must have been enormous. Helen wondered at people like Mel who buy goods that they know to have been stolen past "world class" security systems, yet still retain such touching faith in the systems themselves. Well, Mel's system would certainly foil the average apartment house burglar.

The apartment was in darkness, all the windows covered tight. Mel threw a switch and the place flooded with light from a multitude of unobtrusive halogens. The hall and one bedroom were lined with files, horizontal map and print cabinets, and rows and rows of movable display cases. Mel led the way to what would have been the kitchen.

"That's the stretching and framing studio. I'll be working on that Daumier you brought next. It will need some care and attention after all it's been through. Like to see how I'll work on it?"

It was a tactful way of asking for the mailing tube. Romulu obviously considered that it was due. Agreeably Helen turned it over. He'd earned it.

"Ah, good! It's not in too bad a shape. First I'll have to unroll it carefully, then secure it on a stretcher."

Helen perched on a tall stool and watched as Mel wrapped a pure white apron around his body and put on a pair of disposable gloves. He placed the painting on the wooden bench that bisected the kitchen, switched on an additional overhead light and picked up a pair of magnifying glasses. The scene reminded Helen of a surgery with Mel about to operate. Perhaps he'd been a dental surgeon? Helen wasn't sure. In any case he was enjoying himself.

Mel worked quietly for a few minutes unrolling and flattening the small dark painting, pinning it down on a stretcher. He looked up, satisfied.

"Honoré-Victorin Daumier. Born in 1808. Died in 1879. Lived in Paris all his adult life. Think of it, Helen, this man was at the centre of the European art world when Europe was the centre of the world. Think of the 19th century, what times he lived through! When he was born, Napoleon was Emperor of France! Think of the people he knew!"

"I'll take your word for it. You could stick in your eye my knowledge of 19th-century Europe." Helen had a difficult time even sounding interested. But Romulu didn't care.

"Come look. There is nothing to say that's not an original Daumier. Nothing at first glance, nothing at all. No suspicion is aroused. Nothing that would lead you to look further. That's the first step. Perfect."

"I'll take your word for that also. This Daumier. You're an expert on this guy?"

"Well, yes. In my small way, I am. He's one of my pets, my very favourite artist. Very prolific, in his lifetime he is reputed to have created over 6,500 works of art. Lithographs, woodcuts, paintings, even sculpture. Only one etching, however." Romulu paused, considering this odd fact. "He was a brilliant cartoonist, caricaturist. His people are almost like Goya's. And he's been compared to Rembrandt. A great artist. I love him. I've been collecting his work for years. And everything about him. Books, catalogues. I'll show you my collection later. It's in the next room. Now I've started seriously collecting his oils.

Paintings, like this. Very fine, don't you think?" Helen nodded without enthusiasm.

"Will you be able to tell? Whether it's the real thing or not, I mean. Come on, Mel, can you be sure?"

"It won't be easy. As I've told you already, it might be impossible. To complicate matters, there is another painting of the same subject and title. Let me show you."

Having captured her interest, Mel Romulu ushered Helen into the next room, originally the dining room. Bookcases filled with books, magazine and pamphlet files covered the walls. He took down one volume from a two-volume set bound in blue and red cloth with gilded edges and opened it in front of Helen. Then he went into his lecture mode again.

"One of the most important of my books on Daumier, a prize possession. *Catalogue Raisonné of the Paintings, Watercolours and Drawings,* Volume 1 — Paintings. Look here, Plate number 95, recognize it? Thin man in top hat, hands in pockets standing in front of a display of prints and paintings? French title, *L'amateur d'estampes, The Collector* in English. Right. And next plate is of a very similar composition, almost identical except a fraction larger and lighter in tone. This one is in the Art Institute of Chicago. Now, if there are two so very similar, who is to say there couldn't be three? Or four?"

"Hum. See what you mean. But aren't all his paintings known? Look at this book! Plates, descriptions, exhibitions, details of owners, provenances, catalogue numbers ... this guy is really very well documented."

Romulu smiled. "Oh, yes. Paul Valery wrote that 'everything has already been said about Daumier.' But it's not true. There is much confusion about dating and the genuineness of various works. There are many known forgeries, you know. There are issues about what he signed personally and what others signed for him ... And his works are scattered in collections throughout the world. There isn't one big collection. Even the Louvre has only a few of his works. He is everywhere. So anything is possible."

"Fascinating! I had no idea this was such a complex business." In spite of herself, Helen was awed.

"Live and learn, Helen, live and learn." They were back in the workroom. "But getting back to the question of how good are CHNOPS forgeries. Specifically, how to tell whether this item we have here is a 'real' or a faux Daumier. Well, if I had something to compare it with, like the one the Japanese police are holding, that would help a great deal."

"But these two could both be fakes! Right? And the original back in Scotland where it came from! So ..."

"Yes, but if they both pass all the tests and even side by side it's impossible to tell them apart ... when you know at least one has to be a fake ... see what I mean? And I'll tell something else. I think this one is most likely the original, stolen from the Burrell in Scotland. Because CHNOPS would have held on to it, not returned it or sold it to me in our original transaction. So the police and Burrell have fakes. However, this time round CHNOPS couldn't produce another copy so he had to send me the original. And he wants me as partner, I've told you. So he must persuade me, sell me. What better way? I would love to get my hands on the police reproduction and compare the two! What a coup that would be!"

"Well ... what would you pay me to produce it for you? I can't promise but I think I could."

Mel answered without hesitation: "Ten thousand. I was willing to pay it then, I'm willing to pay it now. Ten." He turned his spectacular eyes and brows on Helen. She nodded.

"We have a deal." Mel stuck out his hand.

"Deal." They shook hands.

"Now I'll put this into a press so it can flatten out again after its long trip here in a rolled-up condition. Right. Now, let us go see my collection of other Daumiers."

"And those legal fakes you spoke about. I do want to see them."

"Absolutely, I'll show you everything. My pleasure."

Helen hadn't known what she was letting herself in for. It took hours to merely skim over Romulu's collection. He wouldn't let her go. Every time she indicated that she'd had enough, he pressed on, insisting she see one more example of fake paintings, or he would open just one more folder of prints, graphics, illustrations or caricatures. All the while he talked, explained, described and commented on what lay before them, digressing and going off into more and more esoteric territory.

He had lunch brought in for them from a local deli. It was well past four before Helen could extricate herself from him. She left thoroughly convinced of two things. One, she had gotten all the relevant information on CHNOPS in Mel Romulu's possession and two, that he was alarmingly obsessive. But the bottom line as far as she was concerned was that he would pay 10 grand to get another copy of *The Collector* by Daumier. Stuck in the rush hour traffic in her rented car on the Don Valley Parkway, Helen sang under her breath "California here I come!"

49
Keiko in Toronto

Perched on the edge of the hotel bed, Keiko fingered the worn chenille bedspread on which she sat and stared out the window. Around her, dust particles danced in the overheated air of the shabby hotel room. A print of a blue jay in technicolour plumage was screwed to the wall above the bed, a pin-up calendar from a hotel supply company decorated the desk-cum-dresser. Keiko's bags lay on the floor by the bed, half unpacked. Wayne had made room for her things amongst his in the skimpy closet, but she'd given up putting them away, disheartened.

Outside the second-story window the parking lot extended south towards what looked like an old warehouse with shuttered windows plastered with For Lease and For Sale signs. Right across from her window two white men in dirty white coats and no gloves threw bags of hotel garbage onto overflowing dumpsters and blue recycling containers. Keiko sighed. This was not what she had expected and certainly not what she had hoped of her new home in Toronto. She had been warned by Julie. And Wayne had even described this room and his work in the third-class hotel in Toronto's tenderloin. Second hand it had sounded romantic and exiting. Reality was something else.

Their wedding and three-day honeymoon in Honolulu had been virtually perfect. She'd wanted to stay longer but Wayne had insisted on returning; he was concerned about his regular job for Glendenning and even more about Romulu's reaction to the fact that all the funds he'd entrusted to Wayne were gone. Ten thousand dollars plus all the expense money! They were broke, Wayne had told her, and lucky to have his old room to come back to. He trusted that Glendenning would take him back (why shouldn't he?) and that Keiko would soon find a job. They couldn't stay in Hawaii and honeymoon forever. They had to return to Toronto and "back to real life, babe," as Wayne never failed to say. To him, Japan was fantasy; Canada was the real thing. To Keiko, who had American Express cheques to the value of three thousand dollars hidden in her luggage and access to 10 times that much on tap from Nagoya, Japan was the hard reality and North America the promised land.

Ever since her early stint in Hawaii, Keiko had longed to escape the restrictions Japanese society imposes on its people in the name of ethnic uniqueness and tradition. She knew that she had highly marketable skills — Japanese accounting experience and fluency in the two most important languages on earth. The world could be her oyster if she could only get away somehow. She kept looking, waiting for any opportunity. A Westerner might well have just up and taken off, but Keiko's alienation from the role of the traditional Japanese female didn't mean she wasn't a product of her society. She couldn't conceive of going it alone. She had to have a man to take her away. Wayne was it.

Wayne Tillion had appeared in Nagoya at a crucial moment in Keiko's life. At Nangi's death the routine of her normal workaday world had fallen apart and she had suddenly been left without a familiar male superior to answer to. Then she was faced with the consequences of having had a part in a yakuza enterprise. Naturally she'd been aware of who and what their clients were but it had been easy to be "professional" about it since her involvement had always been at arm's length, mediated by Nangi. He'd dealt directly with the mob; she did the desk work in the back room. With Nangi's death, all that ended abruptly. There was no ducking the yakuza anymore.

When Wayne fell in love with her and promised to take her away, it was as if in answer to a prayer. He was an attractive young man, a glamorous Westerner, an eager lover, bright enough but hardly intimidating. She liked him, enjoyed being with him and believed she would have little trouble controlling him. What more could any woman expect?

Moving to the bathroom Keiko looked in the mirror, still cloudy from Wayne's shower. Wayne had left early to pick up Glendenning at his home off the Lakeshore Road, halfway to Oakville, and chauffeur him on his rounds. She wiped off the mirror, recalling how unhappy Wayne had looked as he left, and spent the next 10 minutes working on her face. No matter the time, place or circumstances, Keiko had to look her best.

The night before she and Wayne had met Helen and a woman called Alice Caplan for drinks. Keiko wasn't absolutely sure of the relationship between Helen and Alice but Wayne had had no doubts. When they'd discussed the matter in bed later that night he'd said:

"They are both dykes, babe, lezzies. Like, they fuck each other, like you and me."

"Oh, I'm sure you're right about Helen but ... Alice, she's so young and beautiful ... and fun. I really liked her."

"Yeah! That Helen, she sure can pick 'em!" Wayne was admiring. Without realizing it, he'd placed Helen in the category of successful males. Since he liked and admired her there wasn't any other place for her, in his limited experience. Then realizing the implications of what Keiko had said, "Say, babe, what did ya think? That all gay broads are like Helen? Like, old and tough? It's not like that. Anyways, you like Helen, too, don't you? Or are you worried she might come on to you? Now you have me you never have to worry about that, see." He put his arms possessively around her. Keiko didn't react. Her mind was on the two women.

"Oh no, I'm not worried about that! And I do like Helen. It's just that it seems strange. For her and Alice to be lovers. Why, Alice could have any man she wanted! I don't think I quite understand why a woman would prefer another woman to a man."

"You and me both, babe, you and me both." The topic was making Wayne uncomfortable. To avoid pursuing it he did what any man would have done in the circumstances. "Here, let me show you what they are missing. Mmmm?"

His mouth and hands turned eager. Keiko felt his full erection and allowed herself to accommodate it. It was irritating to be forced to drop such an interesting subject but of course there was nothing to be done. Of course.

The subject of Helen had come up again this morning just as Wayne was leaving. They had had breakfast in the coffee shop downstairs and were walking up the one flight to their room. Wayne had said: "Damn it! I sure wish there was a way to swing it so I could go on working with Helen. We made a good team, you know. 'Wayne Tillion, Private Investigator,' how's that sound, eh? Would sure beat chauffeuring that jerk Glendenning around town, let me tell you."

"Why don't you ask her? Maybe it could be possible. We're going to see her tonight, yes?"

"You think? Well, maybe. No harm asking, I guess. At dinner, yes. Well, babe, have a good time seeing good old T.O. Bye." At the door he'd kissed her and departed leaving behind a very thoughtful and determined Japanese wife, ambitious for her husband. Just as well for them both that Wayne's ambitions and Keiko's coincided at that moment.

50

Sashimi for Four

The Sushiman Restaurant for dinner that night had been suggested by Alice Caplan. She'd wanted to demonstrate that Toronto had any number of good Japanese eating places, many more than even Wayne and Helen knew about. Accordingly, they met downtown at the corner of Victoria and Richmond streets, an unlikely part of town for dinner at a Japanese restaurant.

Having picked the place, Alice felt responsible so she arrived early to be sure to be first. She hadn't seen Helen since that morning. They had spent the night together but Helen wasn't staying with her, having quietly moved into a hotel directly on arrival and before even seeing Alice. Alice was relieved but at the same time a bit peeved. She would have liked Helen to have tried to pick up their relationship where they'd left off. Which was when Helen had gone back home to Vancouver at the end of that nasty business at Diamond Plaza Towers. That would have provided Alice the opportunity of telling Helen once again that she "wasn't into long-distance relationships." A dramatic scene could have followed, perhaps culminating in a passionate reconciliation, perhaps not. Either way it would have been much to Alice's taste. However, Helen had preempted the possibility. She called and waited to be asked over. She'd been warm, happy to stay overnight and make love just like in the old days but it was all very properly casual with nothing taken for granted. Which impelled Alice to mention all her affairs of the past year — especially one new lover, Betsy. Betsy was a 25-year-old, sexy, leather punk. Also a doctoral candidate at York University doing her thesis on gay politics in Toronto during the seventies. Naturally she was very pro sex, which she tended to see as having been discovered by her generation. Helen's reaction to Alice's involvement with Betsy was "that's nice," and could Alice take the time to show Keiko around town? From which it was plain that Helen wasn't going to play her part in any scenes of jealousy and rejection; she didn't care a fig whom Alice was seeing. Only a little disappointed, Alice agreed to look after Keiko the next day. She was beginning to be bored by Betsy's fixation on the politics of sex. Helen's adventures in Japan plus the story of Keiko and Wayne were proving more compelling. Taking Keiko around Toronto that morning, showing her the sights, asking her questions about her life in Japan had absorbed all her interest in people and her flair for drama. She was further excited about the possibilities of this dinner, the four of them together. She wished Helen would hurry up and get there.

Sushiman is an unpretentious place with Western tables and chairs and no requirement to go shoeless. Alice sat in the nonsmoking section watching the sushi chef do his stuff behind the counter. He was working and talking without missing a beat, perfect sashimi and sushi flowing from his busy hands as if off an assembly line, production perfectly synchronized with the animated conversation he was conducting with one of his customers at the bar.

Bored with listening to the Japanese conversation, which she couldn't follow, Alice looked up in the direction of the door and there were Keiko and Wayne. (Still no sign of Helen.) Not yet comfortable with Canadian informality, Keiko had dressed up for the occasion. She was wearing a black outfit of light wool that must have cost $1,000, black patent leather pumps, a green silk scarf and silver jewellery. Her makeup was perfection. Next to her, Wayne, in jeans and bomber jacket, looked like exactly what he was — an out-of-work barroom bouncer.

Although Keiko and Alice had just spent part of the day together, effusive greetings followed. The two women smiled and nodded, outdoing each other in expressions of admiration and friendship, Keiko's traditional Japanese formality meshing easily with Alice's theatrical bent. Ignoring the whole dynamic, Wayne retired behind his menu and suggested they do the same. They had better be ready to eat soon, he was hungry enough to eat a horse, he told them unselfconsciously. Keiko and Alice complied, Keiko commenting on the excellence of the choices before them. Wayne ordered a bottle of saki. There was an awkward moment as they waited for it to be served. (Helen still hadn't arrived.) Alice suggested they order a platter of assorted sashimi. Their lively young Japanese server arrived with the saki. She left with their sashimi order. They sipped the warm pungent liquor gratefully.

"Where the hell is that Helen?" Wayne looked at the door impatiently. "She's holding up our dinner."

"She is late," Alice conceded. "I can't think what's keeping her. All I know is she went up to North York to see Mel Romulu this morning. But that was hours ago. She could be stuck in traffic somewhere, I suppose."

"Romulu, eh? What would she want with him?" Wayne still smarted from the dressing-down he'd received from Mel Romulu on his return to Toronto empty-handed. He was edgy in any case. Glendenning had given him a bad time all day. On top of that, Keiko had acted strange when he'd returned to their hotel room. Now, no Helen and no dinner.

Before anyone could answer, the tall, dark figure of Helen loomed over their table. Somehow none of the three had seen her arrive.

"Hi, folks," she said, sitting down and picking up a

menu all in one movement. "Sorry to be late. Got held up. Ah, you've ordered saki. Great! And a cup for me. And here comes our waitress with the sashimi." She poured herself some saki, sipped it and beamed at the other three. She appeared without a care in the world. In fact, she was primed and excited. Clearly her day had been a success.

"Helen! Where've you been?" Alice couldn't help but sound annoyed and proprietary. Helen continued beaming.

"I'll fill you in about it after we eat. What d'you recommend here, Alice? You know the place."

For the next half hour the foursome concentrated on their dinner. They conferred on the menu, ordered, drank saki, ordered more saki and Sapporo beer, sampled each other's dishes. Everyone relaxed as the alcohol did its job of social lubrication. They laughed and chatted. Keiko and Alice described their trip up to the Japanese Cultural Centre. A fine modern complex in a northeastern suburb where Keiko got the shock of her life. She'd asked something of a middle-aged woman whom they'd met in the lobby. Naturally Keiko had used her native tongue, only to find that the woman couldn't speak Japanese and barely understood it! It had never occurred to Keiko that a Japanese adult might not know the language even if living in Canada. Perhaps it wasn't until then that Keiko realized what emigration meant. Helen looked interested at this story; Wayne smiled as if pleased.

"And then where did you go? SkyDome, CN Tower, Eaton's Center?" Wayne asked, reeling off three standard tourist attractions in downtown Toronto.

"Nothing so dreary. I took Keiko to the Island on the ferry, and the Queen's Quay Terminal and Harbourfront. Then I showed her my stomping grounds on Queen West. Then Bloor ..."

"And Hazelton Lanes. Very nice," Keiko added.

"Hazelton Lanes?" Wayne looked at Keiko doubtfully.

"Christ, woman! That's a pretty high-priced neighbour-hood! Hope you don't think we can afford to shop there, babe. No way! You better get used to doing without. You might as well know now that Glendenning offered me a job at $30,000 per. Can you beat the nerve of that creep?! That's not enough to keep me in beer! Sure, I can make another 10 grand on the side, but that's still damn little. I told him where he could stick his lousy job. So as of right now I'm unemployed." Wayne refilled his glass and looked down at his plate. There was a moment of silence. The atmosphere plummeted.

"Not to worry, Keiko will soon get a job," Alice jumped in eager to rescue the evening. Impulsively she put her hand on Keiko's arm. "Honey, with your qualifica-tions, no problem. You'll be able to pick and choose between offers. Banks, consultants, accounting firms, gov-ernments and companies doing business in Japan ... every-one will want you. Major bucks. Shop in Hazelton Lanes as much as you like."

Before the words were out of her mouth Alice realized that she'd badly misread the situation. Wayne only looked gloomier; Helen continued to clear her bowl carefully with her chopsticks. Keiko put down her napkin, stood up, said "excuse me" very quietly and walked quicky towards the stairs leading down to the restrooms. Belatedly aware that she'd only made matters worse, Alice looked at Helen for help. Ignoring her, Helen, in turn, put down her napkin, stood up and followed Keiko down the stairs. Alice and Wayne were left alone at the table. Neither spoke.

Keiko was locked in a cubicle when Helen reached the otherwise empty women's restroom. She stood and waited silently until Keiko emerged.

"You okay?" Helen asked. Repairing her makeup, Keiko nodded. She looked at Helen in the mirror. Finally she reacted.

"You will tell me I should have expected this, yes? Julie warned me about something like this, in Nagoya. But I didn't, I couldn't ... oh, Helen that awful hotel, that room we have to live in! Wayne must get better work! He must! Please help. A man needs money, self-respect. If I get good job and make much more money, he'll never forgive me, I know. Please help us."

Arms folded, leaning against the door, Helen examined Keiko as if for the first time.

"What in the world do you expect me to do for you? Or for Wayne?"

"Hire him as an assistant. Train him. I know he wants to be a private investigator. When he has his own business and feels good about himself, perhaps then the money I make won't matter so much."

"Wait a cotton-picking minute, lady! I don't make enough to hire anyone. And what makes you think I want or need an assistant?"

"Please, Helen. Just for a little while. Get Wayne out of the state he's in in that horrible, horrible place. I will give you money so you can pay him. This way he will have some pay, better than he could make with this Glendenning and you have good help. Why not?"

"Why not?! Well for starters, I'm leaving Toronto in a couple of days. I don't work from here, you know; I don't have an Ontario detective licence, for another. It's hard to get into this racket in Ontario unless you're an ex-cop. Or can find a job with an existing company. I ain't it."

"But you have a licence in British Columbia, don't you? Anyway, it doesn't matter. Take him with you ... where will you be going? Far?"

"You want to know where I'm going and what I plan to do, do you? That makes sense. Now I understand this sudden concern with Wayne's career. Yeah. You had me going there for a minute."

"What do you mean?"

"Set me straight, will you? There could be three reasons for you to marry Wayne. One, because you fell so in love that you couldn't live without him. Now Wayne is a nice enough guy — I'm no expert in these matters, but he strikes me as better than most. You could have done a hell of a lot worse but still I do find it hard to believe that you harbour a mad passion for him. Second, you married him to get away from Nagoya. For any number of personal reasons. That makes sense and that I could buy except that the third motive plays even better. You married Wayne on orders of your bosses. To get next to him and through him to me and perhaps Julie. Very helpful you were in getting her away. It had to be with their connivance. We Westerners are not as dumb as you might think. That's the mistake you make. But it would be obvious to anyone that you work for the yakuza, following orders. Except Wayne, of course. He wants to believe it's his boyish charm, nothing else. Anyway, now you're having problems with the lad, and you hate it in Toronto and you still have to get your bosses what they want. Tough assignment. Too bad. You'll get little sympathy from me. You set it up, you and your bosses. Deal with it."

As Helen spoke Keiko turned towards her, eyes widening. Clearly she hadn't been expecting this.

"No, no! It's not like that! You must, you must believe me! I did want to get away and I do love Wayne. It's so."

"Oh? And your bosses had nothing to do with it? Kusashita didn't orchestrate Julie's 'escape' from Nagoya? He isn't interested in what Wayne and Julie and I were really doing there and how it all fits in with Nangi's death? Give me a break!"

"Yes, of course, that part is true. But it isn't like you say. I can see how it would look like that but it's not why I married Wayne. Please he mustn't ever think that! You must believe me! Help me!"

"If it isn't true, then why is there a Mr. Itami staying in your hotel? The same guy who interrogated Wayne and me in Kusashita's offices back in Nagoya. At the time I thought maybe he was just an interpreter since he speaks almost perfect English, but obviously he's a lot more than that. He knows all about the Nangi business, knows all of us, right? What shall we say he's doing in Toronto? Coincidence maybe?"

"How ... how did you find out about him?"

"I went and checked out your hotel this evening. I had a hunch there would be someone bird-dogging you. It wasn't hard to put two and two together once I knew this guy had checked in. I hung around the hotel lobby — that's why I was late for dinner — till he went out tonight. I saw him and recognized him from Nagoya. That's all I need."

"God, what if they think I told you!"

"I won't let on I know, don't worry. Now, tell me about this Mr. Itami. What exactly is his role?"

"He's my brother."

Keiko turned her head so she faced the mirror again. Helen stared at her reflection.

"No shit! Your brother! Well, well! What d'you know about that. Tell me more."

"I was permitted to marry Wayne and leave Japan only on condition that I reported to them. And Sam was sent to keep an eye on me. You see, he got me the job with Nangi in the first place, he recommended me. Our parents are both dead. So I am his responsibility. If I go against them, he will ... suffer."

"Sam?"

"Sam. He likes to be called Sam. He was born in Hawaii too early ..."

"Prematurely."

"Yes, prematurely. Mother couldn't get back to Japan

253

for the birth as was planned."

"Fascinating. Sam Itami. Your name is Keiko Ueki. Or is it?"

"It is. Itami is just the name he's using here. Please Helen!" Keiko was pleading.

"I'll think about it. Listen, we haven't got much time now to talk. Wayne is bound to start wondering what we're doing here so long and get anxious. I expect one of them down here any minute ..."

"He mustn't suspect ... please!

"... so if we are interrupted, you call me at my hotel, the Redstone on Maitland Street. We'll arrange another meeting. You will have to shake both boys, husband Wayne and brother Sam. I want to hear more. And I'll consider your idea of 'hiring' Wayne. Might just work okay all round."

As Helen was speaking, someone pushed against the restroom door at her back. She moved and Alice poked her head in and looked curiously at the two women. Behind her loomed Wayne.

"Oh, so sorry! Did you miss us?" Keiko plunged in without a moment's hesitation. "We'll be right up. Oh, Wayne, I was just asking Helen about your idea to become a private investigator. We must have her advice, what to do. That would be good. Yes?"

For a few seconds the four of them milled around awkwardly in the cramped doorway. Finally Helen broke through past Alice and Wayne and almost ran up the stairs, saying over her shoulders:

"Enough already. Let's get out of this dungeon and have a beer."

Before they got back to their table, Wayne caught up with her and proposed, very quietly, that they meet together privately the next day to discuss his potential new career.

51

Helen Connives

Helen went back to her hotel room to a restless night. The evening hadn't lasted very long after the restroom episode. After one final beer she had said a terse good night to Keiko and Wayne and declined Alice's invitation to go home with her. She needed to be alone, to think over the happenings of the past day without distraction. And a very eventful day it had been, full of surprises and implications for the future. Sitting up in bed with CBC FM playing softly in the background, Helen considered it, running names and events over and over in her mind like worry beads through fingers.

The crazy CHNOPS, Mel Romulu and his desire for the Daumier. She expected it would be in California with Julie Piper by now. Chasing it down in the southwestern United States felt like a fun thing to do. Fun thing? Why was she kidding herself that getting the painting for Romulu came under the rubric of "recovering stolen property" and therefore ethically defensible, when clearly it was no such thing?

It had always been a matter of pride for Helen not to get conned into doing anything against her personal and/or professional standards. These standards might be highly idiosyncratic, but they were hers and she took them damn seriously. Naturally there have been instances when she'd slipped up, she was human after all, but they were exceptions. So, Helen said to herself, here you are rushing off to California, Nevada or wherever after a painting that was either stolen or faked by the thief. Square that with your precious standards!

It wasn't for the money. She'd never cared that much for money, although always held out for it. No freebies. Getting paid well for what she did was an indication of success, a measure of her worth as an investigator. Money was how you kept score, no more.

So why? Because she was fascinated by the CHNOPS affair, wanted to see it explicated, to understand the who, why and wherefore. Be involved in it. To stay in the game she needed cards and the questionable Daumier painting was her hand. Keep her in play, permit her to act. Simple, eh?

Rationalizations? Sure, to an academic nitpicker. For Helen it was enough justification. She continued running over details of the case.

The yakuza Sam Itami — she was beginning to think of him as "Brother Sam." He could be bad news, but not interesting ... On the other hand, she thought of what a surprise Keiko had turned out to be.

How could Keiko have guessed that I would continue on the case, look for Piper and the painting, carry on untangling the web they had been caught in in Nagoya?

I must be pretty transparent, Helen mused, so Keiko wants me to take Wayne along. So he would be the unwitting pipeline into the CHNOPS business for Keiko, and therefore Brother Sam and therefore the Kusashita yakuza. If Keiko stays in Toronto, likely Brother Sam will also, and Wayne will be their only source of information. I can live with that. They will expect some mis/disinformation from me through Wayne. Naturally. Pipelines work both ways; I bet Brother Sam has some mis/disinformation for me. If not about CHNOPS, then perhaps about Tan — whatever. Must press Keiko on Tan. Keiko. She sure knows more about Nangi than she's told me. Probably more than she'd told them too. Why else did she send me to Tokyo to Aido

Tagata Private Research Bureau? Glad she did. What a time we had! Some woman Miko, wish she were here. No I don't, do I? How about that Keiko? She's ace! Paying me to employ Wayne. Smart. Cute too.

Helen fell asleep smiling.

Next morning Wayne was the first to call. He arranged to come right away, for breakfast. Half an hour later they were in the hotel coffee shop. Wayne ordered orange juice, granola and a soft boiled egg. He was clearly on a health kick. Helen had her eggs scrambled and English muffin. They both had coffee, no sugar.

"You see how it is, Helen. I'm a married man now, I can't work for a sleazeball like Glendenning, doing his dirty work for pennies. Like, I know Keiko will get a good job. I don't mind her making more money than me, I really don't. That out-of-date stuff don't cut no ice with me no more. So, like, that's not the problem. Problem is I need to think about the future. Career path, you know? So what d'you think? I mean us working together, like. You and me, eh?"

"It means going out of town, Wayne. Down to the States. That's where my next job is — getting to Julie. You just got married; sure you want to leave Keiko in Toronto by herself? We could be gone weeks. Never know in our line of work."

"We'll be looking for Julie Piper again, eh? Just like old times. Couldn't take Keiko along, could we?"

"No." Helen was firm.

"You're right, she better stay, find a job while I'm away, get a decent place to live. Alice will help, eh? They seem to be getting along real good. It could all work out for the best. She'd do all that better without me underfoot."

Wayne was exhibiting a remarkable grasp of his marital situation. Helen was impressed.

"Going south with me doesn't provide you with a career as a private investigator. Tough to get a licence in this jurisdiction. Cops are big on 'protecting the public' mostly by keeping the detecting business for themselves. So unless you're an ex-cop, you can't dream of getting a licence to hang out a shingle of your own. So you will have to look for a job with a licensed agency. Then two, three years down the road, if you keep your nose clean, they might, just might, let you. Working with me for a few weeks won't help you with the OPP bigshots. So don't get your hopes up."

"That's okay by me. I'll take it as it comes. Come on, Helen, we made a good team in Japan, didn't we? And you can always use muscle in the States, and I've got lots of muscle. How about it?"

"I'll think about it, Cookie. Let you know. Call me tonight. And if I say 'yes,' be prepared to light out of here, fast."

"No sweat! I'll be ready. So where are we going?"

"Don't be jumping the gun. I am going to L.A."

"Far out. Always wanted to check out California."

Helen went on eating her eggs, ignoring Wayne's enthusiasm. She wondered how genuine it was. She wondered whether to take him along, whether to accept the money Keiko was offering for doing so. Finally she decided to wait with both those decisions until she and Keiko had another talk, preferably not in a women's restroom.

Breakfast finished, they parted. Back in her room Helen found a message from Keiko. She called back immediately, before Wayne had time to get back home, assuming that's where he was going. She arranged to meet Keiko in Allan Gardens just a short walk from Keiko's Jarvis Street hotel.

This was a perfect day in May. At its best, May is early summer in Toronto. The sun shines hot. Ontario's brief, uncertain spring is safely over, woes of winter are forgotten, everything is green and blooming and full of birdsong. Breathing in the urbanscape, Helen walked south on Church Street, then cut east entering the park just south of Carlton. Those who had spent the night on the street or in nearby hostels and grungy rooming houses sat on park benches, turning their worn faces to the sun. Bouncy black squirrels foraged with impunity, easily avoiding the hands of dozens of precocious toddlers. A group of men in fedoras and cloth caps played some board game on a concrete table. Further south, the Parks Department's first lawnmower of the season cleared its throat and clattered into action. Students from Jarvis Collegiate high school walked by oblivious to everything but each other. Helen saw Keiko, wearing designer jeans and a cotton top, standing by the massive doors of the conservatory. Taking it all in Helen wasn't sure she wanted to leave for California.

"Hi! Glad you could make it. Let's go in."

They moved under the glass canopy and entered the soft, moist world of the municipal greenhouse. Walking in silence they found a bench hidden behind a mass of spring flowers and sat down.

"What did Wayne say to you?" Keiko asked once the usual polite greetings were over. "What did you talk about?"

"He seems seriously to want a 'career' as private investigator, sometime. Right now he wants to go down to the States with me, just as you suggested. I don't know about that."

"Please, Helen ..."

"All right, all right, I heard you! I'm thinking about it. Look, Keiko, this won't do. You must come clean with me."

"I will, I am! What can I tell you?"

"Let's start with what the yakuza want from you, exactly. What's their interest?"

"Well, I think that they believe that Mr. Nangi was on to something. Something big. They want to find out what it was. Once they heard about that painting and realized that Julie was a courier and that Mr. Nangi was killed by a professional hitman ... well ..."

"Yes, yes! All that is obvious. What else?"

"That's all, as far as I know ... all I've been told. I had to tell Sam everything I knew about Mr. Nangi and now I am to find out anything I can from you or anybody else."

"What about Mr. Nangi?"

"Very worried man Mr. Nangi was before he was killed. For months."

"What about that report from the detective agency? Did that have something to do with it? He had himself investigated!"

"Of course. Mr. Nangi wanted to find out what his colleagues thought about him and whether Mr. Kusashita still trusted him. Many salarymen who are concerned about their careers do that."

"So what happened to the report, Keiko? Does Brother Sam have it? Or did the police find it?"

"It was in Mr. Nangi's desk. I removed it before the police came."

"And turned it over to Brother."

"Yes. I was afraid to hold back ..."

"Yes, yes! But you read it first, right?"

"Yes."

"That's okay. I understand. Now you can tell me what it says."

"It confirms what Mr. Nangi feared. That he was under suspicion. Mr. Kusashita didn't consider him a good yakuza anymore. He had no future."

"No future?"

"Yes. Mr. Nangi was no longer young. He wanted to retire but now he knew he had no future with the Nagoya yakuza. I think that he decided to, what is the expression ... 'go into business for himself,' yes?"

"Right on! I've had that suspicion for some time. It explains a lot. One more thing you can help me with, I almost forgot. What is the connection, if any, between your Japanese yakuza and Taiwanese triads?"

"Personally I cannot say. No business to or from Taiwan came through my hands. I know that Mr. Kusashita considers Taiwanese very low-class sort of people, without honour."

"But there would have to be some sort of a business relationship. Taiwan is rich and their triads are very powerful. And your yakuza and the Taiwanese triads would share a very anticommunist ideology, right?"

"I think maybe so. Yes, mainland China big target for both, yes, you are correct. Why are you interested in this?"

"General knowledge, like. Now tell me about this mysterious Tan. You mentioned it to me in Nagoya and you scared Julie with it. Who or what is Tan, and why should we be shaking in our boots at the very mention?"

"I don't know what Tan is. Sam just told me to use it to you and Julie. That it threatened her, so she wouldn't stay in Hong Kong but to go somewhere safe."

"Get her to run home, yes. When you want to find out where 'home' is, it's not a bad way. That's just what she did, too. And you don't know anything about it? Never heard of Tan in any connection?"

Helen didn't hide her scepticism.

"No, no, really. I don't know much."

"It's hard to believe, a smart woman like you. Never mind. Now tell me whose idea was it to have Wayne accompany me to California? Sam's or yours?"

"It was my idea but Sam is very agreeable. He thinks we should all go together to Los Angeles. He believes you will be able to trace Julie Piper and find out everything he needs to know so Mr. Kusashita is happy again. What you know we will also know — at least Wayne will and he will tell me. So all Sam needs to do is wait around. That's what he thinks. Now what I think is, supposing you take only Wayne but not me? I have to stay here, Sam have to stay here, yes?"

"Very good, very good, Keiko! Keep him here by all means necessary! I'll take Wayne south with me. No strings."

"Thank you. I'll have money ready for you ... "

"No, you won't. You make sure he has travel and eating money. Just give it to him directly. It's better all round, believe me. I can't really hire him, you know. All I can do is let him come with me. If it all works out as I hope it will, I'll give him a split. But for now he has to come along on spec."

"On spec? What's that?"

"Oh, never mind. Wayne will understand. So that's it, I guess. I'll tell him tonight and we will be on our way in a day or so."

"Oh, thank you!"

"You're welcome. Tell me about Sam. What's he like? And how come both of you work for the yakuza?"

"Sam is a businessman ... you know, like others. He told me not to think of the yakuza as a secret criminal organization. He said that in these modern times the yakuza is just a fraternal organization with secrets."

"Oh, yeah! Like the Lions or the Rotary? Give me a break."

"More like the Masons, I think he means. With a hierarchy, initiation ceremonies, code of conduct, member solidarity, penalties ... "

"Keiko, you didn't buy this, did you? What about the criminal part? How did he get you to work for them?"

"Well, Sam told me that the yakuza isn't any more 'criminal' than other big business organizations. Everyone evades taxes, he said. As an accountant, that's my job no matter who I work for. No difference."

"This guy, your brother, is something else! He deserves an Oscar for such pretty rationalizations. And you bought it?"

"At the time, yes. He's my brother; I didn't want to disappoint him. I wanted what he wanted. He wanted me to work for Mr. Nangi ... "

"... so you went to work for Mr. Nangi. And the yakuza. Well, that's all over with now, right? Is it?"

"Yes. Except ..."

"Except we've got to give Brother Sam what he wants. We will, don't worry about it. First off, once Wayne and I are outta here, we have to have a way of communicating that Sam can't check up on. I bet he's already arranged to monitor your long-distance calls. And he will get first crack at any of your mail or faxes. Wouldn't even cost him much at that crappy hotel. Wayne can write and call you with lovey-dovey stuff and I'll give him enough to interest Sam to keep from following us down. But anything we need to let you know privately will go via Alice. Got that? You should be able to call or fax us directly from someplace other than your hotel, once we let you know where we are. Just make sure Sam doesn't catch you at it."

"I understand."

"Meanwhile just act natural. Go apartment hunting, send out resumés. Alice will help you. Explore Toronto. Go shopping, why not!"

"Yes, yes!"

"Good. You aren't going to miss Wayne too much are you?"

The two women stood up almost simultaneously and stood facing each other.

"I will manage," Keiko said.

"No doubt. Well, see you when I get back."

52

Ms. Khayatt

The following day, Wayne and Helen left for Los Angeles on the 13:40 Air Canada flight. The trip from the heady spring of Ontario to sun-an'-smog-drenched southern California was routine. On arrival they fought their way out of LAX and into a rental car. With Helen navigating, they found and took Lincoln Boulevard, a busy main stem running north to Santa Monica. The white Chevrolet Avis rental wove its way past dreary low-rise commercial buildings, RV and boat storage lots, autoparts stores, bars and gas stations. At Ocean Park Boulevard, they found a motel that didn't look too bad and registered: two rooms side by side on Helen's Canada Trust MasterCard. While Wayne stared gloomily out the dirty window, Helen phoned the office of Master, Powers & Khayatt. She was told to call again the next day for an appointment; Ms. Khayatt was out. After a few more questions, Helen hung up.

"Guess what? This law office is on Wilshire just a few blocks from Lincoln. Luck. Hope it holds."

"You mean this is it, we are in Santa Monica? Sure isn't what I expected. I know parts of Highway 2 near that Toronto look just like this."

"Yeah. It gets a bit more interesting further along. Come on, I'll take you to the beach and the Santa Monica Pier."

"Sounds better. I didn't know you knew Los Angeles! How come?"

"I've been here before, more than once. About five

years ago would be the last time. Used to hang out in Venice and at the various piers up and down the beach. Place hasn't changed that much, just more run down because of the recession, I guess. Riots don't help either. But I know San Diego better. I lived there with my father in my late teens. Long time ago. It was an uptight navy town then, likely still is. You ready?"

"Sure!" They climbed into the Chevy. This time Helen drove.

"So you lived in San Diego with your father! You American or what? Ever wish you still lived here?" Wayne was curious.

"Live in the Excited States? No. I guess I could claim dual citizenship since my father was American. But I don't feel American. I was born in Vancouver. Moved down here when my Mom died. I was 14. Left when I turned 20."

Helen fell silent. It was the most she'd ever said about her origins. She was glad that they had reached the Palisades before Wayne could continue to pry.

Next morning they had breakfast at a neighbouring Denny's. At 9:30 a.m. Helen called Master, Powers & Khayatt again. She introduced herself and was amazed to have Ms. Khayatt agree to see her at 2:00 p.m. that day.

"Interesting. I'm going to go see her alone. You drop me off and I'll walk back to the motel. But Cookie, don't you go far! If our luck still holds, we'll be on our way out of here right soon. Best stay packed."

"On our way where?" Wayne wanted to know.

"To find Julie Piper."

"You don't think she's in L.A?"

"I'll bet she isn't."

"And this Khayatt woman is going to tell you where to find her?" Wayne was sceptical.

"We'll soon know, won't we?"

They drove around Beverly Hills and Hollywood sightseeing until lunch, which they came back to Santa Monica to eat at the Pier.

Promptly at 2:00 p.m., Wayne dropped Helen off at a four-story office building on Wilshire that had seen better days. He turned around in the driveway of an enormous car dealership next door and disappeared. Helen went into the immaculately clean lobby where a bored Latino man let her take the elevator to the top floor.

The offices of Master, Powers & Khayatt, Attorneys-at-Law, either took up the whole floor or else part of it stood empty; it wasn't clear which. The firm itself was either just coming up in the world or on its way down. In the small windowless reception area a tired-looking brunette was in deep conversation with a pony-tailed individual in a jean jacket. The Dell PC in front of the brunette glowed with a multi-coloured spreadsheet, a very expensive pair of roller blades were parked next to the old wooden desk and there were fresh-cut flowers on the table next to the worn client chairs. Unframed posters of art-related events covered the walls.

Before Helen could announce herself a statuesque young woman in perfectly fitting pants, long earrings and a dazzling smile popped her head into reception.

"Are you Helen Keremos? Come in. I'm Martina Khayatt."

They walked down a narrow passage between offices on one side and tiny cubicles — some empty, some occupied — on the other, into Khayatt's office. It had two windows, two desks, two credenzas, two telephones, four chairs, three file cabinets, two bookcases full of law books, one Dell PC and a coffee machine. It looked as if Khayatt shared her office. If so, her roommate was invisible for the duration.

"Sit down." Khayatt sat down behind one of the desks with her back to the window and waved Helen towards one of the facing chairs. "Coffee?"

"Sure."

"Help yourself."

Helen helped herself, then the other woman did likewise. In no hurry, they drank their coffee, slowly taking measure of each other.

"What can I do for you?"

"You are Julie Piper's lawyer. I need her present address."

"Why? Who are you, a friend of hers?"

"Wrong question. You know who I am and you've been expecting me. Julie told you about me."

"She did expect people to be trying to find her. And she did mention you might be one of them. But I have no instructions to give out her address to anybody."

"Good. We are making progress. Tell me then, why did you agree to see me?"

"Curiosity partly. Julie described you as a very interesting woman."

Helen brushed the comment aside.

"And partly you will see anyone who asks questions about her. Am I right?"

"Yes."

"Has anyone? Contacted you about Julie Piper, I mean."

"Just you."

"Nobody else? You sure?"

"Does it matter?"

"It might. What will you do when someone else does?"

"Just what I'm doing. Look them over, tell them nothing and then let Julie know."

"Better and better. You can let Julie know that I will be in Las Vegas." Helen didn't take her eyes off Martina, looking for any reaction, any indication that she was right about Las Vegas. The lawyer gave no sign. Helen pressed on, "Starting tomorrow night. At the Comfort Inn South, near the airport. Ask her to call me."

"I can try to get in touch with her, but I can't promise. She's hard to reach, sometimes. If I succeed, I'll give her your message. Anything else I can do for you?"

"Did the package arrive from the Nagoya Police? Has Julie all her things back yet?"

Martina's smile widened. "I can't answer that."

"Why not? What would be the harm?"

"Sorry."

"Come on, tell me! Were Julie's things returned to her from Japan? I know they were supposed to be sent here, to you."

"Sorry." Martina didn't bother looking sorry.

"Privileged information, eh?"

"No comment. My, but you do press hard!"

Helen stood up and prepared to leave.

"Not really. I just don't back down, is all."

"Good-bye." Martina came round her desk and offered Helen her hand. "And good luck." They shook hands like boxers after a bout.

"Thanks. For the coffee," Helen said.

"Oh, I think you got more than that!" They smiled at each other.

53

Las Vegas

They were on their way east out of Santa Monica by 3:30 p.m., hurrying to beat the rush hour traffic already congesting on the misnamed freeways. Rushing through the intersection with the San Diego Freeway Helen had a momentary qualm. Nostalgia or indigestion? she asked herself only half-facetiously. Did she really want to take the well-remembered road south to San Diego, to see how it had changed? Walk the worn-out Silver Strand State Beach? Check whether the little house near the naval air station on Coronado, her father's retirement home, still stood or was replaced by a flock of townhouse condos? No!

Driving through the tangle of L.A. freeways requires concentration on the part of novices and allows for little sightseeing. Helen drove and Wayne sat with a map on his knees, trying to anticipate junctions and guessing how to stay on the right freeway. It looked easy on the map, and even sounded silly when Helen had said, "Just keep us on I-10, that's all I ask."

With some good management and lots of luck — Wayne spotted the right ramps in time for Helen to take them — they avoided landing in downtown Los Angeles at the height of the rush hour. Instead, together with a million home-bound Angelinos, they fought their way on the San Bernardino Freeway to I-15.

"Cucamonga," Wayne noted, looking up from his map. "Great name."

Tract developments scarred the semi-arid country like

poison ivy blisters. New townhouses with protruding chimneys as primary "design features" and dressed up with plantings of svelte "Memories of Tuscany" cedars crowded the brows of steep hills. Imported flora dominated the sparce native vegetation. Sprinklers sprayed Colorado water over private lawns and golf courses as lush and green as in any rain-soaked land. The hazards of fire, drought, earthquake, mud-slide and evironmental devastation were systematically ignored.

Helen, who had seen it all before, didn't bother noticing. Wayne's reaction was mixed.

"Southern California, eh? Sort of pretty, most of it. Lots of rich folks, I guess. Here anyway, not where the blacks live, I bet. Hey, just look at that house there! Yeah! But ...," and he paused to formulate his next thought, "but it's all one suburb, like. Where's the action? Must be hard to find."

"Suburb, yeah. Nothing is walking distance, as in Toronto or Manhattan even. Have to drive everywhere. Get in your car to get a pint of milk. So the 'action' is like that too. Scattered."

"Not for me. Pity. It would be great otherwise."

Helen didn't answer. She wasn't about to lecture on the madness of millions of people insisting on an affluent, auto-centered lifestyle in a semi-arid, water-short area, situated over a major fault line. The cost of such a life was high even in temperate zones; here it was astronomical. All she said was: "It's a disaster waiting to happen."

"Well, meanwhile it's the good life, I guess. Eh?"

"I guess." Helen shrugged. The subject was dropped.

They stopped in Barstow. Ate and changed drivers. Then Wayne drove through the virtually empty Mojave: miles of bare, yellow dirt speckled with dark creosote bushes surrounded by a rim of pink hills. Virtually no sign of human life. Just the roadway unrolling in front of them, little traffic. They drove in silence.

Wayne hit the Nevada line and sped past the first casino in Jean without a second look. He didn't want to spoil the impact of the Real Thing — Las Vegas! — for himself. He was all prepped up to troll the Strip but Helen had other plans.

"It won't run away, for Pete's sake! Let's check in. Then you can party. Take the next exit number 37 right. Yes, just cross Las Vegas Boulevard and take a right again at Koval."

Grumbling under his breath, Wayne complied. They pushed their way through the Strip intersection past the pointy red and blue towers of the Excalibur looking like a grain elevator with pimples, then the plastic lushness of the Tropicana and relative unpretentiousness of the San Remo. Across the road the monstrous MGM Theme Park and Casino Hotel were nearing completion.

The glitz stopped there. At the corner of Tropicana and Koval was a cheap low-rise motel and next to it lay their destination: a modest, two-story Comfort Inn. Standard horseshoe shape with the office and pool filling in the middle. Across the road it faced an empty, weed-covered field surrounded by a high-wire fence. Behind it, in the distance were the outlaying buildings of McCarran Airport, most prominently a small building with a huge sign advertising sightseeing flights over the Grand Canyon. Wayne looked the place over with disgust.

"Comfort Inn, for Pete's sake! Can't we do better than this? Come on, Helen, gimme a break! This dump could be in Dunville, Ontario. How about a casino hotel, hey? Since we're here anyway."

Helen didn't answer. She left Wayne fuming and went into the office to register for them both.

"Over there. Park right in front of our rooms. This one is yours. I'm next door. With connecting doors. Give me

20 minutes and I'll be ready to go. Okay?"

"Sure, but ..."

"I'm expecting a call." She picked up her bag and went into her room. Resignedly Wayne did the same.

They didn't go far together that evening. They walked to San Remo for dinner (Special! $9.95! Steak and crab legs, with salad and baked potato) following which they moved up the street and sat in and then played at a $5 poker table at the Tropicana. They lost about $30 between them.

"Enough for now. I'm going to bed. You do what you want, Cookie, as long as the car stays where it is. I may need it, anytime," Helen said finally.

Helen walked away leaving Wayne to explore Las Vegas on his own. Which he proceeded to do, finally staggering to bed (alone!) at well past two in the morning. The evening had cost him half the ready cash Keiko had provided.

Wayne didn't surface until 11:30 the next morning. When he did, he found the car gone, Helen's room empty and a note under his door that said: "J. called. I'm off to meet her. Stick around, I'll be in touch." Wayne swore and went out for breakfast. What else was there to do?

Helen had been tasting Comfort Inn's complimentary coffee and Danish when the phone rang. She gulped her lukewarm coffee.

"Hello?" She knew it had to be Julie.

"Helen, damn it, why did you follow me here?! You have no idea ..."

"Save it, Julie. I want to see you."

"I know you want to see me! And I know what you want, too. You made it clear to Martina. The painting."

"Sure, the painting. And I won't give up, so tell me where you are so we can meet and talk."

"Oh, all right! I know it's hopeless arguing with you.

I'll be having coffee at the Boulevard Mall at eleven. Come find me."

"Count on it. G'day."

"G'day, you bitch!"

There is nothing to distinguish Boulevard Mall on Maryland Parkway in Las Vegas from any middle-class shopping mall on the continent. It has four department stores, including the ever-present Sears and J.C. Penny, plus some 90 other retail businesses. A dozen fast-food counters cluster around a large open space going under the name Panorama Cafe. Here the decor is black and white with a frieze of Hollywood characters around the walls. A fountain is featured. The space is filled with spindly tables and uncomfortable chairs and that's where Helen found Julie, sitting over her coffee and crumbling an oversized blueberry muffin.

Helen bought herself a coffee and sat down across the table from her.

"Hello, stranger. How's business?" Helen tried to start the conversation on a light note. It didn't work.

"Oh, Helen. It's not funny!"

"Why not? Okay, I'm sorry. Let's start again. Hi, Julie! How you doing?"

"Fine, I guess, considering how sick I've been. Or fine until you showed up. When Martina called me with your message I was that browned off. Leave me alone, why don't you?"

"Loosen up, Julie. This isn't like you. Maybe I can help."

"Help! Look, mate. Best way you can help is to split, right this minute. Beat it. The painting is a fake, or didn't you know? So what good is it? Anyway ... it isn't safe for you to be here, not safe for any of us."

"So I gather. Who's after you? What are you afraid of?"

"You just won't listen! The situation is complicated.

Back in Nagoya, I didn't realize just how complicated and dangerous it was. Now I know ... more than I knew then, anyway. For both our sakes Helen, go away! Take off!"

"I want the picture, fake or not. And I want to talk to Bob. Bob of *ARTrace*. Arrange that for me, Julie. Else I'll have to start looking for myself, beating the bushes, raising a lot of dust. Could mean more problems for you. It's your choice."

For the first time Julie Piper lifted up her face from the pile of muffin crumbs on the table in front of her and looked into Helen's eyes.

"You never quit, do you? Well, hear this. I don't have the painting. As for Bob, it's up to him. I'll ask him whether he wants to talk to you. Perhaps I call you again tomorrow ..."

"Within an hour, Julie. I want an answer within a hour or I start digging. I'll be at the motel; you have till 12:30. That's generous, I figure."

"An hour! What if I can't get to him so fast ...?"

"You will, Julie, you will. G'day to you, mate."

Leaving her coffee untouched Helen got up and started walking away. She hadn't covered more than five black-and-white vinyl squares on the floor when Julie called her back.

"All right, all right! Wait here, I'll call him now. See what he says."

Helen sat down again. Julie walked towards a bank of telephones adjacent to the outside doors. Although it wouldn't have made any sense, for a moment she had the impulse to just skip out. Leave Helen to find her again. No. She punched in Bob's number. He answered immediately.

"Bob, she's here and she wants to see you. Gave me a hour to produce you. And she asked about *ARTrace*."

"So? We expected all that. What would happen if you refused? I'm not easy to find."

"She would find you. She's real smart, I told you, damn it! You better see her. Talk to her maybe ..."

"All right. I'd better see for myself. Bring her here. Now. I'll show her the setup. The story is quite straightforward, why should she doubt it? Be frank to a fault. Like, there's nothing and nobody else involved. Make her believe there is nothing more. A snow job. Come on, Julie! You're an expert at it!"

"And Helen's an expert at seeing through snow jobs."

"Every time? Nobody's that good. Lets give it a try."

"Okay. We'll be there in ten."

Julie hung up, turned and waved to Helen. They met at the doors to the parking lot.

"Bob will see you. Let's go."

"Now?"

"Now. Why not?"

"No reason. Where we going?"

"We'll show you *ARTrace*. The whole ball of wax. We decided to let you in on everything. Explain. Then maybe you'll see it our way."

54

ARTrace

Julie drove along La Canada Street and crossed Capistrano. The house was only three blocks from the mall. It was in an area of cinder-block ranch houses painted pastel colours with orange and beige predominating, all clinging to the middle class by their fingertips. Five-year-old cars sat in driveways, next to burned-out lawns. At noon on a week-day, no one was about.

The house was beige and seemed uncared for. Helen figured it was rented, furnished. Julie pulled the blue Taurus station wagon into the drive, narrowly avoiding a tricycle. She led Helen into the dim interior. All the windows were shuttered against the merciless sun. The air conditioner hummed gently.

"Hi! Welcome to the Forbes mansion! Sorry my wife isn't here to help me do the honours but she took the kids to visit her mother in California."

Bob was large, blond and soft-looking like an out-of-shape football player. In his early thirties, he had pale, forgettable features, tired eyes and noticeably trembling hands. Booze, Helen decided, and probably fear. Still, he was quick to establish an atmosphere of normality. As if Helen's was just a friendly visit, nothing more. "How about some ice tea? I think there is a jug in the fridge all ready to go."

"Ice tea would be great." Helen was quite willing to go along.

The living/dining room took up the whole front of the

small house. Bob went into the kitchen while Julie and Helen sat down, Julie in an overstuffed armchair, Helen in a straight chair next to the table.

Bob was soon back with drinks, which he handed around like a good host. Then he took a dining chair near Helen and turned to her, his speech ready:

"It's a real pleasure to meet you. Julie told me so much about you. We're real grateful for what you did for her, getting her out of Japan. That was a great rescue! Wish I'd been there."

"Yeah, it was kind of fun. She was in bad trouble. But that's all over now. Or is it?"

Bob laughed politely and passed the ball to Julie. "We sure hope so. Right, Julie?"

"Who knows? Helen followed me here, so can others." Julie sounded genuinely despondent.

"You mean Tan? You know what Tan is?" Helen asked.

"Of course I know! In Hong Kong everyone knows that it's shorthand for 'the Taiwanese will git you.'"

"Why would the triads be after you?"

"If they killed Nangi ..."

"Did they?"

"I don't know who killed him, mate. I didn't know in Nagoya and I still don't know. But it could've been them."

"Could've been Kusashita's mob did him in and are trying to throw suspicion on the Taiwanese. Scaring you so you go to ground. That way they'd know who's behind this scam."

Julie nodded, her eyes on Helen. Bob was being ignored.

"Sure. I figured that out. Either way, I don't want to be found."

"Then why did you agree to see me? And bring me here?"

Julie sighed. "For one, Bob and I aren't behind this

scam, as you put it. And two ... well we need all the help we can get."

"Oh yeah? Back in the mall you told me to leave you alone, to get lost. Now you need me! Consistency isn't your forte, is it Julie?" Helen turned to Bob, "Thanks for the warm welcome, Bob, but I'm not here for the climate or the casinos. Tell me about *ARTrace*."

"I'll do better. I'll show you." Suddenly animated, Bob got up and opened a door leading to a small back room with a glassed-in patio opening onto the backyard. Tucked into one corner was a long narrow office table covered with paper in untidy piles and a work station holding a Mac computer and a laser printer. There was a desk with an expensive fax machine and a copier. Between the computer and the fax stood an office-size shredder. Issues of *ARTrace*, back copies of art-related magazines, gallery handouts, newsletters and exhibition catalogues were stacked against the wall.

"As you can see, it's everything needed for a desktop publishing function," Bob announced proudly. "We are small, neat and efficient."

Helen took her time looking over the contents of the room. She noted the phone and fax numbers. It did look like a going operation; she had little doubt *ARTrace* was produced in this room. She nodded carefully. They walked back into the living room and sat down again.

"Very impressive. Now tell me how Julie came to be in Hong Kong hanging out with the likes of Sonny Burke. And moving stolen paintings around Asia."

"Right. Well, let's see, where shall I start? Julie and I met at some gallery party in L.A. She was freelancing and I threw some business her way. My wife Isobel and I got to know and like Julie so we visited back and forth quite frequently. In fact, Julie stayed with us here and helped out when Ludwig was born. That's our youngest." Bob smiled winningly, the proud Papa. "*ARTrace* was growing and I needed someone to be my California eyes-and-ears and Julie was perfect for the job. It worked out real well, didn't it, Julie? Then ... why don't you take it from there, Julie?"

"Then ... I guess I got sort of restless, you know how we Aussies are, so I took off. Working my way from place to place. First Hawaii, then Kuala Lumpur and Singapore. I had some connections here and there in the art business, you know how international it is. Then I made it to Hong Kong. That's the hub, of course. On the circuit I heard about Sonny, this strange man who never left his bar stool and did all his business by phone. I told you about that, Helen, remember?"

"Go on." Helen said.

"Hard slogging this. Think I'll get myself more tea. Anyone else?" Helen and Bob shook their heads.

With Julie out of the room, Bob turned to Helen.

"I think our Julie feels a bit strange talking about her relationship with this guy Sonny. Getting pregnant and all that ... must be hard for her. Now, I don't know anything about him, except what she's told me. You've met him, right? What did you think of him?"

Instead of answering, Helen smiled at him and left the room in the direction of the bathroom. By the time she returned Julie was also back from the kitchen. Helen said: "Bob was just asking me about Sonny. But what I think of him is irrelevant. Let's hear your story."

She watched as Bob and Julie exchanged a quick look. Julie said: "Well, what happened was that I had to go to Japan on a little job for *ARTrace*. Bob had asked me to talk to this man in Nagoya called Nangi. Yes, he had some information he wanted to exchange. So I agreed to meet him at the mall in Nagoya on the night ... you know about that. Anyway, when Sonny asked me to take a parcel to someone in Tokyo and then go to Nagoya to pay off this same man, I thought it was quite a coincidence." Julie smiled at Helen.

"Coincidences do happen," Helen said, deadpan. "What was the information Nangi wanted to 'exchange'?"

"I better take over here," Bob cut in. "You see, Helen, one of the things that *ARTrace* does is try to keep up with the market for stolen art. Nangi heard of us and got in touch saying he had information about a big caper about to come off."

"'About to'? You mean not happened yet?"

"That's what his fax said."

"Where does that anonymous catalogue of stolen art come in? Julie told me she was carrying it to show him."

"Oh, yes. We'd came across it through one of our sub-cribers and were trying to trace it to its source. We thought that Nangi might know where it came from."

"That's not what you told me in Japan, Julie. You said Nangi wanted a copy of the catalogue all to himself. You were going to use the painting to authenticate the catalogue. That was your story, remember?"

"Well, Helen, what can I tell you? It was a little white lie."

Helen didn't react. She said: "Go on."

"That's it. That's all she wrote. I missed Wayne in Tokyo in order not to miss Nangi in Nagoya. He was most insistent about time and place. The rest you know. I'm sorry I misled you but it wasn't my secret. And I didn't want to get Bob into trouble. Just put it down to journal-istic ethics."

"Journalistic ethics?!" Helen's sarcasm was palpable.

"That's right, mate. Not revealing your sources. Everything got very mixed up. Such a foreign place, Japan. After Nangi got bumped off, I didn't know what to do. Seemed best to keep mum and split as soon as possible. And with your help, that's what I did."

"And the painting? The painting in your umbrella, which Suzuki returned via Khayatt. What happened to it? Where is it?"

"I sent it away UPS to New York. I'm having it examined by experts. I believe it's a fake." Bob jumped in before Julie could open her mouth.

"You didn't waste any time, did you? And by rights it belongs to Sonny. Or a client of his. Not to you."

"Technically, yes. But I believe it's a fake. The original is back in the gallery in Scotland. It was authenticated. Anyway all I want is the story. For *ARTrace*. Then Sonny can have it back. Although he hasn't been asking for it. One way or another it's hot and nobody wants to claim it. It could be a case of possession being nine-tenths of the law."

"Right. I want it. Get it for me."

"I told you, I haven't got it. It's ... on its way to an expert in New York. I'm sorry but I can't let you have it. Now or ever." Bob was firm.

Helen stood up and grinned at them both.

"Let me recap. Correct me if I've gotten it wrong. You are telling me that the painting and the catalogue being in Julie's possession at the same time in Nagoya when Nangi was killed was a coincidence. Second, you are telling me that you don't know who is behind that catalogue. Third, that *ARTrace* and that catalogue are not connected except via this 'coincidence.' Fourth, that you sent that painting out of here to some anonymous expert in New York virtually within minutes of it being returned from Japan. How am I doing?"

"Look, Helen. I know it all sounds unlikely but ... that's the way it is." Bob was all look-them-straight-in-the-eye Boy Scout honour.

"Phewee." Helen said, then ignoring Bob, bent down to look Julie in the face. "I'm not finished yet. Julie, now you tell me why you're so all fired scared. Given the story you've just fed me, there doesn't seem to be any call for all this hide-and-seek. Who or what would such innocent babes as you portray yourselves have to worry about? Why are you hiding? Why is *ARTrace* not listed anywhere? A subscription-based newsletter without an address, hiding its light under a bushel? Give me a break!"

Before Helen was finished, Bob stood up and faced her, interposing his bulk between her and Julie. Helen didn't give ground as expected. Bob stepped back with a nervous twitch and sat down again. He clearly didn't have the stomach for a real confrontation.

"Oh, let it rest. Helen, you really have no business asking us questions. We agreed to tell you our part in all this, whether you believe us or not is immaterial. I think you'd better leave now," he said.

Helen ignored him, still looking down at Julie who hadn't met her gaze. Helen waited for some reaction from Julie. Finally Julie asked: "Why don't you buy what Bob and I told you? Just out of curiosity, why?"

"Come now, Julie, you and Bob just aren't the innocent bystanders you claim to be. You both lie too well, for starters. On the other hand, Bob is no criminal mastermind and neither are you, my friend. So you and he can't be all there is. And *ARTrace*! Well, maybe it's printed, collated and mailed out from that room. But someone else somewhere else actually edits and writes *ARTrace*. The same someone who produces the mysterious catalogue. My guess is that Bob gets the text for both transmitted electronically to that Mac and then just prints them up. Maybe he adds a piece of news from California to *ARTrace* just to make it look really local. But nothing as complicated and expert as the contents of *ARTrace* or the catalogue is actually developed and written in that patio room by Bob!"

"I see," Julie said. Bob was looking down at his shoes

and biting his lip.

"Never mind being coy about it. Just tell me: who or what is CHNOPS? And what's your part in all this?"

There was a moment's silence. Then Julie said:

"I can't tell you about CHNOPS. It's not for me to do that. But you're right about *ARTrace*, of course. Most of its contents arrives on the electronic highway. From ... Europe. I guess I can tell you that much. And that's all Bob does: print and distribute the newsletter and pass on subscription information and any communications about it to ... well, to the principal."

Both women looked at Bob but he kept on staring at his feet saying nothing. Julie continued:

"Bob prints and distributes the *ARTrace* newsletter for someone else who calls himself CHNOPS. He has no connection with the mail-order catalogue. Neither of us knew about it until recently. Then Bob smelt a rat when one of the *ARTrace* subscribers sent a copy of it along with his renewal, probably by mistake. That's how we found out that the subscription list was being exploited. We got no satisfaction from CHNOPS. So we decided to investigate further on our own. I went to Hong Kong ... and all this mess started."

Julie paused, then continued, "I took it on as a journalistic assignment, that was no lie. We found out deliveries were being made via Sonny Burke in Hong Kong. So when I got there I made a point of getting to know him. The rest you know."

"Interesting. How about Nangi? What was that meeting really about?"

"Yes, that was very confusing. Nangi had gotten in touch with Bob. He said he had information about a major art theft that was being planned. It was the kind of tip *ARTrace* gets all the time. Bob passed this information on to ... CHNOPS, we may as well use that title, but again that brought no joy. So we decided to push on with our own investigation on the q.t. Nangi wanted personal contact. He wouldn't tell us anything except face to face. So that's what happened."

"And you kept this quiet all this time out of loyalty to Bob, eh?"

"Yes."

"So why tell me now? Julie, I can see that you're really disturbed about this business. Not knowing whether to tell me any of this or not. But you started out lying. So what changed your mind?"

"Because ..." Julie looked at Bob, then away. "Because we've lost touch with CHNOPS. We can't raise him. He's always been available by phone, fax or bulletin board. Always. It's not like him. We know something is brewing ... oh, Helen I don't like it!"

"So you're just sitting tight, waiting for hear from CHNOPS?"

"Yes, yes! And worrying about this Tan business. What if he's done something that has set the Taiwanese triads after him!?"

"Right, they will find you first. Following Julie's trail. And of course the painting and other stuff from Japan!"

"And you —" Bob broke in, "— they know about Julie and the painting and then they know about you! I wish you hadn't come to Vegas!"

Helen was silent, thinking of the pipeline that Wayne and she constituted via Keiko to Brother Sam and the Nagoya yakuza. Damn. Julie and Bob had every reason to be afraid. And everything they'd told her could be true.

"I see. I'd best split. Don't bother getting up. I'll walk back to the mall for my car."

And she walked out the house and down the driveway stopping only en route to check the glove compartment of Julie's Ford for the rental agreement.

55
Poker Games

Wayne had done 20 laps in the motel pool and was considering starting on another set of 20 when he noticed the loitering man. There was no one else in sight. Checkout was at 10:00 a.m., so all the overnighters were long gone and the maid's cart was over at the other arm of the horseshoe-shaped motel. There were only three cars in the whole parking lot, none near his and Helen's rooms. The man didn't look like a maintenance man or other motel employee. So what was he doing looking into Helen's window and trying the door?

As Wayne watched treading water, the man took something out of his pocket and started to fiddle with the door lock. Heaving himself out of the water, Wayne scrambled onto the rim of the pool. Water cascaded off his body, splashing onto the aquamarine tiles and tumbling back. Startled by the sounds, the man looked around, spotted Wayne standing there looking at him and immediately took off, walking briskly back towards the road. In seconds he'd disappeared behind the building that housed the motel office.

Swearing under his breath, Wayne grabbed his towel and ran back to his room, his wet footsteps evaporating behind him. He fumbled for the key, opened the door and slammed it shut. Inside, he dried himself and struggled into his clothes still cursing Helen for leaving him like this, for not briefing him properly. He didn't know what to do. The man had clearly been interested specifically in

Helen's room. Coincidence? Hardly. In any case, he was gone.

After a moment's thought, Wayne walked over to the office and as calmly as possible asked the cheerful young woman behind the counter whether anyone had been asking for Helen Keremos. She nodded readily.

"Sure. Just a few minutes ago. I gave him her room number but unfortunately she was out for the moment. I guess the gentleman will call again."

"Oriental guy, was he?" Wayne asked.

"No. Caucasian."

He went back to his room and tried to recall what the man had looked like. Short and quite athletic by the way he'd carried himself. Dressed in a light suit. He had been about to pick the lock of Helen's room.

How did anyone know where to find them? In Las Vegas? In this motel? Had something happened to Helen? Did the information come from her? Wayne was fit to be tied. What if she didn't come back? He had no idea where and how to look for her. That lawyer in Los Angeles was the only lead. He looked speculatively at the phone. Call her? Would she tell him anything?

As he was contemplating the instrument, the phone rang. He picked it up immediately.

"Wayne? You're sitting on the phone, I see. Good. I'm on my way back. Just wanted to check and see how you're doing. Any developments?"

"Yes! Some guy came round asking for you, then tried to break into your room! I scared him away ..." Wayne was virtually shouting.

"Whoa there! Easy. Better not on the phone. Listen. You come to me. Let's see. Take a cab to Caesar's. Meet you there in 15 minutes. Just walk by the poker tables, the ones furthest away from the entrance. And take it easy getting there, like you're just going to play a little cards. Now,

Cookie, don't act so spooked. Did this guy seem to know who you were?"

"No. At least I don't think so. I was in the pool and saw him at your door. Then he saw me and split. I could have been anyone. But he'd asked for you by name at the office."

"I see. Now do as I said. See you in 15. And keep cool."

Las Vegas Boulevard South, the notorious Strip, is also just a short piece of Nevada Route 604, more or less paralleling I-15. There are four exits onto the Strip from I-15. Starting from the south they are: Tropicana Avenue, which is where Wayne and Helen exited the previous night; Flamingo Road; Sands Avenue; and Sahara Avenue. With a few notable exceptions, most major hotel casinos cluster on the Strip within sight and sound of these four intersections. Caesar's Palace is at the Flamingo intersection, across from the Dunes and Barbary Coast casinos and kitty-corner from Bally's. It sits amidst the greatest concentration of hotel casinos in the Entertainment Capital of the World, as Las Vegas likes to style itself. If gambling has a centre in this town, this is it.

Caesar's Palace is not the newest or the largest or the glossiest or the most extravagant hotel casino in town. It's no fistful of peanuts either. Its three casinos alone cover 117,000 square feet. It offers race and sports book, four entertainment lounges, showrooms, nine restaurants, health spa, squash and tennis courts, two swimming pools, an Omnimax Theater, video arcades, unending parking garages, 4,500-seat indoor pavilion, 15,300 seat outdoor stadium ... and oh, yes ... 1,518 hotel rooms and full convention and catering facilities.

Those whose pleasure runs to shopping can "mall hop" to ancient Rome. The Forum Shops at Caesar's are advertised as the Shopping Wonder of the World and described as having "the look and feel of an ancient Roman streetscape, complete with columns and arches, central piazzas, ornate fountains and classic statuary."

Naturally there is valet parking, a landscaped streetfront a block long, spacious entrance driveways and, hidden at the back, acres of service buildings and parking lots.

Having a long-standing distrust of valet parking and underground garages, Helen sneaked up behind all this splendour and parked outside in a back lot. She got out of the car and looked around over the tops of innumerable automobiles. In one direction there was nothing but a tangle of wires and in the distance the ring of pink hills that surrounds Las Vegas. Behind a fringe of palms in another direction and blocks away loomed the yellow bulk of The Mirage Hotel Casino. Nearest to her was a windowless circular structure crowned with a cupola. A number of large blank fire doors marked EXIT indicated that inside was a public facility where Nevada Fire Marshal's regulations applied.

Helen should have done the proper thing and walked around the building to find the public entrance. She didn't. She found one of the huge fire exit doors not quite shut, pried it open and found herself in an empty passage high and wide enough for a troop of elephants to pass through comfortably. She carefully avoided the door marked OFFICE and walked decisively in a I-know-where-I'm-going and I-have-a-perfect-right-to-be-here manner to and through a second set of outsize double doors. And found herself in the Caesar's Forum.

The sky-blue painted ceiling embellished with little white clouds soared above her as she walked chuckling to herself over the polished marble floor. The place wasn't busy. A cathedral-like atmosphere prevailed. A few tourists rubbernecked at the marble and plaster splendours and window-shopped. A group stopped to photograph the life-size copy of the fountain of Trevi while an awed young couple gulped their coffee in the "outdoor" cafe next door. Appropriately, the Disney store was doing the most business.

A casino came next. First rows and rows of poker video machines and one-armed bandits. Further on (that is, closer to the proper public entrance) was the serious business of roulette, poker and craps tables. Helen got $20 in quarters from a passing attendant and sat down at one of the poker video terminals where she could watch the traffic around the live poker tables. There was action at only two of them, so spotting Wayne wasn't going to be a problem.

Five card draw. Helen pushed in five quarters and looked at the cards that appeared on the screen. A pair of eights, a queen, an ace and a deuce. She pressed HOLD for the pair, got a pair of jacks this time, and was credited with 10 quarters, double her bet. Good start.

Five dollars up and 10 minutes later, Wayne appeared, strolling casually past the video and slot machines. In jeans, sport shirt and Blue Jay baseball hat, he looked right at home, his clothes matching that of the majority of men in the sumptuous, high-ceiling rooms. Vegas may be full of wealthy high rollers, but, if so, most of them don't dress the part. In fact, Las Vegas seems to belong to the retired couple in an RV, the week-ending insurance clerk on a spree and more and more to the white middle-class family on school vacation. Hotel casinos are where the lower end of the middle class get their taste of the "High Life." And why the hell not, thought Helen watching Wayne looking around to find her, everybody deserves a bit of glitz in their life.

Helen waited until he came past the poker table nearest to her and cashed in her winnings. Coins tumbled into the metal payout box, the cascading quarters sounding like an avalanche. A sound designed by casino managment to raise hope in the losers and greed in the winners and keep both sorts playing. Wayne looked up in the direction of the sound and saw her. Helen nodded towards the seat next to her. He moved there fast.

"Here, play." Helen handed him a handful of quarters and went on to feed coins into her own machine. "Now, tell me exactly what happened."

Helen made Wayne tell the whole story twice; she was especially interested in his description of the man, pressing him repeatedly. Think carefully, Wayne, she said. He'd only had a glimpse. He replied.

"Too bad, but we'll find out soon enough, I expect. Were you followed here?"

"Hard to say. I walked to the corner of Tropicana to get a cab and could've been followed from there if he was watching. But why would he? How could he know who I am and that I'm with you?"

"How did he know where to find me, come to that? If he knows about me, why not you?" Helen fell silent for a second, and then as if changing the subject, asked: "How's Keiko? You called her last night, didn't you?"

"She's fine. Of course, I called her ... Oh, shit Helen! I know what you're implying ... I did tell her where we were, naturally I did! But Keiko wouldn't tell anyone! Why would she? Who's to tell?"

Helen was relentless.

"Sorry, Wayne. But. That doesn't mean Keiko meant to give us away. Phones can be tapped. So don't write her off. Not yet anyway. There is another possibility, you know. Julie Piper and Bob know where I'm staying. So does Martina Khayatt for that matter. They don't know about you being here. As far as we know, anyway, they don't. But Keiko does, of course. So let's see whether someone followed you here, okay?"

It was the best Helen could do for Wayne. Regardless of who and what the guy in the suit was, she thought it was time for Wayne to face a few facts. He had to be told about Keiko and Brother Sam. As she told him, she watched his face grow more and more gloomy. Then angry. It didn't bode well for the fairy-tale marriage.

"I know it's hard, Wayne, but be a mensch. Keiko is who she is. This guy Sam is her family, the only family she has, it seems ..."

"She's got me, damn it! I'm her husband, right? That's what matters. If as you say she really wants to get away from the yakuza sleazeballs, then why ...? It doesn't make sense."

"It makes sense to her. We don't know what's in her head, but you've got to see that she's got her own agenda and her own rationale for what she does. It's not yours, that's all. Doesn't make her any worse than you are."

"I wouldn't sell her out, ever! Bitch."

"We don't know that she's sold you out! Get a grip! It's not the end of the world. Anyway, we have a situation here we have to deal with, first. We have to find out who this guy is and what he wants. Are we agreed about that?"

Helen looked at the five cards on the screen, made a face and held two diamonds, discarding the rest. Replacements were no better. She put more quarters in the slot. Wayne was too preoccupied to play. He jiggled the coins in his hand nervously.

"Yeah, yeah, sure. Let's get him away someplace and beat the shit out of him." Wayne was eager to find someone to take out his anger on.

"It might come to that, you know."

"What the hell is going on here! Christ! I thought we came here after Julie Piper and that painting. That's all. I wasn't counting on ..."

"Them's the breaks. In this business you never know where you're going to end up. You better learn fast, Cookie."

They fell silent, each trying to figure out where they stood. Finally Helen put a hand on his arm and dropping her voice to a conciliatory murmur said: "I am really sorry, Wayne, to have gotten you into this mess. It just happened that way. And I didn't tell you everything I know or guessed ... well, that's because I'm not used to working with partners. I just go ahead and do my thing, regardless. Sorry."

Wayne nodded. He seemed bemused but not angry any more. At least, not at Helen.

"Yeah, that's cool. I get the picture. You never really wanted me along anyway. You did it for Keiko. And Keiko wanted me here as a pipeline for her brother to whatever you turn up. Shit, have I been a fool! But now ... I'm here. You can count me in. Let's fix those scumbags, whatever it takes. So. What's our next move, boss?" He smiled and flexed his muscles.

"Well, right now just keep your eyes open for the guy at my motel door. Spot him here if you can. If not, good. You looking? Yes? Right. I better start by telling you what happened this morning. In a nutshell, I found Julie and a guy called Bob who publishes *ARTrace*, a newsletter about art for collectors and such. At first, their story was that Bob is the brains behind, and the sole proprietor of, *ARTrace*. Follow?"

"Go on."

"Which was bullshit. So now their story is that while *ARTrace* is a front for the mail-order stolen art scam, Bob knew nothing about it. He's just an innocent front man for some guy who really runs it. Also, according to them, they don't have the painting any more. Bob says he sent it to New York for authentification. Which I don't for a moment believe. Bob strikes me as the type of guy who lies for the sake of lying, almost. Like, he's got a tricycle out on his driveway and talks glibly about his wife and children. But I bet anything you like that he lives in that place all alone. I checked the bathroom and the two bedrooms. I am sure no kids live in that house. There is no mistaking a house that small kids live in. Of course, nothing makes a man look as innocent as a tricycle in the driveway. Next point, they're nervous and worried. Could be they're scared of Taiwanese — Julie certainly knows more than she's telling about that — but perhaps it's someone else. Like their boss, CHNOPS."

"Chops? What ... ?"

"Never mind, let's just call him 'Chops,' for short. This is the mastermind, sort of. My guess is that both the Taiwanese triad and the Nagoya yakuza want to run him down. Find out who and what he is. And then either close him down permanently or offer him 'protection' or something like that. I wish I knew which it is."

"Why? How does it matter?"

"Oh, it could matter a great deal. To our health among other things. Liquidating CHNOPS might be easier than negotiating with him, if you see what I mean. Or they might want something from him, like a piece of his action. If so, then we might be useful. As intermediaries, for instance. Like I said, if all they are interested in is putting him out of business 'permanently,' then who needs us? It's always safer to be needed, Cookie."

"I guess. Sounds very complicated. All I want to know is, what do we do next?"

"First off, I think we'll move and this time not tell anyone where we are."

"You mean not even Keiko, eh? Okay. Where shall we go?"

"What's wrong with right here — Caesar's? You wanted a casino hotel. This one is as good as any."

"Great! Gimme the car keys. I'll pick up our bags and check us out of that crummy motel."

"Ha! You should live so well all your life," Helen said, handing him her keys. "Register us in your name. I'll wait here. The car's parked on the back lot; you can get there without going out the main door. And don't get followed back here."

"No fear. Okay. We move here, then what? What's your plan?"

"Then, it depends."

"That's not much of a plan. It depends on what?"

"On what happens next. On who makes what kind of move. Cookie, 'it depends' is the name of the game. There is no other. Ever play chess?"

"No."

"Me neither." Helen laughed, her lined face turned to his. There was excitement in the sound, the sound of adrenalin starting to pump.

"Ever bungee jump, Cookie?"

"No."

"Well, what we're about to do is jump, possibly without a bungee. Possibly. What say?"

Wayne's answer wasn't in doubt. Of course, any risk that this old woman was going to take he was ready for. But why was she doing this?

Wayne had often thought of Helen as a witch. Witches were post-menopausal, unknowable women. Sexless and dangerous. But also unimportant, irrelevant, out of sync with the real world. Powerless in any way that mattered. Now looking at Helen, Wayne knew that he'd gotten it wrong somehow. He shook his head as if discarding the thought.

"Let's do it. Whatever," he said.

"Right."

56

A Death

With the engine and the air conditioning turned off, the car was hot. Helen and Wayne sat in the sticky silence listening to the night noises. After what seemed like hours but was really only a few minutes, Helen pulled two pairs of latex gloves out of her bag and handed one to Wayne.

"Let's go," she said.

Closing the car door quietly, they walked like black shadows around the corner and across the sleeping intersection towards the beige *ARTrace* bungalow. Not a light showed anywhere. It was 3:00 a.m.; even in Las Vegas that's the dead of the night.

Except for the tricycle, the driveway of the run-down house was empty. Julie Piper's rented car was gone. Without breaking stride Helen led the way around the building to the back door. Now out of sight of the surrounding homes they stopped and listened for a second, holding their breath. Nothing, not a dog or late-night TV. The only sound was the occasional automobile speeding some blocks away on Desert Inn Road or Maryland Parkway.

"So far so far ..." Helen smiled up at Wayne who stood grim-faced beside her. She pulled the gloves on her sweaty hands. His were already on. In their dark clothing, with their hands now white and ghostly in the gloom, they looked like characters in a mime.

"Oh, oh! This door isn't locked. Why, I wonder? I don't like this." Helen turned the handle and pushed open the door. They stepped into the kitchen and stopped again, listening and adjusting their eyes to the different light level.

"Flashlight." Helen spoke softly. A large white cone of light sprung from Wayne's left hand. Two doors led from the kitchen into the rest of the house. As Helen was aware, one door led into the combined living and dining space, the other into a short passage from which the bedrooms and the bathroom opened.

"Right. Let's check the bedrooms first, see that Bob is safely beddy-byes, I hope."

But both bedrooms stood empty. One had clearly not been lived in, as evidenced by a thick cover of dust over every surface, and remained perfectly untouched. But the larger master bedroom was in total disarray: bedding on the floor, closet and dresser spewing out their contents, clothes and odds and ends in ugly heaps.

"He's split! Hey? And took with him that damn painting we've come all this way to get. Right? So now there's nothing here for us. Let's get out of here," Wayne hissed in a loud whisper.

"Could be. But since we're here, let's check the rest of the house." Helen turned and made her way across the passage into the living room. "May as well have some light on the subject. Where's the light switch? Ah, here!" The shabby room sprang into focus.

"Looky, looky! Bob wasn't just packing! This place's been trashed!" Wayne gasped.

But Helen wasn't listening. Stepping around the chaos of overturned tables and ripped armchairs, she moved swiftly towards the open door to the *ARTrace* room. And stopped so suddenly that Wayne, who was close behind, bumped into her.

"What ...? Christ!"

They were looking down at the body of Bob Forbes.

He lay on his back, his nondescript face contorted in a grimace of painful surprise. Blood from two small holes had congealed black on his shirtfront. His pockets had been turned inside out.

For a good minute or two they stood close together, their eyes busy examining the room.

"He was shot from the direction of the backyard door with a small calibre pistol. Probably he heard someone, started to investigate and was shot as he opened this door. Whoever shot him didn't give him a chance. Bam, bam." Helen said eventually as if to herself.

"Yeah. Then the shooter trashed this place. Look at it! What a mess! Someone sure as hell didn't like this guy."

The *ARTrace* office was unrecognizable. Helen and Wayne picked their way through the debris. File folders and back issues of old magazines covered the floor, the computer lay with its back torn open next to a pile of broken diskettes. Every single piece of equipment was torn out of the wall, destroyed beyond repair. Every chair, table and box overturned. The only thing left standing was the overflowing shredder.

"Someone sure demolished *ARTrace*. Killing Forbes wasn't enough" was Helen's comment. "Well, Cookie, what d'you think we should do, eh? Call the cops and stay around to be interrogated? Or vanish?"

"Vanish, you said it, vanish! We wasn't ever here!"

"Yeah. Let's go. There isn't a working phone here anyway."

In seconds they were out of there, into their car and away.

"Where? Back to Caesar's or what?" Wayne asked, his voice shaky. He was driving. Helen considered. She shook her head.

"No. Just drive around and let me think."

"Right." They drove up the Strip in silence. Finally

Helen said: "Julie. Let's find Julie before we do anything else."

"Good idea, but how do we find her?"

"I know the address she gave to the car rental company. The Airport Inn. It's worth a try. Stop at a public phone."

"Right."

Julie had indeed checked in at the Airport Inn three days previously. But the receptionist, polite and unsurprised at 4:20 a.m., told Helen that Ms. Vanessa Hood had checked out. At 1:20 that very night.

"Well, well." Wayne said when Helen got back into the car and told him. "So she split! Listen, Helen, maybe Julie did this guy in. What'd you think? Is it possible?"

"Could be, I guess. But why? Yeah. What is our favourite Aussie up to, I wonder? May as well go back to Caesar's, Cookie. I'm bushed. Hard to think straight."

"Right," Wayne agreed. He made a sudden illegal U-turn. Helen froze as a police car sped past them. Wayne, who hadn't noticed, said: "This is kinda creepy. Hell, I've never seen a dead body before. Let's go back home soon, eh?"

57

Back Home

Twenty-four hours later, sitting in her Toronto hotel room, Helen still couldn't think of why Julie would have killed Bob. But if she hadn't, then why had she skipped without a word? And if she hadn't, then who had? The yakuza? The Taiwanese? CHNOPS? Some parties unknown? All of the above seemed possible, even probable, but none much more than any other.

Helen Keremos was very tired and very unhappy with the turn of events. She was mad at herself. Surely she must have missed something vital that day at the *ARTrace* house with Bob and Julie. And then again perhaps she'd led the killer(s) to Bob. The murder had occurred within a day of her and Wayne's arrival in Las Vegas. It could be a coincidence ... .

Wayne and Helen's return back home to Toronto from Nevada had taken on all the elements of flight. They had return empty-handed, and as Alice put it, "with their tails between their legs." In the end, Helen had placed an anonymous call to the police from a public phone at Caesar's and reported Bob's murder. They couldn't bring themselves to leave Bob's body unreported, but on the other hand, neither Wayne nor Helen could handle staying around to be interrogated by the police. Helen just couldn't face what she knew would be an ordeal that might keep them in Vegas for weeks. She and Wayne made such splendid suspects. For Wayne the experience in Nagoya was enough; he wanted to get home as soon as possible and didn't give the ethics of the matter much thought. Sneaking away had been an easy decision.

With Wayne safe in the arms of Keiko, Helen allowed herself to drift into a depression. She hadn't seen Nangi alive or dead and, besides, his death had taken place before she'd become involved. This was different. She'd met Bob Forbes, instantly judging him a lightweight. His killing was all the harder to bear. With this murder somehow all the fun had gone out of the "game" for the sake of which she'd gone down to Nevada in the first place. Her easy rationalizations lay in ruins.

Mel Romulu's attitude hadn't helped. He'd sounded quite uninterested and unconcerned at the news that she'd struck out, that she was unable to procure for him the Daumier he wanted. Helen couldn't help wondering what had changed in the intervening days. She couldn't understand it. She seemed to have lost her grasp over what was happening. On top of it all, she was paying the price of the stress and strain of the past weeks — the travel, time changes, late nights, fast food. Her body was wracked by fatigue, her back and knees hurt, she was conscious of a cold coming on.

For three days Helen sat in her hotel room like a zombie, watching TV, reading magazines and sustaining herself on single malt scotch and takeout. Wayne called once or twice to give her his news. Keiko had found an apartment on Front Street East, very upscale: she'd ordered new furniture for it; movers were coming first of the month. He had tickets to a Jays game, how about it? Having gotten nowhere, Wayne gave up. Alice dropped in with an invitation to dinner, plus yards of gossip about various lesbian couples Helen might have known. She also went away shaking her head.

Helen continued to brood. About CHNOPS, about Mel and the Daumier, about Sonny Burke, about Nangi and the Nagoya yakuza, about Tan, Keiko and Brother Sam, about Ladrone and Bob Forbes. She twisted and turned everything she knew, guessed or suspected every which way. Trying to see it clearer, to get a new perspective on all the elements of the puzzle. Time and time again she came up with an explanation, only to discard it.

Finally on the third evening, the phone rang. It was Mel Romulu. "Ah, good. You're still here. I was afraid you might be gone. Back to Vancouver. Aah ... I wonder if I might persuade you to come up to see me. Right away, if possible. I know it's an imposition ... I'll pay your usual rate for your time, of course. If you could come ... immediately. Now."

"What d'you want me for?"

"I need your advice. Please." Romulu sounded unsure of himself. It was all most un-Mel-like.

"I'm not bound by any Hippocratic oath. I'm willing to give advice over the phone. So what's your problem?" Helen wasn't prepared to be gracious.

"Actually there is someone I think you might be interested in meeting." Craftily.

"Who?" Suspiciously.

"CHNOPS." Deadpan.

"Why didn't you say so in the first place?"

As if liberated from a spell, Helen brushed aside the remains of a barbeque chicken, got up, showered, dressed and was out of there within half an hour of Mel's call. She pushed her rental car — oh! how tired she was of rentals, when will she get her own wheels again! — north on the Don Valley Parkway, over to Highway 401 and up to 2800 Braymount Avenue: Diamond Plaza Towers.

With a nod at the security staffers on duty she crossed the once-familiar lobby to the elevators. Up to the 16th floor. Full of anticipation she pushed the buzzer on number 1609. Mel answered immediately.

"Come in, come in. Thanks for coming. What will you have?"

"Beer would be nice," Helen said and followed Mel, ignoring the art on display around them. She looked around the office to which he'd led them. Nobody.

"So where is he?"

"Upper Canada Ale okay?" Mel asked, reaching into the mini bar.

"Sure, sure! Damn it, Mel, you promised me CHNOPS. Produce him."

"Come now, Helen. I only said that I thought you might be interested in meeting CHNOPS; I didn't promise he would be here tonight. Sit down, have a beer and I'll explain."

"You suckered me! Oh, well." Never one to fight the inevitable, Helen sat down and accepted the drink. Relieved, Mel Romulu settled his skeletal form behind his desk with a glass of brandy. This evening he was fashionably all in black, in a designer sweatsuit.

"I do want your advice and yes, it's about CHNOPS. He's in town. Here in Toronto."

"No shit. Have you met him? Who is he? Tell me!"

"Let me tell this story my way, one thing at a time. A few days ago I received a fax signed CHNOPS."

"When? And where was it sent from?"

"Four days ago. I guess it was the day before you got back from the States. Well before you called me to report your lack of success in getting hold of another Daumier for me. It came from Atlanta. You can see it later, if you like. Now, please don't interrupt any more." Having gotten Helen's undivided attention, Mel took a sip of his drink and continued: "'The fax was brief but pithy, you might say. First of all, CHNOPS reiterated his interest in doing business with me. Then he asked what he could do or supply to persuade me to go into partnership with him. In other words, what evidence did I need to help me decide? So I told him. Produce another copy of the Daumier and let me examine it side by side with the one I've got. His answer was immediate: 'It's on its way. I'll bring it myself,' signed CHNOPS. So I waited. And today I received a call, a local call, and spoke to a man who claims to be CHNOPS. He said that he'd bring me the Daumier any time and any place I chose. I told him to be here tomorrow at noon. Then I called you. Quite frankly, Helen, I feel a bit insecure about all this. Rather unusual for me, I know. What do you think about this business? I value your opinion."

"I guess I should feel flattered. Sorry but I don't. You set all this up without reference to me, then you get cold feet and now you want my 'opinion'? Opinion on what? Whether to go through with this charade? Whether this guy is really CHNOPS? Whether to go into business with him? What?"

"Yes, I see. I'm sorry if you feel slighted. I guess I was hoping you would help me. Just for ... old time's sake. And perhaps out of curiosity. You do want to know about CHNOPS, don't you? Well here's your chance. Help me deal with this situation. Plan our moves. Be here when he arrives tomorrow at noon. Come on, Helen! You know you want to!"

"Oh, I want to, all right. But I'm not sure I like the way this is unfolding. What evidence do you have that this guy is CHNOPS, that he isn't stringing you along? He could have acquired his Daumier just like you did yours. This 'partnership' offer could be a con job."

"Exactly why I want you in on this! Your cool head to help me keep things in perspective. Because if this other Daumier proves as good as the one you brought me from Sonny! ... well, I just could get carried away. By the way, I've had it X-rayed. Among other things. It's superb! Look, Helen, I know you went down to get that painting on your own risk but I want to pay for your time, at least. And, of course, for this consultation and your attendance here tomorrow. How about it?"

"What you are willing to do to get your hands on this other painting? What if this guy wants a 'deposit' to let you examine it? How much? Is it going to stay here in this building, in your workroom downstairs? Do you intend to bring in an outside expert, have it X-rayed presumably elsewhere? Or what? We'll be negotiating with this guy, right? I need to know what's involved, what's the margin. That's number one. Number two, if I'm to participate, I want backup. That okay with you?"

"Absolutely. I rely on your judgement and your expertise in these matters. Now, about your first question. Yes, it would have to go to an outside technician whom I trust for chemical and X-ray examination. Not an art expert; I don't want to take the risk of a leak. I would pay a reasonable 'deposit,' as you put it, based on my own examination of the painting. I certainly know enough to judge if it's a 'no go' or if it's worth going further. That is not what bothers me. What does, is that ... well, I don't want to go into business with CHNOPS even if he's for real. I don't intend to be partners with him, no matter what. I just want this other painting. That's all. You see our difficulty?"

"*Our* difficulty! You want to con this guy! Who might or might not be CHNOPS. He thinks he's dealing with a potential partner, a rich partner, and all you want is to get your hands on this painting. Then kiss him off! Wow! Hope your insurance is paid up. Mel, you are aware that this CHNOPS scam has produced two murders? At least."

"So you tell me. But surely there is no reason to believe that CHNOPS himself was directly responsible for either of them? Surely ..."

"Directly or indirectly, what's it matter? Nangi and Bob Forbes are just as dead. Get real, Mel. This is very dangerous ground."

"If you say so, Helen. Make what arrangements you think necessary, but let's do it."

"Okay, I hope it won't be your funeral."

"That's my risk. Good, good! How's about another beer? No? Right. Now about tomorrow ..."

For the next half hour they discussed how to proceed at the meeting with CHNOPS. Helen finally left bemused and unconvinced but determined. Driving back to midtown through the night traffic Helen didn't notice a little car that followed her right to her hotel.

58
Julie Calls

"Julie! Where are you? What happened to you in Vegas?" Still wet from her shower, Helen answered her phone the following morning. And there was Julie Piper's Australian twang.

"They killed Bob, for Pete's sake! Of course I got out of there double-quick. You found his body too, didn't you? Well, I was in that trashed house and found him before you did. It was horrible! You didn't know him like I did, wouldn't affect you as much. And I was scared. I would be next. I drove to L.A. all night, stayed with friends until now. D'you blame me?"

"I see." Helen considered. "And where are you now?"

"Here, here in Toronto! I want to see you, Helen. Can you meet me soon?"

"I guess." Helen refused to sound enthusiastic. "Answer me one question first."

"Sure."

"Did Bob really send that painting to New York so soon after it arrived from Nagoya? I could've bet it was still in the house when I left that afternoon."

There was a short pause on the other end. Julie wasn't prepared for the question.

"I'm not sure. He might have. On the other hand, maybe not."

"Really? You don't know? Come now, Julie! I've heard enough of your lies. I can't count the different stories you've told me since we met. This one I don't believe.

Period. You know what happened to that painting."

There was another silence.

"Why did you ask that question?"

Helen ignored the query and pressed on with her concern.

"Who was it sent to? Bob mentioned some 'expert.' That part doesn't make sense. Who?"

Pause.

"Bob's uncle. Jason Forbes. You might have heard of him. He's a world-renowned art expert."

"Aha! But is he also CHNOPS? Because someone calling himself CHNOPS is flogging that painting in Toronto. That painting or one just like it, and how many can there be? Does that make sense to you?"

"Yes, yes. With Bob murdered and *ARTrace* kaput Jason would need some way to dispose of that painting. Mel Romulu would be a prime potential client. It is Romulu, isn't it?"

"It is. That wasn't difficult to guess. I seem to remember that you and Bob told me that you've lost touch with CHNOPS. Was that true? Is Jason CHNOPS? How can I believe a word you say!"

"You think I'm lying about finding Bob dead. You think I killed him!"

"It has crossed my mind."

"Helen, I'm not a killer! No matter what you think of me, I didn't murder Bob. He was my friend. Please, please believe me on this."

"You don't make it easy to take your word for anything."

"All right! I know I haven't always been frank with you. But look at it my way. In Nagoya I was sick and confused. I didn't know who was who or whom to trust. But I'm no murderer. And now, come on Helen, you don't really think that of me!"

"How about being up-front about Jason Forbes? Is he CHNOPS?"

"Damn it, Helen!"

With this Julie hung up.

Puzzled at this abrupt ending to the conversation, Helen looked at the receiver in her hand for a moment. Had she been outmanoeuvred? It felt like that. Julie had called ostensibly to arrange for them to meet. Yet she'd cut the conversation short and without leaving her phone number. Maybe she really was hurt and upset at being suspected of murder. However, Julie was a manipulator; her reactions couldn't be taken at face value.

How had she known where I was staying? She'd called to find out something from me, all the rest was window dressing, Helen decided. So, once she had the information she wanted, she hung up.

What had Julie been after? Or more precisely, what had Helen told her that she'd wanted to know? That was easy. One, that someone calling himself CHNOPS was in town, claiming to have the Daumier. Two, that Mel Romulu was negotiating with him for it. It hadn't all been one way, however. Helen had also learned a few things from Julie, lies or not. The one thing that wasn't at all clear was what Julie's purpose was in Toronto. What was she doing here? And what was she going to do with the information she'd gained from Helen?

There wasn't any more time to worry about Julie, her motives and plans. Helen had a date with Wayne for breakfast. Once again they met in the coffee shop of her hotel. She had hired him for the day. He was to be her backup at the meeting between Romulu and the mysterious CHNOPS.

59

CHNOPS, The End

Julie Piper sat in her car across from the Diamond Plaza Towers. Just after eleven, she saw Helen arrive, drive into the grounds and park around the side in the visitor's parking lot. As Helen walked back to the main doors into the lobby, Julie gave a sigh of relief. Not that there could be much doubt about it but still ... it was good to be sure that Jason, Helen and Romulu were going to meet in latter's apartment. Now what she needed to do is wait for Jason to arrive. After a minute, she started up the engine and drove to the ramp, using a pass card to the underground garage clearly marked For Residents Only. On the strength of an opportune sublet, Julie had become a resident of DP Towers two days previously. Since then she'd sat outside and waited for either Helen or Jason himself to appear, as she was sure one or both of them would, on their way to Romulu's place on the 16th floor.

The previous night she'd been proven right. Helen showed up and left after an hour or so. Julie had followed her to the Redstone Hotel in midtown Toronto. Initially Julie hadn't been sure that it was a good idea to call Helen that morning. Why let her know that she was in town? But it had worked beautifully. Her hunch was right; Jason was in Toronto negotiating with Romulu. She could get to him. Two hits, no errors. When Jason showed up it would be a home run. (After years in North America, Julie's sport metaphors tended to be from baseball rather than cricket or rugger.)

Having parked her car in the slot allocated to her temporary apartment, Julie made her way to the basement elevators. She pressed the button for the 18th floor, holding her breath as it travelled up. Her luck held. The elevator passed the lobby floor and ascended to the 18th without stopping. She was now free to walk down the emergency stairs two flights and, hidden in the stairwell behind the fire door, watch for any movement on the 16th floor. As far as Julie was concerned, no one had seen her even enter the building, never mind be able to find her in her hiding place.

She settled down to wait, sitting huddled on the cold stone stairs, her long elegant legs in serviceable denim folded under her. What exactly she would do once Jason arrived, she wasn't certain. Something drastic that was for sure.

If Julie thought herself invisible, she was, of course, quite wrong. A security camera had seen her safely from the garage into the elevator. Another had been activated by the opening of the 18th floor fire door leading to the stairs. The security guard on duty in the lobby had idly wondered what the striking new tenant of an apartment on the 10th floor was doing up there. When she'd showed up on his screen sitting on the stairs on Dr. Romulu's floor, he'd routinely reported it to the supervisor, Feng. Dr. Romulu was an important tenant with valuable property. Feng, ever conscientious, immediately called Romulu's apartment, just to be sure. After a moment, Mel turned the phone over to Helen, "Here, you deal with this. Feng has something to report."

"Right." Helen listened carefully as Feng described what the tall lady called Vanessa Hood from apartment 1004 was doing. Did Ms. Kerémos want Feng to go up and check on her?

"No, Mr. Feng, thank you. I know who it is. We'll

manage. Thanks for calling."

"No problem. Nice to have you with us again, Ms. Keremos." Feng never neglected professional courtesies.

"Nice to be here again. How are you doing?"

"All is fine for me, thank you. And you?"

"Not too badly. Thanks again, bye."

Helen put down the phone and smiled at Mel Romulu and Wayne Tillion. They were in the largest of Mel's gallery-like rooms, in tones of brown to black. It housed primarily museum artifacts rather than "art" objects as such: a perfectly preserved Haida totem held pride of place, an Italian-designed leather sofa against one wall with an Andian lama-hair tapestry behind it, a cossak saddle on a wooden stand next to a Japanese armour on a brown-faced mannequin, a beautifully restored French 17th-century harpsichord lit by a trio of bronze art nouveau lamps, a set of African drums, an English crossbow and many, many more. Romulu's collection was nothing if not eclectic.

Wayne sat on the sofa, while Mel stood by the window. Today he wore a bright red outfit of vaguely Chinese cut. With his bony frame and Stalin-like eyebrows, Romulu seemed to be playing Lord High Executioner in *The Mikado*. His looks were guaranteed to throw Jason Forbes (or whoever) for a loop and carefully designed to heighten any drama the day might bring.

The phone rang again. A Mr. Jason Forbes was downstairs to see Dr. Romulu.

"Send him right up," Mel ordered. Helen nodded at Wayne, who immediately took his place out of sight. Mel and Helen waited.

The doorbell rang. Mel moved leisurely to open the door and allow Jason Forbes to enter.

He came in silently and examined his hosts and the apartment like a cat might new premises. Without asking, he wandered from room to room, stopping and looking, his head cocked as if listening, his steps careful and hesitant. He touched nothing and said nothing for what seemed a long time. Amused and interested, Helen and Mel watched his progress from one gallery room to another.

Jason Forbes a.k.a. CHNOPS was disappointing to look at. There was nothing here of the movie mastermind; nothing about him indicated an individual who could organize burglaries, set up international stolen art networks, operate sophisticated communications. The immediate impression was of a slight, grey, rather insignificant individual.

Jason Forbes was a small-boned man with thinning sandy hair and virtually colourless eyes. He wore a conservative London suit, highly polished black shoes, white shirt and an unfashionable narrow tie as becomes an English gentleman who happens to be an international art expert. His narrow face seemed almost purposely forgettable. Trying to find something to latch on to with this man, Helen noted only an extravagant Rolex watch.

Back in the brown room and continuing to ignore Helen, Forbes finally turned to Mel Romulu. He looked the tall man up and down like a farmer at a cattle sale. Then he smiled, showing small, even teeth.

"Perfect, absolutely perfect. Yes, indeed. Now I'll take a drink. Coffee." He sat himself down on the sofa recently vacated by Wayne. Without a word, Mel left the room. Helen picked up an antique chair, carried it closer and sat down in front of Forbes.

"CHNOPS? You are CHNOPS?" She pronounced it "knops" the first time, then when he didn't react, tried "chops."

"Yes, yes. But that's all over now, of course. I'm Jason Forbes. And you are Helen ... Keremos. You work for Dr. Romulu."

"At the moment."

"Dr. Romulu and I will be working together from now on. Your talents might be of use to us. We'll call you when we need you. Now go and make me coffee."

Helen didn't move. Instead she said in a steady voice: "I think Mel is making the coffee. What makes you think you and Mel will be working together? That's his decision to make."

"We will, of course, we will. But never mind. You cannot be expected to understand any of it."

Helen refused to react.

"What do you have to offer him? Your whole network is shot. *ARTrace* is gone. Two men have been killed. What is more, I bet you're broke! If you play your cards right, Mel might offer you a handout. That's all."

Jason didn't turn a hair.

"As I said before, you cannot be expected to understand. Dr. Romulu is a collector. He wants a painting I own and he will do anything to get it. Collectors are like that. I know."

"Oh, he might make you an offer for the Daumier. But he will want to see it first. But as to working with you! I wouldn't count on it, if I were you."

"This conversation is at an end. Get Dr. Romulu for me and leave us."

"I'll go see how the coffee is doing. I could use a cup."

She found Mel in the next room leaning against the wall. He'd been listening to her conversation with Forbes. They moved into the kitchen where the coffee had just finished dripping.

"The man is mad. Quite mad!" Mel said.

"Not certifiably so, I'm afraid. Strange, I grant you. And dangerous. His price for the Daumier is a 'partnership.' He never had any intention of giving it to you to test or even of selling it."

"What does he mean by working together? I hate to think what sort of 'partnership' he has in mind. He did indicate that the CHNOPS thing is over, correct?"

"Correct. He seems to have written that piece of his life off, including Bob Forbes and *ARTrace*. I bet he has brand-new plans for this partnership. His ideas, your money."

"Quite. We better get back to him. Take the pot." Mel picked up three cups and marched back into the brown room. Forbes still sat on the designer sofa, his feet together, his hands folded. His icy stare followed them.

"Coffee, good," he accepted a cup, sipped appreciatively and continued, "Dr. Romulu, I cannot tell you how pleased I am with you. I couldn't have hoped for a better junior partner. This fabulous place, your collection! Toronto is a perfect location. You characterization is very well done too. It all fits perfectly into my plans. Congratulations."

"Aren't you jumping ahead a bit? My understanding was that I will receive for examination a duplicate of the Daumier that I bought from you via Sonny Burke. On the basis of what I find, I then make a determination whether or not I will help finance an expansion of your replicating business. That's as far as I'm prepared to go." Mel Romulu's voice was firm, his clown face serious. He loomed over Forbes and rustled his picturesque costume for emphasis.

"There is no need for that now. Surely you are intelligent enough to see that."

"I'm afraid not. I want to see the painting. Otherwise no deal."

"You will change your mind."

"Indeed. I will, will I? I don't think so. However, I'm prepared to consider buying the Daumier from you. Or at least give you a deposit while I have it examined."

"No."

"Why not?"

"I do not negotiate. I never have."

"Consider starting. Helen and I have been discussing you, Mr. CHNOPS," quite suddenly Mel's tone turned sarcastic, "Your whole scam is in tatters and your very presence here indicates that you've nowhere to turn but to me. You're in trouble and in no position to dictate terms."

"An illusion. CHNOPS is no more; the slate has been wiped clean. My knowledge and my powers are undiminished, that is what matters. My offer to you is most generous. You may participate with me in my next venture. You will."

"Wiped clean? What do you mean?" Helen entered the conversation.

Jason Forbes's colourless eyes fastened themselves on her face.

"There is nothing and nobody to connect me, Jason Forbes, with CHNOPS. What you know or think you know is of no account."

"I agree that Mel and I are no danger to you in that respect. But what about Sonny Burke? And the Ladrone partners? What about Nangi?"

"Nangi is dead. The others never heard of Jason Forbes."

"Yes, Nangi is dead. And so is Bob Forbes, your nephew I believe. Most convenient."

"Yes. The slate is clean. My new plans are made and it remains only to carry them out. Dr. Romulu, I give you one more chance. He who isn't with me in my endeavours is against me."

"That sounds like a threat."

"I do not negotiate. I do not threaten."

"My answer is no," Mel said after a short pause. "I want no part of you and your crazy schemes. Helen, have you anything to add?"

"There is someone I would like you to see, Mr. Forbes.

Not everyone who knew you as CHNOPS is dead. There is always Julia Piper," Helen said and raising her voice, she called for Wayne.

The door swung open and Wayne Tillion and Julie Piper burst in. Taking in the situation with one swift glance, Julie shook Wayne's hand from her arm and with no preliminaries approached Forbes.

"Still have the gun you killed Bob with, Jason you murderous bastard?" she demanded.

Nobody saw him move, but in an instant Jason Forbes was holding a small automatic in his hand. It pointed at Julie and didn't waver. She took an instinctive step backwards.

"Yes, I do," Jason said.

"You murdering bastard!" Julie repeated. "Why did you have to kill him? Bob was harmless."

"He was *ARTrace* and *ARTrace* had to be liquidated. He was a compulsive gambler, not to be trusted once the money stopped coming. He knew I was CHNOPS. Even you should be able to understand that I couldn't let him live." Forbes spoke in a tired voice as if explaining the obvious to a child. This was the closest he ever came to justifying his actions. "That's enough of that. I'm glad you're here, Julie. There is much that you can yet do for me. You and I will leave here now." Without moving the gun, his eyes swung towards Mel. "You have made a mistake in not joining me, Doctor. Together we would have been unstoppable. You will regret this. Good-bye."

Forbes was up from the sofa and moving, his gun still aimed at Julie who was between him and the door. He ignored the other three people in the room.

"I'm not going anywhere with you!"

"Oh, yes, you are. Turn around." His gun hand steady, he gestured briefly with the other. Julie didn't move. He came closer, still ignoring the others; clearly, he realized

316

that his was the only gun in the room.

Unable to handle the feeling of powerlessness, Mel made a sudden move towards the crossbow on the wall next to him. Forbes smiled and unhurriedly shot him.

The room exploded with action. Julie Piper threw herself at Forbes, crying "I'll kill you!" Her attack was so sudden and unexpected that Forbes lost control of the weapon. She wrestled it out of his hand, turning the tables. As she seemed about to carry out her threat, Helen shouted, "Cookie!"

Her shout galvanized Wayne, who had initially been taken by surprise by the gun and astonished by the sight of Julie attacking Forbes. Now he grabbed Julie in a bear hug from behind, immobilizing her arms and easily removed the gun from her hand.

"Cookie!" Helen warned again as Forbes attempted to take advantage of the situation and dodge past Wayne to the door.

"No, you don't!" Wayne grunted and hit Forbes with his own gun on the forehead as he went past.

After that it took a while for matters to get sorted out. Forbes was deposited on the leather sofa where he lay silently holding his head, with Wayne standing guard over him. Mel's wound turned out to be minor. Although passing within a few inches of his head, the small calibre bullet merely grazed his shoulder. Helen took a shaken Julie aside and gave her a cup of coffee. A few minutes passed as she pulled herself together, then Julie said: "Thanks you two! I'm glad you didn't let me kill that creep, I guess. But what do we do with him now? Can't just let him go."

"Let him go! No way. You wouldn't be safe."

"I know. So do we call the cops? He did shoot Dr. Romulu." Julie smiled at Mel, who seemed more concerned about the damage to his fancy dress than to his shoulder. "Let me introduce myself. I'm Julia Piper. I've heard so much about you; it's a pleasure to meet you finally." She put out her hand. Mel laughed and shook it.

"How do you do, Ms. Piper! A pleasure indeed. But you should have shot him, you know. He quite ruined my *Mikado* outfit. But no cops, please. This is just a scratch, not worth the bother the police would cause. Anyway since he's a murderer, self-admitted at that, I think he should go down for murder and not for ruining my fancy dress. Don't you think so, Helen?"

"Right. He hasn't killed anyone in Canada and he isn't wanted in Nevada. As far as we know anyway. So what are our options?"

Julie lifted her head and looked at Forbes.

"Bet Nagoya cops would love to question him. Wish we could send him to Nagoya and offer him to Suzuki!"

"Something like that might be possible," Helen said, after a moment's thought. "Wayne, how about calling Keiko and telling her and Brother Sam whom we've got here. Kusashita should be very interested in Jason Forbes, a.k.a. CHNOPS. With luck they will take him off our hands."

Across the room Forbes stirred. "What a good idea! I should have thought of going to Mr. Kusashita myself. We can do business. I did him a favour by disposing of Nangi. He will be appreciative," he said.

No one spoke. Helen waved to Wayne to make the call.

An hour later, Jason Forbes was gone from DP Towers. A big bruise on his forehead had slowly turned blue but otherwise he seemed his usual self. He had willingly accompanied Wayne's brother-in-law. Wayne and Keiko went along in case Forbes changed his mind and decided that being taken to Nagoya wasn't a such a good idea after all. As they left, Helen wondered how Kusashita would react to the principle of "no negotiation." She wasn't ready to bet that Forbes would survive until his next birthday.

"Where is that painting? By God, we've forgotten all about my Daumier," Mel exclaimed after the door closed behind the four.

"No, we didn't. I don't think Forbes ever had that painting. Right, Julie?" Helen said, turning to her, "Bob never sent it to New York or Chicago or wherever. Forbes wasn't in New York in any case. He was in Las Vegas. Murdering Bob, destroying *ARTrace* and looking for the Daumier. He didn't find it in that house because you took it with you. You've got it now, don't you, Julie?"

"It's in my apartment downstairs. You can have it. Mel can have it. I never want to see another fake painting again! Especially not a Daumier."

"Really?" Mel sounded pleased, but tired. His whole body sagged like a broken-down scarecrow. Even a minor gunshot wound will finally take its toll. "Helen, can I ask you to look after that little matter? Thank you. You ladies will excuse me but I'm feeling a little weak around the knees. Better lie down before I collapse. Oh, dear, tomorrow I'll have to get that bullet hole patched up. What an exciting morning this has been! I haven't had so much fun ..."

"Go to bed, Mel! Shut up and get some rest. Take two ASAs and hit the sack," Helen interrupted him. "Give me your apartment keys. I'll take care of things."

Down in apartment 1004, Julie immediately produced the "umbrella Daumier," the one Suzuki had studied so carefully on his desk in Nagoya, and handed it to Helen. Helen didn't bother taking it out of the mailing tube in which Martina Khayatt had sent it to Julie at the Las Vegas Airport Inn, much less unrolling and looking at it. Like Julie, she'd had enough of paintings, whether fake or genuine. Instead, she dropped it along with her handbag on the floor next to the couch, sat down comfortably as for a lengthy stay. Julie read this body language perfectly. She brought two bottles of beer and a dish of mixed nuts from the kitchen and settled herself next to Helen.

They spent the first few minutes chatting and catching up. Julie explained how she found Romulu's address, sublet the apartment in DP Towers, then followed Helen the night before to find out where she was staying. Helen didn't need telling that Julie's aim in this was to confront Jason Forbes as a murderer when he came to call on Romulu, as Julie was sure he would. That wasn't what she wanted to hear about.

"You want my story, don't you? And you won't leave till you get it, right?" Julie asked finally.

"Something like that."

"What specifically do you want to know? ... Oh, but first tell me how you knew that this painting wasn't sent to New York but stayed with me?"

"It didn't scan. You wouldn't have let it out of your sight except to return it to CHNOPS. You told me that you had no way of reaching CHNOPS if he didn't want to be reached. Which sounded plausible. So how come New York and via UPS? UPS doesn't deliver to box numbers so there would have to be an N.Y. address. Anyway it figured that CHNOPS operated out of Europe. Plus the way Bob volunteered that information about sending it to an 'expert' in N.Y. He was a fantasizer, but unlike you, not a good liar. That's how I knew. Your turn now."

"Interesting. It proves that you're hard to lie to, even by an expert 'like me.' We'll get back to that, I'm sure. One more question, if you don't mind."

"Shoot." Helen relaxed and started to enjoy herself. She took a sip of beer.

"Why didn't you fall for the Tan story? You know, triads, mob killers. How did you know it was Forbes?"

"I didn't. I didn't know Forbes as such existed, remember? Just CHNOPS, who could have been anyone. I did take Tan and the Taiwanese triad stories seriously at first. Triads are quite real and I still think they play some part in all this. But having Tan be responsible for killing Nangi was all just too, too pat. First Keiko telling me about Tan, then scaring you out of Nagoya with it. Tan exists all right but anyone can use that term. By the time I saw Bob's body, I was sure that neither the Taiwanese triads nor Japanese yakuza murdered Nangi. It would have played very differently had either of them had a hand in it. To me it was clear that mob involvement was peripheral at best." Helen stopped and considered her next words. "You were one of my suspects for Bob's murder, you know. There was that mysterious Caucasian who somehow knew that I was staying at the Comfort Inn. How? I figured he was either CHNOPS or a flunky of his. And he'd found out either from Khayatt or directly from you. It was Khayatt who gave Jason Forbes my address, wasn't it? She knew at least a little of what you were into. She's more than just your lawyer, she's a friend, right? So it was either you or that guy who murdered Bob Forbes; I couldn't see how anyone else would be involved. Next the look of that house. It wasn't just trashed. It was searched. What for? The Daumier seemed the most likely treasure. But by then I tended to believe that you had it so why would you be looking for it — even if you had killed Bob. See how complicated it gets?" Helen stopped.

"Go on."

"Okay. When I saw that overflowing shredder in the *ARTrace* office it came to me that CHNOPS, whoever he was, was closing up shop. Who else would take time to so completely destroy any paper trail to the head honcho? Both the triads and the yakuza would have taken that stuff with them in case it proved valuable. Only CHNOPS, and possibly you, had a motive for wiping out *ARTrace* so thoroughly. What Forbes just told us confirmed it. How am I doing?"

"Ah, beuwdy! You're good at this, Helen, yes you are! All that is right on, you didn't miss a thing! So smart." Julie's eyes shone in admiration.

"Enough flattery. How about your side of the story, eh?"

"No worries, I'll tell you the lot. I knew Jason was behind *ARTrace*. Bob couldn't have managed anything like that to save his life. Wow, an unfortunate metaphor. Anyway, originally I thought that Jason was just being charitable setting up his nephew in a small business in the place where he wanted to live, which of course was Las Vegas. Bob was a heavily addicted gambler, that's why his wife Isobel left him. By the time I first went to Asia, it was clear that Bob was being used by Jason. Then I met Jason." Here Julie stopped. The going would be tricky from now on. "It's hard to explain in hindsight but I went along and for a time I really enjoyed the ride. It all sounded very exciting at the time. The art world is so full of fakery, hype, rip-offs and generally bullshit in any case. A little light burglary, selling fakes to rich collectors, scamming insurance companies seemed like, well, victimless crimes ... and great fun. So why not?"

"Life is 'Sex, Drugs and Rock 'n Roll' you told me once."

"When did I say that? Oh, yes, when I described Sonny to you, I remember now. I don't think I will ever see it that way again. Too many bad things you never expect come along with it. Death. I admit I didn't care much about Nangi; I only met him the once. In Nagoya I was just ill and shit scared. But Bob's murder really threw me. I knew immediately when I walked into that house that it was Jason's doing. Then all I wanted was to get him, the heartless bastard! His own nephew! I can still hardly believe it."

"Well, you got him, kind of. I understand what happened in Las Vegas. Tell me more about Hong Kong and

Nagoya. Just what were you up to with Nangi?"

"I have to go back a bit. Jason was in Nagoya last year, something to do with some show at their art gallery; he was an invited speaker. He met Nangi in a bar called 'FineFun,' I think it was and they got to talking, you know how it is. Apparently Nangi liked hanging out with foreigners. Anyway, Nangi was very interested in the art biz, also in getting out of working for the yakuza. After Jason left, they corresponded; Nangi would send him tidbits of news from the Japanese art market. Jason dropped hints about his CHNOPS scam. He even sold Nangi some stolen Japanese prints — he was very proud of that I recall. Then Jason called me in Hong Kong and told me to go recruit Nangi."

There was silence again.

"As partner? Or what?" Helen helped out.

"Yeah, as partner. I didn't realize until later that things weren't going so well for Jason, his CHNOPS deal was more flash than cash. It was expensive to run. But you've met Jason; he's a megalomaniac in spades. He wanted to expand and needed financing. He elected Nangi to supply it. But Nangi was cagey. Once he found out that Jason's big score was to be on the National Museum in Taipei, he nixed it. He wasn't going to mess with the Taiwanese. To cut this sordid story short, by the time I got to Nagoya, Nangi had no intention of going into any partnership with Jason. He intended to go into business for himself, some modification of Jason's CHNOPS scam on his own turf. The night we talked in that awful underground mall, I gave him a copy of the catalogue and promised to show him the actual painting, which he insisted he had to see. Of course, I didn't know he was just stringing me and Jason along to get his hands on anything he could. See, Jason was around, just waiting for me to give the word that Nangi had taken the bait. I didn't call so Jason knew something was wrong. He and Nangi were to meet the next night to do the heavy negotiating. Well, you've seen what negotiating with Jason is like. He either killed Nangi himself or hired someone locally to do it. Take your pick."

More silence while Julie fetched two more beers.

"I feel awful about all this, Helen. Like it's all my fault. I was such a patsy for Jason. I took money from him. What an idiot I was!"

Helen interrupted, "Relax. Now I know the tune I don't need all the verses. Your story sure puts a different slant on what happened in Nagoya. So CHNOPS was in town all the time! What d'you know! Where was he staying?"

"He didn't actually stay in Nagoya; it was too dangerous since they knew him at the art gallery. He stayed in Kyoto, just a short train ride away. Plenty of tourists make that trip every day." Julie took a deep breath and plunged on. This time Helen didn't try to stop her. "Listen, I appreciate that you aren't giving me hell for my part in this mess. When I woke up in that hospital bed I didn't know what had happened. All I wanted was out of there, fast. So I lied to you, like you say ... but I never pretended to be any better than I had to be."

"Meaning?"

"Meaning, how good do I have to be now? For you."

There was no mistaking where Julie was leading them. For a fleeting moment Helen considered nipping the situation in the bud and leaving. Only she couldn't think of a reason why she should. Julie was trying to seduce her. And why not?

"What do you want from me?"

"Do you ever sleep with straight women, Helen?"

"Sure. Members of the trendy set do hit on an old dyke like me once in a while. Little lesbian adventures are quite fashionably chic these days." Helen laughed. "Not my preference, however. Is that what you had in mind? To try something new and different, like ants in chocolate?"

"No. I've tried ants in chocolate. Will you sleep with this straight woman?" Julie's hand moved across the back of the couch towards Helen. Their eyes held.

"What if you get a taste for it? Are you sure you're ready to give up the 'straight' life?"

"If I like it, I could be 'bi,' like Sonny."

"Don't count on it." Helen imprisoned Julie's wandering hand between her palms. Her tiredness and depression had lifted as if it never existed.

"I hope you've brought your toothbrush," Julie whispered wickedly as they kissed.

"Never leave home without it." Helen mumbled.

60

Epilogue

Inspector Suzuki read the letter over again, slowly. It had been delivered by courier, written in English and unsigned. Its contents allowed him to conclude that the writer was Helen Keremos. It said in part:

> ... the Nangi case will probably never be resolved in a lawful fashion. Privately you should know that the murderer has been identified and your home-grown mobsters are taking care of him. It's not an ideal solution but then when are any solutions ideal? Nangi died because he was meddling in the stolen art business on his own account. As we both know, the theft of original art from public galleries and museums is only half the story. The other half is the passing of forgeries as original masterpieces. In the next few years, expect more and more collectors and experts to be taken in by ever-increasing numbers of virtually perfect fakes. Japan is a large and lucrative market for top-flight art so this trend will inevitably affect your jurisdiction ...
>
> ...
>
> The following may not be news to you but I think I will spell it out; Kusashita has a pipeline into your department. At the very least he knows the content of your 'Nangi' file ...

Suzuki pondered. The document wasn't evidence; it had no standing. He debated whether to destroy it, file it ... or ... It went against all his training and instincts, but he folded it and put it in the inside pocket of his jacket. He hoped one day to have a long talk with its author.

✦

Sonny Burke rubbed his hands. It had been a good day. In the mail there had been a letter from Julie. She was in Vancouver apparently hanging out with Helen and planning to stay there for a while. She invited him to visit. He debated trying to overcome his fear, leaving this place of safety to check out that city as a possible replacement for Hong Kong should things not work out after 1997. Maybe he would send Bill on ahead to prepare the ground or something. On the other hand, Bill could be an asshole and resent Julie ... better not. He would go himself and go alone!

Sonny found himself excited as he hadn't been for years. Suddenly the Matilda and the world he'd built for himself appeared small and, yes, claustrophobic.

Meanwhile, business was picking up. There were scores of icons looted from Russian, Ukrainian and Serbian churches to dispose of and a list of clients eager to buy. Sonny's talents and resources were stretched to the fullest, which is how he liked it.

He rubbed his hands again. Things were definitely looking up.

✦✦

Ray Choy sat at his desk with his head in his hands. This was the first time since his father's death a month before at 95 that he had really accepted that the old man was gone. Ladrone Investigation had been virtually inactive for most of the time since then. Twenty-three relatives had arrived from all over the world for the old man's funeral. Although his older sister Ruth had done most of the work of looking after this influx, still Ray had the responsibilities that accrue to the eldest and only son. The younger members of the extended family were happy to go shopping in the richness of Hong Kong, but he had to spend time with the older generation of the family from places as diverse as Sydney, Bangkok, Denver, Singapore, and Richmond, British Columbia. There were even two elderly relatives from a small village in mainland China. The cost of all this in money and time was incredible, not that Ray begrudged any of it. Still, it was a relief the funeral was over and they'd all gone back home.

Well, not quite all: one of the cousins from some little place near Denver had insisted on staying on and was angling for a job with Ladrone. He'd questioned McGee's role in the organization, wanted him out of what he called "the family business." Ray found himself defending the old Scot! Now that his father was dead and Angus could be jettisoned, Ray didn't want to part with him. McGee was a reminder of the old order that would pass soon enough, Ray knew. The pushy young buck from Colorado represented much that Ray disliked. Damn it, no! He wouldn't take him into the business, no matter what the family had to say. And Angus McGee could stay at Ladrone as long as he liked.

Decision made, Ray lifted his head stood up and went next door to see his old colleague. Ladrone had to be put to work again full blast. Thank goodness there were lots of jobs out there. And thank goodness they hadn't heard from CHNOPS in ages. Never again, Ray vowed. Then he wondered what that Helen Keremos was doing. He'd kind of admired her. Maybe they would meet again in the line of business someday.

◆◆◆

As soon as they'd finished, Keiko got out of bed and made for the bathroom as she always did. Wayne watched her bare back, slim legs and round firm behind disappear through the door. He swung his feet to the floor looked down, removed the wrinkled condom and wiped himself. The sticky tissues clung to his fingers. With an impatient gesture, he got up, pulled on a pair of jockeys and stomped into the still-unfamiliar kitchen. In the bathroom the toilet flushed and moments later Keiko appeared dressed in her best *yukata*.

"Would you like some tea?" Keiko asked. "I will make it." Wayne said nothing, standing in the middle of the kitchen half-naked. She worked her way around him until he got the message and disappeared into the bathroom. When he emerged wrapped in a terry-cloth bathrobe, tea was ready. Keiko carried the tray with pot, cups, sugar bowl, milk pitcher and chocolate cookies into the sparsely furnished living room and set it down on the coffee table. She knelt down beside it and looked up at Wayne.

"Please sit down. Now, some tea." Carefully, Keiko poured the Earl Grey into two cups. It was her favourite and she took it clear. Wayne sat down on the brand-new couch just delivered from Ikea, put sugar and milk in his cup, stirred and waited. He wasn't crazy about tea but at least he could make it more palatable with sugar and milk since it wasn't Japanese, thank goodness.

This is what married life was like, he thought, sex followed by tea!

After Brother Sam had left Toronto, taking Jason Forbes back with him to Nagoya, they had had it all out between them. Many times. About her Sam, about her connection with her ex-employer in Nagoya, about ... how he'd felt betrayed. Somehow he wasn't able to properly articulate his feelings, perhaps because by now he himself wasn't sure what they were.

While he'd been away in California — just four days! It had seemed much longer — Keiko had found this apartment, ordered furniture and made contacts about a job. Clearly she was preparing for a life with him, together. She wasn't stingy about sex, seemed always ready, available. She loved him!

And even that awful trip to Las Vegas had turned out okay after all. At least money-wise. Just before she left for Vancouver, Helen had given him three grand for his share. Apparently Romulu had paid up.

He could have his job back with Glendenning if he wanted it. He didn't, but still it was good to have something to fall back on. Meanwhile, there were prospects of a job in a major international security firm. He had nothing to complain about!

So why wasn't he satisfied?

✦ ✦ ✦

Helen looked out of the window of their rented cabin overlooking Long Beach and Pacific Rim National Park on the west coast of Vancouver Island. Another whole week to go. A real treat. Expensive but worth it. More than worth it: necessary. She'd started out the holiday completely beat, having lost six pounds since her trip to Japan. Her knees had ached every morning and she got tired much too quickly. Already she felt rejuvenated. Another week of rest, no phone and lots of TLC would complete the transformation.

Soon the mist would burn off with the sun of late June and the beach would stand revealed. They would walk the strand and clamber up the rocky outcrops, then drive in to

Tofino and do their grocery shopping and pick up beer, fresh bread, mail. They would stop and chat with some chance acquaintance about the weather, the fishing, the provincial government, the logging in Clayoquot Sound. Then come back for another long walk, maybe even a dip in the cool Pacific waters. One of them would cook a meal; they would eat, read, listen to the CBC. Make love. Sleep.

Helen stretched and looked back at Julie curled by the fireplace deep in a monograph called *Art and Survival.* Since arriving on the coast, Julie had caught the bug of environmental causes. She read voraciously on the subject and already held firm opinions about what strategy the movement should adopt. Her personal aim, as she explained exhaustively to Helen, was to use art and her knowledge of art in the cause of environmental survival. She had extensive plans. Helen, ever the sceptical nonactivist, listened silently, concentrating on the smooth planes of her new lover's face, the eyes full of energy and eagerness.

"Julie's young and smart; life's her oyster. She'll be off and away anytime now. Good luck to her," Helen thought, feeling immensely fortunate. "Miko, I wonder whether Miko would like to come out here for a vacation. Even one week. Once Julie takes off, I'll write and suggest it. We could go island hopping ..."

Then the mist cleared, Julie lifted her head and smiled at Helen. "Let's go, mate," she said. "Time's a wastin'."

Helen thought, "One day soon I must settle down. Get a mate more my own age, buy a house, tend a garden, worry about taxes, keep a dog ... but not yet. Not just yet."